Praise for Jon Courte

'Raymond Chandler for the 21ˢᵗ century . . .'
Esquire

'All brilliant light and scorching heat . . . Grimwood has suc-
cessfully mingled fantasy with reality to make an unusual,
believable and absorbing mystery'
Sunday Telegraph

'Deftly told and laced with neat ideas'
Time Out

'His best to date . . . A deeply original work, carrying within
it the seed of Grimwood's vision of an alternate future. Strange
indeed and quite wonderful'
Alien Online

'Set to cement his position in both critical and public opinion.
The pacing of this book is near perfect'
Murder One

'A tremendous read that is every bit as good as you would
expect from a writer with Grimwood's standing'
Enigma

'A novel which pulls you in and doesn't let go . . . If this is sf,
then bring it on, I can't wait for the next instalment'
South Wales Echo

Born in Malta and christened in the upturned bell of a ship, Jon Courtenay Grimwood grew up in Britain, the Far East and Scandinavia. He currently works as a freelance journalist and lives in Winchester. He writes for a number of newspapers and magazines, including the *Guardian* and *SFX*.

Visit the website
http://www.j-cg.co.uk

Other books by Jon Courtenay Grimwood

neoAddix

Lucifer's Dragon

reMix

redRobe

Effendi
The Second Arabesk

Felaheen
The Third Arabesk

Pashazade

The First Arabesk

Jon Courtenay Grimwood

POCKET BOOKS

LONDON · SYDNEY · NEW YORK · TOKYO · TORONTO

First published in Great Britain by Earthlight, 2001
This edition first published by Pocket Books, 2003
An imprint of Simon & Schuster UK Ltd
A Viacom Company

3 5 7 9 10 8 6 4 2

Simon & Schuster UK Ltd
Africa House
64–78 Kingsway
London WC2B 6AH

www.simonsays.co.uk

Simon & Schuster Australia
Sydney

A CIP catalogue record for this book is available
from the British Library

ISBN 0-7434-6833-3

Typeset in Me⋯⋯⋯⋯⋯⋯⋯⋯ on Limited,

Prin⋯⋯⋯⋯⋯⋯⋯⋯ y
Cox⋯⋯⋯⋯⋯⋯⋯⋯ e

For the girl with red hair
standing in the cold under the bridge at Waterloo
and for the lead guitarist with the Sepuku Chihuahuas.
Same as it ever was . . .

'However many ways there may be of being alive, it is certain that there are vastly more ways of being dead . . .'

Professor Richard Dawkins *The Blind Watchmaker*

Part One

Chapter One

6th July

The sound of fountains came in stereo. A deep splash from the courtyard below and a lighter trickle from the next room, where open arches cut in a wall over-looking the courtyard had marble balustrades stretched between matching pillars.

It was that kind of house.

Old, historic, near-derelict in places.

'Ambient temp eighty-one Fahrenheit, humidity sixty-two per cent . . .' The American spoke clearly, reading the data from the face of his watch, then glanced through a smashed window to what little he could see of the sky outside.

'Passing cloud, no direct sunlight.'

Dropping clumsily onto one knee, Felix Abrinsky touched the marble floor with nicotine-stained fingers, confirming to himself that this statement was correct. The tiles were warm but not hot. No latent heat had been stored up from that morning's sunshine to radiate back into the afternoon air.

Bizarrely, it took Felix less effort to stand than it had done to kneel, though he needed to pause to catch his breath all the same. And the silver-ringed hand that came up to wipe sweat from his forehead only succeeded in smearing grease across his scalp and down his thinning ponytail.

Police regulations demanded he wear a face mask, surgical gloves and – in his case – a sweatband to stop himself from accidentally polluting biological evidence. But Felix was Chief of Detectives and so far as he was concerned that meant he could approach the crime scene how he liked, which was loose, casual and lateral. Not to mention semi-drunk. All the

3

virtues that first got him thrown out of the police in Los Angeles.

Besides, if you wanted to talk about *should have been*, then he *should have been* on holiday. And he would have managed it, too, if this particular buck hadn't been bumped up the line so fast it practically hit the wall parking itself right outside his office door.

The body in the chair was fresh, still warm to his touch. Stiffness had set in to the arms – but then, rigor happened fast when a victim was borderline anorexic. And even without the woman's thinness there was North Africa's heat to add into the equation. Heat always upped the rate at which rigor gripped a corpse.

On his arrival Felix had considered obtaining an immediate body temperature. But habit made him do the crime-scene grabs first, then work a grid through the victim's office, tweezering up clues. And technically, since she was obviously dead, he'd already broken his own regulations by checking under her jaw for a carotid pulse.

'Covering the body prior to site shots.'

Some cities used electronic observers, 360 degree fish-eye vids, wired for movement and sound. El Iskandryia used the human kind, when it bothered to use observers at all. The silksuit Felix had selected stood in the doorway, doing exactly what he'd been told, which was shut up and stay out of the way.

From a foil packet Felix extracted a sheet of tissue-thin gauze designed to protect the woman's modesty in death, as surely as a scarf round her head would have hidden her hair on the streets in life. Except there was no scarf, because the woman had been stabbed in her own house, at her own desk, in her own office . . .

'Starting location shots,' said the fat man and lifted an old Speed Graphic. The camera was linked to his even more ancient LAPD-issue chronograph, which would back up each shot as it was taken, just as the camera would automatically stamp *time*, *date* and *orientation* across the bottom edge of each new shot.

15.30:
July 6:
SouthSouthWest.

All the same, Felix dictated a description of what he was doing, working fast to photograph the little office from every angle. Only when this was done could he start work on the body.

'Exposure five. Al-Mansur madersa. Upstairs. Interior. West wall and corner of office taken from door. Speed Graphic Digilux. Fifty-millimetre lens. K400-equivalence.'

The dictation did no more than tell the court what camera had been used, what the shot showed and what the light was like: something the camera readouts told them anyway. But he'd learned his craft back when Speed Graphics still took acetate and defence attorneys jumped on any conflict of technical information, no matter how small. And besides, Felix spoke not really to his camera or watch but to himself.

These days defence attorneys weren't an issue. If the Chief of Detectives said someone had committed a crime that was usually good enough for a judge. The suspect went down. Unfortunately it had taken Felix a few months to realize this and there were three cases from his early days in El Iskandryia which still gave him sleepless nights – four cases, if he was being unusually hard on himself.

'Exposure eleven. Al-Mansur madersa. Upstairs. Interior. Open door to office, taken from broken mashrabiya window in south wall adjacent to Rue Sherif . . .'

Mashrabiyas were, originally, shaded balconies where water jugs could be left to cool. But the term had long since come to signify both the balcony and the ornately carved screen that hid those in the balcony from the street below. Marble was commonplace for the screen, as was gilded or painted wood.

The smashed mashrabiya at the al-Mansur madersa had been carved two hundred years before from a single slab of alabaster and now lay in shards on the floor, apparently kicked in from outside. That the balcony was fifteen feet above a traffic-laden street only made the break-in more unlikely. Unless one factored in the *Thiergarten* who apparently could move unseen, kill silently and climb walls like flies . . .

Felix sighed. Whatever else Berlin had to buy for its agents abroad, their deadly reputation came free.

Officially, of course, Berlin was El Iskandryia's ally. Merely an equal partner in a bigger, three-way alliance with Stambul and Paris. Unofficially, French influence kept itself to Morocco, while Berlin's advisers flooded the rest of the littoral and Stambul banked its takings from the Suez Canal and did pretty much what it was told.

Politics – now there was one subject Felix spent a lot of time trying to avoid.

Grunting crossly, the fat man wiped fresh sweat from his face and grabbed two shots of a ridiculous rag dog, quite out of keeping with the cold elegance of the Khedivian desk on which it sat.

And then, having put off what came next for long enough, Felix turned his camera on the corpse.

'Exposure thirteen. Al-Mansur madersa. Upstairs. Interior. The body, taken from front of desk . . .' Felix whipped off the modesty cloth and took his second look at the dead woman's wounds. They were no more pleasant than first time round.

Once started, he worked swiftly on the crime grabs, moving in to get specific shots of the ripped-open blouse, the nails broken on one hand, the trickle of blood dried to a stark black ribbon down her side.

The woman was in her early forties. Middle height. Brown eyes staring blankly at the ceiling. Black hair cut short and expensive – elegant, obviously. The very fact her eyes were clear and the cornea unclouded told Felix that she was less than six hours dead, but he knew that anyway and put her death at two hours ago at the most.

One of her elbows was flopped across the arm of her chair and her head had tipped right back, the muscle relaxation that precedes rigor having smoothed her face until it looked more serene in death than it ever did in life: infinitely more serene than it did glaring out from that afternoon's *Iskandryian* open on the desk in front of her.

'*Berlin furious as society widow slams RenSchmiss.*'

And those in El Iskandryia's German community who believed in the legal right to slash open each other's face for the sake of highly-prized duelling scars had slammed right back, from the look of things . . . Punching a button on the side of his Speed Graphic, Felix reduced the depth of field until it showed only what he wanted the judge to see. The injuries in sharp focus.

To him the victim was no longer human: that was where he differed both from his boss and underlings – and from Madame Milla, the coroner, who would already be on her way. To them, what slumped in that chair was still a woman. Deserving all the respect and modesty that the law allowed.

Which was why Felix had put the rest of his day on hold to make it to the scene of the crime first. Back in the City of Angels where Felix had trained, he'd have grabbed a few more corpse shots, lifted dabs, collected up handleable bio like hair and stashed it in evidence bags and then vacuumed the victim's clothes, one garment at a time, again putting the dust into separate sachets.

And then, with the victim's original position recorded beyond all possible doubt, he'd have had a medical technician take the body some place near but non-critical and remove the clothes so Felix could photograph the naked corpse, wound by wound and bruise by bruise.

But that wasn't the way crime against women was handled in El Iskandryia. At least, not officially and this, regrettably, was unquestionably a very official crime. The victim had once been married to an important man, there were rumours that she was badly in debt – to whom nobody seemed to know – and she'd been outspoken enough to upset the young khedive's German advisors.

This was the kind of crime that required press conferences, photo opportunities and fancy political footwork, all of which would get in the way of actually solving the murder.

Reaching into his pocket, Felix palmed a silver hip flask and opened it by flipping back its spring-loaded top with a single flick of the thumb. Like most things in his life, practice was all it took.

Chapter Two

3rd July

Three days before Chief Felix found his holiday plans suddenly ruined, the silent observer from the doorway of the al-Mansur madersa had been sitting at a café table, thinking. Of course, back then the observer hadn't yet met Felix and still mostly thought of himself as ZeeZee.

Though this was in the process of changing. As for what he would become, he hadn't yet decided. And he had no good reason to be sat in the sun anyway.

Which took care of *who*, *what* and *why* . . .

Where? was simpler. According to the fox, looking down from space revealed a green wedge of delta driven into yellow sand. Nature fighting the elements. Or rather, nature fighting itself . . .

'The fox was big on *who, what, why* and *where*. That had long been one of its more irritating functions. The fox lived inside ZeeZee's head. Most of the time it stayed there.

It used to ask him those kind of questions all the time when he was a child. But foxes live faster than humans and it was old now, tired. Mostly, though, he could still sense it lurking behind his eyes, and occasionally it took over. ZeeZee was fine with the fox. He had been ever since he'd realised it was meant to be there. And sometimes, back in the early days when they used to talk a lot, what the fox had told him was even interesting.'

. . . looking down from space revealed a green wedge of delta driven into yellow sand. Stretching a hundred miles from south to north, over 125 miles at its topmost point and far longer than that if measured along the inlets and lakes of its almost fractal coastline, the delta fought back against a parched wasteland that dropped 2,000 feet into the desolate Qattara Depression only a day's drive away.

Far to the delta's south-west was the Great Sand Sea, an area so blasted in places by heat that the silica of some dunes had melted to chunks of clear, green-yellow glass. More than 1400 tonnes of the purest natural glass in the world lay strewn across the surface of the Sand Sea like fist-sized jewels. With a melting point 500 degrees higher than most natural glass, the sand-sea variety was so tough that a standard geological party trick was to heat a lump of the stuff until it was red-hot and then drop it into cold water. The interest was in what the glass *didn't* do . . . which was splinter.

Scientific argument raged about whether the glass had been formed when an ancient meteorite had hit the desert full on or whether a meteorite had cut through Earth's atmosphere at a shallow angle to skim the surface of the Sand Sea like a stone skipping across water, creating glass from the friction of its contact.

What was known was that a piece of the glass had been taken from the desert and carved into the shape of a sacred scarab, set into gold and given to a king. The scarab had been found by Wilhelm Dorpfeld in the tomb of Tutankhamen and was now in the Khedival Museum at Umm el-Dunya.

The green of the delta spread in a silt-rich patchwork of rice fields, date palms, villages and towns opening out like a fan from just north of Umm el-Dunya until it hit the southern edge of the Mediterranean where, in winter, waves crashed along barren, deserted beaches.

Three main roads cut through the delta, supports for the giant fan. And though one route led direct from the capital to El Iskandryia, few of those who used this road journeyed its full distance. People either flew over the delta or took the faster desert highway – a long strip of blacktop whose convict road-gangs engaged in a ceaseless war with the wind-shifted gravel that tried to eat the road at its edges.

The free city faced north, at the westernmost edge of the

delta, limited on its northern side by the Mediterranean and
to the south by a lake as long as the city itself. Necessity had
made the inhabitants build and then build again on their narrow
strip of land, until Iskandryia stretched over twenty miles from
one side to the other but was never more than five miles deep
at any point.

Looked at from any one of the spy satellites that hourly
passed overhead, Isk appeared as a long grey rectangle bounded
top and bottom by blue, with verdant green on the right and arid
grit-grey to the left.

Increasing the magnification produced recognizable districts,
from El Anfushi's narrow side streets (built on what had once
been an ancient causeway jutting between Western and Eastern
harbour) to the ornate Victorian offices of Place Manshiya and
the stuccoed villas and Moorish follies lining the Corniche:
that elegant coastal strip which ran east and featured houses
so exclusive their owners could afford to keep them staffed all
year but use them for only six weeks in high summer when the
capital became unbearably hot.

There were two gaps in the grand buildings lining the
Corniche. One gap formed Place Orabi, which stretched from
the shore back to a statue of Khedive Mohammed, the point
where Place Orabi intersected with Place Manshiya, a different
square that ran west to east along Orabi's southern end.

To the east of Orabi was the second gap, which intersected
with nothing at all. Place Zaghloul was named after the
nationalist leader who in early 1916 had personally negotiated
the Berlin Accord with Kaiser Wilhelm.

The political descendants of the Zaghloul party stressed that
their man's actions had led to Iskandryia's status as a free
city and Egypt's return to enlightened Islamic government as
an autonomous, khedival province of the Ottoman Empire.
Opponents pointed out that – well over a century later – the
Kaiser's supposedly temporary German advisers were with
them still.

The French were a newer addition to the North African
cabal. Their place in the alliance cemented fifty years back by

judicious marriages between Bonaparte princelings and both the Hohenzollerns and descendants of Mehmed V Rashid, Sublime Porte at the time of the original treaty.

South from Place Zaghloul ran Rue Missala, a thorough-fare lined with restaurants. And right on the corner, with entrances on both Zaghloul Square and the rue sat Le Trianon, Iskandryia's most famous Art Nouveau café. On its walls were equally famous paintings, a series of seven increasingly unlikely tableaux depicting full-breasted dancers, naked save for open shirts and jewelled slippers.

The fox didn't like the paintings. But then, the fox was a purist and had problems with Orientalist kitsch. And the fact that the fox was invisible to everyone but ZeeZee didn't make it any less real. Though it wasn't real, of course, not in the way the yellow cabs lurching along Rue Missala were real. ZeeZee had come up with a number of explanations for its existence. The fox's favourite was that it was an autonomous construct of unprocessed dark memory.

In other times it might have been regarded as a ghost . . .

Sitting outside Le Trianon in an area roped off from pedestrians, the thin blond observer with the flowing beard and tangled dreadlocks washed down his second croissant with the dregs of his third capuccino: and wished that what passed for breakfast at the madersa where he was staying would feed more than a stray mouse.

Ashraf al-Mansur – known as ZeeZee to the police, his therapist and a Chinese Triad boss who was undoubtedly even now searching the world to have him killed – had hated the interior of Le Trianon on sight. But since he'd needed to find somewhere to spend his mornings, this café was where he'd taken to eating. Now he just found the interior irritating.

'Another capuccino, your excellency?'

Adjusting his Versace shades and brushing pastry flakes from the sleeve of his black silk suit, the young man nodded. 'Why not,' he said slowly. It wasn't like he had anything else to do.

'Very good, your excellency.' The Italian waiter bustled away, totally ignoring two English tourists who'd been waiting ten minutes for him to take their order. It was Saturday morning, four days after he'd arrived in the city, two days after he'd first met the industrialist Hamzah Quitrimala and one day after he'd finally agreed to marry the man's 'difficult' daughter. And every day, bar the the day he'd actually arrived, he'd visited the café.

So now he was being treated as a regular. Which made sense, because by treating him as such, the patron hoped that was what he would become. Besides, once the patron had discovered that the excellency with the matted beard and odd hair would be working upstairs, it became inevitable that ZeeZee should take his place in a magic group who got tables when they wanted, exactly where they wanted them.

Situated directly over the café were the offices of the Third Circle of Irrigation, famous as the department where Iskandryia's greatest poet, Constantine Cavafy, once worked. What the Third Circle actually did ZeeZee had no idea, despite having arrived on time at the offices every morning for the last three days. He was beginning to think they did nothing.

Certainly his assistant had looked deeply shocked that first morning when ZeeZee suggested he be told how the office operated. Politely, speaking English with an immaculate accent, the older man had made a firm but smiling counter-suggestion. His excellency might like to try Le Trianon, which was where many of the other directors spent their mornings – and their afternoons, too, come to that.

ZeeZee's office occupied a corner site and his excellency had done enough corporate shit in the US to know the prestige *that* carried. What was more, it overlooked Zaghloul and Missala, making it prime real estate. And everyone in the office was polite, way too polite, which meant Hamzah Quitrimala had a big mouth. Albeit no bigger than ZeeZee's own, because his had been the throwaway comment that started a rumour-become-certain-fact that he was a traumatized survivor from one of the greatest fundamentalist atrocities in living history.

'Your Excellency . . .' It was the patron himself, rather than the waiter who'd taken the original order. Putting the capuccino carefully on the table, the patron picked up a crumb-strewn plate and hesitated.

'Did your excellency enjoy breakfast?'

ZeeZee nodded, adding, *'Mumken lehsab,'* as he instinctively scrawled an imaginary pen across an imaginary payment slip in the universal demand for the bill.

'Of course . . . Although perhaps his excellency would like to keep a tab?'

'Perhaps he would.'

Make like a chameleon. Acclimatize, was what the fox said. If you had time, that was, and ZeeZee was making time. Whether his position with the Third Circle made the difference or the fact that he ranked as a bey, life in El Iskandryia was proving easier than he'd ever dreamed possible when he stepped off the plane. But then, after prison, almost anything was going to be an improvement.

He just wished he could remember at what point the fox had disappeared. He was pretty sure it had been there right up to the point they hit Immigration. And ZeeZee always hated it when the fox went invisible on him. It was like suddenly not being able to see in the dark.

Chapter Three

29th June

Tiri had definitely been there when ZeeZee first landed in Iskandryia, twisting itself in and out of people's legs, sometimes so thinned by distance that ZeeZee lost track of everything but the fox's silver tail and hacking cough.

Too many cigarettes, a biology master had told him years before, when ZeeZee had asked why a cub stood choking in a distant field, shoulders hunched as it tried to throw up a splinter of bone. The other men present had laughed and one had rumpled the small boy's blond hair.

My own little wild animal, the visitor called him. That was just before ZeeZee decided to fail all his exams . . .

'Read this.' An immigration officer in khaki thrust a green embarkation card into ZeeZee's hand and waved him towards the end of a queue. There were several queues, all moving inexorably towards a row of desks where simple polygraphs stood waiting, their guts exposed to the air. A golem-featured man from the line alongside glanced over and ZeeZee thought for a moment he was going to nod or say something. But he just stared at ZeeZee's matted hair and then looked away.

It was one of those evenings.

On the card was a list of statements to be read aloud, in a choice of French, Arabic, German or English . . .

He wasn't a drug addict.

He wasn't infectious.

He didn't plan to overthrow the khedive . . .

So far so good. ZeeZee skimmed his eyes down the next three prohibitions against entering El Iskandryia.

He wasn't planning to purchase for export any classical or Pharaonic artefacts.

He didn't belong to a proscribed fundamentalist group.

He'd never been charged with murder. *Except he had . . .*

It might have been the last prohibition that made ZeeZee sweat, or it could have been the lack of air-conditioning. Whatever, he was still sweating when he reached the head of his queue to find himself facing a middle-aged man who wore a fez, an oiled moustache, a gold lapel pin shaped in the name of God and a rectangular tag that announced he was Sergeant Aziz.

'Where did your journey begin?' demanded the sergeant.

'America,' said ZeeZee and Aziz nodded. Given the bleached dreadlocks, hobo beard and beige elephants stampeding across an ill-fitting sports shirt it was unlikely the thin man came from anywhere else.

'Make your declaration,' the sergeant said. So ZeeZee put his hand on the plate and let Aziz click shut a wrist band. Then he swore his beliefs away, only stumbling when he reached the final prohibition.

'Again,' demanded the sergeant.

'I have never murdered anybody,' said ZeeZee flatly and every diode on the cheap Matsui lie detector stayed green. On the far side of the desk the fox grinned like the fox he was and, without thinking, ZeeZee grinned back.

Drugged or drunk, Aziz decided, his eyes flicking from the passenger's darkened armpits to his bead-slicked forehead. Either way, he was suspect.

'ID card?' Irritation made the sergeant snap his fingers.

'I've got this,' ZeeZee said apologetically. The document he proffered was unmistakable, its cover pure white and hand-stitched from Moroccan leather softer than velvet.

'*Excellency . . .*' In place of a sneering NCO stood a man in shock, career options cashing themselves in right in front of his own eyes. The diplomatic pass he now held was registered to a *pashazade*, the son of a pasha, senior grade. Basic survival instinct made Sergeant Aziz forget everything except his need to make the sweating tourist someone else's problem.

Not even bothering to stamp the *carte blanche*, the sergeant clicked his fingers for a jellaba-clad orderly and ordered the underling to escort the important pasha to the fast-track desk and quickly.

Eyes like a maniac, beard like a dervish and a pair of combats that were way too long in the leg . . . plus the man kept looking round for something he obviously couldn't see. Captain Yousef was worried. He had an apartment in a block off Rue Maamoun that needed repairs to its balcony, he'd only just made Captain and – God be praised – his wife was pregnant for the third time. He couldn't afford to make a mistake.

But which would be the mistake? To hold a notable with a *carte blanche* for questioning or to let through someone who couldn't look less like a real bey? The call was impossible to make and the implications of getting it wrong were horrific – for himself and his wife, for his children, his home . . .

'Sir . . .' Captain Yousef's accent was elegantly Cairene. His words those of someone born not in El Iskandryia but in the capital. All the same, his voice shook as he asked his question. 'Do you have some secondary form of identity?'

The notable in the elephant shirt and shades said nothing and did nothing except shrug. It was obvious that his answer was no.

Looking from slumped man to the elegant Ottoman diplomatic passport, Captain Yousef had real trouble reconciling the dishevelled mess in front of him with the photograph encrypted on the *carte*'s chip that gave his family as al-Mansur and his place of birth as Tunis.

The passport was five years old, almost expired. The encrypted picture showed someone clean-shaven, neatly dressed, who stared hawk-eyed at the camera. While this man looked like the worst kind of American, the poor kind.

And yet.

And yet . . .

'Ashraf Al-Mansur?'

ZeeZee began to shrug, caught himself and smiled for the

first time since he'd entered the airport. It was a rueful, what-the-fuck-am-I-doing-here smile. Not the kind that the Captain had ever seen from a real bey.

Casually Captain Yousef adjusted his red fez with one hand, while touching a discreet buzzer on the underside of his desk. Trying to enter El Iskandryia on a fake passport was a serious crime. Pretending to be a notable was even worse. And when that passport was a diplomatic one, then . . . The Captain didn't waste time worrying about it further. No point. His decision was a good one and besides, it was no longer his business. Orders specifically said to pass this kind of problem straight to the top.

Chapter Four

29th June

'Merde, merde, merde . . .'

The dark-haired girl hit a key and switched search engines. Looking for one that worked. So far she'd spent twenty highly illegal minutes learning precisely nothing about her future husband, who was probably even now at the al-Mansur madersa, delivered there from the airport in some smoke-windowed Daimler stretch.

al-Mansur
Nothing.
Ashraf Bey.
Nothing.
Pashazade Ashraf.
Nothing.

It was enough to set off another litany of swear words. Zara bint-Hamzah spoke Arabic but swore in perfect Cairene French for the simple reason, established in childhood, that neither of her parents understood it.

She also spoke English, as did her father, though she spoke hers with a New York twang. Two years studying at Columbia did that to you. Only that bit of her life was dead now and she was back home. And didn't she know it.

Ashraf Bey might as well not exist for all the record he'd left of his life to date. *'Putain de merde . . .'* Without thinking, Zara gulped the last of her slimmers' biscuit – rolled oats, rolled wholewheat, glycerol, sorbitol and xenical – total calories fifty-seven – and ruined any calorific benefits by pouring herself another coffee and mixing the liquid with a large teaspoon of what looked like dirty diamonds but was really raw sugar.

Just looking at the ragged crystals made Zara long for a few good old-fashioned pop rocks of freebase, something to heighten her courage or stupefy her nerves: because misusing the Library's LuxorEon3 terminal didn't come easily – not to her, anyway. Only these days she was clean, had been since she was fifteen, and all she had for courage was a Sony earbead. So she upped the volume on DJ Avatar and went back to her flat panel.

The fact that Ashraf couldn't be found on the empire-wide voting list held at the Library of Iskandryia Zara put down to his rank as a bey. Sons of emirs were probably too rarefied to be recorded on an openly accessible database. More puzzling was his complete absence from the Library's proscribed database and from the web itself. Out there Ottoman law meant nothing. So, on the web at least, there should have been some ghost of a record.

This was a man who'd spent seven years in America. That was the point her father had used to sell the marriage: how much they'd have in common. (By which he meant they'd both been corrupted by the same culture.)

But according to every credit agency she'd accessed, the bey's rating wasn't so much bad as simply non-existent. No charge cards, no bank account, no mortgage had ever been issued in his name. More bizarrely still, he'd never posted to any internet newsgroup, never chatted, never had an e-address – at least, not under his own name. The man to whom she was days away from becoming very publicly engaged had left no trace of his life to date, no shadow. Not out there in what Zara now thought of as the real world, and not in the Ottoman world, either.

It wasn't a good feeling.

Her own entry in the city register was brief, short and depressing. Though flesh would be added to its bleak bones at the end of the week when data was updated to take account of her father's new rank.

Zara had no illusions about how he'd attained the rank *effendi*. A bey could not be expected to marry the granddaughter of a *falah*. So her elderly, half-blind grandfather was to be moved from his mud-brick home in Siwa to a new house on the outskirts of Isk. With the new house were promised orange trees he couldn't see, irrigated lawns he'd consider a criminal waste of precious water and the honorific *effendi*. The fact that *his* father was now effendi made her father effendi, which made her respectable enough to marry.

Zara was the price and her dowry was the prize. Love didn't enter into it and nor, for once, did complicated family alliances. The only alliance that interested the bey's aunt was with her father's money. The deal stank and was morally wrong; but as her mother had angrily explained, this was how things were done. And the very fact that – for once – her mother managed to keep her hands to herself told Zara just how worried the woman was that her daughter might do something stupid, like refuse.

Mind you, first off, they'd been worried that if they let her go to Columbia she wouldn't return when her two years in New York were over. Then they'd been worried she might *disgrace* herself while over there. Now . . .

Merde indeed.

A mouthful of now-cold coffee warned Zara that she'd over-run her own safety margin. It was time for her to log off and go pack up her little cubbyhole before Zara's boss realized what she'd been doing with her last day in the department. Breaking every regulation she could find, starting with unauthorized use of a LuxorEon3.

There was only one computer matrix in the city: IOL. Available through subterranean snakes of optic that crawled in conduits beneath the sidewalks to feed everything from cheap edge-of-network devices in local schools to the complex hierarchy of information appliances used in the Library itself.

The network was wired with optic rather than relying on radio because cable withstood EMP and those inconvenient, mujahadeen-inspired charged-particle things that scrambled radio signals elsewhere in North Africa. The wiring of the city had been done in record time, with roads ruthlessly ripped up, rivers drained and inconvenient buildings bulldozed. What

Ove Arup had insisted would take twelve months minimum had been finished in six and even then General Koenig Pasha, the city's governor, hadn't been happy: he'd wanted it done in three.

And though the city streets were an open and fluid mass of architectural styles, crammed with all races and religions, the network running beneath those streets was anything but . . . It was utterly hermetic, completely sealed. Only the room where Zara sat, a cupboard-like alcove of the Library, acted as a node for those with permission to swim in the wider, wilder waters where information apparently wanted to be free but mostly seemed to expect you to buy it.

Zara clicked her way out of a credit-check site that kept demanding an account number for a charge card she no longer owned and shut down the connection.

If she was traced then Zara could undoubtedly count for help on the fact she had no previous record. Besides, the new marble floor of the triangular foyer below came directly out of her father's pocket. Disgrace her, and the director definitely wouldn't get his new roof.

Money was power. Zara was about to add *Even dirty money*, then amended it in her head to *Especially dirty money*. Dirty money carried with it the threat of unpredictability. Of course, *dirty money* eventually turned into *new money*, with all the scrabble for respectability that the term suggested. And *new money* lay on its back and opened its legs, *or did it by proxy*.

Zara shuddered.

Somewhere out of sight, beyond the sweep of the Eastern Harbour and beyond where the peninsula of the old Turko-Arabic quarter jutted into the sea to separate the Eastern Harbour's elegance from the warehouses and squalor of the West, somewhere out there flames lit the approaching evening like dancing devils, signature of the Midas Refinery.

A \$1.8 billion complex that processed 100,000 barrels a day.

Out there on the edge of the desert, low-value heavy oil got an upgrade to petroleum gas, naphtha, aviation fuel and diesel for export to Europe. Though the public face of Midas was a minor Napoleonic princeling, her father owned 27.3 per cent through a holding company. It was more than enough.

Reaching into her bag, Zara pulled out a page torn from an American student magazine and began to read it for the fifth time. This was how she had to erase her traces from the network to become a ghost. There was much talk of command lines, Linux and Mozilla which she ignored, skimming down the page until she got to a paragraph for users prepared just to do what they were told.

Zara did exactly what it said. If the article was right she was now in the clear. If not, well, too bad . . . Did they want a new roof or didn't they?

When she returned to her job – if her new husband ever allowed her back – it would be to a different department of the Library. None of her male bosses would talk to her, except to give orders or collect information. Most of them would not even look in her direction in case their glance was seen and misinterpreted.

She'd made plenty of mistakes in her nineteen years, but the biggest by far was ever turning up at the airport in New York. Her parents had been right to be worried, whereas she was just naive for not wondering why they wanted her home for the summer. Leaving Columbia for Isk because she was touched they'd been missing her was about as stupid as anyone could get.

Now she was stuck with an arranged marriage and Zara could just imagine to what . . . Some spoilt, prissy little coke-head dressed in PaulSmith International. She'd watched enough episodes of *Rich & Famous* to know what to expect.

Chapter Five

29th June

First isolated as a pure chemical in 1820 but sourced from shrubs long before that and spread across the littoral a thousand years earlier by the armies of Islam, caffeine was the North African drug of choice and something of a local vice. Which was fine with ZeeZee. He'd spent time at both Scottish and Swiss boarding schools and could think of worse ones . . .

Lifting the airport cup to his lips, ZeeZee winced as the scalding black mud burnt his lips. The taste was of sweetened silt and *arabica* beans that hadn't been gently roasted so much as charred to death in their very own *auto-da-fé*.

'Best let it cool,' announced an elderly, whipcord-thin man who was sat opposite facing him over a low table.

'Yeah,' said ZeeZee. 'Thanks for warning me.'

General Saeed Koenig Pasha smiled and sipped from his own cup. Until thirty minutes ago the General had been bored. And then serendipity had seen him arrive at the airport just as all the fools on the scene started to panic about having breached diplomatic protocol.

Now he had the object of their worries in front of him, and the General had to admit he could see their problem. Not that he would ever, under any circumstances admit that to any of them. All the same, in his long and detailed experience as Governor of El Iskandryia, beys came in three types.

Old ones who lived in rambling palaces and wrote to him complaining about the laxity of the young.

Middle-aged ones who were too worried about their expanding bellies and nagging wives to have time to trouble him.

And young ones who drove too fast, lived hard and had

acquired bad habits in foreign countries, without acquiring the necessary wisdom to realize that was where their bad habits should have been left – at least, when it came to displaying them in public.

This last type was what he half been expecting to meet. Someone elegant and urbane, if somewhat louche. Instead the young man opposite looked, sounded and smelled like an American hobo. He had ill-fitting clothes, his hair was twisted into ugly locks and his face was hidden by a long, matted beard. Luckily the General had visited West-Coast America enough to know that this was a look often adopted by the children of the very rich.

He hadn't introduced himself to the al-Mansur boy and didn't intend to do so. All the same, it *would* have been his signature that bounced the boy out of the country, had him sent to jail or even killed; if he'd followed the first instinct of a certain Colonel Gasparin, instead of doing what the idiot Colonel should have done right at the start. Place a call to Lady Nafisa at her madersa.

Besides, if his staff really believed it was coincidence that saw the General arrive at the airport at exactly that point, then they really were fools and he'd be replacing the lot of them. He had his own reasons for being interested in the family of Lady Jalila al-Mansur.

'You could formally complain,' said the General. 'You have that right.' He didn't say anything more, just cocked his head to one side and waited to see which way the boy would play it.

'Not worth it,' said ZeeZee, standing up. He was in a hastily-cleared VIP lounge at Iskandryia airport where Gasparin had escorted him as soon as the Colonel had been told ZeeZee's passport was genuine. 'The man was just playing his part . . . That's all any of us can do.'

He smiled at the older man's sudden sideways glance.

The area around them was done out in ersatz Rococo Islamic, all mirrored arches, peacock-blue tiles, white marble slabs and a splashy alabaster fountain that sounded like a woman pissing.

ZeeZee got the feeling that the General couldn't wait to get away either.

Too close, thought ZeeZee as he headed for the exit. Way, way too close. He slipped the *carte blanche* into the breast pocket of his pug-ugly sports shirt and headed for a gap in the barriers.

Near the front of the barrier stood a chauffeur wearing peaked cap and polished boots, with a printed board that read *Ashraf al-Mansur* resting in the crook of his elbow. ZeeZee walked past the man without even breaking his stride.

First things first, and that meant hitting the local shops.

ZeeZee's other clothes were on their way to Zanzibar in an overhead locker, courtesy of Ottoman Airways. At least he sincerely hoped they were. He'd left his briefcase behind at Cairo aboard the Seattle/Zanzibar flight for exactly that purpose.

Everything he stood up in had been bought duty-free on the plane, paid for with a platinum HKS that had arrived along with his passport. And yellow shirts with beige elephants weren't his first or even second choice of clothing. The garment was what the Boeing's on-board boutique had had in his size.

Cairo was where he'd switched planes, to a Lufthansa local flight. There'd been one moment in a steel-and-glass corridor between Cairo arrivals and local departures when he'd been tempted to keep walking and lose himself in the chaos of the capital.

Quite why he hadn't was a question ZeeZee would ask himself later, when he finally stopped moving long enough to think. But first he needed new clothes and then he had to find the al-Mansur madersa, whatever that was . . .

Chapter Six

29th June

'Now the graveyard was haunted by Ifrits who were of the Only True Faith,' announced Hani. Her new uncle was late. Her aunt was furious about something, as always. So the small child was busy amusing herself.

'And in that night, as Hassan lay sleeping with his head leaning against his father's grave, came an Ifritah who marvelled at Hassan's loveliness and cried, "Glory to the True God. This is a creature from paradise." Then the Ifritah spiralled high into the dark firmament as was her custom and there met a Djinn on the wing who saluted her and she asked, "Where hast thou come from?"

'"From old Cairo," he replied.

'"Wilt thou come and look at the loveliness of the boy who sleeps in yonder graveyard? For thou wilt see no boy more beautiful."

'And the Djinn nodded and said, "I will . . ." And together they descended through the chill night sky to where Hassan . . .'

'Stop talking to yourself,' demanded Lady Nafisa, as she swept through the door of the haramlek's nursery and frowned at the sight of a puppy sat in the middle of a spreading puddle. If there was anything she hated worse than Hani wasting her time on computer games it was that animal.

'I'm not talking to myself, I'm writing a story for Ali-Din.'

The child's tone was scrupulously polite. But her dark eyes were defiant and she looked at her puppy with pride.

'And I've already warned you,' said Lady Nafisa firmly, 'not to bring that thing up to the nursery.'

'But it's my nursery and I always mop up after him.' At nine Hani already considered herself too old to beg, so she kept her voice steady, as if she really couldn't see why there should be a problem. This was an old argument. One that had got her slapped at least twice and sent up to her room more times than she could remember.

'Ali-Din belongs in the courtyard and besides . . .'

'Yes, I know,' Hani said heavily, 'Ali-Din is a boy dog.'

Nothing male was allowed on the third floor of the al-Mansur madersa, Aunt Nafisa's house on Rue Sherif. In the five hundred years it had been standing no man had entered the haremlek. Now there was no one but Hani or her aunt to use the echoing rooms, where dust gathered in a dry fountain and geckos died and desiccated, unnoticed and unmourned.

'Disobey me again and I have him destroyed.'

'What if I change his name?' Hani demanded, not even prepared to acknowledge her aunt's threat. 'Then can he be female?'

'No,' Lady Nafisa hissed in irritation, resisting the urge to re-check her watch. A Cartier case with Swiss mechanical movement, it was elegant, tiny and unfailingly accurate. Which hadn't stopped her checking it every five minutes for the last hour, ever since the driver she'd hired at unnecessary expense had called in to report that her nephew was not on the plane.

And when she told him firmly that Ashraf was very definitely on that flight because she'd had a call from the General himself, the driver had replied tartly that, in that case, perhaps the bey didn't want to be collected and had put the phone down on her. No doubt he'd want paying, too, even if he'd failed in the job he was hired to do.

'Why can't Ali-Din be female?'

'Because I say so,' Lady Nafisa snapped. 'Now take Ali-Din down to the courtyard.' And she left before the child had a chance to defy her openly.

Chapter Seven

29th June

Between Iskandryia airport and Place Orabi ran a Carey bus. It made stops on the way at Shallalat Gardens, Masr Station and the Attarine Mosque, but Place Orabi was the terminus and that was where all the remaining passengers but ZeeZee clambered off.

At least three conflicting varieties of Rai drifted in through the open doorway of the bus, blasting from cafés in the square. But ZeeZee couldn't even recognize the instruments, never mind the styles. He was tired, cross and hot. He hadn't slept since he'd snorted his last line of crystalMeth two days before and was trying very hard not to think about the approaching comedown, and that was making him more edgy still.

All he knew was that he needed to look his best.

A new identity needed a new look, because personality was a performance put on by the self for the self, or some such shit. ZeeZee felt much too wasted to remember the fox's actual line.

In fact, ZeeZee would happily have stayed on board the bus and shuttled his way back to the airport. Only that didn't seem to be an option. A recording in three languages was telling him it was time to leave. When that didn't work, the driver took to turning the inside lights on and off to signal they'd arrived.

'Yeah, yeah,' said ZeeZee and levered himself out of a plastic seat, leaving sweat marks where his back and buttocks had been. 'Where can I buy some decent clothes?'

The driver looked up from punching digits into a logbook but said nothing.

Wearily, ZeeZee peeled a $5 note from the roll in his back pocket. 'Clothes?'

'Rue Faransa,' the man said, lifting the note from between ZeeZee's fingers and making it disappear as if by magic. 'Have a nice evening.'

'You shouldn't be here,' ZeeZee told the man with the knife. In Iskandryia tourists had more chance of being run over by a taxi than being mugged. It said so in a travel short on ZeeZee's internal flight. Though maybe that wasn't such a comforting statistic, given that taxi accidents seemed to be a regular occurrence. And the golem-faced man from the airport certainly seemed to be real enough.

'Just give me your wallet.'

Golem features nodded down to a glass blade he was holding at his side. A deep groove ran along both sides, put there to help blood flow freely.

'I don't have a wallet,' said ZeeZee, which was the truth. He had an iris-specific platinum HKS card in one back pocket of his combats and his *carte blanche* in the other. Other than that, nothing. No rings, not even a watch. Well, only the Omega he'd bought duty-free on the plane and the G-Shock in his pocket, and he wasn't about to give up either of those. For the average mugger, ZeeZee was a big disappointment. Actually, as a mugger's target he was bad news, full stop.

ZeeZee kept his voice soft, unthreatening. For good measure he tried a small half-smile. But darkness visible already drew an unseen circle around them both and inside his head the fox was smiling as it memorized the layout of a tiny alley, a street at the back of Rue Faransa, so narrow and insignificant it appeared on no maps and the panniers of long-dead donkeys had managed to scratch grooves into both walls at once.

'Wallet,' repeated the golem features. There was a dogged determination to his voice but his small eyes were clean. Whatever need he was feeding it wasn't chemical. '*Now*.' He raised the knife slightly to show he was serious.

'And I've already told you,' someone said, using ZeeZee's

voice, 'he doesn't have one.' Most people would have stepped back, away from the sharp blade. ZeeZee stepped in close, until he could see tiny broken veins on the man's nose and smell stale garlic on his breath. It was definitely the man from the neighbouring queue at airport, and he was still staring at ZeeZee's hair.

'No wallet. No cash. And besides . . .' ZeeZee smiled. 'If you need a knife, you're batting in the wrong league . . .'

The man opened his mouth.

'No,' ZeeZee said firmly.

Golem features shrugged. 'Too bad,' he said. And then his blade whipped up, aimed at a point behind ZeeZee's diaphragm – except that ZeeZee was already some place else. Pain blossoming across his side as he pivoted sideways to let the knife scrape across his ribs. *Ugly but not life-threatening.* The status report concerned his wound, ZeeZee realized, not his opponent.

Dodging the next blow was easier. All ZeeZee had to do was pivot to take the putative knee to the groin on his hip.

'You're going to die,' said the attacker flatly, seeing ZeeZee's gaze flick round the deserted and darkened alley.

ZeeZee laughed.

'I died years ago,' he said and unravelled in one fluid sweep, a sideways twist creating exactly the right amount of space to let him bring his palm up under the man's chin, snapping back his skull so hard the sound of teeth breaking echoed off both alley walls. Without further hesitation, ZeeZee buried his forearm in a suddenly exposed throat and crushed the golem's larynx.

The follow-though, where ZeeZee's elbow swept back to crack a skull and drop the man to the dirt was unnecessary, but he did it anyway. The old Rasta he'd learnt from had been very strict about always completing each sequence.

In all, it took less than two seconds. And had there been anyone else in that alley to watch, which there wasn't, they'd have been presented with moves so fluid, so controlled that they could have passed for some deadly ballet.

'Shit,' said ZeeZee, blinking hard. Two courses of primal

therapy, a complete twelve-point plan and three years of anger management straight down the drain. Personally, he blamed the fox.

Under a blue blazer golem features carried a new ceramic Colt in a flashy leather shoulder holster, the fancy saddle-stitched kind with a chrome buckle just guaranteed to show up under a full body scan. So maybe he wasn't such a professional after all.

Apart from that, the idiot was clean, right down to labels cut out of his clothes and no keys of any description in any of his pockets. The only other thing of interest, was a polaroid in a crumpled manila envelope. ZeeZee knew exactly what the shot would show even before he examined it. But he was wrong.

He wasn't the man in the photo staring out at the world through hooded eyes, because he'd never worn a goatee beard like that or had elegant hair swept back behind his ears. And he'd definitely never worn a drop pearl earring. But the man in the picture *was* him. The high cheekbones were his, the heavy nose, the whole shape of the face was the same, right down to his mouth.

And in the background of the picture, just out of focus behind the man, was a soaring minaret outlined against a shockingly blue sky. The mosque to which the minaret was attached was impressive, heart-breakingly beautiful and undoubtedly famous but ZeeZee could honestly say he didn't recognize it.

Pocketing the polaroid, ZeeZee rolled the body against a wall and left it there.

'Head south towards the equestrian statue of Khedive Mohammed Ali, turn right at Place Manshiya and walk briskly on. The road directly ahead is Rue Faransa . . .'

ZeeZee thanked the map without thinking, not noticing the glance he got from other tourists waiting their turn. Talking to machinery was a prison quirk. Even in soft habitats like Huntsville it could be the closest anyone got to a day's decent conversation.

Walking briskly was out, what with the gash over his ribs

taped shut with instant skin from a chemist behind the bus station, but he managed a slow stroll through the square towards the waiting statue.

From the Khedive's bronze turban and fierce beard, to his gut bound round with a vast cummerbund, and the ornate horse pistol hanging from his saddle, Mohammed Ali was impossible to miss. Though his mount looked unnaturally square at the corners, as if the sculptor had used up all the roundness available to replicate the Khedive's impressive bulk.

ZeeZee stopped rubber-necking Mohammed the moment he realized he was the only person on Place Mohammed paying Khedive the slightest attention. He didn't want to look the tourist, even when that was so obviously what he was.

The first three shops in Rue Faransa sold bric-a-brac masquerading as antiques. A Bakelite radio in one window caught ZeeZee's eye but when he went inside to examine it he discovered that someone had replaced the original valves with a cheap Somali chipset. So he put the radio back in the window and retreated under the shopkeeper's watchful eye.

Two clothes boutiques followed, both in the process of closing for the night and both featuring short dresses in washed-out silk by designers ZeeZee had never heard of, though given the prices displayed in pounds Iskandryian, US dollars and Reichsmarks everyone else obviously had.

The next shop looked much more promising. It sold menswear, was still open and, even better than that, had an industrial-strength air-conditioning unit sticking straight out into the street. ZeeZee couldn't tell how expensive the suits in the window were from their price tags because there weren't any such tags – which probably made the garments concerned seriously upscale. But since it wasn't really his charge card he could live with that.

Something tastefully restrained was playing on the sound system as he entered. Gorecki probably. One wall was matt black, the rest sand-blasted brick. All of which left ZeeZee as singularly unimpressed as the intimidating elegance of the boutique's French manager, the simplicity of her stark granite desk and the three obsidian-topped work tables.

ZeeZee might heal unnaturally fast but he was still in too much pain from his ribs and far too strung out to take note of the shop's expensively understated detail. All he noticed was a framed page from *Esquire,* showing a man wearing a black tee under a loose lightweight black coat with matching trousers. The shoes the model wore had Cuban heels and sloped to a point at the toes. The outfit looked elegant, sophisticated and just slightly threatening. But most of all it looked cool. Not fashion-victim cool, just as if the model wasn't overheating.

'That,' said ZeeZee, nodding at the cover and putting his card on the counter. 'I want that.'

The glance the woman gave his card was so fleeting ZeeZee almost missed it. 'Good choice,' she said. 'Good choice.' Pushing herself up off a silver chair, the manager stepped quickly behind ZeeZee and ran one slim hand across his shoulders and then down his spine from his neck to the small of his back. And even as ZeeZee tensed, the manager was across the other side of the boutique, standing next to a rack of jackets, muttering measurements under her breath.

'Smart silk,' she told ZeeZee, returning with a coat. 'Double-stitched, jet buttons, silk half-lining. Ideal for this weather.' She slung the garment across ZeeZee's back, not bothering to get her only customer of the evening to thread his arms through the sleeves. 'If it hangs okay like this then the fit is good. I'll check sleeve length later, but it will be fine.'

She stepped towards ZeeZee and hesitated as he stepped swiftly back. 'I need to check your waist,' she said. 'If that's a problem I have a tape . . .'

'No problem.' ZeeZee stood as the woman touched her fingers together over his spine and deftly smoothed the tips around his waist until they met slightly below his navel. If she noticed the heavy cross-hatches of tape coming down from his damaged ribs she didn't mention it.

'Thirty, maybe thirty-one. We'll try both. Okay, now the length.' She skimmed one hand up ZeeZee's inside leg and nodded. 'Thirty-three . . .' A pair of silk trousers joined the jacket, leaving only a black cotton tee that the woman selected from a pile on the obsidian-topped table. Shoes came last.

'The changing room's through there.'

'There' was a black curtain screening off a tiny corner of the boutique, a CCT camera bolted baldly to the bare brick wall.

'How about shades?' ZeeZee asked when he emerged, his duty-free clothes and shoes crumpled into a bundle in his hands.

She shrugged, the merest hint of an apology. 'Afraid not, but Versace's across the street . . .'

ZeeZee initialled the slip she handed him without checking the amount, dropped his old clothes in a bin and took a small silver-and-red business card the woman was offering. It was only when he felt its weight he realized the card really was silver, the hallmarked kind.

'We make hotel calls,' said the manager. 'If your itinerary is too crowded to allow for a revisit. Our number is in enamel.'

Chapter Eight

29th June

'I don't usually . . .'

The boy with the cats-eye contacts nodded like he understood and Zara took a good look and realized that he did. Which was just as well, because someone had to understand that she had her reasons for not wanting to be back.

'Where are we going . . . ?'

She knew the answer to that because he'd already told her, but asking again was easier than trying to remember, particularly as remembering might bring back something best forgotten.

'My place,' said the boy.

Her answering smile was wry, almost ironic. There were a dozen reasons why this was an extremely bad idea.

'Okay,' said Zara and climbed onto the waiting tram.

Where?

The elderly woman who stumbled into ZeeZee from behind when he suddenly stopped dead took one look at the foreigner's scowling face and decided to keep walking, in another direction. Not that ZeeZee even noticed: he was too busy stripping down his memory, deleting taste, smell and extraneous movement to find a simple primary colour.

There.

It took ZeeZee a split second to reassure himself that the people on tram weren't staring at him because he was dripping blood (he'd already sealed the knife cut with surgical glue from his complimentary Pan American medical kit before taping his ribs with skin from the all-night pharmacist). And it wasn't his suit that worried the people on the green tram, even though most of the other men wore flowing jellabas. It was his beard and dreadlocks. Or maybe it was the shades.

Too bad.

And yes, once they'd been a trademark of his but that had been by accident – and besides, it had been in another country. He wore shades from necessity because without them his eyes swallowed too much light. Just one of the little childhood modifications for which he had his mother's friends to thank.

Lately he'd taken to wearing polarized contacts but his supply was back at Huntsville along with his stash of crystalMeth and the rest of his life. Except it wasn't just life he'd been doing at Hunstville, it had been all day *and* all night, life with no option of parole. Which was still a pretty good result, given the district attorney had been going for throwing the big red switch.

'Excuse me.' ZeeZee stepped carefully across some market trader's outstretched boots and slid between two thick-set construction workers in concrete-splashed jellabas.

His brain was headed for what the fox would call a five-car crash and he needed that seat. Besides, that was where the girl sat, the girl he'd seen hesitate, then get on a green tram. The one whose sadness was flash-frozen to the inside of his eyes like lightning.

Though maybe that was just the meth.

ZeeZee knew immediately why his seat had been left free when the tram braked suddenly and the girl shot forward, straight into him. No amount of cologne could hide the reek of alcohol.

'I'm sorry,' said the boy beside her. He half stood, then sank back into his seat and turned away with the embarrassment of the still-young. Fourteen, thought ZeeZee, fifteen at the most. Silver hair, gold tear, lazer tattoo. Not as hard as he wanted to be.

Politely, ZeeZee put one hand on each of the girl's shoulders and pushed her back into her seat. The slightest of nods was all he got by way of acknowledgement. And it was obvious that she didn't trust herself to speak. As if sitting very still could hide the fact that she was too drunk to stand. A birthday or leaving do, ZeeZee decided, noting the card clutched loosely in her fingers and the bunch of orchids wilting on her lap.

Birthday parties gave good access. He'd used them back in Seattle. People's guards came down, making it easy to get close. Much closer than they mostly wanted: but then that was ZeeZee's speciality, getting close to targets who spent time and money keeping people like him at arm's length.

Style was a key factor and ZeeZee could do style. Looking right got you through doors that remained closed to others. Neatness, youth and an ability to blend. There'd been few places he couldn't enter if needs must . . . There was even a name for it. Negative capability . . .

ZeeZee smiled.

He was still smiling when the girl hunched forward and dribbled vomit from her mouth onto the tram floor between his shoes. She didn't do anything as vulgar as actually throw up, she just let the alcohol make its own return trip.

'Sorry.' That was the boy again.

ZeeZee shrugged. 'It happens.'

At Rue Sherif, ZeeZee pushed himself up off his seat and paused. He needed to know who she was, but he also needed to get off at this stop. Most of all, he wanted to tell the boy not to worry. But anything he said would have drawn attention to the girl's plight, so ZeeZee just nodded and kept going. He'd been those people, both of them. Just not for a long time.

Chapter Nine

29th June

Lodging House & Eating Shop read the old sign at the corner of Abu Dadrda and Rue Cif, though the building in question showed nothing but empty spaces where windows and door should have been. At ground level even the floorboards were missing, long wooden joists stretching out over darkness that dropped to a cellar below.

A plank had been nailed crudely across the open doorway as vague warning of the dangers that hid inside. And over by the far wall in the darkness something glittered that might have been glass reflected in the headlights of a car but proved to be a fox when ZeeZee removed his shades to take a proper look.

'Later,' said ZeeZee and the fox grinned toothily, saying nothing.

The man didn't believe in omens and of his many childhood demons only the arctic fox remained untamed. And Tiriganaq was more afraid of him than ZeeZee was of the fox. Because, if necessary, ZeeZee could stop answering and then it wouldn't matter if the fox called itself *Tiriganaq*, *Smoke* or *Earl Grey Malkin*, it would be alone.

Still, they'd always faced trouble together before, so ZeeZee couldn't imagine how he might have thought the fox would lie low this time.

Above them both, three storey walls gave way to a thin night sky, softened and faded by a sodium glare that didn't stretch far enough down to reach the side walk, had there been one.

East of El-Gomruk and south of Manshiya, but way too far north to be Karmus or Moharrem Bey, ZeeZee wasn't sure what this district was called. It had been blank of any name on the map at the tram station, its streets cross-hatched to tell cash-rich tourists that here was where they could find Iskandryia's famous souks.

ZeeZee could see the map clearly in his head, right down to the pink cross-hatching, but that meant nothing. There was very little from his life that he couldn't see in his head once he'd remembered where it was filed.

The entrance ZeeZee wanted turned out to be a narrow arch between two shops, one of which sold beaten brassware, the other old computers in shades of pastel. Between them was a door without a knocker. At head height was a peeling sign that read *On ne visite pas.*

Straightening his shoulders, ZeeZee rapped hard on the ancient door and then regretted it as noise crashed like thunder down both sides of the street. So he knocked again, more gently this time.

'What do you want?'

At least, ZeeZee imagined that was what the man on the other side of the door said, though he didn't recognize the language.

'I'm looking for Lady Nafisa,' said ZeeZee.

Nafisa. The voice turned the word over as if tasting it.

'Yes,' said ZeeZee. 'My aunt.'

'Why didn't you say so?' In the space where the door had been stood an old man, the stub of a cheroot gripped between his right thumb and skeletal first finger. Dark eyes examined ZeeZee's face and then the man stepped to one side. 'Our house is your house.' This time round he spoke in French, with a voice raw from a lifetime of cheap cigars.

There were five bolts on that door and the old man secured them all, including one that fixed straight up into the top of the arch and another that drove into the worn surface of a stained flagstone.

'This way.'

An arch in the side of the entrance room led left, followed by an immediate right turn through a second arch, which was when ZeeZee realized the shabby corridor he was in was really the start of a small, very simple maze leading to an ugly, obsessively-neat garden immediately beyond.

On either side of the garden stood open-fronted rooms, little more than flat roofs supported by sandstone pillars over a cracked terracotta floor. And at the far end of the garden was an ornate marble arch set in a simple brick wall. Once the formal garden had been naked to the sky but someone, years back, had roofed it over with steel and glass, panes of which were now cracked and dirty.

That the glass roof was old was obvious, because the frame supporting it was riveted to crossbeams that were held in place by cast-iron pillars, and a century's worth of paint had crusted round the rivets and smoothed the Doric decoration on the plinths to a bland ripple.

'This way.' The old man vanished through the marble arch into a cavernous, empty room where water didn't so much fall from a fountain as run bubbling down a free-standing slab of marble.

'*Shazarwan*,' announced the man and ZeeZee guessed he was naming the strange object.

Open arches on the far side of the room led into an open courtyard, smaller than the garden and tiled with white stone. In the centre stood a fountain carved from a single block of horsehair marble. But what ZeeZee noticed was the impossibly ornate four-storey house that rose at the far end of the courtyard.

Soft uplights pulled detail from a carved balustrade and threw its huge arches into shadow. If the al-Mansur madersa was meant to impress, then it succeeded.

Jerking his chin towards stairs that started up the outside of the madersa, then turned in under an arch to continue inside, the thin man stood back.

'Nafisa . . .' He said simply.

ZeeZee went.

'You're late,' said a voice that ZeeZee tracked to a small woman angrily pacing near the top of the stairs. Backlit by wall lights,

Lady Nafisa looked thin and birdlike, a neat faceless shadow but an angry one.

'Am I?' ZeeZee's first reaction was to apologize, then insist his flight was late, even though she'd know from her driver that this was untrue. But he didn't let himself do either. Instead, he shrugged and kept climbing, as if not caring if he walked straight through her.

'Shit happens,' he said as he reached the top and stared round at a huge room, open to the night through its arches on one side. Since heights and he didn't agree with each other, he didn't go look at the view. 'And besides, someone wanted a word.'

Lady Nafisa stopped suddenly. 'You saw somebody you knew?'

'Other way round,' said ZeeZee. 'He thought he knew me.'

They spoke French because that was the language Lady Nafisa had first used. Yet when it came, her switch to English was so fluent ZeeZee wasn't even certain she was aware of making it.

'I sent a car for you. A stretch Daimler-Benz.' She was doing her best to smile but there was real anger in her eyes. Which was fine with ZeeZee because he was pretty sure that, behind the expensive anonymity of the Versace shades she'd unwittingly bought for him there was real anger in his too.

Families had that effect on him and no family more strongly than his own. If she really was family, which remained to be proved.

'I make my own way,' said ZeeZee.

The woman stared at him. And behind the fashion-plate suit she saw ghosts of her husband backed up like reflections in a mirror. 'Later,' she said hastily. 'We can deal with this later . . .'

As if on cue, the skeletal porter from the rear entrance strode in clutching a brass tray that he placed on a three-legged wooden contraption which seemed to be waiting for it.

'This is Khartoum,' said Lady Nafisa, as if talking about a dog. 'He's from the Sudan so *you* can say anything you like in front of him.'

Meaning he didn't speak English, presumably.

'Unless, of course,' said ZeeZee, 'I say it in French, Arabic or whatever that other language was.'

Nafisa sighed. 'German,' she said heavily. 'I can see you're going to be like your father.'

Father? ZeeZee stared at her.

'Precise to the point of irritation.'

ZeeZee hadn't meant to be precise, merely glib. And since he'd never met his father and the last time he'd seen her, his mother still regarded the truth as something so fluid that identical sentences could mean opposite things on different days, he had no idea if Lady Nafisa even knew who his father was. Somehow he doubted it. Some undiscovered theory of chaos seemed to be the only thing that made sense of his family life to date.

Aim to please, shoot to kill. That had been one of Wild Boy's phrases back before Huntsville when he and Wild were still not quite enemies. 'We aim to please,' said ZeeZee.

'We?'

Yeah, we . . . ZeeZee clicked his heels and bowed slightly, almost as if he meant it. *Me and the fox.*

'Stupid that is,' the sudden voice behind ZeeZee was cutting in its contempt. 'Clicking your heels. No one really behaves like that in Iskandryia. I knew you'd be stupid.'

'*Hana.*'

'Hani,' corrected the girl.

Lady Nafisa sighed.

'Anyway, *Hani* what?' the child asked angrily, walking into the light. She had oil smeared across the palms of both her hands and bare ankles from where she'd slid down an elevator cable.

'You've got the floodlights on,' she said to Lady Nafisa and stalked over to a balustrade to examine the courtyard below. '*And* the fountain . . .' The small girl turned her head to stare at ZeeZee. 'You're honoured.' Her voice was bitter. 'She doesn't turn the lights on for anyone. She wouldn't even turn them on for my birthday party.'

'They were broken,' Lady Nafisa said fiercely.

'And now they're mended.' It didn't look like she believed her aunt for a minute.

'I'm Raf,' said ZeeZee.

'Ashraf,' corrected the child, scornfully. 'Don't I know it. She's talked of nothing else for days . . .'

'*Hani*.' Lady Nafisa's voice was hard.

'Yes, I know. Hani, be good. Hani, disappear . . .' The small girl turned round and stamped back towards the lift. 'You don't look like you're worth all the fuss,' she said cuttingly and slammed the grille, leaving ZeeZee with the impression of a small, furious animal glaring through the bars of a cage.

Chapter Ten

1st July

Dawn came in low, the sky clear and turquoise blue. And Hamzah Quitrimala knew exactly how it would look out on the water. The breaking light would catch one wave after another, until a ribbon of sun stretched from the horizon to the glass-sided cockpit of his 15,000bhp VSV. Fifty feet long, maybe ten at its widest, the boat was ex-police issue, chisel-prowed but flared at the stern. Stealth-sheeted and proof against infrared sensors.

It ran every month, midweek, without fail.

Diamonds carried to a pick-up point south of Iraklion/medical supplies brought back – Hamzah had captained the run himself when he was younger. Of course, in his day the boats had been nothing like as fast, but they had still done the job and been back before the second daybreak – which was more than Hamzah could say for his current crew.

He was going to have to find himself a new captain. But first he had a bey to see . . .

'Ashraf al-Mansur,' repeated ZeeZee. 'Known to his friends as Raf.'

ZeeZee emptied his mind and let the name roll over him. When he opened his eyes five minutes later the change was made and he was someone else, though boiling fog still filled the *hamman*, making it impossible for whoever he was to see the door.

In fact, so thick was the steam that Raf could hardly see his own feet, which might also have had something to do with the slick of sweat running down his forehead to drip into his eyes.

He stank, though not as much as when he woke first thing the previous morning, in a pool of perspiration that smelled sweet as blood and sour as dysentery. That was twenty-four hours ago, when his piss had been black. Now the colour was nearing normal as his body began to adjust to its lack of crystalMeth. It was his mind that was still addicted.

Raf was naked. In a domed room filled with naked women. Except the women were on the walls – pictures only, depicting a dozen dancers, their breasts full and bare, each plump *mons* hidden behind a wisp of fabric fashioned from tiny tesserae, marble fragments glued into place more than a century before by some artist keen to preserve a slight air of decency.

In Huntsville, in the days before Dr Millbank, recalcitrant convicts were broken by being locked in a hot-box and broiled. In El Iskandryia, even first thing in the morning, people had to book for the privilege.

Raf wasn't sure he understood why his aunt considered a Turkish bath the ideal place for him to meet Dr Hamzah Quitrimala Effendi. But here he was, still waiting for the man to show.

Sweat beads almost bubbled from his stomach and chest, and already he felt dehydrated.

'Your Excellency?'

Raf opened his eyes to see a man whose shoulders would make those of most sumo wrestlers look puny. A blue suit hung tent-like from his frame, its fabric already gone limp in the steam. In one ear was a gold Sony earbead, the kind you were meant to notice.

'Your Excellency?'

That was him, Raf realized. He nodded.

'The boss will be with you in a minute. He apologizes for being late.' Job done, the huge Russian took up position against the opposite wall, apparently impervious to the heat that soon had sweat rolling down his pink face.

'You Ashraf?' A thickset man strode in, hand already outstretched, gut protruding. 'Good to meet you.' He too was unashamedly naked, his uncovered genitals at eye height to where Raf sat on a marble bench.

Raf stood.

'Dr Hamzah Effendi?'

A lightning grin flashed across the man's face, then vanished, leaving only a wry, almost self-mocking smile. Lady Nafisa had insisted that Raf should remember to add the honorific to Hamzah's name. It was a neat touch.

The newcomer had the kind of handshake Raf expected. Strong but slightly clumsy, and brief as if he'd finally learned not to grab the hand of every contact and wring it heartily. Heavy gold links circled one wrist and on his middle finger was a huge ring set with a cauchabon ruby. Both screamed money but neither said anything about restraint.

Hamzah was rich and obviously enjoyed the fact.

Reading people was one of Raf's skills, like eidetic memory and night sight: he knew that and accepted it. It came from living in institutions . . . Swiss boarding school from the age of five, a Scottish school after that, three years working for Hu San in Seattle and then Huntsville. He'd been inside institutions all his life and only one of them had been a prison – the others just felt like it. They also felt safe. Raf wasn't stupid enough to deny that.

'Nasty scar,' said Hamzah.

'Yeah.'

'Recent.' Hamzah added. It wasn't a question. He examined the cut along Raf's ribs with a practised eye, taking in the double strip of plastic skin.

'Slipped and cut myself,' said Raf. Which was possible. Not true, admittedly, but no less unlikely than being mugged by golem with a photograph of him that wasn't. 'My own fault,' Raf added. 'Should have been more careful.'

'And that?'

Raf's shoulder looked, at first glance, like a map of some capital city of damaged flesh, lines radiating out from a densely scarred centre. 'Long story,' said Raf. 'Maybe some other time.'

* * *

If the steam room was hot, the plunge pool outside was so cold that Raf thought his heart would stop and his lungs never unfreeze.

'Lovely isn't it?' Hamzah said happily as they both bobbed to the surface. Raf scowled, but only because he had no breath left to speak.

'Strange,' said Hamzah as he kicked his way towards marble steps. 'I would have thought your father had a dozen Turkish baths . . .' He let his words trickle into a silence that stretched ever longer – until Raf finally realized the man wasn't just making conversation, he expected an answer.

Which was fair enough. Hamzah undoubtedly wanted to know what he was getting for his money. Raf's big problem was that he didn't have an easy reply.

'I lived with my mother,' Raf said, then stopped, because that wasn't strictly true either . . . For a start she wasn't really his mother and he hadn't really lived with her. Or maybe she was. Her opinion on that changed with the wind. And maybe he had . . .

'I boarded at various schools. England, Scotland, Switzerland.'

'Your ma was American?'

'English, living in New York.'

Hamzah shrugged as if it was all the same. Which it probably was to him. 'I'm told her name is well known . . .'

'Not unless you're a fan of the National Geographic channel,' said Raf. 'She campaigned for animal equality and worked on documentaries. Remember that film about meerkats?' Hamzah looked blank until Raf put his hands up like paws and swung his head from side to side, as if watching for danger.

Hamzah nodded.

'She did the camera work,' said Raf, clambering out of the water ahead of Hamzah. 'Syndicated in six continents. You can still get the screen saver. She took a flat fee of $1,500 and used it to fly down to Brazil to film vampire bats. Remember the baby panda trying to eat bamboo . . . ? The young fox playing in the snow? The white tiger cub with the empty Coke bottle? Well, she did camera on those, too.'

Animal porn, just a different kind. Cuddly images for a cold planet, used to fund the stuff that really interested her, like filming predators. Not that he was bitter or anything. 'She did a lot of the work for love,' said Raf, forcing himself to be fair. It had to be for love, because, God knew, there'd been little enough money in it. And it probably wasn't her fault the only way she could cope with a damaged world was by examining it through a lens or the bottom of a vodka bottle. But then, nor was her life his fault either, whatever she might have said . . .

'Let's go back to the steam room.'

Hamzah smiled. 'Getting a taste for it, eh?'

Sitting side by side and naked in the boiling mist, both men knew the real interview was beginning. But Lady Nafisa hadn't made clear to Raf who had final approval. All she'd said was that he shouldn't commit to any fact that could be checked, that he should keep answers vague and always return a question with a question.

She might know that Raf had spent years locked in a Seattle jail but there was no reason why Hamzah had to know too.

'You've been in America?' The industrialist's voice was studiedly relaxed, almost urbane. He hardly glanced at an ugly slash of scar tissue above Raf's right hip and when he did it was fleeting. Raf could have told him about the operation he'd had at five on a kidney but that story was as boring as the month he'd spent wired to machines.

'Were you working over there?'

'Something like that.' Raf stood and stretched, twisting his head to one side like a man with a bad crick in his neck. It fooled neither of them.

'Lady Nafisa mentioned that you were an honorary attaché.'

Did she? Reluctant to lie outright, Raf retreated into something close to the truth. 'To be honest,' he said, 'most of my time was spent on a doctorate.'

Behind bars, with limited web access and no on-campus visits.

'Finance?' Hamzah asked, looking suddenly interested.

'No,' said Raf. 'Alternative timelines. They've very big in

the US right now.' That, at least, was true. 'It's a way of understanding what happened by looking at what didn't but quite easily might have done . . . You know, say America had actually joined the Third Balkan War . . .'

'They stayed neutral. So did we.'

'Not the 1966–75 conflict,' said Raf, 'The *Third* Balkan, 1914–15. Say Woodrow Wilson hadn't cut a deal between Berlin and London but had sent in troops on Britain's side. London might have been victorious. The Kaiser might have been fatally weakened . . .'

'The Kaiser was always going to win,' Hamzah said flatly. 'History is what God writes.'

Raf sighed. 'Just imagine,' he said. 'The Prussian empire breaks up in 1923, just as the Austro-Hungarians almost did. Might the Ottomans have fallen? What would have happened to Egypt's Khedive?'

'*The Khedive* . . .' Hamzah knew better than to accuse a bey of treason. Especially not one who was about to marry his daughter. And no doubt, all this *what if* was merely some sophisticated game played by people without real jobs. But it sounded like treason to him.

Besides, Hamzah knew what *had* happened. Every schoolboy across North Africa knew that Islam had trampled colonialism into the ground. On Suvla plain, the English king's own servants from Sandringham had been killed to the last man. The slaughter at Gallipoli broke the warmongers' spirit.

Fatally weakened, the British were driven from Egypt by General Saad Zaghloul. Having stolen Libya in 1911, Italy was forced to give it back six years later, and the French relinquished Tunis.

Fifteen years of smouldering unrest followed. Nationalists, fundamentalists, Bolsheviks . . . but money from the Arabian oilfields bought them all off in the end. Mosques were built, hospitals erected and schools set up to educate the children of the poor. His grandfather had been one of them. The child of a *felah* who sharecropped a single strip of Nile mud far to the south of Iskandryia and resented bitterly the interference of *effendi* who demanded his child attend class when there was *bersim* to gather and irrigation channels to be kept open with a broad-bladed hoe.

From *felah* to *effendi* in three generations. That was worth something. And Hamzah's doctorate was in engineering. Which was worth something too. The industrialist nodded to his bodyguard and stood up to go. He had bribes to pay, building contracts to negotiate, a new captain to find for the Iraklion run.

Olga, his PA, would be waiting at the office with a long list of people to see and calls he should make. Most of which he would ignore.

'Where were you an attaché?' The final question was asked from politeness alone. Beys were obviously different and Hamzah made no pretence of seeing any value in the theories expounded by his future son-in-law.

'Seattle,' said Raf.

Hamzah sat down again. This time when his gaze flicked to the slash across Raf's ribs they stayed there. And when he looked back again there was something in his eyes that looked very like guilt.

One heavy hand came up to rest briefly on Raf's shoulder. 'I had no idea. No one told me.'

Raf said nothing because that was what someone who'd worked unofficially at the Seattle consulate would have said.

'That's confidential, obviously,' Raf muttered finally. 'So please don't mention it to anyone.'

'But I have to tell . . .'

'No,' said Raf, looking Hamzah straight in the eyes. 'What I did was insignificant. An *honorary* attaché is just someone's unpaid assistant.'

'And the person you worked for is dead.' It wasn't a question. Hamzah had watched the official broadcasts. And even if he hadn't, the bombing of the consulate in Seattle by Sword of God fundamentalists had filled the world's newsfeeds, swamped the radio stations and briefly turned even pirate TV into rolling 24-hour news channels.

Image after image had been bounced round the planet. Bodies

being pulled from the wreckage of a concrete building with heavy balconies. Viewers only knew the consulate once had balconies because CNN researchers had found 'before' shots to emphasize the horror of what came after.

One car bomb alone would have caused structural damage. But the consulate had main streets on three of its sides and the delivery trucks had been perfectly synchronized, their drivers in constant communication. The police deduced that the suicide bombers had been in regular radio contact from several charred fragments of circuit-board and the say-so of a thirteen-year-old band scanner, who'd been irritated to find crypted static where he was expecting juicy neighbourhood gossip.

Chapter Eleven

3rd July

The free city was not just built on the rubble of its own history, it used that rubble in the rebuilding. Greek columns reshaped by Roman artisans now formed part of mosque doorways, having been ripped from an earlier Byzantine church. So, too, the cultures had mixed. Until the rich mix became its own culture.

Berlin thought El Iskandryia barbarous, the White House feared it and Baghdad dismissed the metropolis as decadent and forgotten by God. But *realpolitik* demanded a Mediterranean free port where oil, cotton and particularly information could be traded. And El Isk got the job.

Roman, Byzantine, Coptic, Muslim . . . If ancient Babylon was the whore, then El Iskandryia had long been the courtesan: though for Islam's conquering army she was a sister to be brought back into the family. Napoleon called the city five shacks built over a dung heap. Nelson, being British, couldn't even get the sex right and dismissed the city as a crippled dog. But the insults meant nothing to Isk . . .

For Isk was hermaphrodite, ageless. A vampire of a city. Venerable and elegant, with a taste for fresh blood – a taste that it kept hidden behind stately boulevards and impeccable manners, in daylight at least. Night-time found the city stretching itself and yawning to reveal ancient fangs. Though the half-smile never left its face and the dark glint never left its eye.

And to assume Isk had a single identity was to misunderstand the Gordian complexity of its personality. The vampire existed parallel to the blonde innocent-eyed victim, the virgin inside the whore. There never had been only one city at any time in El Iskandryia's history. And for all its ancient glory, there were days when Isk was afraid of its own shadow, of the tarnished side of the mirror it held up to the world.

Days like now, when all that showed inside on Le Trianon's bar screen was a rerun of that morning's executions in Riyadh. A Saudi paedophile and a Sudanese found guilty of sorcery, both losing their heads in the flash of a sword blade, then losing them again in slow motion.

Family.

Ashraf al-Mansur, who was doing his best not to think of himself as ZeeZee, rolled the word round his mouth and spat it out. He'd never had one and wasn't sure why he'd want to start now. As a child, in Zurich, he'd known boys at the Academy with families. Seen the strange effect it had on them. They cried from homesickness at the start of term and then no longer felt at home when they went back for the holidays. Their parents were worse. The kind of people who talked about roots and forgot those were what kept vegetables in the ground.

Besides, Raf didn't need roots. He came with a 8000-line guarantee that promised his *genetic heritability* would always outweigh *social calibration*. Whatever the fuck that meant.

At first, given the number of zeros after the first number in the price, Raf thought that his mother must really love him . . . But later, when he looked at her accounts for the year of his birth, he found that ninety-five per cent of the cost of the genetic manipulation had been met by Bayer-Rochelle and the rest she'd written off over five years against tax.

Oh, and the pharmaceutical company had totally funded her next three expeditions and made a sizeable one-off donation to a pressure group for which she was official photographer. It was around that time she'd stopped campaigning against non-transparent genome research.

On the evening he arrived Lady Nafisa had made clear the payment she intended to collect for digging him out of Huntsville. Though what she talked about was the need for family members to help each other, to accept their responsibilities.

'I don't have a family,' Raf had said. 'I *had* a mother. And when I wanted to talk to her I'd call her agent.'

Lady Nafisa had looked at him. 'Your father is my brother-in-law. That makes us family.'

Her brother in law . . . 'My father was a backpacker,' said Raf. 'From Goteborg. My mother didn't even get his name.' The man had apparently been hired for a week to drive his mother across the Sahel when she was filming the Lybian striped weasel, probably because she was too wasted to steer the vehicle herself.

'No.' Lady Nafisa shook her head. 'You must listen to me. The Emir of Tunis is your father.'

'Yeah, right,' said Raf. 'That well-known Swede.'

'Blue eyes, white hair, high cheekbones. You're Berber,' Lady Nafisa told him crossly. 'Look it up . . . And while you're at it, take a good look at this.' Only Raf didn't need to take a good look because he'd seen the picture before – the palm trees, the minaret, the man with the drop-pearl earring.

'Your father,' said Lady Nafisa.

Raf wanted to say that she was talking to the wrong man: but then suddenly realised he was the one who'd got it wrong. It wasn't his responsibilities they were discussing – or not just his – it was her responsibilities to him. An odd and uncomfortable thought.

'I knew he had a brat by an American,' Lady Nafisa said. 'And that he paid your mother a small allowance, but he does that for all his bastards, he can afford it. But he also told me you were illegitimate. And he lied.'

She handed Raf a letter.

Beneath the words *Isaac and Sons. Commissioners of Oaths*, a rush of Arabic flowed right to left across expensive paper like tiny waves. Raf could no more read it than fly. 'What does it say?' Raf asked, handing it back.

'On 30 April . . . Pashazade Zari al-Mansur, only son of the Emir of Tunis, married Sally Welham at a private ceremony in an annex of the Great al-Zaytuna Mosque,' Lady Nafisa recited from memory. 'She was his third wife. He divorced her five days later.'

'My mother was already married.'

Lady Nafisa made no pretence of scanning the paper. 'My informant says not . . . Your real name is Ashraf al-Mansur. Under Ottoman law you hold the rank of *bey*, which entitles you to a senior post in the Public Service.' She glanced up. 'We'll talk about that later. You have *carte blanche* anywhere in Ottoman North Africa from Tunis to Stambul and you have diplomatic immunity everywhere else in the world, for any crime except murder . . .'

Raf pushed his empty coffee cup aside and prepared to stand, but the moment he began to ease back his chair a waiter materialized at his side and shifted it for him. Seconds later the *patron* himself appeared.

'Will we be seeing Your Excellency soon?'

'Monday morning, I would imagine,' said Raf and the small man smiled.

'I'll reserve your table.' He glanced at the English-language newspaper Ashraf had downloaded from a stall. 'And I'll have a copy of *The Alexandrian* waiting . . .'

A sluggish breeze rolling lazily off the sea faded as Raf headed inland. Away from the Corniche the hot midday air was muggy, with humidity high enough to merit a warning on the local newsfeed. Common sense said grab the nearest air-conditioned taxi, but Raf ignored the sweat beginning to build under his thick beard and headed south on foot towards Lady Nafisa's house.

Between Le Trianon and Rue Abu Dadrda, Raf found one *boulevard*, four *rues* and a quiet tree-lined *place* named al-Mansur, historical detritus of the family to which he now belonged.

And Raf was more than halfway across the *place* before he finally realized why Nafisa's roofed-over garden inspired in him such hatred.

Chapter Twelve

Seattle

Out at Huntsville the rain did more than merely drum on glass: it fell like buckshot. But before there could be Huntsville, the city of Seattle had to exist – and the fox blamed that on a man called Asa Mercer.

On 16 January 1866, Mercer left New York with thirty-four unmarried girls bound for a new settlement at Puget Sound on the Pacific coast. He'd hoped to bring more than 700 but, all the same, it was an improvement on his first expedition to collect marriageable women. Then he had persuaded only eleven to make the dangerous trip. Maybe it had been the rumours of rain that put them off, maybe it had been the distance, or the fact that the war was only recently over . . . Whatever, that had been then and this was later.

It still rained though, because in Seattle this was what the weather did – even ZeeZee knew that. And the rain drummed off city sidewalks, or beat on sun canopies raised in hope over empty tables outside cafés.

But out at Huntsville the rain did more than merely drum, its buckshot fell on the glass roof of the jail, twenty-four/seven. At least, that was what it felt like to ZeeZee those first few months he was there. Until the snow came and with it silence.

A masterpiece of nineteenth-century iron and glass, built twenty-five years after Paxton first led the way by using prefabricated sections for London's famous Crystal Palace, Huntsville Penitentiary was a monument to man's ingenuity – and stupidity.

Not the stupidity of the convicts who ended up there but of the architects, philanthropists and politicians of Washington State. Men who wanted their names immortalized in a correctional glass cathedral that turned out, in practice, to function as little more than an ice house.

Two riots in three winters went some way towards convincing the governor that the design was not as humane as he'd been led to believe. But since five identical penitentiaries had already been built in other states to the same plan, and all had been unsuccessful, this didn't come as a surprise to his critics.

By 1930, nearly sixty years later, all were ruins except Huntsville. In 1979 Huntsville was finally decommissioned. And then, in the final year of the twentieth century, Californian therapist Dr Anthony Millbank published his revolutionary work on lux therapy.

Crime, said Dr Millbank, wasn't merely a matter of incorrect socialization, food allergy or genetic malfunction, which in animals was called bad blood. Therefore social therapy, healthy meals and carefully selected drugs were not the complete answer.

Most crime was urban. What most urban dwellers lacked was natural light. It was therefore obvious that light-deprivation was a contributory factor in crime. Since most of middle America believed that original sin rather than genetics, allergies or lack of breastfeeding led to crime, they paid little attention to the latest addition to the list of contributory causes. Though a teenage serial killer who drained, labelled and later drank the chilled blood of his victims mixed with Stolichnaya gained brief notoriety by claiming his murderous tendencies were caused by an aversion to food, shopping malls and daylight.

But Dr Millbank persisted, helped both by appearances on Oprah and data-showing that the gene cFos (a marker for the human internal clock) peaked only once – under artificial light, at dawn, but expressed at dawn and dusk in natural light.

There was, in Dr Millbank's opinion, a distinct and irrefutable correlation between artificial light and crime.

The gradual shifts in light-intensity and wavelength that caused humans to adjust peacefully to the transition between night and day were missing in urban society. And basic research showed that under the artificial conditions imposed by electric light, even lab rats and gerbils became restless and unsettled.

How much better, then, for naturally unsettled people – like prisoners – to benefit from lux therapy rather than live under a regime governed by harmful artificial light . . .

No state in the US would fund a new penitentiary based on the ideas of Dr Millbank so he applied for a private licence and founded his own prison, buying Huntsville cheap from the city of Seattle which was delighted to offload its responsibility for a decaying Victorian masterpiece.

Dr Millbank's price was that five miles of forest and scrub around Huntsville should officially be declared a dark-sky preserve, with light-pollution strictly controlled within this perimeter. Heating was installed, lifts, carpets . . . a gym, a weights room, an Olympic-size swimming pool.

Huntsville wasn't just unique in being run according to the theories of Dr Anthony Millbank. It was the only penitentiary in the US allowed to charge its inmates hotel fees. To be incarcerated at Huntsville cost money: about the same as sending a child to a good Ivy League University. Everyone loved the place, except the police. The state saved money on prisoners, those incarcerated mixed with a better class of criminal and there was none of the gang violence endemic in most other American prisons.

The kind of people who belonged in gangs couldn't afford the fees. It wasn't that the inmates were all white, all Anglo-Saxon or all Protestant. From the very start, right from the turn of the century, there was a rich mix of embezzlers, capi di capi and drug barons of every ethnic origin. The only thing they had in common was that they were all very definitely not poor.

Justifying the existence of Huntsville, however, proved a politician's nightmare. Democrats hated the prison's elitist credentials, Republicans loathed the softness of its regime: but when a senator from one party was caught bribing a congressman from another, Huntsville was where both elected to serve their sentences.

Statistics put inmate violence at almost zero and for once they were accurate. Violence happened, but not often, and violence between prisoners and staff was literally unknown. Which was why ZeeZee Welham's unprovoked attack on the elderly, white-haired Dr Millbank sent shock waves through every elegant Huntsville walkway.

Merely punching any member of staff would have been horrifying enough. But to grip Dr Millbank himself by his scraggy throat and drag him across his own desk to plant a blow that split his lip as if it had been a ripe plum was beyond belief. So far beyond belief that Dr Millbank announced on the spot that what ZeeZee needed was not punishment but psychiatric help. His words left a fine spray of blood across his attacker's tangled beard and broad chest, but even then he handed ZeeZee a Kleenex from a box by his desk.

It made ZeeZee want to punch him all over again.

All of which explained how ZeeZee found himself in the passenger seat of a Lincoln Continental coming off the 522 onto Interstate 5, with Lake Washington on one side and Puget Sound on the other, on his way to psychiatric assessment at a hospital in Takona.

The man driving him to Mount Olive Hospital was Clem Burke, a bull from a downstate prison who was undergoing compulsory rehabilitation at Huntsville after taking a nightstick to the skull of an inmate at his old jail. Making Clem Burke work as a warder at Huntsville was probably constitutionally illegal: he certainly regarded it as cruel and unusual.

'You know what I'd do with you?'

ZeeZee looked across as Clem swung the heavy Lincoln out into the fast lane and overtook an old Beetle, nudging so close the VW got almost buffeted off the freeway.

'Let me guess . . .'

'Nah,' said Clem. 'Don't bother. You couldn't begin to imagine.' He shifted down a gear and slid past a truck on its nearside, angrily flicking it the finger when the Mack hit its brakes and flashed its lights.

'This Shitville do-gooding crap. It's just toss. You don't just hit the Governor and get away with it.' The Lincoln lurched forward, closing up a gap before anyone could pull into it.

'Rehabilitation not working, then?' ZeeZee asked innocently.

He enjoyed watching the veins stand out on Clem's fat neck and his face turn an even deeper shade of purple.

'Solitary,' snarled Clem. 'That's what you need. Stripped naked in a sweatbox; till you as pink and pretty as a baby. Then I'd give your ass to some Boss Nigra . . . That's what. That's the way any real prison would do it.'

A real prison probably would, too. But then, someone was paying ZeeZee's fees precisely to ensure stuff like that didn't happen. And ZeeZee had a pretty good idea where that money came from. A Chinese woman who knew who really put a .22 through the back of Micky O'Brian's head and watched him crumple as the sub-sonic slug ricocheted around the inside of his skull, scrambling what was left of Micky's brains after a $15,000-a-month crack habit had magimixed its share. And Hu San wasn't someone ZeeZee wanted to upset. Not now, not ever . . .

Mentioning her name in public would have been a quicker way of committing suicide than standing up in court to claim he'd killed Micky, he'd meant to kill Micky and, given half a chance, he'd kill Micky again. And which way should he go for the electric chair?

All of which would have been a lie.

ZeeZee kept his eyes on the interstate. Watching the approach signs for SeaTac Airport and the other cars. Which was more than Clem Burke did.

'What do you think of that, then?' Clem asked. He was chewing the inside of his lip at the thought of ZeeZee pegged out in some sweatbox or on his knees tossing salad for a war daddy.

'Well?' Clem demanded.

'It's not going to happen,' said ZeeZee. At least, not now. He'd spent a lot of time in the remand centre worrying about what came next. Wondering what the rippers inside might *have in mind for a polite blond boy with a nice English accent.*

So he did his own attitude adjustment, before anyone else got the chance. Within a month his prissy accent was gone – still obviously English, but flatter and harder. He took up exercise in his cell. And then, when his shoulders had developed and his arms had grown stronger, he braved the gym. In the weeks that followed he let his hair grow, gave up shaving and stopped washing until his skin finally found its balance.

His life was a xerox, a copy. And the original wasn't his. Never had been. He was a mirror, in which people saw what they wanted to see; and in him they soon saw a J-Cat, ready for the Ding Wing, walking the very edge of psychosis.

He took up tai chi – minus the sword, obviously. Volunteered to act as kick bag to a hard-ass elderly rasta with a thing for Capoeira. He learned ginga, rabo de arraia and queixada as well as esquiva and a few other basic defensive moves, but mostly he learned blade technique, though to the badges and white-shirts it just looked like dance. But then that was the whole point of a martial art which had survived by disguising itself as something else.

'Do your own time,' warned the rasta and ZeeZee did. He kept himself to himself, didn't pry, didn't boast, lost the fights he couldn't win or absolutely couldn't avoid, until one week he won, then won again, earning himself space. And when the rasta nicknamed him after some hick redneck band, ZeeZee took it as a compliment and waxed his own matted hair into embryo dreadlocks.

But as age nineteen slid into twenty and a date still wasn't set for his trial, ZeeZee kept on fretting, right up to the morning a suited lawyer turned up in his holding cell at Remand3 and put the basis of a cast-iron insanity plea in front of him.

It was elegant, it was sweet and all ZeeZee had to do was agree: but it was only when the lawyer mentioned 'ville that ZeeZee nodded and reached for a pen.

'I didn't kill anyone,' he told Clem suddenly.

'Yeah,' Clem hawked out his window, just missing the windscreen of a passing saloon. 'That's something else I'd kick out of you cons at Shitville. All that "Poor me, I'm innocent" shit. If you weren't guilty you wouldn't be there. How fucking simple do you want it?'

ZeeZee silently shook his head. In his case guilty didn't come into it. He was either innocent or mad, not that Dr Millbank used such words. Hysterically amnesiac was what had made it onto ZeeZee's files. He knew: the doctor had powered up a screen just to show him.

The insanity plea on offer was simple. ZeeZee couldn't be convicted of murdering Micky O'Brian because he didn't know he'd done it. His fingerprints might be on the Wilson Combat thrown down by Micky's body, they might also be on a couple of .22LR in its magazine and all over the conversion unit that had replaced the Wilson's usual .45 barrel, but ZeeZee genuinely didn't know he'd fired the shot.

Even though the police had found him in O'Brian's house overlooking Puget Sound, standing in the hallway with Micky dead in the gallery at the top of the stairs.

Every lie-detector test ZeeZee took came up clean, and he'd taken five, three of them in sterile-lab conditions. He'd had CT and MRI and, according to the expert witness lined up for his trial, the scans revealed fear and anxiety but absolutely no guilt. At the demand of the police, he'd undergone full hypnotic memory-recall. He recalled nothing.

The defence was simple.

ZeeZee believed he was not guilty, except all the evidence said he was. Ergo, to use his lawyer's phrase, he was innocent through insanity. Except that ZeeZee knew the lawyer realized that wasn't how it went. ZeeZee might not be guilty but he wasn't insane. Insanity would involve naming Hu San.

'Hey!' ZeeZee nodded at a black pick-up only inches from the front of Clem's Lincoln. 'What gives?'

'Asshole won't pull over.'

'Look,' said ZeeZee, drawing his knees up into the brace position. 'We're in the slow lane, Chief. Where's he going to move?'

'That's not my problem,' Clem announced, but he edged back slightly. And just as ZeeZee was about to sigh with relief, Clem hit the gas again, lurching the Lincoln straight into the back of the pick-up. Metal shrieked and locked, and then the Lincoln twisted sideways, did half a revolution and came to a halt on the hard shoulder fifty yards later. Fifty yards in which ZeeZee sat in the passenger seat aware he was going down the interstate, backwards . . .

Very sensibly, the pick-up truck kept going, dragging the ripped-off remains of a Lincoln's bumper behind it in a flashy display of sparks.

'Jesus,' said ZeeZee when he could say anything at all. 'You trying to kill me?'

'No,' said Clem. 'Nothing that simple.' He fished in the car's glove compartment and came out with a matt black Para Ordnance .45 – the 15-round, police-issue model.

ZeeZee didn't register the make, finish or calibre. He was too busy looking at the void of its muzzle, which pointed straight at his head.

'This is where you escape,' announced Clem. 'And over there's where you run, towards that nice big sign saying Flight Departures.'

'And just about here's where you shoot me in the back,' said ZeeZee, nodding to a spot ten paces from the car.

'No,' Clem shook his head as he leaned across and shoved open ZeeZee's door. 'I'm retiring and you're my pension plan.' Reaching under his seat, Clem yanked out a briefcase. 'The combination's your DOB.' He grinned sourly. 'I don't want to know what's in here. Just make sure you open it well away from my car . . .'

'Who's paying you?'

Clem didn't know, but he had no intention of admitting that to ZeeZee.

'Tell me,' ZeeZee insisted. What with remand, taking the plea and developing his designer mad-fuck persona, he'd put a lot of effort into staying alive.

Clem pulled back the slide on the Para Ordnance.

Stay and get shot, run and ditto. It had been a day full of shit choices. But what really scared ZeeZee was that the whole wired-out scenario had Wild Boy stamped all over it and ZeeZee didn't trust Hu San's deputy. The Boss – now, she'd have done it differently, smoothly.

'I'm not going unless you tell me,' ZeeZee said, slamming shut his door. No one tried to escape from Huntsville because no one could afford to. A bond was posted prior to arrival. Any attempt to escape automatically forfeited the bond, which was a multiple of the number of years in the sentence times a sliding scale according to the severity of the crime and the perp's previous . . . Killing a police informant – ZeeZee didn't even want to think what his bond would have been set at.

Unless it really was Hu San organizing this, busting out of Huntsville was just a quick way to commit suicide. Marginally less dramatic than standing up in court to name the woman. But only marginally . . .

'Your choice,' said Clem, raising the automatic. He was smiling.

The briefcase was retro Alessi, with a numerical lock and little purple LCDs that glowed through black glass: Fooler loops were built into its sides and the handle housed a semi-AI whose sole job was to inform airport scanners that the contents were covered by diplomatic protocol.

Holding his breath, ZeeZee started counting to ten in his head and lifted the lid. He reached seventeen before he realized he could stop now. His initial haul from the case was a plane ticket, a white passport and a strip of photos from one of those Kodak booths found at stations. The smiling girl in the shots was young, dark-skinned, middle Eastern. Four different poses, but each frame showed the same wide-eyed teenager.

ZeeZee flicked open the ticket and scanned the details. All the real data was encoded in a strip running along the outer edge of the front cover: the printout inside was just a reminder. It was made out to Ashraf al-Mansur, OA-273 flight to Cairo, with a connecting flight to El Iskandryia, taking off—

In about fifteen minutes, according to ZeeZee's watch. He checked the passport and blinked as his own face stared up at him, only shaved and without the dreadlocks, surrounded by a sea of unreadable foreign type. That the photograph had him wearing a suit and tie he'd never seen before was weird, but what really weirded him out was the simple English phrase across the top of each page.

Everyone had heard of diplomatic immunity.

In a small pocket in the lining of the lid was a platinum HKS, with a holo of his face on the reverse, stamped over with a mesh of laser thread. Finding the card was enough to make ZeeZee ransack every slot, pocket and zipped compartment in the case but he discovered nothing else, except a crumpled Mexican quality-control slip and a torn sachet of silica gel.

The check-in desk for the flight had already closed but ZeeZee stared round in such obvious distress that a girl two desks down trotted off to get an Ottoman Airways official.

'I'm on flight OA-273.'

'I'm sorry, sir, your gate's closed.'

'But I have . . .'

'It shut twenty minutes ago.'

Mutely, ZeeZee thrust his ticket at the American woman who took it with a frown, as if actually touching the thing might commit her to something. She flicked back the cover to glance at the counterfoil, then looked at ZeeZee: taking in the blond biker beard and beeswaxed dreadlocks, the pale blue Huntsville jumpsuit and tatty trainers.

'Something wrong?' ZeeZee had trouble keeping anxiety out of his voice.

Yes, there was, but not in the way he meant. Counterfoils were discreetly colour-coded for priority, to avoid bouncing the wrong people off over-booked flights. The scale ran green up though red. ZeeZee's ticket was coded gold.

'Can I see your passport, please, sir?' Her face was white with hostility.

She didn't even bother to take the small booklet ZeeZee tried to hand over. Instead, she made sure her fingers didn't touch his as she handed ZeeZee back his ticket.

'I'll see what we can do about stopping the plane.'

He was waved through Security, which was probably just as well. And then a black kid with three gold nose rings hurled ZeeZee through the crowds filling Departures, horn beeping as ZeeZee gripped tight to a rail that ran around the back seat of the little electric buggy.

'Man, I love that,' announced the kid as he slammed to a halt.

'Some ride,' agreed ZeeZee, clambering off.

'Yeah.' The driver did as near to a skid turn as he could manage with an electric cart on the carpeted floor of an embarkation tunnel. 'A rock god in a hurry. It's the only thing makes my life worth living.'

Once aboard the Alle Volante, ZeeZee was shown to his cabin. A tiny cubicle with a shower stall, chair and the kind of double bed that might just fit two people if both were fashionably thin and intended to spend most of the flight on top of each other. For one person it was ideal.

The catalogue of duty-free goods was the same as it ever was – full of overpriced and ugly items that probably seemed a good idea at the time. ZeeZee skimmed through a dozen screens, adding to his basket a shirt, combats, new shoes, a silver Omega, a black G-Shock and hair clippers, along with a choice of complimentary medical kit that came free because he'd racked up more than $2500. He chose number three, which claimed it was for essential in tropical emergencies and came with malaria patches, surgical glue, unbreakable condoms and a generalized snake-venom antidote.

When the screen asked for payment ZeeZee fed it the number on his new card and in reply got a smiling cartoon valet who assured him all the goods would be delivered within five minutes.

Halfway across the Atlantic, ZeeZee turned up the screen again and found a local Seattle newsfeed. Any reference to his *own escape had been relegated to non-news by the murder in Kabul of the mujahadeen general Sheikh el-Halana.*

ZeeZee knew all about Sheikh el-Halana: the whole world knew. Two weeks back, fundamentalists had bombed the Ottoman consulate in Seattle, killing thirty-five and destroying the consulate, its computers, its listening centre and most of its records. The FBI had spent twelve days saying nothing, then announced there was little likelihood of getting enough evidence to convict. And now, two days after that announcement, the man widely suspected of being behind the bombing was dead.

Somewhere on the outer edges of ZeeZee's tired brain a plan began to gel. Reaching for the complimentary in-flight notebook, he scrawled seven words on the first page, crossed one word out, added another two and circled them all individually before joining them together with a rapid flurry of lines. His next identity now had a little flesh on its bones.

Chapter Thirteen

3rd July

When Ali-Din was bored he peed on the tiles. Hani didn't have that option. She wasn't even allowed to visit the lavatory when Aunt Nafisa had company. She wasn't allowed books and she certainly wasn't allowed her Nintendo gamepad.

Wiping up Ali-Din's puddle with her shawl, Hani screwed the sodden cloth into a bundle and stuffed it under her chair for Khartoum to find. Hani was bored, too, and lunch hadn't even started. To make things worse, it looked as if lunch might not start for ages. Ashraf was late and everyone was pretending they didn't mind.

Well, she *did* mind, she minded a lot . . . Aunt Nafisa had forced her into a dress and kept at the knots in her hair until Hani's scalp hurt.

The woman Ashraf was going to marry didn't look that happy, either. She was prettier than Hani had expected – dark, though, with black hair cut so short it probably didn't need to be brushed at all. She wasn't wearing a proper dress, either . . . just a long scarlet coat with baggy trousers underneath. There were three holes in one of her ears but no earrings in any of the holes.

Zara caught Hani staring and forced a smile. Instantly the child snatched away her glance, then looked back. When Hani married it was going to be to a pasha, rich and handsome, Aunt Nafisa had promised. Ashraf was a bey, which was almost as good, but he looked weird. Aunt Nafisa said that was because he'd been doing secret work for the government. And no, Hani wasn't allowed to ask him about it.

Everyone in the *qaa* was sitting on silver chairs, except for the big man leaning against a pillar. Probably he was worried he might break his if he sat on it. The chairs were classically French, made a hundred and fifty years earlier when Third Empire was what families like theirs had wanted, so Aunt Nafisa had told her.

But instead of the cabinet maker covering each chair-back with walnut veneer, he'd finished the entire frame – legs, back and sides – with a tissue-like sheet of beaten silver. And the matching chest of drawers, divan and semi-circular occasional tables had their own share of similar ornamentation. All of the madersa furniture on display in the public rooms was *haute* Third Empire, refracted through Ottoman eyes. It looked ugly to Hani but she'd learnt to keep that opinion to herself.

'Sorry . . .' Steps rang on the marble stairs leading up to the *qaa* and Hani forgot furniture at the same moment as she stopped being bored.

'Ashraf!' Lady Nafisa's voice hovered between fury and thinly disguised relief that he'd shown at all. Smoke had been twisting up from the kitchens for at least an hour. And while Nafisa's cook Donna might have been spit-roasting a goat over an open fire of juniper twigs, Hani's money was on something in an oven beginning to burn.

'I'm sorry,' said Raf, looking round the *qaa*. 'I was at my office.'

'On a *Saturday*?' Hani snorted, not bothering to disguise the disbelief in her voice. Even she could lie better than that.

'*He went to his office.*' She hooked Ali-Din up onto her lap and rubbed her nose in his fur, ignoring her aunt's scowl. It said something about how determined Aunt Nafisa was that things should go smoothly that she didn't immediately order Hani to take the puppy outside.

'Yes,' said Raf. 'And then I walked home.'

'Doesn't look far on a map,' growled a voice he knew. 'Rather different against the crowds.' Hamzah Effendi left his place at the balustrade, wrung Raf's hand heartily and retreated back to his pillar.

'Lady N doesn't like it,' he said, waving a fat cigar. 'Nor does my wife. Don't blame you going to the office. Probably the only place you can get some peace. Still,' he said, 'you're here now and that's what counts.' Dropping his cigar to the floor, Hamzah ground the butt under heel.

Lady Nafisa tried not to wince.

'My nephew, Pashazade al-Mansur, Ashraf Bey,' she said to a short thickset woman loaded down with more gold than the federal reserve. 'His father is the Emir of Tunis.' Lady Nafisa sounded as if she was selling a horse at auction.

'Ashraf, this is Madame Rahina . . .' It was obvious from the shock on the fat woman's face that her husband hadn't warned her about Raf's beard or dreadlocks.

'. . . And you know Dr Hamzah Quitrimala Effendi, who owns HZ Oil . . .'

'Bloody hard work,' said Hamzah, tapping a fresh cigar from a leather case that looked like it should contain shotgun shells. 'Pity you took that job at the Third Circle. Could have done with a good man on board. God knows, Kamil's never going to be up to—'

Both Lady Nafisa and Hamzah's wife suddenly found something else to talk about, so Raf never heard who Kamil was or what he wasn't up to. But from the frown on the face of Federal Reserve and the quarrelsome expression of Hamzah Effendi himself, Raf guessed that, whoever he was, they argued about him a lot.

'And this is my daughter,' said Madame Rahina hastily. 'She has a very good job at the New Alexandrian Library.'

'We've met,' said Raf.

Madame Rahina looked at him in shock.

'Four days ago,' said Raf, talking to the girl. 'On a green tram. Going south, heading for Rue Derida. You were carrying flowers.'

'It can't have been Zara,' Madame Rahina said firmly. 'She stayed over with a friend in Abukir. They both caught the most terrible food poisoning.'

'Then I must be wrong.' Raf peeled off his glasses and dropped them in his pocket. 'Still . . .' he shrugged, 'I'm surprised there are two such attractive girls in El Iskandryia.'

Zara shot him a look that mixed relief with outrage and her mother smirked. But it was Hamzah Effendi who spoke. 'Nasty stuff, food poisoning,' he said, looking at Zara.

'It's disgraceful,' said Lady Nafisa firmly from her end of the table. 'Completely disgraceful that we let immigrants mutilate each other in the name of *RenSchmiss*. I've written to General Saeed himself and asked him to complain to the Khedive . . .'

She glanced to her right, as if daring Hamzah to argue. There was no fear the person sat to her left would disagree. So far, Madame Rahina had nodded fiercely every time Lady Nafisa opened her mouth.

The big man just shrugged, though from his position at the other end of the table Raf couldn't tell if this was because Hamzah couldn't be bothered to argue or because he genuinely didn't concern himself with Germans.

'What's *RenSchmiss*?' Hani asked.

The table went very still.

'I'll tell you later,' Lady Nafisa said, in a voice that meant she wouldn't.

'I want to know *now*,' Hani demanded. She dipped sticky fingers into a bowl of warm water and rose petals, shook them dry and sat back. Everything about her said she wasn't going to rest easy until someone had answered.

'*Hani*,' said her aunt.

'Well?' The small girl tugged Raf's sleeve and when he shrugged she turned to Zara. Hani could put up with Ali-Din being banished while they ate but didn't see why she had to put up with not understanding what everybody else was talking about as well.

'You tell me.'

Zara smiled as she dipped her own fingers in a rose bowl and shook them. 'Have you seen those gashes German boys have on their cheeks?'

Hani shook her head.

'We think it looks ugly but it's tradition for them,' said Zara.

'*Renommer schmiss*, the scars prove their bravery. When boys like that get to about fifteen, they go to a gymnasium, put on special jackets, helmets and metal goggles. And then they stand absolutely still, while an opponent slashes open their face . . .'

'Zara wrote a paper on it at Colombia,' Madame Rahina said hastily.

'Not to be encouraged,' Lady Nafisa said. She might have been talking about *RenSchmiss* but, equally, her comment could apply to letting girls go abroad to college. 'Cousin Jalila and I have also sent a letter to *El Iskandryia* demanding the practice be banned.'

'We also have our traditions,' Zara said quietly, 'ones which they could call—'

Lady Nafisa set her mouth into a straight line. 'No,' she said. 'There is a difference between barbarism and the medical demands for a healthy life.'

Hani giggled. The mention of healthy living having brought a smirk on her face. 'You know where my Aunt Jalila goes?' she whispered to Raf when he bent to listen.

He shook his head.

It involved hoses and bottoms.

Lunch was in the *qaa*, at an oval table cast from marble dust and inlaid along the top with swirling Persian-blue tesserae arranged as a peacock displaying its tail. Matching benches curved down both sides of the table. Only Lady Nafisa had a chair.

The main part of the meal was goat, split open and spit-roasted until the flesh was so tender no knife was necessary and hot mouthfuls could be pinched off between finger and thumb. Two French waiters from a local café carried the dishes from the kitchens, Lady Nafisa having promised to pay what they demanded, provided they wore their uniforms from the café and the uniforms were clean.

Food as politics and food as blackmail: both theories had been regurgitated more times than anyone could remember. But food as an elaborate dance, somewhere between etiquette and preening display, that was new to Raf. Though not to Isk, where the conspicuous consumption – not of rich or rare ingredients, though both were there – but of time itself was as ancient as the elaborate laws governing hospitality.

Time given was what was on display.

In Isk, just as in Tunis, Marrakesh or Fez, ceremonial food required preparation: the more preparation, the greater the respect being offered to guests. Tradition also demanded that ingredients be divided into small portions, wrapped in filo or hidden beneath pastry in pies, rolled in crushed nuts or stuffed into vegetables that had been lovingly hollowed out or cored. Food bought at a stall or fast-food joint was different. No one expected Burger King to be anything other than cheap, swift and anodyne. But in the home, it was almost an insult to offer guests food that looked as if preparing it took anything less than total commitment.

Served with the roast kid was a silver-edged clay bowl of saffron rice, plus a dish of red couscous, a chicken tajine where the juices had been sweetened with honey and reduced to a sticky syrup, fried red mullet with marjoram, and fresh matlou bread, which Lady Nafisa asked Raf to break and portion out in order of precedence. Hani got her chunk last, being both female and a child.

All the recipes chosen were classically Tunisian: which was to say that they were really from Andalusia, carried to North Africa when the defeated Moors finally retreated from Spain in the fifteenth century. Except that Andalusian cookery had originated in North Africa in the first place, having been taken to Spain several centuries earlier by the armies of Islam. Its complexity of flavour a response by Islamic cooks to the new ingredients they suddenly found surrounding them.

Lady Nafisa had decreed the cuisine be Megrib to remind everyone of Ashraf's heritage. And every dish relentlessly reinforced the fact. Even the fried *brieks*, small paper-thin pastries stuffed with vegetables, eggs or chicken, were a Tunisian staple. Raf's aunt was making sure Hamzah appreciated exactly what he was getting. A genuine Berber princeling, a real bey.

If Hamzah hadn't decided to talk up his own end of the bargain, then disaster wouldn't have struck; but he did and so it began, with a compliment from the girl's father.

'She's a good kid,' Hamzah said firmly.

'*Dad.*'

'She doesn't make a fuss. Doesn't cry over stupid things.' He paused. 'Actually, she doesn't cry at all. Gets wound up occasionally, like girls do. Usually over animals or children. Stuff that can't be changed . . .'

Zara snorted.

'You don't agree?' Raf asked. 'That things can't be changed?' He only meant to make conversation but it was obvious from Madame Rahina's sudden silence that she didn't think he'd like Zara's answer.

'What's to agree?' said Zara. Her slate-grey eyes came up to meet his and for the first time that afternoon she didn't blink or look away. 'And what does it matter if I believe things can be changed or not? In Iskandryia, daughters don't have opinions . . . Or rights.'

'Zara.' Her father sounded more concerned than angry.

'No rights?' Raf's voice was gentle. 'Why not?'

'Tradition,' said Zara bitterly. She stood up from the table. 'You see Dad's case over there?' The briefcase was Calvin Klein, black crocodile skin. 'That contains ten per cent of my dowry. You get a further fifty per cent when we marry, minus whatever your aunt's already had for expenses. The remainder you don't get for twelve months.'

From the surprise on Raf's face it was obvious he hadn't known money was involved at all.

'Twelve months . . . ?'

'Apparently that's meant to stop you beating me.' Zara stepped away from the bench. 'Well, for the first year, at least . . .' She turned to her father. 'I'm sorry. I need to get some air.'

'*Go after her,*' Raf's aunt hissed as Raf stood watching Zara go.

'And say what?'

'Anything you like.' Lady Nafisa was almost shaking with fury. 'All girls get nervous before their wedding. Make something up. Tell her whatever she wants to hear.'

Raf nodded. 'Okay,' he said. So he did.

As soon as Raf saw Monday morning's newsfeeds, he tried to ring Zara. But she wouldn't take his calls. Raf knew she was at Villa Hamzah because the butler who answered made no pretence of her being anywhere else. The girl just didn't want to talk to him.

He kept calling and by that evening the butler could recognize Raf's voice without him having to give his name. But she still wasn't taking his calls.

'No luck,' said Raf and tapped his watch strap, breaking the connection. He was in the *qaa*, his back to a wall. And it was obvious from the anger twisting Lady Nafisa's face that she'd dearly have loved to have him lifted bodily, carried to the edge and tossed to the flagstones below. Hani had been slapped and sent to the haremlek for nothing more than being there when Lady Nafisa finally and completely lost her temper. So far, Lady Nafisa had tried ordering and begging, now she was trying moral blackmail.

'You've ruined her. You know that, don't you?' Fury and three arguments had worn Nafisa's voice to an ugly rasp. The first had begun as Madame Rahina stormed out, dragging Zara behind her. The second took place the following day, when Raf angrily told his aunt there were no circumstances under which he would marry the girl. And finally there had been today's, the third and worst.

Raf skimmed the evening paper she'd just handed him. The compulsory box-out on page two featured General Koenig Pasha's new crackdown on smuggling, with separate pix showing the young Khedive, the General and sunrise over Western Harbour. General Koenig Pasha's was the biggest picture by far. The rest of the paper was filled with what interested Lady Nafisa.

'Oil heiress jilted . . .' The story wasn't going to go away. That morning's Zaghloulist tabloid had been more upfront, less pleasant. *Dumped dumpy* read the kindest comment. Above it an unflattering and outdated grab showed Zara in a voluminous swimming costume, aged about fifteen, all expanding chest and puppy fat. The fact she no longer looked anything like that was nowhere mentioned.

'Do you realize what you've done?' Lady Nafisa asked furiously.

Raf sighed. Her question was entirely rhetorical. He'd tried several times to explain himself but Lady Nafisa wouldn't even let him reach the end of a sentence.

'She's disgraced,' said his aunt. 'Unmarriable. You think anyone in El Iskandryia wants your cast-offs?'

'She's hardly a cast-off,' Raf said angrily. 'Besides, her father's worth millions.'

'Billions,' Lady Nafisa corrected him without even thinking about it. 'That's not the point. No one who matters will marry her now.'

'Maybe she doesn't want to marry *someone who matters* . . .' Raf said between gritted teeth. He put as much scorn into the words as possible. 'Maybe she doesn't want to get married at all.'

'That's not how life works,' said Lady Nafisa. 'You know nothing about it.'

'No.' Raf tossed the paper onto the marble floor. 'You're right, I don't. But I don't like what I've seen so far.'

'And I suppose you prefer prison?'

'To this?' said Raf. 'Yes, I do.'

That wasn't entirely accurate. There were brief moments when Raf looked out along the heat-hazed sweep of the Corniche and El Iskandryia felt bizarrely like home. But liking or not liking Isk wasn't Raf's big problem. His problem was Hu San and Wild Boy. They would be looking for him and when those two went looking, they found . . . All Raf had going for him was they didn't yet know where he was or who he'd become.

Which meant Raf needed to keep on being Ashraf al-Mansur the way he needed to keep breathing. And, unfortunately, it looked like the two states were inextricably linked.

Disappear into the night?

That was a definite possibility. Isk was full of foreigners running bars, brothels and dubious businesses, doing the work pure-born Iski regarded as beneath them. The only flaw there was that Lady Nafisa would undoubtedly call the police. It didn't matter what version of the truth she told them. She was *someone who mattered*: they'd find him.

Killing her or staying close were his safest options, maybe his only options. Either way, he kept ahead.

'Ashraf?' The question was a whisper.

He spun, fast. 'How the fuck did you . . .'

Wide-eyed, Hani held up her hands so he could examine the grease smeared across her palms, then lifted her arms to show the oil smeared down the front of her flannel pyjamas. 'It's a bit slippery,' she said seriously. 'It gets easier when you've done it a few times.'

Like using the glass sword in *Dragon's Bane III* or writing your own level for *Imperial Assassin*. Hani didn't really distinguish between what she did on screen in her nursery and what she did in life, it was all real. Sort of . . .

Raf said nothing. Telling the child that climbing wires was dangerous wasn't his job and besides, judging by the stubborn glee in her eyes it would have been pointless anyway. The danger was precisely why she did it.

'You off to feed Ali-Din?' he asked eventually.

Hani looked at him with a new respect. 'That too,' she admitted. 'But I also came to see you.'

'Well, here I am,' said Raf.

'They work like speaking tubes,' Hani said, pointing towards the lifts. 'Stand at the top and you can hear everything . . .' She paused to consider what she'd just said. 'That's why we should whisper . . .'

'I'm whispering,' mouthed Raf and Hani giggled.

'Stupid.'

'Yep,' Raf glanced round the silent *qaa*. 'You're probably right.'

'Why were you in prison?'

To answer or not to answer. 'For killing someone.'

Hani looked appalled, shock swallowing her small face as she struggled for something to say. And then she relaxed slightly. 'They must have done something very bad.'

'No,' said Raf. 'They just talked too much.'

'And you killed them?'

Raf shook his head. 'At least, I don't think so. But I got the blame.'

'That's not fair.'

'No, it isn't.' Raf smiled. He could remember when he too used to believe in 'fair', right up to the day he'd been driven, aged five, through the gates of a Swiss boarding school. And he'd kept wanting to believe. Making excuses for the arbitrary beatings, cold baths, sly hands, the randomness of lesser punishments . . . He was seven the first time he ran away. The last time was the day before his eleventh birthday, but that was from a different school. Out of five attempts, three were briefly successful.

In the end, his brain had to admit what his gut already knew: there was no justice, no fairness, only rules. Those who used, twisted or kept to the rules got by, those that didn't were marked down as enemies of order. It was a very thorough training. 'Emotional institutionalization' was how Dr Millbank described it.

And in his own fashion Raf had been keeping to rules ever since. What was his taking the fall for Micky O'Brian but playing to the rules of the world in which he found himself?

'Aunt Nafisa said you were a spy,' Hani said, tugging his sleeve. 'Spies kill people. It's their job.'

'*Assassins* kill people,' said Raf. 'Spies collect secrets.' But Hani wasn't listening. She was already working out another justification in her head.

'If it was your job that would make everything all right.'

Chapter Fourteen

6th July

Lady Jalila rolled sideways off the couch and wrapped her gown tightly round herself. Her stomach was cramping and she wore the tension in her neck and shoulders like a heavy body cast. It hadn't been an easy final half-hour.

'You know where . . .'

She nodded abruptly at the slim Greek woman and walked hurriedly from the consulting room to the lavatory next door, squatting just ahead of a spasm that emptied her bowels in a long squirt of almost clear water. That final ritual was as much a relief as it was undignified. Lady Jalila could put up with the anal speculum and lying on her side with her knees pulled up and buttocks exposed as gravity forced water into her colon and out again, emptying her lower gut of faecal matter. She could even stand those five minutes of intolerable pressure towards the end, when a warm herbal infusion replaced cool water and Madame Sosostris locked a crocodile clip round the tube to keep the infusion inside.

It was the uncontrollable gripe in her gut immediately afterwards that upset her. Those few seconds between the couch and the lavatory pan when she feared she might disgrace herself.

As for the rest of it, Lady Jalila made a point of never considering how she looked when she was on that couch or what the Greek woman thought of her endless visits. The beneficial effects of cleansing were too valuable to give up. And though she knew her husband the Minister didn't really approve for a number of reasons, none of which included the substantial cost of her frequent visits – she could handle him. Literally, if that was what it took.

Better.

Sighing, Lady Jalila squatted again, double-checking that her gut really was empty. It was. As empty as her abdomen was flat and her stomach just slightly, attractively curved. Even her hips looked thinner now that her colon was no longer a sausage stuffed full of poisonous waste.

If only all life's complications could be flushed out that easily.

Wrapping the paper gown tight about her, Lady Jalila returned to the consulting room of the relentlessly old-fashioned third-floor clinic set between Nokrashi and Rue Tatvig, in a not-at-all-salubrious area of El Anfushi.

She'd been the first to discover Madame Sosostris, back when the herbalist was pulled in for questioning. In those days Lady Jalila had been just plain Jalila, a uniformed recruit in the *morales*. Recognizing someone useful, she'd amended the arrest sheet from performing abortion to practising unlicensed female circumcision and kicked Sosostris free with a warning. Two months later, she'd gone looking for the woman with a search warrant in one hand and a business proposal in the other.

Now everyone Lady Jalila knew came to the clinic – even Coroner Mila, the new City Magistrate for Women, who usually regarded matters faecal as being beyond mention, like sex.

Lady Jalila smiled sourly. Everybody fucked. The coroner-magistrate just withheld her approval because Lady Jalila didn't bother to hide the fact.

'All done, then?' asked the Greek woman, looking up. Tall, hipless and small-breasted to the point of clinical androgyny, Madame Sosostris had the body most of her clients secretly craved, whether or not they realized it. Her very shape gave them a target at which to aim. A reason to keep coming.

'Then I'll let you dress . . .'

Madame Sosostris always waited for the client to return before leaving them to change back into their clothes. Of course, Lady Jalila was more than just a client. She'd quickly become Madame Sosostris's dear friend and ally, an invaluable patron for a woman practising therapies not entirely approved of by

Islamic mullahs. Her husband was Mushin Bey, Iskandryia's Minister for Police, respected deputy of General Koenig Pasha himself.

Madame Sosostris left the room at an elegant glide.

Next Tuesday, decided Lady Jalila climbing into a white CK thong that no longer felt tight round the hips. That was when she'd visit next. She shuffled her full breasts into a sports bra and looked round for a mirror, forgetting there wasn't one. Though it didn't matter: she'd still be thin enough to check her shape in the glass when she got home for lunch, after she'd dropped in to check on Nafisa.

All in all, a good morning's work. Her white jacket now clung in the right places without bulging in the wrong ones and the matching silk skirt hugged her hips without wrinkling. Lady Jalila wore white because white went with her swept-up blonde hair and her husband liked clothes that emphasized the difference in their age. Thirty-one might be old enough for all of her friends to have large families but to the sixty-five-year-old Minister of Police it seemed positively childish. But then, Mushin Bey still thought of her as the seventeen-year-old she'd been when she first joined the women's police force. All blonde hair, blue eyes and innocence.

Lady Jalila pushed her feet into a pair of Manolos, then picked up the Dior bag that contained her credit cards and smiled.

Long may it remain so.

Lady Jalila let herself into her cousin's madersa, frowning at the door Khartoum had left unguarded. Nafisa always had been slack with her house boy.

The glassed-over knot garden was hot as a steam bath, bringing Lady Jalila out in an instant flush. She knew her cousin claimed not to be able to afford air-conditioning except in her own little office. But what was the point of owning a famous garden if it was uninhabitable for most of the summer?

'Nas?' Lady Jalila used her pet name for Nafisa.

Nothing.

Passing the *liwan* with its cooling marble slab now dusty and dry, she stepped out into the open courtyard and stopped to breathe deeply. Early July in El Iskandryia was often humid and hot, but nothing like as cruel as that covered garden.

'Nas?'

The silence was complete. Made deeper by the absence of running water in the courtyard in front of her.

Lady Jalila started to climb the *qaa* steps, hearing her heels ring on the stone slabs. Cousin Nafisa didn't approve of Lady Jalila's kitten heels: they made scars in the marble. At the top of the stairs, she hesitated. To her left was the large tiled expanse of the *qaa* proper. While straight ahead was the cubicle of Lady Nafisa's office, cool and air-conditioned, created by filling space between arches with sheets of smoked glass.

That was where Lady Jalila went first . . .

'I don't care who he's with. Tell him I'm at the al-Mansur madersa and I need to talk to him *now*.' For once Lady Jalila didn't have to raise her voice. The urgency in her tone was obvious even to his idiot PA and, seconds later, her husband's worried face flashed up on her tiny silver Nokia. As ever, he looked just like a small startled rat.

'What's . . .'

'Wait,' said Lady Jalila suddenly, snapping off the camera option on her mobile. Something silver and sickening had just caught her eye. Let him read about it or look at the crime-scene photographs later if he must. Nafisa dead with her blouse ripped open — there were some things she didn't think her husband needed to see.

'Nafisa's been murdered,' said Lady Jalila.

'*Nafisa?*' His horror was absolute, obvious. There were several things the Minister immediately wanted to say. But he said none of them, contenting himself with a simple 'I'm so sorry.' He glanced beyond the edge of her screen to a group of people she couldn't see and waved his hand, dismissing them. A muted question filtered into her earbead and she heard her husband's grunt of irritation. 'Tomorrow,' he said crossly. 'It can wait.' And then she had his full attention again.

'How did she die?'

'She was stabbed . . . with her pen.'

Lady Jalila heard him punch buttons on his desk. 'Don't touch anything.' That was the policeman in him speaking. 'I'll get my best man onto it now.'

'Mushin.'

The anger in her voice stopped him dead.

'You really don't get it, do you?' She didn't care if all his calls were taped or not. Or what his PA thought when the little tramp typed up that day's transcripts. 'Nafisa was stabbed with her pen, understand? She wrote that letter and someone stabbed her.'

He understood now. She could see that from the sudden tightening of his jaw.

'You know who else signed that letter,' said Lady Jalila. 'Don't you?'

He did. He knew only too well.

She had.

'I want you to put Madame Mila on this case,' Lady Jalila said fiercely. 'It's an attack on our values.' By 'our', she meant women's.

The Minister's lips screwed into a tiny moue of irritation but he nodded. 'I'll do it now,' he promised.

'Good,' said Lady Jalila and punched a button on her Nokia, consigning her husband's rat-like feaures to a flicker, then darkness.

Chapter Fifteen

New York

It was ZeeZee's childhood therapist who first suggested that, since the small boy had hated his time in Switzerland and New York obviously didn't suit him, the best answer might be to find him a place at a specialist boarding school in Scotland.

So, four months after he first arrived in New York, the child who would become ZeeZee left again, at the suggestion of a therapist that ZeeZee knew, even then, he didn't need. And the boy knew why he was being sent away too. He kept fusing the man's neural-wave feedback machines . . .

The next time ZeeZee arrived in America he was eleven. The Boeing had come in low over Long Island and sank onto the runway at Idlewild in a simulation-perfect landing. It was the first time ZeeZee had ever flown in an Alle Volante. He travelled executive-class with his own tiny room, and though the cubicle walls were veneered from a single peel of Canadian maple and his bed had a frame made from the same extruded magnesium alloy found in Japanese racing bikes, the cubicle was still no bigger than the inside of a small van.

ZeeZee hadn't minded about the size at all. After a term in a dorm with nine other boys – the largest of whom thought Welham sounded enough like wanker to be interchangeable – the privacy and silence of his cabin was enough to make him drunk with the luxury of it all.

There was a stewardess who arrived every time he pushed the button, and who smiled and didn't mind because he was travelling on his own and looked just like she thought English children were meant to look – blond and blue-eyed, the way they did in films.

The fact he wore grey flannel trousers and a cotton shirt with a striped tie helped fix the image in her mind. As did his thick tweed jacket, which he called my coat. *His shirt even had links at the cuff made from Thai silver, with tiny dancers embossed on their black domed surface.*

The stewardess let the boy be first off the plane, passing him into the care of a second attendant, who smelled strongly of roses and took him straight to baggage reclaim.

'Is that all you've got?' she'd asked, examining the single case he pulled from the executive-class carousel.

He nodded. There was no point telling her the case was almost empty and he'd only brought the thing because leaving it behind would have been rude. The case was a leaving present from his tutor's wife.

'Over there,' he'd said suddenly as they walked into the Arrivals hall. Beyond a vast wall of glass stood a line of white Cadillacs on the slip road outside, their drivers standing by open doors while inside the hall excited families waved frantically. ZeeZee waved back.

'I'll be fine now,' he said firmly and thrust out his hand.

Any fleeting doubt the attendant might have had lost out to the novelty of shaking hands with a serious, immaculately polite eleven-year-old boy. 'If you're sure,' she said.

'Of course.' ZeeZee sketched her the slightest bow.

The woman with the warm scent smiled and shook her own head in disbelief. 'Okay,' she said, 'enjoy your stay.'

'It's not a stay,' ZeeZee said seriously. 'This is where I live now . . .'

Chapter Sixteen

6th July

Felix felt like a candle melting.

He was tired, he'd had his holiday cancelled and he'd been at the al-Mansur murder scene just long enough to confirm that a woman was dead, there was a traumatized child sat wide-eyed in one corner of the *qaa* and the Minister's wife, who'd apparently called in the crime, was missing from the scene itself . . . And just when it looked like his afternoon couldn't get worse, some dreadlocked trustafarian in shades and a stupid suit came hammering up the *qaa* steps, puffing like a lunatic.

'Hold it,' Felix barked.

'I live here,' announced Raf, stopping to glance at the fat man blocking his way. From the rye on the man's breath to his thinning hair gone grey and tied back in a lanky ponytail, the fat man had 'American cop' written all over him. Which was weird, given this was North Africa.

'Prove it . . .'

Raf had left his office at a run, over-tipped a cab to jump two lights and pounded straight through Nafisa's knot garden, leaving shredded shrubs behind him. He'd made it from office to steps in five and a half minutes. Obstruction wasn't what he needed right now. Instead of stopping, he began to squeeze between the fat man and the door frame.

A finger jabbed his chest. 'Identity papers,' the man demanded. Even speaking bad French he had an air of authority – derived from more than just age or experience.

Raf hated him on sight. So he made quite sure he got in the first move.

Faced with having his knuckle rupture or stepping backwards, Felix retreated with Raf still twisting the offending finger. Some of the moves Raf had learned on remand were so simple a child couldn't screw them up. That was the idea, anyway.

'*Ashraf . . .*' Hani's shout meshed with a blur of movement, the cold click of metal and the touch of a police-issue revolver to Raf's head. Very slowly, Raf let go of the fat man's finger and stepped back.

'You know this person?' the fat man asked Hani, sounding disappointed. As if that somehow meant he wasn't allowed to beat his target to pulp.

Hani nodded, eyes wide. 'That's my new uncle.'

'Identity papers,' Felix said. His left hand kept the Colt pushed against Raf's skull while his right reached for the card Raf extracted from his inside jacket pocket.

'Fucking terrific.'

Definitely American, Raf decided, watching the fat man return his revolver to its hip holster. First language Brooklyn, second Arabic, third very bad French. Which was one better than him.

'Colonel Pashazade Ashraf al-Mansur . . . *Pashazade*? Your dad's a fucking Pasha?'

Your dad. Now there was a concept with which to conjure.

'No,' said Raf, grabbing back his Third Circle laminate. 'He's the Emir of fucking Tunis.' Stepping round the fat man as if he wasn't there, Raf knelt beside Hani.

'You all right?'

'No.' She nodded towards an open door. 'Aunt Nafisa . . .'

'Don't let the kid go in there,' said Felix heavily. 'Don't touch anything. And don't even think of getting in my fucking face.' With that he stamped his way downstairs to tape off the crime-scene entrances before anyone else decided to appear.

It took Raf nearly a minute to spot the platinum pen rammed hard between her ribs, its metal end protruding beneath one breast like a witch's third nipple; but then he was stood in an open doorway, on the other side of a rustling strip of police tape that had been hastily strung across the door.

'Shit.' There didn't seem much else to say. And besides, it was hardly the first corpse he'd seen. All the same, it was his aunt, supposedly, and he was surprised at how unmoved he felt. The wound was ugly, the small office was a mess. That was it.

'They murdered her,' whispered a voice behind him and when Raf looked back Hani was there, eyes vast as she stared up at him.

'Who did?'

'The foreigners.'

Somewhere inside Nafisa's office a lavatory flushed, a lock clicked open and before Raf could react an almost-elegant blonde stepped into the tiny room, still wiping her mouth. The door she'd used was hidden behind a Persian rug that hung on the wall from a wooden pole. Except the pole wasn't really attached to Nafisa's office wall: but to the top of a door. Behind her came the sound of a cistern filling.

'Lady Jalila,' said the woman, introducing herself.

'I'm Raf.'

'Yes, I know . . .'

They stared at each other in silence. She'd done a good job of cleaning herself up but the scrub marks on the front of her white jacket didn't quite hide vomit stains. And she very carefully avoided stepping anywhere near the desk as she crossed the dead woman's office.

Her composure held for as long as it took the child behind Raf to turn on her heel and clatter away down the *qaa* steps. Lady Jalila looked startled.

'You let Hani see this?' The woman's voice was suddenly brittle, her hands shaking. To Raf it looked like the onset of shock.

'No,' said Raf. 'That was you.'

Lady Jalila shot him a puzzled look.

'You were obviously here first,' Raf added.

'I imagine that I was in Nafisa's loo being sick when Hani

appeared.' Whatever else Lady Jalila intended to say was lost in a sudden tread of heavy feet below.

'Up here,' she barked. But Felix had got there first. The two uniformed police officers were halted in the courtyard, listening intently to whatever it was the fat man wanted to say.

'Hey, Boss,' said the younger, when Felix finally stopped talking. 'Control said to tell you you're showing up as off-line . . .'

'His Excellency?'

Both uniformed officers nodded as one.

'Felix here,' the fat man announced, flicking a switch on his watch and then punching a button. Other than that, he said nothing for the next few minutes, just turned a deeper shade of red. 'Yes, sir,' he said when the call was finishing. 'I'll make sure she gets every courtesy extended. And, yes, I'll remember it's easier for you if I don't turn off my connection.'

'My Lady.' When Felix looked up to where Lady Jalila stood staring down into the courtyard, the politeness in his voice was at odds with the contempt in his eyes. 'The Minister thinks it might be best if you went straight home.'

'Does he indeed . . .' Lady Jalila headed for the *qaa* steps, nodding for Raf to follow.

'Presumably he's sending a car?'

'No,' said Felix. 'He's sure one of these officers will be delighted to drive you. That is, if you don't mind travelling in a squad car?'

Lady Jalila sighed heavily. 'If I must.'

'So all I need now,' said Felix, 'is to know when it would be convenient for me to call on you . . . ?'

'*On me?*' The woman stopped in her tracks. Her voice made it sound as if Felix had suggested they book into the nearest Ramada for a quick afternoon of bestiality and child abuse.

'There *has* been a murder.' Felix glanced from Raf to Lady Jalila and then at Hani who was coming out of the kitchens with Donna in tow. What he thought about having his crime scene littered with a bey, children, cooks and the wife of his boss was obvious, if unprintable.

Chapter Seventeen

Seattle / New York

The third time ZeeZee arrived in America he was almost sixteen and his previous trip was a memory he didn't take out of the box and dust down too often . . .

There'd been no waiting stretch limo that earlier time, no one to meet him, not that he'd expected either and not that he minded. And besides, he'd proved quite capable of catching a Carey Bus and unloading his almost empty case outside Grand Central. He ditched the case in a gash bin on 42nd. There was nothing inside except a school coat and he didn't need that any more.

The yellow cab he stopped to take him to the apartment his mother was borrowing on the Upper East Side parked up illegally while he ran inside to get the fare. And when he discovered his mother wasn't home, he borrowed the $10 from a uniformed doorman and was vaguely surprised when the elderly black man assured him that his Seiko automatic wasn't needed as security for the loan.

It seemed she'd remembered to tell the front desk that her son would be sharing the apartment, even if she hadn't remembered to meet him at the airport.

By the time his mother came home, he'd found a room he assumed was his – from an almost-new copy of Vampyre Blade III and an old Sony console – and had a long shower, eaten a slice of cold pizza from the fridge and slept right through to the following morning.

She came in as he was cooking toast under a grill he could hardly reach because whichever designer her latest friend had employed hadn't factored eleven-year-olds into his equation.

But then, the apartment wasn't designed as living space, more as a public statement of identity. And even the kitchen was bigger than his old dorm and it was only a fifth of the size of the new living room, where one complete corner had been ripped right out and replaced with glass to look down on Central Park. ZeeZee figured that when she borrowed the flat, she must have forgotten he hated heights.

The living-room fireplace was machine-cut from some grey stone he didn't recognize and along both of its sides stretched elegant steel shelves packed untidily with master disks of her trips and large, tattered books full of her photographs. Other disks and books were crammed sideways into the narrow gaps above.

Rugs, oil paintings and an antique leopard skin completely covered the other walls, but those didn't belong to her. On the floor itself, newspapers competed for space with empty plates, glasses, and half a dozen camera bags that did . . .

'Darling. How good to see you.'

She held a pair of shades and wore a crimson scarf tied over hair that needed washing. Her black jeans and jersey looked like they'd been slept in, except that one look at her eyes told him she was too wired to have slept in days.

They had both smiled, slightly tentatively.

'You found it, then?'

ZeeZee nodded, then went back to cooking his toast, leaving her to make conversation.

'I've booked you into a school,' she said. 'It's over on the other side of the Park. There's a prospectus around here somewhere.' Her black-nailed hands fluttered at a clutter of papers covering the sand-blasted steel kitchen table. 'You can start when you want. I hope it will do . . .'

He looked at her then.

She shrugged. 'They took a year's fees up front.'

While his mother took a shower and then fixed herself a line, ZeeZee set up the reconditioned Sony console. He got as far as skimming the 'read me' before he realized there wasn't a television in his room to plug the console into. Moving the huge

TV from the living room into his bedroom seemed impractical. As did moving himself and his bed into the living room, so he decided to worry about it all later and instead took a lift down to the foyer to see the doorman.

What ZeeZee remembered most about that year with his mother was watching screens with Max the doorman. Inside Max's office was a bank of video monitors linked to hidden CCTV cameras in the foyer, lifts, corridors and parking bay. The cameras were chipped for sound but Max liked to watch them with the volume turned down. Creating stories for the people he saw.

By the end of the first month, ZeeZee's mother was just one of a dozen characters ZeeZee and Max watched lock up their doors, then promptly check their hair, cleavage, teeth or waistlines in corridor mirrors. ZeeZee learned which men were going into flats they shouldn't be going into. He saw elegant women kiss men who weren't their partners. He watched an Italian girl who didn't even know he existed hurriedly change her tampon in a lift, secreting the old one neatly in a tissue. And he stayed glued to a monitor as two drunks screwed on the hood of a black Cadillac in a corner of the underground garage, even though one of them was his mother and the other the man who lent her the flat.

ZeeZee made it to the end of the year and then did what he'd always said he wouldn't do, went back to Roslin in Scotland. Neither he nor his mother really discussed it. Life just happened that way, as if all the necessary conversations had already been had and all that remained was to fix the ticket. It was hard to know which of them found his leaving the greatest release.

Chapter Eighteen

6th July

The crime perimeter was secure, no press were present and a junior detective was out on the sidewalk, trying to determine the perpetrator's entry and exit routes. So far without success. Lady Jalila had gone and Felix was busy trying to persuade Raf to do the same.

Below them, guarding the bottom of the *qaa* steps was a tall young man with the flawless skin of a Nubian and the upset eyes of a recruit not yet grown used to death. The young uniformed officer had given a length of tape to Hani, who was twisting it endlessly so that sunlight caught a holostrip of lettering which read *EIPD – do not cross*. And as she flipped the tape back and forwards, making it sparkle in the hot sun, the child looked almost happy.

Felix shrugged. Kids weren't his area and the idea wouldn't have occurred to him. True enough, he had a daughter in Santa Fé. Only Trudi lived with her girlfriend, three tabby cats and a gun under her pillow; and the last time he'd seen his kid she'd probably been younger than the one sitting by the fountain playing with the tape.

These days his daughter had cropped hair, a razor-wire tattoo that wound up her arm from elbow to shoulder and nipples pierced with silver spikes, one tiny spike going across and the other down . . . He knew about those because her last but one Christmas card had a picture of her and Barbara on the front, taken at a Gay Pride barbecue in San Francisco. They were stripped to the waist and holding bottles of Bud. Only the bottles were closer to their button-flied groins than they were to their mouths and Barbara had pierced nipples too, linked together by a chain.

Trudi looked hot and tired, so he'd written back saying he hoped she was taking vitamins and that if she had to go out like that in public he hoped she was wearing lots of sun cream. That earned him a postcard of a tram. Only three scrawled lines on the back but one of them was her new e-address. They wrote to each other now, not often but a couple of brief paragraphs once every few months. And she sent him more photographs of herself, fully clothed this time, with one of the cats sitting on her lap.

There'd been a time of no photographs at all, when Trudi was in her early teens and her mother was going through a religious phase, if that was what you could call moving state and announcing to her new neighbours that no, she wasn't divorced, her husband was dead. It had taken the ghost cancelling her alimony for five months to start the pictures flowing again. Before they did, he got a stiff letter from her attorney to which he'd had his own reply in Arabic. The photographs had restarted pretty soon after that.

'It would be best . . .'

'No,' said Raf. Not waiting for Felix to finish the sentence. There were a number of reasons why he didn't want to leave the crime scene and go back to his office, only one of which he could tell Felix.

'I can't just leave Hani.'

That, at least, was true. Without Lady Nafisa the girl was a scrawny nothing. She wasn't pretty, she was way too young to be married off and, anyway, the kid was without a dowry. She had to be: Islamic law said girls couldn't inherit in their own right. So unless Lady Nafisa had left everything to a favourite charity someone other then Hani was going to inherit and the chances were it was him. And that wasn't what Raf wanted either.

A murder, money, the recent appearance of an unknown heir. Arrange into a winning combination . . .

Before the murder, *RenSchmiss* was just one middle-aged

woman's obsession. Now it would be debated in drawing rooms and cafés across North Africa.

If the fat man wanted to keep talking about *Thiergarten* killers, that was fine with Raf but he knew what conclusion most people would draw from the evidence. And that was before he factored the press into account. The press were there to service the newsfeeds, which meant pictures, syndicated to local feeds all round the world, including Seattle.

Raf sighed.

The beard, hair and any thought of polarized contacts would have to go and the shades make a long-term reappearance. It was just a pity he didn't have time for a completely new face to go with his new name and nationality.

'I'll stay . . .' He held up one hand, stopping Felix in his tracks. 'Lady Nafisa was my aunt . . .' He was about to say something crass, like *duty demands it*, when the fat man's mobile started beeping.

It kept beeping while Felix searched his trouser pockets and finally tracked the watch down to his jacket, which was upstairs in the *qaa*, slung over a silver chair.

'What?' Felix demanded. He made no attempt to keep the irritation out of his voice.

The Minister was on the other end again. Raf knew that from the way the Chief of Detectives suddenly straightened up, pausing mid-stride. One hand came up to smooth his hair, thick fingers once again slicking sweat across his scalp.

'Yes, sir. I'm glad your wife got home safely. I sent one of my best men with her . . .' If the Minister noticed the criticism implicit in the fat man's words it didn't stop his list of questions.

'Exactly when did it happen?' Ripping aside the tape that closed off the study door, Felix walked over to the dead woman's desk and half closed her paper, making sure the sticky pages didn't actually touch. It was the midday edition. 'So far all I can say is that it happened after twelve noon,' said Felix. 'Yes,' he said, 'I *can* state that categorically.' Felix listened to the next request and instinctively shook his head,

sending sweat trickling down the bridge of his nose.

'No, Your Excellency. I don't think we should turn the site investigation over to Madame Mila.'

'Yes, I know the General is . . .'

'No, I'm not . . .'

'If I can just . . .'

'Yes, he's still here . . .'

It was a one-way conversation after that, Felix's protests fading into silence, broken only towards the end when he nodded abruptly.

'Whatever you want, sir . . .' Felix tapped a button to end the call, scowled balefully at his watch and stabbed a switch that put it back on standby.

'You should have got out when you had the chance,' he told Raf. 'The Minister wants you as my official witness.'

'Which means what?' Raf asked, pushing back his own hair. The wind that seeped in through the smashed mashrabiya was hot and sticky, and Nafisa's precious air-conditioning unit would probably have been reaching meltdown, if someone hadn't already ripped its thermostat from the wall, leaving wires trailing.

It might have been Raf's imagination but he was sure her body had already begun to smell.

'What does it mean? It means you stand in that doorway and watch me commit professional suicide. You don't come in the room, you don't interfere and you definitely don't talk while I'm working. Understand?'

No, he didn't. 'What am I witnessing?' Raf demanded.

'Me. While I do this.'

On the marble table where Lady Nafisa had given her lunch for the parents of Zara bint-Hamzah, Felix dumped a battered leather case with reinforced corners and a webbing strap to hold the top tight shut. The words on the strap read *Property of the LAPD – do not remove without authorization.* Yanking off the strap, Felix waved his hand in front of something that might have been a human head, had it not been made of clear perspex and filled with jumbled electronics. Chunks of crystal memory had been crudely glued to the back.

Its eyes briefly lit red.

'Meet Dr Dee,' said Felix. From the other side of the case Felix pulled a battered camera, a Speed Graphic digiLux so old it had a separate flash unit and came minus a removable memory dump, which was where Dr Dee came in . . .

'First off, I'm going to sweep the scene, do crime-scene shots, then body shots. And finally I'm going to examine the body . . . Your job is to see I don't plant or remove evidence and that I don't molest or defile the woman's corpse. You got any problems with that?'

Silence.

'Good, then let's get started . . .' Felix slid out his hip flask, flipped its lid and downed the flask in one. 'Beats holding your nose or saying prayers every time,' he added sourly, noting Raf's undisguised shock.

Only when Felix was certain that the tiles directly in front of him were clear of clues did he lie flat and sweep the floor with the beam of a tiny maglite. Two blouse buttons showed up immediately, both near the wall. Other than that, there was only debris from the mashrabiya. Lady Nafisa had been as fanatical about outer cleanliness as she had been about the inner kind.

'Why aren't I surprised?' Felix asked, but he was talking to himself. Lifting both buttons using tweezers, he dropped them straight into separate evidence bags, carefully dating and labelling each bag.

It took him no more than fifteen minutes to take positioning shots, with another ten for body shots and five for close-ups of the wound itself. In that time he stopped twice to drink from a second flask and when that ran out he calmly switched to a third and used that instead.

Perspiration rolled from the fat man's face as he worked, and the air around him stank of whisky and sour sweat. But never once did he stumble or even look drunk. He just snapped off each shot, checked the quality on the little screen at the back of the Speed Graphic and moved on, looking for the next angle, his next shot. He had a professional's tolerance for the drug of his choice. Raf had seen it before, up close and way too personal, every single day of the year he had spent in New York with his mother.

Chapter Nineteen

Seattle

Hitting America aged fifteen was different. So different as to be unforgettable in a life where everything was unforgettable. No flight attendant held his hand on the trip out and he travelled regular, legs cramped into a tiny gap between the edge of his seat and the sloped chair-back of the passenger in front.

Next to him sat a black-eyed girl wired into a Sony Dance-Master, the thud of Hold Me Down *hissing from earbeads as her long fingers danced over the touchpad of a Nintendo to an entirely different beat. She smelled of toothpaste and a cheap powdery scent. Beyond her was a window seat, empty except for a Tibetan bag with an untouched magazine poking out of the top.*

ZeeZee desperately wanted to ask if she'd mind if he took the window seat but didn't know the words . . . It wasn't that she didn't speak English. She did. Confidence was his problem. His school outside Edinburgh was strictly single-sex. Which meant tarting the smaller boys was a regular pastime for most of his year: talking to girls wasn't.

PanAmerican called the seats regular *but most of the regular passengers were further forward, drinking free vodka shots and eating complimentary cashews while watching Hollywood's finest on the screen in the wall of their bunks.*

The seats at the rear of the Boeing were for students, casual workers, girls hoping to find work as nannies: the kind of people who didn't travel often, bought their own tickets and couldn't believe just how few US dollars they got in exchange at the bureau de change. Not that ZeeZee had forked out for his own seat.

Providence had paid for it.

Providence in the form of a man in the Lyons Coffee Lounge at Heathrow who walked away from his table and forgot a leather pouch he'd put on the chair beside him. Until then ZeeZee had been running away to Paris to find bar work. By the time the man hurried back to where he'd been sitting, ZeeZee's plans had changed and Seattle was on the cards, almost literally.

While the man filled out a form to reclaim his pouch from Lost Property, where ZeeZee had left it, ZeeZee was off buying dollars from a FirstVirtual auto-teller in Arrivals, using a deposit card he'd extracted. Selling half those dollars back to a different machine in Departures took him a minute and gave ZeeZee enough paper money to buy a cheap, one-way ticket to Seattle-Tacoma. He had to show the girl at PanAmerican his permanent US visa. But once she'd swiped his passport through a reader and the visa came up valid she was all smiles, even when he bought the cheapest stand-by she had.

The deposit card he flushed away in a men's room on the way to his gate. Some kind of warped morality made him buy a cut-price ticket. And it was only after take off that he realized the owner would just claim a full card against insurance and ZeeZee could have travelled first if he wanted.

'You wanna borrow this?' The girl was holding out her magazine, one hissing earbead carefully cupped in her hand where she'd half unplugged herself from the music. He didn't recognize the accent.

'Hold Me Down,' ZeeZee said, nodding at the bead, 'the ice-hot FP remix . . .'

She looked at him then. Glanced, without realizing it, at his white shirt and grey trousers. He'd ditched the jacket and striped tie but nothing could make what he was wearing anything other than what it was, half a school uniform.

He didn't mention that he only recognized the mix because some jerk in his common room had downloaded the Belize Sleez compilation and had played it to death.

'End of term?' she asked.

ZeeZee shook his head. 'Just had enough.' He took the offered magazine and was surprised she didn't immediately pull away when his fingers accidentally brushed her hand.

'What about you?' ZeeZee tried to make it sound like he always talked to strange girls on planes.

She smiled and named some city he didn't recognize, except to realize it was probably in the neutrality corridor between the Soviets and the Berlin alliance. 'I've got a student visa,' she added, 'but I intend to find work in Seattle. You don't know anywhere?'

He didn't, but she still told him her name and lent him a spare set of earbeads, toggling the DanceMaster onto split so they both got the full mix. Twenty minutes later, when the lights dimmed and an attendant came round with covers and all the couchettes tipped back, ZeeZee and Katia ended up under the same blanket.

The blanket was PanAmerican blue, logo-laden along all edges, with holes all over to trap air. It came vacuum-wrapped in foil and it was only after they had both struggled to rip open her packet that Katia discovered the easy-release tab.

'Dumb,' said Katia and ZeeZee smiled slightly nervously. He kept on smiling as he pulled the single blanket over both of them. And if Katia noticed his fingers shaking she didn't let him know. Instead she just rolled onto her side, facing away from him, and curled up with her head rested on her arm.

'Listen,' she whispered.

So ZeeZee did.

The new track was like nothing he'd heard before. A young boy's voice soared in a language he didn't recognize above a famine-sparse synth line that bled into a gull's cry and ended with a softly-building loop of whale song. BaghavadGhya. Not his taste, but it went with the ying/yang tattoo on her wrist and the grey titanium stud piercing the bridge of her nose.

Settling down, the girl shuffled herself backward until her bare heel just touched ZeeZee's ankle. And it seemed natural, somehow, for him to rest one hand on her leg and gently stroke the brushed surface of her chinos, feeling her warmth beneath as he moved his hand in time to the music.

When she didn't complain he kept going. And the next time she shifted, he suddenly found it easier to reach the seam that his finger had been tracing along the inside of her knee.

'That's neat . . .'

He wasn't sure that was what she actually said, but he muttered agreement anyway and shifted his fingers higher. He didn't quite have the nerve to trace the seam all the way to the top, so he settled for smoothing his hand gently up over her hip.

'No.' She tensed as his fingers reached the softness of her very slight stomach, only to breathe out again as ZeeZee hurriedly moved his hand, finding instead the swell of one breast through her thin green T-shirt.

She wore no bra.

She didn't move and nor did he, seemingly flash-frozen to the spot. Then, infinitely slowly, she moved his hand softly, letting her suddenly erect nipple write a line of fire across his palm.

ZeeZee started to breathe again.

Gently he reached under the cloth of her T-shirt to find a breast that was was full and warm, smooth to the touch. Close to, her long dark hair smelled of resin and oil, unwashed and almost animal.

'God.' ZeeZee sucked in his breath as he found her nipple with his thumb and first finger.

'Softly,' she said over her shoulder and he nodded, even though he knew she couldn't really see him.

Much later, when the Boeing was halfway across the Atlantic and most of the other cabin passengers were sleeping, ZeeZee smoothed his hand back across her hip and ran his fingers gently up that seam. And only the fact she opened her knees slightly told him that she wasn't also asleep.

One button fastened the band of her cheap chinos and the fly was a simple nylon zip, nothing fancy or expensive like tiny straps, toggles or invisible velcro. Katia couldn't afford designer clothes, even if they'd been available in whichever unpronounceable city it was she came from.

Terrified she'd say no, ZeeZee began to ease the zip, as if undoing it extra slowly meant she might not notice. Then he popped the single button at her waist. When she still didn't protest, he let his fingertips creep gently down her abdomen, reaching for the waistband of her knickers. What he found was tight body hair, then dampness and finally heat.

Katia wore nothing underneath, not even a basic thong . . .

She wouldn't look at him when the cabin lights came up. Her jeans were already buttoned and zipped, her T-shirt smoothed down. She'd rearranged both herself about an hour earlier, just before she drifted into sleep.

ZeeZee was more relieved than hurt by her sudden distance and put the earbead he'd borrowed politely but silently into her hand. Despite himself, he was grinning as he left the Boeing.

He was fifteen. He'd never yet kissed a girl – but he'd had one tighten frantically around his fingers and then, when her gasps were safely swallowed, push her hand back into the waistband of his trousers to squeeze until her wrist was sticky with his release.

Seattle was definitely the right place for him to be.

Chapter Twenty

6th July

'Guard the door for me,' Felix told Raf, resting his Speed Graphic on Lady Nafisa's desk and pulling a foil packet from his hip pocket. Ripping open the foil, he pulled out what looked like a large condom, shaking it between first finger and thumb until a tissue-thin glove was revealed.

'Surgical,' Felix told Raf, ripping open a second packet. 'Nanopore latex, anti-static. I get them from the hospital. The standard-issue stuff round here is crap.' Felix shrugged. 'I could always change manufacturers, but they're probably paying kick-back to the Khedive's second cousin . . .'

'What am I guarding against this time?' Raf asked as he watched the fat man struggle to force his thick fingers into the tight gloves.

'The coroner,' said Felix cryptically and knelt beside the seated body. With his fingers out straight, he ran his right hand over Nafisa, never quite letting his fingertips get close enough to touch either flesh or clothes. It was as if he was feeling for something that wasn't there.

Taking his tiny maglite, the fat man swept its beam across Nafisa's skin as she sat in the chair. 'No fibres, no animal hair . . .' He was talking to his watch, to Raf and to the weird back-up device in the room outside, but mostly he was talking to himself. Getting himself ready for the bit the coroner wouldn't like.

The leather case Felix took from his pocket contained a Saez scalpel, the old-fashioned titanium-edged kind, a handful of glass thermometers, tiny combs, surgical swabs and glass holding tubes that could freeze themselves. He only planned to use the first two.

Lifting the edge of Lady Nafisa's skirt, Felix checked the dark bruises on her buttocks and lower thigh.

'Obvious lividity . . .'

He pushed the bruising and watched the skin go pale beneath his fingers as the blood that gravity had pooled in the tissue moved aside. Within another couple of hours that would be fixed in place.

'. . . lividity still blanches.' That confirmed his time frame.

All he needed now, for thoroughness, was a core temperature reading. The simplest way of getting that was use a rectal thermometer, but Felix knew better than to even consider the idea. Instead he reached for his Saez scalpel, moved the skirt higher still and punched his scalpel through the skin of Nafisa's abdomen. Extracting the blade, Felix took a surgical thermometer and worked it deep into the tiny wound. Ninety seconds later he broke the red tag off the top of the thermometer to fix the temperature and withdrew the sliver of glass and silicon, dropping it into an evidence bag, which he initialled.

A human body lost roughly one-point-five degrees an hour, depending on surrounding temperature. The reading was within the limits he'd expect.

'Initialling postM wound . . .'

Using his pen, Felix drew a circle around the wound on Lady Nafisa's abdomen, signed his initials and added the date and time. The coroner-magistrate would have a fit about it, there'd be another strong memo to the Minister mentioning desecration of the dead and Felix would get told not to do it again.

Again.

To which he'd reply, as he always did, that if he wasn't allowed to use the orifices that Allah provided, then he'd have to make his own. As yet Madame Mila hadn't come up with an answer that . . . Mind you, she hadn't forgiven him either.

'Toxicology report . . .' Slamming a sterile plastic reservoir into a syringe, Felix picked a vein in Nafisa's wrist and drew blood. Circling and initialling the puncture mark. Let them complain about that, too.

The corpse felt warm through the latex of his glove as he

lifted a breast to examine the pen buried beneath it. He felt for the edge of her ribcage and then counted up, already knowing what he was going to find.

'Penetrating wound to chest, between third and fourth . . .' The blow was perfectly placed to puncture her heart. And it was a single stab wound, highly professional. Amateur assassins often missed. Suicides left hesitation cuts, little lacerations and half-hearted weals while they jabbed or slashed at themselves to see how much it was going to hurt.

Yet no defensive wounds were present to indicate that Lady Nafisa had even tried to fight for her life. And this was a woman notorious for fighting for everything she considered her due. One fact contradicted the other, Felix decided glumly, chewing at the inside of his lip as he always did when conflicting evidence ate away at the insides of his mind.

Lifting her right hand to recheck unbroken skin between the woman's thumb and first finger, Felix almost hissed with irritation. 'No defensive cuts to finger web, nor across palm or wrist . . .' He stopped, turned over the hand to look at her nails. The cuticles were still manicured and immaculate, that morning's lacquer as dark and glossy as a blood trickle but the nail ends were badly chipped and ripped back, all of them.

If she'd been a girl locked in a cellar to starve to death, then that was what he'd expect her fingers to look like at the end of the first day, before they stopped being something used to scrabble at a locked door and became food instead. And it did happen, even in El Iskandryia – but only among the poor, out in the slums, to daughters and sisters who hadn't been as careful as their fathers or brothers expected. It didn't happen to the middle-aged and rich.

Besides, her office wasn't a cellar and her door had been found open.

Felix shook his head, thought briefly about starting his fourth hip flask, the emergency one, and rejected the idea. Every year new morality laws made his life that much more difficult. It was hard enough being Nasrani in a North African city, even worse to be so obviously fat and pink in a country full of elegant Arabs, rugged Berbers and sophisticated Levantines. And his own Catholicism might now be almost residual, but it still made for difficulties in an Islamic metropolis where a male officer wasn't supposed to touch a female corpse.

But then, this was a city where the police test for rape in the outer boroughs was to sit the victim on a rough wooden stool to see if she squirmed with pain. If she didn't, she hadn't fought back and it wasn't rape. Most fought back. Many died rather than submit. Not surprising when most *felaheen* still chose to kill their daughters for being disgraced rather than kill the rapist and risk starting a blood feud.

Sod it. Felix took the swig anyway, aware without looking that the nail of the thumb he used to flip up the top was bitten to the quick, just like all his others. He'd have to go back on the *Sobranie* soon, whatever the medics said about ghostly shadows haunting his lungs. Logical deduction was hard enough without self-inflicted nicotine withdrawal.

So what had he got?

At first glance the attack appeared frenzied. But any attacker in a real frenzy would just have punched the pen straight through whatever clothes Lady Nafisa wore, which meant the open blouse signified something. Unless, of course, what it signified was not frenzy but passion and the stabbing came later, when the widow's defences were down.

That wasn't an avenue Nafisa's cousin Jalila or her husband would want explored with too much thoroughness . . . Or any thoroughness at all, come to that, Felix decided sourly as he listened to heels that clicked regular as a metronome across the courtyard outside. That would be Lady Jalila's friend, the new coroner-magistrate.

Felix waited for the sound of her and Hani's footsteps on the stairs. Then, when they didn't come, he tuned out the distant chatter of Hani's voice and went back to examining the body, using his last few seconds of peace to search for anything he might have missed. Something obvious.

There was a tiny stigma right in the centre of her left hand, a dark crater-like indentation that bled slightly along one edge.

Significant? Possibly. He grabbed a shot anyway and hurriedly thrust the dead woman's hand back in her lap where he'd found it. Then Felix smoothed the skirt down round her knees and stepped back. He left the blouse as he'd found it, torn open at the front. He didn't want anyone saying he'd been messing with the evidence.

'Chief Felix . . .' The coroner-magistrate's greeting was borderline polite, but brittle. 'No one told me you'd be here.'

'Didn't they? Then you've been talking to the wrong people.' The fat man took his time to straighten up, rolling his heavy shoulders to ease their stiffness. And then, when he could put it off no longer, he turned to face the ebony-skinned woman who stood glaring from the doorway.

Madame Mila, with her hair pulled back, her nails worn short and unvarnished, her black trousers and coat cut from local cotton, not even off the peg but off the shelf from Walmart. She wore no jewellery.

Word was, Madame Mila dressed simply because of her job. Felix's view was that she'd dress like that no matter what job she did.

'We've done everything according to regulations,' said Felix. 'His Excellency here is my witness to that . . .'

The woman raised her eyebrows but didn't bother to reply. Instead she stepped over to the body and touched her finger to the throat of the stabbed woman, checking that there was no pulse.

'Dead,' she announced. Felix nodded. The official time of death was now, not when Felix estimated she was killed but when the death was formally recorded by a medical officer.

Carefully, Madame Mila closed the open blouse. Then she stooped for the tissue-thin modesty shroud Felix had earlier discarded and spread it over the dead body. Only after that did she turn back to the door, nodding for Felix to follow her.

'Body's released,' Felix said to his watch. Formalities complete, the corpse could now be removed and the fingerprinting brigade sent in. Felix took a last look round the crime scene, a token glance for anything he might have missed.

'Chief . . .' The voice was unnecessarily impatient.

'What?' Felix demanded. 'What's your problem this time?'

'The pashazade.'

'Using him as my witness was the Minister's idea,' said Felix flatly. 'You got a problem, take it up with Mushin Bey. Ashraf and I are out of here.'

Which was the first Raf had heard about it.

Madame Mila shook her head. 'He goes nowhere,' she said. 'At least not with you. As of now, he's under arrest. Suspicion of murder.' She tightened her grip on the shoulder of the small girl stood beside her. 'And this is *my* witness.'

Chapter Twenty-one

Seattle

Red on white inside, grey on grey without, where the Pacific beat on jagged rocks and gulls circled like sailors' souls over a stark concrete bunker that made the work of Mies van der R look soft and fluid.

Micky O'Brian lay inside on a white silk carpet that cost $340 a square yard and could only be ordered over the web from Beijing, cash in advance. Outside, through a long window that ran the length of his precious first-floor art gallery, gunmetal waters could be seen lapping the shore of Puget Sound. Drizzle made the sky as dull as the sea and reduced visibility to a few hundred paces.

The jetty in front of Lodge Concret was bare. A thin strip of factory grating held above the rocking waves by anodized posts. The clinker-built pleasure boat that should have been there was long gone. So was a Matisse nude, a Christo abstract and one of the most important early works of Cézanne still to be in private ownership . . . Farmhouse at Auvers had been painted in 1873, the year after Cézanne moved to Pontoise to be close to Pissarro.

White on red.

Seepage from a bullet hole in the back of Micky O'Brian's head had formed its own abstract, more Rorschach blot than Rothko. A vivid red splash that would fade to black as blood soaked into silk and eventually dried. There was a message in the colours, and the message was that the man wouldn't be testifying to anything.

At first glance it looked like Micky was grabbing a nap, half curled on his side in slacks, gold slippers and a Chinese dressing gown with a five-toed Mandarin dragon on the back. But that was only at first glance. His wide-eyed glassy stare told a different story. One that ZeeZee picked up only in fragments, as he checked the long gallery and found it empty of any killer, with its picture lights turned down to 'dim' and a still-chilled bottle of Mumm Cordon Rouge open on a side table.

There were macadamia nuts and chilli olives in little bowls alongside the bottle. An open but untouched box of Partegas corona had been placed nearby, along with a neatly rolled spliff placed ostentatiously on a silver ashtray. A very Micky O'Brian touch. The air in the gallery was heavy with scent from a huge vase of black tulips. Debussy drifted from flat wall speakers. Clair de Lune or something similar. Something lightweight, in keeping with Micky's acting abilities.

The visitor Micky O'Brian had been expecting was ZeeZee. But someone else had definitely got here first.

ZeeZee carefully put the fat manila envelope he'd been delivering on the arm of a white leather sofa and considered his options. He could call the police or he could just leave, quietly and quickly. Returning the way he'd come, on the back of his 650cc Suzuki. And why not? He now had no one to meet. No reason for being there.

'Shit.' ZeeZee picked up his envelope and headed downstairs, the Debussy nocturne looping in his head. He made it as far as the sand-blasted glass front door before someone yelled his name.

'Hey, ZeeZee . . .' The amused shout came from behind him. 'Going somewhere?'

He turned to see two bulls he knew in SPD jumpsuits flanking a woman who wore a black Chanel suit, black shoes and Shu Uemura make-up. Not that she needed it: even naked, her face would have been flawless, her eyes bright, brown and hard as glass. He had no idea who she was.

All he knew was the woman had to have practised that contemptuous, deadpan stare. It was too convincing to be real. The grins on the faces of the uniformed officers were *something else entirely. Certainly not real smiles, more grim-faced got-you-you-bastard kind of expressions.*

'Micky O'Brian . . .' ZeeZee began, breaking the silence.

'Yeah,' said the woman. 'Why don't you take us to meet him?'

'He's . . . When I got here . . . I didn't know . . .'

She looked at ZeeZee without saying anything. Just waited until his words stumbled to a halt and then kept waiting while the English boy skidded around in his head for the right approach to take to what was about to happen – and realized there wasn't one.

'Don't tell me,' she said finally. 'You got here a couple of minutes ago and found the front door open. You knocked but no one came, so you went inside. And guess what, you found Micky O'Brian shot through the skull . . . Or was it the throat?'

'A head shot,' ZeeZee said, without thinking.

The two uniformed officers looked at each other. As if that only confirmed what they expected.

'And you were on your way to call the police?'

ZeeZee nodded.

'So why didn't you use the hall phone?' The woman nodded to a Sanyo fixed to the wall by the front door, its screen black but one diode flashing lazily in the lower left corner, to signal the system was set to standby.

'I didn't see it,' said ZeeZee hastily. 'I was too shocked.'

'Which is why you were whistling . . .' She hummed back at him the main motif from Clair de Lune. 'I can see the headlines now. The whistling hit man . . .'

'I haven't killed anybody,' ZeeZee protested.

'Of course you haven't,' she said sourly. 'So why don't you come and show us the person you didn't kill?'

Micky O'Brian's body was where he'd left it. The blood seemed a little darker, Micky a little more obviously dead. Other than that, walking into the gallery could just have been a bad attack of déjà vu.

'So you found him lying there like that?'

ZeeZee nodded.

'And you touched nothing?'

He shook his head, then hesitated.

'Yes?' she said, drawing out the word until it ended with a hiss.

'I touched the wine bottle. To check how cold it was . . . And I turned off the music.'

'How thoughtful of you.'

'But I didn't touch anything else. I didn't kill him. And I didn't take the paintings.'

The detective flicked her gaze to a blank space on the wall. Then back to the body. So far none of them had checked Micky for a pulse. But maybe they'd decided it wasn't necessary, given the very final expression on his face.

'So you're trying to shift the blame to an accomplice, right? He shot Micky, took the paintings and left you to lock the front door . . . Yeah, I know,' said the woman, as she held up her hand to still ZeeZee's protest. 'You didn't kill him and you don't know who did.'

Shrugging, she walked over to Micky and looked down for a while, then bent to free something trapped under him. 'Here,' she said, tossing it to ZeeZee. 'You left this behind.'

The fat envelope he'd been carrying hit the floor as ZeeZee fumbled to make the catch. And then, while he was still worrying about what he'd dropped, ZeeZee realized what he'd just caught. What he'd just tagged with his sweat, fingerprints and oil. An old Wilson Combat, its usual barrel replaced with a .22 conversion. The deep scar of an acid etch where the barrel's identification number should be.

'Ditch the gun.'

ZeeZee heard her words but he wasn't really listening. Had he always been the patsy: or was he only now surplus to requirements? He looked in disbelief at the weapon in his hands, knowing exactly who it belonged to . . . Wild Boy had just, very firmly, taken him out of the loop.

'Drop it.' The woman nodded to the man beside her, who

flipped his service-issue Colt out of its holster and trained the sight on ZeeZee's chest before the English boy realised what was happening.

'Put it down real slow.' The man holding the revolver had a Southern drawl and a liking for theatrics. The trigger on his gun was already pulled, his knuckle white from depressing the trigger to its fullest extent. Only his thumb was holding back the hammer.

'Your choice,' the woman said coldly.

Wasn't it always?

ZeeZee kneeled slowly and placed the Combat flat on Micky's white carpet, muzzle pointed safely towards the wall. He didn't want any misunderstandings.

'I didn't kill Micky O'Brian. I didn't . . .' He wanted his voice to sound decisive and confident but instead it sounded shrill, as if he was trying to convince himself.

'Switching to .22 was a good move,' said the officer with the gun. 'But, you know what . . . ?'

ZeeZee shook his head.

'You really should have used a silencer. We got a call about the shot right after it happened . . .'

ZeeZee looked through the gallery's long window, taking in the rugged coastline, the choppy grey waters, the sheer isolation of this stretch of Puget Sound. Yeah, he'd bet there'd been a call, but not made from around here. There was no other house within miles. He couldn't wait for the part where they looked in the envelope and discovered Micky's delivery: half a kilo of uncut coke.

Chapter Twenty-two

6th July

300–3500 Hz (with harmonics peaking above 3500), is an average frequency-range for the human voice. And the sensitivity of human hearing is pretty smooth between 500–5000Hz, with 110dB being usually as loud as a voice gets.

The prisoner in the next cell was breaking 120dB, his screams emptying in a single breath that ended as swallowed, choking sobs. And though the air in Raf's small room now stank of sweat, everyone was being positively polite.

The bey was good – Felix had to give him that. He hadn't tried to claim immunity or demanded to talk to the Minister. He'd even allowed an embarrassed sergeant to wire him to a polygraph, fastening the band round his own wrist and placing his right hand completely flat on the plate. Not that the bey was exactly cooperating, either.

He hadn't yet removed his black jacket, which still looked immaculate after hours of questioning: and he'd only just taken off his dark glasses, after Madame Mila finally agreed to lower the brightness of the overhead lights.

It had been hypocritical of the fat man to have put on record at the outset that he hoped the coroner-magistrate knew what she was doing – because he didn't hope that at all. What he actually hoped – very much – was that Madame Mila was making the worst mistake of her short but impressive career.

'Hani heard you shouting at each other.' The sergeant kept his voice reasonable. At Madame Mila's earlier suggestion, he'd tried hectoring but that only made the man in front of him shut down. Emotionally autistic.

'Arguing,' stressed Madame Mila. 'All of last night.' That was the fact to which she kept coming back, time after time. The one fact Raf couldn't deny.

'She wanted me to marry Zara bint-Hamzah,' repeated Raf. 'I refused. She was cross.'

'Oh, she was *way* more than cross.' As ever, Madame Mila's voice was cutting. 'She threatened to disown you because you betrayed that poor girl. So this morning you went home and stabbed her. Rather than take the risk . . . That's what happened, wasn't it?'

'No,' said Raf. 'It wasn't . . .'

'So how did it happen?' The young police sergeant fired his question, but it might as well have been Coroner Mila speaking. This was definitely her show.

'I was in my office all morning.'

'No,' said the sergeant, looking at a screen, 'we've been over this. You left at 11.30 . . .'

'And went straight to Le Trianon,' Raf shrugged. 'That's the same thing. You can check at Le Trianon.'

'We have. You left your capuccino undrunk and your paper on the table.'

'While I went for a stamp round Place Saad Zaghloul.'

'Which was at what time?'

'Noon,' said Raf. 'Maybe later. As I said, I didn't look at my watch.'

Heartbeat, blood pressure and limbic pattern all held steady. Every diode on the Matsui polygraph lit a peaceful green. They might as well have been discussing the weather. *Hell.* The sergeant sucked at his teeth. *The weather might have got more of a limbic reaction out of the man.*

The officer glanced bleary-eyed down at his screen. 'According to the maître d' you were gone for an hour, at least.'

Raf shook his head. 'I got back slightly before that, then waited to catch someone's eye. I wasn't in a hurry . . .'

Madame Mila snorted.

'Besides,' said Raf calmly, 'you know there isn't time to walk there and back, from Zagloul to Sherif, inside an hour, never mind murder somebody and fake a break-in. Which I didn't.'

'So you took a taxi,' the sergeant announced tiredly.

'Then where's the driver?'

'We're finding him now.'

'No,' said Raf, looking straight at Madame Mila. 'You're not, because there *was* no taxi. I went nowhere near the Al-Mansur madersa at lunchtime and I didn't kill my aunt – as that machine has already verified . . .' He nodded contemptuously at the primitive polygraph.

Felix pushed himself away from the wall. 'Time to call the Minister,' said the fat man. He was talking both to the coroner-magistrate and to a fish-eye unit she'd placed on the plastic table between Raf and her sergeant. 'You had your eight hours. You blew it . . . I'm releasing him.'

He glanced at Raf and grinned.

Raf sat next to Felix, his back to a sea wall, staring inland over the dark expanse of dust and shut-down kiosks that was Place Saad Zaghloul. The café where they'd just bought supper was the only place still serving at two a.m. and Felix had been hungry. In front of him rested a half-full bottle of Algerian *marc* and a paper plate that had, until recently, been piled with grilled chicken breasts drenched with harissa sauce. It was as near as the fat man could get to a genuine McD chick&chilli burger.

Raf was improving his life with a third styrofoam cup of thick black coffee laced with rum. He didn't think of it as using caffeine to release dopamine in his prefrontal cortex, but he felt the hit all the same. This way he could tell himself the shakes weren't really about having been locked up in a cell.

'You know,' said Felix, 'you could have told me . . .'

Just what Raf could have told him the fat man left drifting on the sticky night breeze blowing in from behind then.

'. . . don't you think?'

Raf said nothing. Instead, he drained his coffee to the dregs, only stopping when his mouth filled with grit from coarse-ground beans. He wasn't going to sleep anyway. The image of Hani's guilt-stricken face was pixel-clear in his brain.

'If you had,' continued Felix, 'I could have got the coroner-magistrate off your case right at the start, before we hit the station. If only I'd known.' The fat man's conversation seemed to be going round in circles. Or maybe that was just the sky.

'Known what?' Raf asked tiredly.

'I made a call to Hamzah Effendi. You know what he told me?'

No, Raf didn't. In fact, he couldn't begin to guess. The last time he and Hamzah had talked, the thickset industrialist had been standing on the upper steps of the *qaa* and had threatened to have Raf's legs broken for disgracing his daughter.

'He said you were an attaché at the Seattle Consulate . . . Said I wasn't to mention that he'd told me.'

Raf went very still.

'It's okay,' said Felix as he leant back and drained off a beaker of Algerian rot-gut brandy. 'Look, fuck forbid I should get all touchy-feely. But I've been there . . . Smoke, flames, flying rubble. I'm not saying you should talk any about what happened but, all the same, telling me would have spared you that shit with Mila.'

'You think I killed Lady Nafisa?'

'The bloody *Thiergarten* killed Nafisa.' Felix slapped Raf heavily on the shoulder. 'All the same, until this is over I'm going to have to take that passport from you. And the gun. General's orders'

'Gun . . .' Raf looked as shocked as he felt.

'Hani told Madame Mila you sleep with an old revolver by your bed.' Felix smiled sourly. 'Someone should tell that kid to keep her mouth shut . . . Anyway,' he shrugged, 'drop them both off tomorrow, before the autopsy.'

'Tomorrow . . . ?'

'This morning, whatever . . . All bodies get buried by the following noon, murder victims included. Shari'ah Law.' His tone made it clear exactly what he thought of the Khedive's new deal with the mullahs. 'Five a.m. then,' said Felix. 'Nice and early.' And he pushed himself to his feet, then staggered off across Place Saad Zaghloul without a backward glance.

Chapter Twenty-three

7th July

Felix didn't mention the tattered state of Raf's beard or hair. Most of both were gone, cropped short with kitchen scissors from the madersa. The job wasn't yet finished, but then he'd only had two hours between arriving home and having to leave again, and most of that had been taken up with Hani.

'How's the kid?'

Raf paused, remembering.

At 2.30 a.m. she'd been a shaking little bundle, crouched on the *qaa* steps with a blanket wrapped round her and Ali-Din clutched tight in her arms like life depended on it. 'She'll survive.'

Felix sucked at his teeth. 'That bad, eh?'

'Yeah,' said Raf. 'The kid wouldn't sleep in the nursery because Nafisa's room is next door, the kitchens were out because Khartoum sleeps there. And she said she couldn't sleep in my room because it's on the men's floor and she isn't a boy . . . So we turned on the fountain, dragged out a carpet and she crashed in the courtyard under a tree.'

Raf didn't mention any Arctic fox he might have left curled up by her head to guard the kid while he was away. Mostly he didn't mention Tiriganaq because he didn't yet know what, if anything, the fox's dawn reappearance meant. Besides, Felix didn't look like someone who'd understand about inner ghosts. Crawling ants and pink elephants were more his style.

They were waiting outside a steel door in a dark underground corridor that was to-the-bone cold, something Raf hadn't previously felt in El Iskandryia. The occasional shop or café might be air-conditioned but this was different. Cold grey walls and cold stone floor, even cold overhead strips that had a light thinner than the washed-out blue of dawn outside. For once Raf wasn't wearing shades: Versace wraparounds didn't seem appropriate in a morgue.

'You know,' said Felix slowly, 'you don't really act like a bey.' From his hungover growl it was hard to tell whether this was meant as a compliment.

'Most of the time I don't feel like one.'

'Then you'd better start pretending,' said Felix seriously. He curled his fingers into a clumsy fist and punched Raf lightly on the shoulder. 'Okay?'

Raf was still wondering exactly how he felt about becoming the fat man's unofficial adoptee when Felix hammered hard on the closed door for a second time.

'All right, all right . . .' Bolts drew back inside and someone in a mask peered through a sudden gap. Over her shoulder came a blast of blood and formaldehyde.

'You're late.'

Felix checked his watch. 'It's only five a.m. . . .'

'I did it at four. Still, you might as well come in and see.' The woman stepped back, then stopped dead at the sight of Raf, her face suddenly indignant behind her mask.

'It's okay,' Felix said hurriedly, before she could slam the door. 'This is the dead woman's nephew. They were very close, and he's as desperate as me to find her killers . . . Raf, meet Kamila. Kamila, meet Pashazade Ashraf al-Mansur.'

'This is not fair,' the girl protested tightly, backing away from the door as Felix gently pushed his way into the autopsy suite. 'I'm taking a risk just talking to you.'

'Kamila works for Madame Mila,' Felix told Raf. 'Her father works for me. Sometimes these things are useful.' He ignored the cadaver of an elderly woman laid out on a mobile cart and made his way towards a steel autopsy table where another ripped-open body lay covered with white gauze. Holes had been punched in the table's surface to let liquid drain down to a collecting tray underneath.

'What did you find?'

'The cause of death was a puncture wound to the chest. The mechanism of death was—'

'*Kamila!*'

'This wasn't what we agreed,' the girl said furiously. 'It's bad enough that you're here. As for him . . .' She glared at Raf.

'*How did my aunt die?*' Raf kept his question short and his voice as cold as the mortuary in which they now stood. Somehow the dark glasses in his pocket had found their way onto his face. Pretend, Felix had said. Raf could do one better than pretend: when necessary, he could *be*.

'Well?' Raf demanded. Even the fat man looked shocked at the sudden anger in his voice. 'I want to know . . . How did she die?'

'Heart attack,' Kamila said quietly. 'The pen severed her left main coronary artery. Which produced a big ischemic area. Tamponade was absent since the pericardium was punctured, but she—'

'You know what the fuck this means?' Raf demanded, swinging round to Felix.

The fat man nodded. 'The pen spiked her heart. Not much blood on the outside, quite a lot on the inside but, technically at least, still death by heart attack. How am I doing?'

The girl gave him a grudging nod.

'Seen it before,' Felix said cryptically. He yanked away the covering gauze without asking Kamila's permission.

Despite his best intentions, Raf looked. He couldn't help himself. All the same, he knew that from now on it would now be impossible to think of Nafisa as anything other than so much jointed meat. What had once been human was human no longer. The body had been sliced open in a Y that began at each shoulder to shoulder, met below the breastbone and ran in a single slash down to a depilated pubis. The intestines were still in place but heart, lungs, oesophagus and trachea were a black and gaping cavity.

'Any signs of rape?' he asked abruptly.

'No.' The girl's answer was brusque. As if that was exactly the kind of question she'd expect someone like him to ask.

'Then why was her shirt open?'

In answer, Kamila turned her back on him. 'I'm about to repack the body,' she told Felix. 'You can indent the coroner-magistrate for a copy of my report. She may even let you have one.'

Felix nodded. 'What about other wounds?'

'What did you have in mind?' She'd spotted where Felix had lanced into the dead woman's abdomen to take a core temperature, though the fat man hoped that the fact wouldn't make it into her final report. And that wasn't what he was asking about, anyway.

'Anything . . .'

The girl started to shake her head, then paused. 'Maybe this,' she admitted, lifting one of Nafisa's hands, which moved unwillingly beneath her grip. Detritus had been scraped from beneath each split nail and bagged and labelled. The tips of each finger still showed traces of staining where prints had been taken.

'Could be nothing,' said the girl. She nodded at the circular bruise that the fat man that had already noticed on the dead woman's palm.

Felix nodded to a small metal trolley. 'Okay to touch this?' He lifted Lady Nafisa's Mont Blanc pen, transparent bag and all, from a metal kidney dish and held the blunt end to the bruise, without letting pen or flesh actually touch. The end was way too small.

'Anything else?' asked Felix.

Raf wondered if the Chief and the pathologist had noticed the pen was missing its top, then realized both of them must have done. Which made his not mentioning the fact significant. Some kind of interdepartmental dance was going on between Kamila and Felix that Raf didn't begin to understand . . .

But he would. Raf was making it his business. Secure the circle, the fox always said. So if the coroner-magistrate had him pegged as culprit, well, he'd bring Felix on-side as protection. And if staying close to Felix meant involving himself in Iskandryian politics then he could do that too, and play out his role of Bey. Life's absurdities existed to be milked for all they were worth. And besides, anything was better than being returned to Seattle to face Huntsville or Hu San. Which was exactly what would happen if anyone discovered who he really was.

'Answer the man,' Raf ordered. 'Anything else?'

'Nothing,' said the girl firmly.

Felix smiled. 'Normal stomach contents?'

'Chief!' Her voice was exasperated, as if she expected him to ask the ridiculous but still found it irritating. 'This is a minimum-invasion autopsy – boss's orders, minister's orders too. Simply confirm cause of death. Repack body, sew along dotted line. You know how this goes . . .'

'Simply *confirm* cause of death,' Felix said slowly. 'Sweet fuck. You know how worried I get when I hear those words?'

'Cause of death *pen*. Mechanism of death *torn heart muscle*. Manner of death *homicide*.' It was obvious Kamila considered their visit well into overtime. She'd had enough of the two men trespassing on her territory and wanted them off it, just as soon as possible. All the same, she was willing to compromise. 'Look,' she said as she herded them towards the door, 'you can indent me direct for a copy of the report.'

Felix nodded thanks. 'About those stomach contents,' he added softly. 'Just tell your father the results and let him pass them to me. Okay?' Felix smiled sweetly and dragged Raf from the room before Kamila had time to refuse.

Chapter Twenty-four

7th July

'La ilaha illa Allah . . .'
   . . . Glory be to the Most High.

The small hand that gripped Raf's had fingers of steel, nails sharp as glass and a palm clammy as that of a drowned child. Which was what she was, only Hani was drowning in ritual and other people's pity. The hand in his shook so rapidly that her shakes were practically invisible.

All through the funeral she'd been tightening her grip, until by the final round of prayers she was alternately hanging on as if for dear life and digging her nails deep into his skin. Though it was hard to tell whether Hani was angry with Raf or herself.

The funeral was brief: divided into four parts and quite obviously following a template that, equally obviously, he didn't recognize. The opening verses of the Quran had been read first, followed by another reading. An intercession was made and finally a plea that the gates of Paradise be wide enough to allow Lady Nafisa entry and therein that she be washed with water and ice, purified as a garment is purified of corrupting filth . . . It was a sentiment Raf briefly found himself wishing he could believe.

'Not much longer,' he whispered. Reassuring himself as much as Hani. They'd arrived together, straight from the madersa, accompanied by a weeping Khartoum and Nafisa's cook Donna, who stopped at the gates of the necropolis, crossed herself with undisguised fervour and refused to take another step.

And as he stood dressed in black and waiting in the blazing sun for the interment to finish, Raf could almost feel Donna's fierce gaze on the back of his neck. But then, almost everyone was watching him – except for Hani, who wouldn't lift her eyes from the ground.

He'd shaved, trimmed the remains of his beard down to a short dark-blond goatee and taken clippers to his skull, because that was the quickest way to get rid of dreads. All of which turned out to be a bad mistake. Apparently, not shaving was a North African mark of respect, a signature of mourning. Lady Jalila couldn't even bring herself to talk to him. Unfortunately, the same couldn't be said for everybody else.

'Okay,' said a voice at his shoulder. 'Ready to go?' That was Felix, more smartly dressed than Raf had seen him before. His ponytail washed and his shoes so shined and polished he'd even blacked the heels. Though the suit he wore, newly pressed or not, still looked as if he kept it hidden at the back of a cupboard and dragged it out once or twice a year when he had a colleague to bury or needed to attend the funeral of some victim. It went almost without saying that the cloth, colour and cut were at least fifteen years out of date.

'Come on.' The fat man touched Raf's elbow. 'Time to move.'

Felix had been the one to collect them from the madersa and driven them out to the necropolis in his pink Cadillac with white-walled tyres. And Raf got the feeling it was only the fat man's presence that was keeping Madame Mila at bay. He hadn't expected to see her at the funeral. But then, Raf had naively thought it would be just Hani, himself and Felix, not realizing that fifty of Iskandryia's great and good would turn out into the airless rising heat of a Wednesday morning to see the cloth-wrapped body of Lady Nafisa carried into her family tomb.

'Ashraf,' hissed Lady Jalila, materializing beside him like a bad smell. 'You have to lead.' Dark patches of sweat showed under the arms of her white linen suit, but her make-up was still immaculate and the few strands of hair that escaped from under her Hermès scarf glinted prettily in the sunlight.

'Come on,' Raf said and turned to Hani. Only to stop at the sight of her face.

The child had her legs set apart, her heels dug deep into the grit of the path. Everything about her body language roared defiance except for the hurt in her eyes. Raf recognized that, the exploding bleakness, which wasn't the same as remembering it. Though he remembered well how hard he'd had to learn to forget.

'We need to move,' Raf said softly.

Hani shook her head. No question of compromise.

'*Hani.*'

Heads flicked round at Lady Jalila's rebuke, until most of the mourners were gazing at the child. There was something hungry about the gathering. Lady Jalila held out her hand to Hani and waited.

Nobody moved.

'*You* lead,' Raf suggested, taking in the crowd of strangers and knowing they listened to his every word. 'You were her closest friend and you found her. Besides, you can see the child is terrified.'

He dropped to his knees on the gravel path. 'We're staying here, aren't we?'

Night-black eyes stared back at him, then arms thin as sticks fastened themselves tight round his neck as Hani clung to him and her butterfly trembling exploded into full-blown shakes. Sobs shook her body but Raf had no need to look to know the child was crying: the tears were trickling into the collar of his shirt.

When he looked up, a good half of the onlookers were gazing sympathetically at them both. The Minister of Police even had a sad, tolerant smile on his face.

'If you insist.' Something ghost-like flitted across the face of Lady Jalila as she turned to face the mausoleum door. And she walked away without waiting for her husband.

'Poor child,' said Mushin Bey sadly. 'Such a loss.' Raf figured the Minister of Police was talking about Hani and not his wife, but it was hard to tell.

One by one, the other mourners followed Lady Jalila and the body until they were all swallowed by darkness and the necropolis suddenly felt empty. From a nearby bush came the bubbling call of a common bulbul and beyond a high wall cars could be heard grinding gears at distant traffic lights.

'About bloody time,' said Felix, with feeling. The flask was out, flicked open and tucked safely back in the fat man's jacket in an instant. 'Needs must,' he said, looking oddly shamefaced. 'It's either grab the odd refuel or not turn up at all . . .' He glanced towards Hani − folded into Raf's arms, her eyes screwed tight, her face buried in his shoulder − and nodded thoughtfully. 'Good man,' said Felix softly. 'Now find out what she really knows . . .'

The al-Mansur mausoleum was elegantly simple. Its very simplicity a sign of the design's antiquity, which easily predated both the city's invasion by Napoleon in 1798 and an earlier seventeenth-century plague that had swept the streets of life and briefly reduced Isk to a handful of dilapidated dwellings occupied by obese rats.

A low door, cut into the side of a marble base, led down to a deep crypt. Rising up from the square base, basalt pillars at each corner supported a roof that rose, in its turn, to meet at a point in the very centre. A short metal spine that jutted from this point ended in a simple crescent. Though it was difficult to see from the ground what material the crescent had been hammered from, as winter storms had weathered the metal to a deep black.

Under this roof, centred on the base itself, was a simple memorial. A rough-hewn slab of stone, balanced on its side and apparently held upright at either end by a short square pillar, one of which had once been broken and repaired with stone of a slightly poorer quality.

'What are you doing?'

'Looking at the building,' said Raf, slowly stroking the child's hair. She didn't quite pull away, so he stroked again, more slowly still. Years back that had worked for a different animal, a wounded one, when no other boy at his school could get near it.

'It's a *kiosk*,' Hani said. She nodded to the mausoleum. 'And that thing's a *cenotaph* and those are *stelae*.' The upward jerk to her chin told him she was talking about the narrow pillars.

'*Yesterday I was as you, tomorrow you will be like me . . .*' Hani recited from memory the inscription on the base. 'How old do you think it is?'

Raf looked round at other, more ornate tombs. A few of which had similar square roofs, though most had little domes, cupolas of stone decorated either with starburst motifs, herringbone patterns or intricate, intertwined arabesques. Even the newest ones looked as if they'd been there for centuries.

'I've no idea,' he said, 'tell me.'

Hani's lips twisted. 'Twenty years . . . Donna told me. My aunt built it for her husband. The pillar broke in the first year and she made the builders replace it for nothing.'

'But the site . . .' Raf scanned the necrotic jumble that crowded in on itself, bent by age and gravity, some of the funerary monuments so close to collapse they looked as though they were trying to shoulder neighbouring tombs out of the way.

'Bought an old tomb and pulled it down.' The child shrugged. 'Of course, she had to pay someone to carry away the old bodies.'

'Of course . . .' Raf nodded at a heavily bent cork tree nearby. 'It's too bright for me,' he said. 'Are you all right with moving?'

They walked over to the shade together, Hani never once releasing her grip on his hand. She'd been holding on without break from the point they stepped into Ruc Cif and climbed into the back of Felix's open-top car. Quite what she thought would happen to her if she let go Raf had no idea, but it was equally obvious Hani didn't intend to find out.

Just getting her out onto the street had been difficult enough. Getting the kid into the car had taken a major miracle. Though it wasn't until Hani had appeared in a dress, her straight black hair carefully tied back, that Raf even realized he had a problem.

She'd walked easily enough from the *qaa* through the courtyard, and less easily from there into the oven-like heat of the covered garden, which was already beginning to wilt after only one day without Lady Nafisa's attention. But by the time she'd reached the madersa's final squat passage out onto Rue Cif, Hani was shaking with fear.

'Come on,' Raf had said, tugging slightly on her hand. Her answering yank almost took his arm out of its socket. And as he stared down to where her face was setting into a mask of stubbornness made flesh, realization hit.

He didn't hear her whisper first time so she said it again.

'I've never . . .' Hani's voice trailed away into silence.

'You've never left the house?'

The truth was confirmed in the eyes of the old Sudanese porter who stood watching the anxious girl stand frozen on his doorstep. Self-imposed boxes, that was what life produced, thought Raf bleakly. Simple and basic or complex and jewelled, it made little difference. Prison was still prison and exile was exile, internal or not.

'Are you afraid?' he asked Hani.

Her answer was a fierce scowl.

'Well,' said Raf, 'are you?'

'No. Of course not.' She bunched her fingers into fists and pressed her hands hard at her side. 'I'm never afraid.'

He would be. Nine years without leaving the madersa where she'd been born. Without stepping beyond the rear door into Rue Cif, never mind using the carved front portal that led from the house to the busy mayhem that was Rue Sherif. Not that anyone still used the Rue Sherif portal, of course. The sun-blasted street doors might remain in place, but the actual archway behind them had been bricked up ten years before Hani was even born, on Lady Nafisa's orders. The few visitors Lady Nafisa had allowed into the madersa since her husband's death use the entrance in Rue Cif.

Dropping to one knee, Raf forgot about his new suit. 'Not afraid?' he said. 'Everyone's afraid . . .' He was aware of Felix watching him from the waiting Cadillac. 'It's what keeps us alive.' He'd almost said *human*.

Hani looked doubtful.

Raf sighed. He didn't want to run the *duty* routine, but he was going to anyway, because that was what would work. He and the kid shared a number of the same buttons in common.

'She was your aunt . . .'

'Your aunt too,' Hani said sullenly.

Yeah, right. That was somewhere he didn't plan to visit. 'But you knew her properly. Much better than I did.'

The nod was tiny.

'And everyone will expect you to be there . . .'

Hani looked doubtful.

'I'm sorry,' Raf said softly. He stood up, slipped on his dark glasses and struck a pose, one hand tucked into his silk jacket, as if holding a gun. *Imperial Assassin* V.

'Hey,' he said, 'Stick with me. You'll be safe.'

Hani's lips twisted. Only the briefest twitch, but it was almost a smile.

Chapter Twenty-five

Seattle

The long blade shone silver. Not as bright as sun on the water in the harbour beyond the shop window where a new Japanese super-yacht sat looking smug and sleek, but bright enough to make the newly arrived English boy glance away.

Behind a wooden counter at the back of the shop was a Chinese woman hard at work removing a scratch from the mirror-black lacquered scabbard of a Honshu wakizasi. Her shop mostly sold reproduction Japanese swords because that was what tourists in Seattle seemed to want and could afford. The sword held by the boy was real, a fact reflected in its price.

Cotton bound the ray-skin hilt, its tsuba was pierced and simple, the scabbard was lacquered wood with traces of crazing, where an under-lacquer showed through. But it was the shinto blade that made that particular sword special. Even the fact her great-grandfather died at Nanking wasn't enough to stop her appreciating the katana's stark beauty.

Hu San Liang had already decided the young tourist would walk out empty-handed. He liked the sword but couldn't possibly afford it. If he'd had that kind of money the boy would have bought the weapon already.

Instead he was taking a last, regretful look. A few more minutes and he would be gone. Buying a coffee at Starbucks next door, most probably. Some small consolation for not being able to afford what he really wanted.

Hu San was used to it. The prices in her shop were higher than elsewhere. Partly that was because harbour-front sites in Seattle were expensive, occupied mostly by hotels, franchise chains and exclusive bars. The other reason was that Hu San didn't sell rubbish. She shipped the reproductions from Osaka to Seattle through her own small import/export company. Cheaper reproductions could be bought from Spain or Taiwan for a fraction of the price but she had her own motives for sourcing material from Osaka. Quite apart from an obvious one, which was that her lover was Japanese.

'How old is this?' The boy's voice was polite, his accent definitely not local. Hu San had watched him come into her shop every day for a week and silently pick up the same sword and pull it respectfully from its simple scabbard to examine the hamon: that wavy temper line where the blade was coated with clay before firing, so that variations in heat would produce a hard but brittle cutting edge, backed by softer but more flexible steel.

It was the best sword in the shop. Hu San suspected the English boy knew that. She also knew the boy had blanched the first time a price was mentioned, but still kept coming back.

'How old? Three-fifty years, maybe a bit more.' Hu San's voice placed her as second-generation Chinese-American. More Seattle than anything else.

'And the scabbard?'

'What do you think?'

The boy picked up the scabbard thoughtfully. When he thought Hu San wasn't looking he flicked a thumbnail across a gold mon on the scabbard's side. The circle peeled rather than flaked away.

'New,' said the boy, looking at the handle. It was all new except the blade.

'The blade is the sword.' Hu San said shortly. She waited for the question but the boy just nodded.

'Beautiful,' said the boy. Then, to Hu San's relief, he put the blade back in its scabbard, put the scabbard back on its daisho stand and left her shop. Which was as well, because the Chinese woman was expecting a visitor. And not one she looked forward to meeting.

Taking a pen from its tray, Hu San moistened a block of ink

and began to practise writing her name. She'd practised every day since she was four, which was now just over thirty-five years ago. One day she would get it exactly right, but hopefully not too soon.

Her Korean visitor wore a dark suit, white shirt and red tie. The uniform of money-men or gangsters. He came in just as Hu San finished her third attempt. Neither bowed to the other and the Korean made no effort to hide his contempt at the smallness of the shop or at how Hu San was passing her time.

'Try writing an epitaph,' he suggested, 'if you must do that ethnic crap.'

But Hu San had no intention of dying. At least, not that day and not to any timetable worked out by a Korean. She knew the Korean's name, of course, but wasn't prepared to do the man the honour of using it, not even in her head. She'd known his father and that one had also been stupid.

'You know why I'm here?'

Hu San gave the briefest nod.

The Korean put his hand into his jacket pocket. 'Agree our terms,' he said, 'or else . . .' The rest of what he planned to say was lost in the ring of a bell as ZeeZee walked back into the shop and headed straight for the sword. Hu San had been right. The boy had gone next door to Starbucks and nursed a regular latte – at the shelf by the window – while he came up with his proposal. He would put down a deposit on the katana, *pay every week and collect the sword when its price had been met.*

He wasn't about to mention that he didn't yet have a job.

Taking the sword from its rack, ZeeZee slid free the blade and held it out in front of him, feeling the perfection of its balance. Only then did he notice Hu San was not alone and that her visitor was gaping bug-eyed at him like some fish out of water.

'Go,' ordered Hu San. 'I'm shut now. Come back tomorrow . . .'

'You heard her,' said the suit. 'Move.'

ZeeZee was never quite sure why he didn't just walk out of the shop. Stubbornness, maybe. Disappointment at not being

*able to make his eminently sensible proposal. Sheer chance,
perhaps. Some half-remembered butterfly stamping its foot way
back when he was born. Although, later, the fox told ZeeZee it
had snapped awake, sniffed the air and tasted something sour.
Tiri was like that, unpredictable. Whatever the reason, ZeeZee
lowered the blade and started towards the counter. There was
something he really needed to discuss.*

*'Out,' said the Korean, jerking his head towards the door.
He had a gun in his hand that hadn't been there a second
before.*

*Inside the boy's head an animal growled and ZeeZee heard
a low whisper that hadn't spoken since he was seven.*

Raise the sword . . .

*Without pausing to think, the boy lifted his blade, cavalry-
sabre-style, and stepped forward. 'Are you being robbed?'*

*Hu San glanced from the boy to the Korean and then
nodded.*

The growling got louder.

*'Call the police,' ZeeZee's voice was hoarse, way too high.
He took a slow breath to steady himself. 'Call them . . .'*

*Most of his weight ZeeZee rested on his left heel, leaving his
right leg forward and heel slightly raised, as he took up the
two-handed position taught at school. Man with gun versus
man with sword. In theory it was a straight stand-off, but the
idea he might actually have to use his blade raised questions
of the kind the boy didn't want to answer.*

*'Fuckwit,' the Korean said flatly. He was talking to ZeeZee, or
rather he was talking at ZeeZee, because his hand was already
bringing up the revolver.*

*Sun flashed on metal, time slowed, and a katana blade slid
through flesh and bit through bone showering the boy with
hot rain.*

'Bow,' ordered Hu San.

*For a second the Korean's severed head remained on his
neck. Then it tipped forward and fell to the floor. Death
smoothing away the man's sudden expression of disbelief.*

The Korean would probably have crumbled forward anyway,

though to ZeeZee it looked as if the blood pumping from the man's neck was what forced him to his knees. It rained down around ZeeZee as he stood staring in shock at the razor-sharp blade resting unused in his hand.

'Could you have killed him?' Hu San asked as she wiped her own blade on a corner of her jacket.

Could he? ZeeZee didn't find the question odd. But then there was very little in life that he found odd. And it was a good question, even if he didn't yet know the answer. He'd never killed anything, not a fish from a lake or a sparrow with a BB gun, and yet . . .

He shrugged.

'No matter.' Hu San, elder sister of the Five Winds Society, pulled a tiny Nokia diary from her blood-splattered jacket and flipped it open. Her conversation was soft, unhurried and authoritative. ZeeZee didn't understand a word. Just as he didn't really understand how a middle-aged Chinese woman could manage to vault a counter and unsheathe a sword in less time than it took the Korean to raise his gun.

Stepping round the blood-splattered boy, Hu San walked to the shop door and flipped round a simple sign, from open to closed. Then she pulled down two bamboo blinds and locked the door. 'Shut for stocktaking,' she announced lightly.

Chapter Twenty-six

7th July

Lady Jalila blinked as the crypt's darkness gave way to sudden daylight. Beside her walked Madame Mila, head turned slightly towards the older woman. There was probably only five years' difference in their ages, but the Minister's wife had a confidence that came with money, good clothes and power, even if that power was vicarious and by right belonged to her husband.

By contrast, Madame Mila felt ill at ease and bitterly resented the fact. She had intellectual brilliance, striking looks and an unbroken run of victories in court from her recent career as a public prosecutor. What she lacked was connections. Lady Jalila knew that. They talked, or rather the Minister's wife talked and the younger woman listened intently, occasionally nodding.

Both of them were headed towards where Raf and Hani sat in the shade of their borrowed cork tree, backs pressed hard against another family's tomb. Reluctantly Raf climbed to his feet and brushed gravel from his suit. Hani clambered up after him.

She didn't look at her aunt or the coroner-magistrate.

'You have my sympathy,' Lady Jalila told Raf. 'And, of course, if there's anything I or the Minster can do to help . . .' She smiled, then shrugged as if to stress she wished there was more she could offer. But Raf still caught the point when her eyes slid across to Hani and noticed that the child was clinging to his hand, her fingers glued firmly inside his.

'Thank you,' Raf said politely, nodding first to Lady Jalila and then at the stony-faced woman stood beside her. 'I'd better get Hani home . . .'

'Your Excellency . . .'

He was the person addressed, Raf realized, turning back. The coroner-magistrate was staring after him, her elegant face at once flawless and utterly cold. Her eyes between darkness and a void.

The woman was attractive and regretted it. Her brittleness a warning at odds with the warmth of a perfume that featured musk mixed with some botanical element so elusive Raf decided it had to be synthetic. Chemical analogues that fell midway between spices and fruit were big business, even in a city that prided itself on having the finest spice markets in North Africa. He'd seen the hoardings on his way through Place Orabi.

'. . . Yes?' Raf said finally.

'You didn't know your aunt very well, did you?'

'I hardly knew her at all.' Raf kept his voice cool, matter-of-fact. 'Why?'

'Madame Mila was just wondering,' Lady Jalila said.

The younger woman nodded. 'She must have been surprised when she first heard from you. Pleased, obviously . . .'

'She didn't hear from me,' said Raf. 'Until last week I didn't even know she existed . . .' And here came today's understatement. 'My father's family isn't something my mother talks about . . .'

'So how did your aunt know where to find you?'

How indeed?

'Good question.' Raf let his gaze flick over Madame Mila, taking in the neat row of tiny plaits, her perfect skin and her scrupulously simple suit, which was immaculately pressed but nothing like as expensive as Lady Nafisa's outfit or the suit he was wearing. It was a gaze Raf had watched Dr Millbank use at Huntsville to bring unexpectedly difficult inmates into line. And the beauty of it was that its effect was almost subliminal.

'I believe my father keeps an eye on my progress.'

This time when Raf walked away no one called him back.

Felix offered to drive them home from the necropolis. But his *drive home* turned out to be an extended tour of the city that involved a slow crawl along the Corniche, beginning at the crowded summer beaches at Shatby and taking them past the grandeur of the Bibliotheka Iskandryia (where a rose-pink marble façade hid 125 kilometres of carefully ducted optic fibre) round the elegantly curved sweep of Eastern Harbour so Hani could see the fishing boats and horse-drawn caleches and then north along the final stretch of the Corniche towards the new aquarium and out along the harbour spur towards Fort Qaitbey, which had once been the site of the Pharos Lighthouse, one of the seven wonders of the world.

Pointing with one hand and steering with his other, the fat man kept up a running commentary that made up in jokes for what it occasionally lacked in historic accuracy. He didn't stop or even suggest they stop, except once on the return trip, when he pulled over an ice-cream van and Hani was given her first ice cream.

Heading south down Rue el-Dardaa at the end of Felix's impromptu tour they hit afternoon traffic. Squat, brightly carapaced VWs, sleek BMWs, the odd Daimler-Benz mixed in with an occasional bulbous-headed Japanese vehicle, apparently designed around some idealized memory of a Koi. By then, the kid was asleep on the back seat, her head against Raf's side, and Raf was running over his future options and getting nowhere fast.

There'd be a will to be read. Legal requirements to be observed. But he already knew from something the fat man had said that he was the sole heir. The house was his and so, it seemed, was responsibility for Hani.

'Sweet Jeez.' The fat man grabbed a hip flask, gulped and put it back under his seat. 'Can't be doing with this.' He spun the wheel hard and Raf suddenly found himself out of the crawling traffic and cutting the wrong way up a one-way route. The fish van headed in the other direction very sensibly mounted the sidewalk and scraped a wall rather than tangle with Felix.

The fat man was right. The traffic really was tight as a nun's ass.

'Which reminds me,' said Felix. 'You saw who else was there?' He tossed the words over his shoulder.

'No,' said Raf. 'Tell me.'

Felix grinned. 'Quite pretty, very rich, spent most of her time glaring at you . . .'

Oh, *her*. 'Hamzah's daughter?'

'Yeah,' said Felix. 'I wondered who'd show.' He glanced in his rear-view mirror, catching Raf's eye. 'All respect to your late aunt and everything, but that was the real reason I went. It's the old dog-to-vomit syndrome. If killers can't manage a nostalgia trip to the crime scene they sometimes attend the funeral.'

'Zara?'

Felix sighed theatrically, shook his head and flipped his vast car into Rue Kemil, then hung a right into Rue Cif, completely blocking the narrow street as he killed his engine outside the nondescript madersa door. 'Not Zara. The man who wasn't there, her father. We've wanted to rattle Hamzah's cage for months.' Felix grinned. 'I'm going to be bringing him in personally first thing tomorrow. See what happens if I poke him with a stick . . .'

Chapter Twenty-seven

7th July

'We're here . . .'

Situated out beyond Glymenapoulo in a formal garden that ran down to a rocky beach, the Villa Hamzah was a bastard cross between the Parthenon and a Sicilian palazzo. Only three storeys high, but each one heavy with grandeur, colonnaded and porticoed like a riotously expensive wedding cake baked in brick and iced with grey stucco.

At its back stood the sea. At its front the Corniche . . . though an expanse of expensive lawn and a short length of drive kept the villa and road separate. Steps led up to a huge portico that rose two full storeys, with the portico's flat roof forming the floor of a balcony that jutted from the front of the house as proud and heavy as any conquistador's chin.

Double columns on either side of the balcony rose higher than the balustraded roof of the house itself, to support a smaller portico decorated at its centre with an Italianate and recent-looking coat of arms.

The windows at ground level were small and rudimentary, in keeping with Iskandryian tradition that put serving quarters on the lowest floor rather than in the attic. It was the windows of the second and third floors that were grand. Each one peering imperiously at the world from under a colonnade that ran round both sides and the rear of the house.

Villa Hamzah was the house of an industrial conquistador. Arrogant and assertive, but also bizarrely beautiful and with proportions so perfect the plans had to have been drawn up using the golden mean. Not at all what Raf was expecting –

though he wasn't too sure what he had been expecting, except that it wasn't this.

'You want me to wait?'

Raf glanced both ways along the Corniche, seeing cruising cars, noisy groups of expensively dressed teenagers and an endless row of street lights flickering away into the far distance. It was late but there were empty yellow taxis every seventh or eighth vehicle and he was unlikely to be at the villa long enough for the traffic to die away completely.

'No, it's fine.' Raf peeled off an Iskandryian £10 note and then added £5 as a tip. He could always call the driver back if he needed to, and besides, it was still cheaper than having him wait.

'I'll take your card.'

'Yes, Your Excellency.' The cabbie pulled a crumpled rectangle from his pocket and handed it to Raf, who immediately scanned both sides to check that a number was given in numerals he could understand. It was.

The wrought-iron gates were already open. And there was no sentry box, bulletproof or otherwise for a smartly uniformed guard, which surprised Raf even more. Flipping off his shades, Raf adjusted his eyes and ran the spectrum from infraR to ultraV, but got nothing unusual. So far as he could see, security was completely lacking. No linked web of laser sensors, no bank of infrared cameras, not even a single starlight CCTV mounted on one of the huge pillars.

Hamzah was either very trusting or his reputation was all the protection he needed. Which wasn't as unlikely as it sounded. Three years back, while Raf was in Huntsville, a Seattle street kid on Honda blades had put a cheap Taiwanese rip-off Colt against Hu San's head and taken her bag. From start to finish the heist took less than thirty seconds and no one got hurt. Fifteen minutes later the kid turned himself and the bag in at the precinct on 4th Street and made a straight-to-video confession.

Hu San still had his legs broken, but cleanly, and the blue shirt who took the contract doped the kid up with ketamine before he began.

Gravel crunched under foot as Raf walked to the front door and knocked hard. 'I'd like to see Hamzah Effendi,' Raf said to a sudden gap, which would have been backlit if the Russian bodyguard standing in the way of the hall light hadn't taken up the whole doorway. Raf kept his voice bored, like a man who knew he would be seen.

'I see,' said the bodyguard. 'Is he expecting Your Excellency?' It was obvious he already knew the answer.

'No,' said Raf. 'But tell him Ashraf Bey would like a word.'

The Russian grinned, the first sign that he had more than iced water in his veins. Until then the man hadn't recognized Raf, not minus dreads and beard. 'Right,' he said. 'I'll just see if the Boss is in . . .'

Stepping inside the door now being held open, Raf waited politely next to a portrait of Hamzah so new Raf could smell paint drying while the big man walked solidly away across a vast chessboard of a hall paved in white and black marble.

'*Ashraf!*'

Raf opened his ears a little wider, jacked up his hearing or whatever he was meant to call what happened when he turned the volume up in his head. The outrage was Madame Rahina's and he heard Hamzah's answering growl, but not Zara . . . Voices blossomed into a brief argument that many would have missed. But Raf followed it just as he followed the Doppler effect of footsteps approaching down a corridor.

The man approaching stank of cigars and Guerlain aftershave, too much of it. His brogues had hand-sewn leather soles that creaked on the tiles. In the painting, he wore impossibly shiny black boots and stood against a balustrade, the background behind him an out-of-focus blur of green and blue. A gold Rolex was recognizable on one wrist. The little finger of his left hand sported a red-stoned, high-domed signet that could have been mistaken for a graduation ring. He wore a frock coat that reached the top of his boots and carried a rolled blueprint, signifying his profession. On his head was the red-tasselled tarbush of an effendi.

'Karl Johann,' announced a deep voice behind him. 'He was

due to paint a Vanderbilt but I made it worth his while . . .'

'It's good,' said Raf.

'Given what I paid him it should be.' The industrialist glanced round his hall, checking it really was empty. Or maybe he was listening to the sound of breaking glass echoing up a corridor. If so, he seemed resigned to the damage.

'My wife wants you killed,' he said. 'Or maybe your balls removed.' Hamzah shrugged. 'I've explained you don't do that to beys. Not openly, anyway, unless you're very stupid. But that's not the reason I refused her demand . . .' Shrewd eyes watched Raf and when Raf didn't ask *What is?* the man nodded slightly, as if he expected no less.

'My daughter told me about the tram.'

What tram? Raf almost asked. But he kept his mouth shut and after a second the man twisted his heavy lips into a slight smile.

'Discreet, aren't you? Well, it probably goes with the job.'

Which didn't answer the question.

Through the haze of that morning's funeral and yesterday's murder appeared the chill ghost of a memory. Zara with the flowers. Zara vomiting neatly onto a rocking wooden floor, the worried black kid with the nose piercings who'd reached for her hand, then noticed Raf's open gaze. *That tram.*

The first time that ever I saw your face . . .

'Her mother still believes she spent the evening with a work friend,' said Hamzah. 'The kid works at the library you know . . .' Even when facing embarrassment full-on the man couldn't keep his pride in Zara out of his voice, and he *was* embarrassed. 'Thinks she got shellfish poisoning too. But I know a hangover when I see one and wherever Zara spent the night I'm damn sure she didn't sleep over with . . .'

The sentence trailed away as Hamzah forgot how he'd intended it to end. 'Don't entirely blame you,' he said finally, his voice blunt. 'You can have the pick of North Africa. Why go for trouble? But she's a good kid for all that.' He bit on his cigar and then considered the smoke for a minute as it eddied towards the distant ceiling.

'Can't tell her mother why you rejected her, obviously.'

'Wait,' Raf held up his hand. 'That had nothing to do with it,' he said. 'How old is she?'

'Nineteen.'

'Fine,' said Raf. 'I'm twenty-five. I don't intend to get married to some stranger. And nor, I imagine, does she . . .'

Hamzah's answer was a laughing bark. 'That's exactly what her mother's afraid of,' he said.

There wasn't much Raf could say.

'Now,' said Hamzah, 'you didn't come here to discuss my daughter. So what do you want?'

'First off, to ask you a question.'

'Then fire away.' The man looked darkly amused.

'Okay,' said Raf, watching a pulse point on Hamzah's temple, the man's mouth, his eyes. 'Did you kill my aunt?'

'No,' said Hamzah. 'I didn't.' His dark pupils remained exactly the same size, neither expanding nor contracting. The corners of his mouth remained firm and the pulsebeat on his temple stayed regular as a metronome. Raf didn't need access to a polygraph to be certain the man hadn't killed Lady Nafisa.

'Of course,' Hamzah added, 'I could always have hired someone else to do it for me . . .'

They sat in a panelled study overlooking the Mediterranean. Waves broke on a headland away to the right, ancient blowholes spewing white plumes high into the air: while on a beach below the window, waves just lapped against the sand and then retreated, soft as a caress.

The coffee they drank was laced with cognac. Raf could taste it on his tongue, though the alcohol wasn't mentioned when a uniformed maid brought in a silver jug on a heavy silver tray. Raf refused the offer of a cigar, waiting while his host bit off the end of a fresh Partegas only to swear when he remembered he was meant to be using a cigar guillotine.

So,' said Hamzah, trimming the ragged edges of his cigar into a crystal ashtray. 'What else do you want to know?' Smoke swirled around his head like evaporating dry ice around some pantomime devil. The effect was studied, Raf understood that. Everything he'd seen told him Hamzah was making a Herculean effort to be something he wasn't – quiet, urbane and softly mannered. What interested Raf was *Why*? He was already impressed: the house and its very location saw to that.

'Well,' Hamzah growled, 'you going to ask? Or just sit there and look at my decorations . . . ?' A flick of his hand took in the dark oak panels and carved marble fireplace, the polished floorboards and Art Nouveau windows that stretched from ceiling to floor.

'It's about my aunt . . .' Raf drained his cup and sat back in a red leather chair. Intelligence told him to approach the matter obliquely, so he did. By asking a direct but different question.

'What did she hope to get out of my engagement?'

'You're a bey,' Hamzah said flatly. 'I'm rich. What the hell do you think she got out of it?' He was no longer smiling.

'But the dowry gets held in trust,' said Raf, trying to remember what he'd learned from an afternoon in front of Hani's screen, skimming legal sites. 'To be returned in case of divorce, if the marriage is unconsummated or not blessed with children. All that's on offer is interest and that would have gone to me . . .'

'She had heavy expenses.'

'You paid her?'

'In this city,' said Hamzah, 'everyone takes commission.' He stubbed out his cigar and took another one from the mahogany humidor. This time, though, he remembered to remove the end using his little gold guillotine. 'She took two and a half million US dollars.'

'Two and a— What proportion of that was her commission?'

Hamzah Effendi just looked at him. 'That *was* her commission. The dowry itself was a billion . . .'

Raf whistled. As responses went it was entirely instinctive.

'And you,' he asked. 'What did you get out of it?' Given the massive villa, the Havana cigars, the uniformed maid and frock-coated bodyguard, it seemed extremely unlikely that Hamzah's need was anything physical.

'Respectability,' Hamzah said bluntly. 'You'd be surprised what a title can do . . .'

No, thought Raf, thinking back to Felix's reluctance to let the coroner-magistrate sweat him properly, he wouldn't be surprised at all. 'The khedive can't take the *effendi* back?'

Hamzah's grin was wolfish. 'I'd like to see him try . . .'

Raf nodded, slowly, carefully considering his words. 'I've got a problem,' he said, 'and so have you. Actually, I've got two problems, both complicated. But yours is worse.'

'Tell me mine first, then.'

'The police. Khartoum heard you threaten Lady Nafisa.'

'I threatened you, too,' Hamzah reminded Raf. 'That was my daughter you rejected.'

'But I'm still alive,' said Raf. 'And Nafisa's not. The police are going to pull you in at dawn tomorrow. See what they can pin on you.'

'How do you know?'

'Chief Felix told me.'

'And now you're telling me . . .' The man paused to stub out his second cigar and didn't light another. 'You're certain?'

Raf nodded.

'Get me Sookia, Son and Sookia.' The order was barked at a Sony unit on a table by the wall. Seconds later a little flat screen flickered into life. The conversation was short and one-sided, and ended when Hamzah clicked his fingers so the screen went dead, cutting off a pyjamaed young lawyer in mid flow. The man would arrive at the villa within the next half-hour as Hamzah had demanded, Raf had no doubt of that.

'What will you do?' Raf asked.

'Go down to the station tonight, with my lawyer, and sort this out. What do you think . . . Okay,' said Hamzah. 'Now it's my turn. You've got thirty minutes to tell me your two problems and if I can help I will, whether my wife likes it or not.'

'First off,' said Raf, 'do you know if Lady Nafisa had debts?'

'No idea. Why?'

'Because her account is empty.'

Hamzah blinked. 'Gone?' he asked. 'Two and a half million just gone?'

'One million in and out on the same day, according to her notebook . . .'

'Through a one-use-only blind account?

Yeah, according to Nafisa's book that's exactly how it was done. Raf nodded his agreement. Not stopping to wonder what Hamzah knew about one-use accounts because he'd realized instantly that it was probably rather a lot.

'And the other one and a half?' Hamzah asked.

'Not even mentioned.'

The industrialist nodded. 'Those were drafts from Hong Kong Suisse,' he said. 'Redeemable anywhere.' And for a few seconds they both thought about redeemable bankers drafts and didn't like where it was leading.

'What was your other problem?'

'Can you recommend a good builder?

They talked for the remaining ten minutes about what Raf wanted done in the *qaa*, which was to get rid of Nafisa's office altogether. For all its smoked-glass pretensions it was no more than an expensive prefabricated hut dumped down in one corner of a large living space. He'd like to have got Hani out of the madersa completely but Felix thought that would look bad. Besides, Raf had another problem that made it a bad idea.

When it came down to it, Raf's salary from the Third Circle was no more than token. He had no money and owned nothing except the suit he wore: at least, not until the will was granted probate and, even when that went through, all he'd have would be a ramshackle house and no means to maintain it.

None of which he mentioned to his host, the man who'd put the price of a billion dollars on his daughter's dowry. With Hamzah, he stuck to practicalities like explaining what he wanted doing with the *qaa*, and why . . .

So when Hamzah suggested getting the *qaa* blessed and then immediately amended his suggestion to getting the whole house blessed, Raf was surprised. He didn't have the industrialist pegged as religious. It turned out that Hamzah wasn't, but it was a good point all the same.

'My mother died in a fall,' said Hamzah. 'It was only after a mullah blessed the site I could bear to go back into the garden. I was nine. At nine you can see things that aren't there.'

And at twenty, thought Raf ruefully, *and twenty-five*. And, for all he knew, thirty . . . Maybe for life. Maybe with some things, once they were in there, they were in there for ever, like Tiriganaq. Further conversation was cut off by a distant bell. The lawyer had made it from one side of the city to the other inside twenty-five minutes.

'Look,' said Hamzah, 'I can't pretend I liked your aunt but Hani's okay, so here's what I'll do for you . . .' He smiled at his own words. 'I'll get a team over there tonight. Because what's the use of owning a construction company if you can't rustle up a few builders?'

Walking over to a pair of French windows, Hamzah shot two bolts, then neutralized an alarm by tapping five digits into a small keypad next to the window frame. Raf's time was up. 'Leave this way,' he said, opening the door to let in a warm night wind. 'You'll find the walk more interesting.'

Chapter Twenty-eight

7th July

For the girl in the water, illumination came not from the city lights strung out along the shore nor from far-distant stars whose distance was measured in countless millennia, because those were half hidden behind fat clouds. No, illumination dribbled from her fingertips in fractured Morse and spun in nebular swirls around her feet. Whole constellations burned around her shoulders and flowed over her skin like glittering smoke in a high impossible wind. She was the night and the night was her.

Zara had been coming to this beach to swim at night since she was seven, though it wasn't until three years ago she'd started smoking blow to make the liquid constellations come closer.

She'd brought Avatar out here once, one evening just before she went to New York. Some ideas needed to be left as ideas and that was one of them. He'd hated the water, he hadn't wanted to get undressed in front of her and one of his new ear-studs had rusted and given him an infection. And later, when she was on a plane and it was too late to say sorry, she realized he'd resented being asked to come out to the villa anyway. So would she, if she'd been born in a slum and Villa Hamzah was where she wasn't allowed to live.

So Zara went back to only coming here late and only coming alone.

Getting here from her room was easy. A short drop from her window, little more than her height even back then, five easy paces across a strongly made tiled roof, then down a short length of heavy iron drainpipe, the old-fashioned kind complete with regular brackets bolting it to the wall. Chance worked in her favour sometimes.

Swimming like this had been the one thing she'd missed while living in New York. No pool came close. As a child, she used to believe that she'd have been happiest being a street kid, if she could still have come here at night. Now she knew it was only money that gave her the freedom to swim like this, in the salt dark, alone, naked . . . But even money had its flip side, though you probably had to be there to believe that.

This was her world. Alone, untroubled, with the whole amniotic Mediterranean as an immersion tank. Her mother hated the sea.

Zara sank under a wave, letting warm blackness close over her head as air dribbled from her lips, and felt herself slip slowly until her toes touched the bottom. The rocks were velvet with algae, seaweed flicked around her calves and ankles like sharp grass.

Raf was shouting, only he didn't shout, he never shouted . . . He stopped, thought about that for a split second and then started shouting again. Waves lapping dark rock were his only answer.

Triangulation: he had the concept before he had its name. Noting where he now stood, Raf next glanced back to where he'd been standing, triangulating the position of the head when he first saw it.

It should be . . .

Eyes skimmed the dark water until they saw a figure break surface. Somewhere nearby the shouting started again. And inside his head came a rolling litany, mostly composed of *Oh, fuck, shit* and *God* . . .

'Present and correct,' said the fox.

Raf's suit ripped across the shoulder as he yanked off his jacket, sleeves revealing red silk as they turned inside out like snake skin. Kicking off his shoes Raf pulled the black tee over his newly cropped head, dropping cloth onto wet rock without thinking. His heart was a steady hammer.

'Chill,' ordered the fox and Raf's cardiac rhythm steadied. He couldn't see the animal but it sounded near. Sounded full-size, too, as tall as he was, with a voice that stuck its claws into his memory and ripped.

'Nictate your inner eyelids.' Raf did what the fox suggested. Experience showed this was usually safer. 'Now get out there.'

The water was warmer than Raf expected, salt like blood, and phosphorescence clung to him as he swam. The swimmer was further out than Raf had thought and the heavy cloth of his trousers dragged Raf back like a chute, slowing him down. But he swam steadily, closing the distance between them.

Clear the mouth of vomit, lift the chin . . . pinch the nose, take a deep breath and blow . . . take your mouth away and watch the chest fall . . .

He was pretty sure he could do mouth-to-mouth. Resuscitation too, if necessary. *Find the top of the arch of the ribs . . . two fingers on it and heel of the hand on breastbone . . . press hard on the lower half of breastbone . . .* The number of apparently random facts Raf could pull out of his head always surprised him. Not least because he'd never been that good at turning up to lessons

When Zara broke the surface she was behind him. She didn't stop giggling until Raf turned and moonlight suddenly lit his face.

'*You.*' Zara sounded genuinely shocked.

'Yeah,' said Raf tightly. 'Me . . .' He was about to say something truly vicious but Zara's shoulders broke the surface as a wave sucked back in the undertow. Bare skin, no strap for her costume. It took Raf a second to process what his eyes had seen and his adrenal system had reacted to already.

She swam naked.

'Who did you think it was?' Raf demanded.

She didn't answer, not at first. 'This is my beach,' Zara said finally. 'You're trespassing.' That's who she thought it was, some idiot trespasser.

Raf shook his head. 'Your father told me to . . .'

Shit and double shit.

Did Hamzah expect this – and what did it say about him if he did? Raf lent back into the water and kicked for shore, still swearing at his own stupidity. Back on shore, he didn't bother with shoes, jacket or tee-shirt, just rolled them into a untidy ball and stamped off towards the Villa. He didn't care how many lawyers the man had in there.

'Where are you going?' Zara shouted from the water.

'To get a lift home,' Raf said angrily. 'You think a taxi's going to pick me up in this state?'

'Try walking,' she called. 'It's what ordinary people do.'

Raf turned back and stared. 'Hani's at home,' he said coldly. 'Her aunt got murdered yesterday. This morning Hani left the house for the first time ever, to watch her aunt be buried. We're sleeping in the courtyard because she's too frightened to go back indoors. It's late. I've been away longer than I said I would. Which bit of that don't you understand?'

Raf's face was ice, his words utterly uninflected. He could have been talking to a particularly stupid child, except he would never talk to any child in that way.

'Five minutes,' said Zara. 'Meet me at the gate.' When she hit the beach it was thirty paces up shore, where her clothes waited in a neat pile. Then she was running for the Villa and swearing inside her head, mostly at herself.

It was the sun that did it. Sports convertibles were big in North Africa, even locally made ones. Morocco had its own air-cooled Atlas, Algeria imported a three-wheeled Soviet Benz knock-off and the Ottoman countries made do with a sub-licensed Ford that leaked oil, belched smoke and was so simple to service it could be stripped back by a ten-year-old and repaired by a blacksmith.

Of course, almost everybody who could afford something more upscale imported a Japanese machine. One of those enamel-and-chrome cut-down copies of old American beasts, all retro fins and goggle headlights. They looked great, told you when they needed gas and practically booked themselves in for servicing, never mind downloading their own tweaks for tuning. Which, with twelve tiny cylinders and forty-eight valves, was just as well.

Zara's car was different. Its 240-horsepower V6 engine had been turbocharged way up beyond three hundred. The headlights were sharp multi-element clusters, using light-guide technology. A speed-tuned aerofoil in the nose and a fixed diffuser tunnel at the rear kept the wheels glued to the road.

It was low, silver and spartan inside. The two-seat cockpit was stripped back, a simple array of controls with an unmistakable utilitarian elegance. The fascias, fillings and switches were machined from solid aluminium. It was the first racing F-type Jaguar that Raf had seen outside of the one in Seattle Museum.

'Get in and hold on.'

Raf grabbed a side handle and she was away, ramming the clutch through a crescendo of rapid gear changes rather than use automatic. Then it was near-silent running all the way, the Jaguar's engine never rising above a growl as the F-type burned up night traffic on the Corniche, hung a tight left into Place Orabi, tyres leaving burned rubber on the blacktop.

Khedive Mohammed Ali appeared and vanished in a blur of grandeur, the Place des Consuls streaming by on either side. A right skid down a short alley between Catholic and Greek Orthodox cathedrals fed her through to Rue Kemil. The unlit shops either side reflecting only each other in darkened glass windows, until the car roared between them, headlights picking out peeling script over locked doorways.

'I didn't do that for you,' said Zara firmly, as the car screeched to a halt at the entrance to Rue Cif. And then she was crunching her way through the gears again, leaving him alone on a street corner, fifty paces from where Hani waited on the other side of a wall.

Chapter Twenty-nine

Seattle

All matter moved. At a basic, base level atoms resonated, electrons could simultaneously occupy contradictory positions in space. What the eye regarded as solid was anything but . . . Of course, at a human level, movement was also what you got when people were too empty to stay still. That was the fox's opinion, anyway.

Wild Boy rode a red 650cc with a custom-built exhaust pot no larger than the silencer on a Ruger rifle. The bike was Japanese like Wild Boy himself, which had no significance (the same bike was ridden by ZeeZee, standard issue for all lieutenants in Hu San's street militia). And Wild Boy was on his way to see ZeeZee, which did . . .

The Japanese kid dressed smart but flashy in silk suits that flattered his rough-cut hair and emphasized his slim shoulders and narrow hips. At the front, Wild Boy's hair was razored to frame wide green eyes and high cheekbones. That was the way Hu San liked it.

He wore a brushed-steel Tag Heuer, lace-up Louis Vuitton boots, cotton shirt from Abercrombie & Fitch, a white Moschino coat over his dark suit and wide Alain Mikli spectacles fitted with tinted glass. Even his cigarettes were Gitanes, carried in a black enamel case with a Gucci clasp. Everything about Wild Boy had a label except the position he occupied in the Five Winds.

It took ZeeZee two months to work out what Wild Boy did. At first he figured Wild Boy and Hu San were somehow family, then that Wild Boy was her bodyguard. Though why Hu San would need a bodyguard when she could wield a blade that way wasn't clear. Unless it was a matter of face. As it was, ZeeZee didn't really work it out for himself at all. Hu San's Croat enforcer Artan told him. 'They're lovers, fuckwit, he's her pretty boy . . .' Wild Boy didn't protect Hu San. She protected him.

Wild Boy hated ZeeZee from the start.

Maybe it was simply the fact that Hu San took ZeeZee on at all. Given he was the only Caucasian in Five Winds, except for Artan and Artan didn't count. Hu San got through enforcers like Wild Boy got through Chinese take-out, which was often how her enforcers ended up looking after she'd sent them to a disputed area of town. Though those areas got fewer by the day.

The only branded thing ZeeZee carried was a small .357 Taurus, with a rib grip and two-inch ported barrel, in matte Spectrum blue. And even then he carried that in a cheap $10 neoprene holster from Gunmart. He didn't want the revolver and only carried it because Hu San insisted. Unlike Wild Boy's gun, ZeeZee's weapon was legal, clean, licensed and never-before-fired, and ZeeZee aimed to keep it that way.

The job Hu San had chosen for him was pig-simple. A hundred years back, in a harbour-side bar, an English ex-policeman called Charles Jardine met a Seattle attorney named Angus Bannerman. Several whiskies later they came up with Jardine&Bannerman, an agency that would handle both the legal and investigative sides of life's personal problems, plus deliver subpoenas and do a little underwriting of bail bonds on the side.

By the time ZeeZee became a junior partner, the legal and investigative side was a memory held only in mouldering ledgers in the basement, bail bonds were a minor side-line and thrusting subpoenas into dirty hands made up the bulk of the business, especially subpoenas that were hard to deliver. On paper, which really meant on microfiche at a warehouse out on the city edge and on a thumb-smeared DVD in City Hall, the company was recorded as stand-alone and independent; majority-owned by its partners. In practice, Hu San owned and ran it, and always referred to the company as Jade&Bamboo,

smiling at the words. As with most of her jokes, ZeeZee didn't get the punchline.

All ZeeZee had to do was dress neatly, present himself at the reception desk of some gilt-edged outfit in Houston, Los Angeles or Seattle (though mostly it was Seattle) and talk his way up to whatever floor was necessary. Either that or stroll casually through the doors of some exclusive club as if he belonged. His English accent and manners usually did the rest.

Once inside, he apologized for disturbing his quarry, handed them the court order and, whipping out a tiny Nikon, immediately apologized again for snapping a shot of them holding the papers. There would be a click, a faint ping and the evidence would be uploaded to J&B's secure databox before the person holding the subpoena had even worked out what was happening.

And all the time, ZeeZee thought people were polite because he was polite, not realizing until he was in Huntsville that the bulge of a revolver slung under his left armpit said more about him than a floppy haircut, elegant clothes or any credit card ever could.

For a year or so, what Hu San got out of owning J&B eluded ZeeZee. Until he began to realize that for every fifteen or twenty supposedly difficult subpoenas he managed to deliver, there was always one job where the target had vanished like early-morning mist before the sun. Sometimes the target left his or her old life behind in uneaten toast or unwashed clothes. And sometimes their possessions were gone as well, gutted out of an apartment or house that echoed with absence.

There seemed no logic, at first, to which person on the list would suddenly vanish but slowly ZeeZee began to develop a sixth sense. So one autumn morning he reversed the order of two jobs and turned up early at an art brut concrete lodge outside Seattle.

ZeeZee left his red Suzuki and black crash helmet at the top of a rough earth track that fed off the crumbling backtop and walked down towards the house and Puget Sound's pale waters beyond.

The man on the jetty wasn't expecting to see him. That much was obvious from the way he froze, heavy suitcase still clutched in one hand.

'Sorry to disturb you . . .' ZeeZee held out his hand and when Micky O'Brian put down his suitcase, ZeeZee slipped the court order into the hand that reached out, watching the fingers close from instinct. ZeeZee relied on that reaction a lot in his line of work.

'Smile.'

By lunchtime the sudden breakdown of Micky O'Brian was leading the local news and had third slot on Sky. A feeding frenzy was about to begin. Ravaged by drugs, or maybe by pleurisy brought on by Aids, by alcohol and painkiller addiction, by paradise syndrome . . . Journalistic diagnoses were made from positions of absolute ignorance; conflicting, contradictory, as many irrefutable facts offered as there were commentators.

Shots of a private ambulance with blackened windows appeared first on Celebrity Update. *As did footage of a grey-haired woman in a white coat who spoke sincerely and at great length to the camera without actually giving out any information at all.* Confidentiality *got a name check, so did* courage, hope *and* recovery. *The name of the clinic got mentioned three times, but that information was redundant. Everyone watching the CU channel already knew where celebs got their lives, health and shit back on track.*

The fact was, Micky O'B would be in there forty-eight hours max, seventy-two hours at a push. The clinic operated a high-profile arrivals policy, while arranging the world's quickest and most discreet departures.

The only thing on which every single commentator agreed was that Micky O'Brian's agent had signed him into a clinic that morning and the head of the clinic was now refusing to let cameras past the gate. That Micky had recently been served with a summons regarding a major drugs bust went unmentioned.

Wild Boy slid to a halt outside ZeeZee's apartment as dusk hit, rolling darkness and soft mist through the streets. Hanging his helmet from a handlebar, the Japanese boy took the stairs two at a time on his way up to the third floor. He didn't knock, just kicked the door out of its frame with some fancy footwork and stood in the gap, glaring.

'Hey, fuckwit . . .'

Been here. *Fear filled ZeeZee's throat like mercury rising in an old-fashioned thermometer.*

'. . . Who the fuck do you think you are?'

It was the wrong question. But only because ZeeZee couldn't answer it. So Tiriganaq answered it for him. Using the English boy like a puppet.

'I know who I am . . .' said ZeeZee's voice, 'and I don't give a fuck who you think you are.' Then ZeeZee found himself scrambling off the bed to grab his holster and yank free the Taurus.

When ZeeZee woke up he was standing in an approximation of Wild Boy's usual stance, shoulders relaxed and one hand hanging loose at his side. In the background, on a screen next to the damaged door, the newsfeed kept running unwatched; flickering like a sad ghost at the edge of his vision. It was old footage of Micky O'Brian, back when he could still act.

Wild Boy looked at the gun and smiled. 'You don't have the balls.'

The click of a hammer being thumbed back was ZeeZee's answer. Some of Hu San's people filed their hammers flat to stop the point snagging on clothes. Not ZeeZee. His revolver was factory-perfect. And when ZeeZee had first started working for Five Winds, Wild Boy had delivered a box of fifty bullets. Only seven of them were missing. They were the bullets in his gun.

'Try me,' said ZeeZee, and raised the gun. The Arctic fox's growl behind his eyes was enough to make the world resonate like a struck glass. He could feel Tiriganaq's grin leaching through onto his own face.

'I've got a message,' Wild Boy said. 'Hu San is very disappointed in you. And she thinks you should be disappointed

in yourself.' He hooked a long strand of dark hair out of his eyes, concentrated on delivering his message and tried not to worry too much about the weird smile on ZeeZee's face.

Then he left.

Chapter Thirty

8th July

Hamzah kept his promise. The builders arrived at five the next morning in a Mack diesel with *HZ Industrial* logoed down the side. They parked up in the Rue Sherif and a Taureg foreman in a striped jellaba walked round to the back where he hammered on the door until Raf appeared, bleary-eyed and squinting.

Khartoum should have gone but he sat unmoving in one corner of the courtyard, not far from where Hani slept. From what little he'd said, Raf gathered he was terrified the killers might come back.

The young Taureg glanced doubtfully at Raf's tattered dressing gown, which came from an old wardrobe on the second floor and was a testament to the late Lady Nafisa's private frugality. Anyone else would have thrown it in the bin. 'Your Excellency?'

Raf smiled. 'Ashraf al-Mansur,' he agreed. 'Hamzah Effendi sent you?'

'Yes, Your Excellency . . .' Shrewd eyes glanced over Raf's shoulder at the madersa's narrow entrance with its portor's bench and traditional blind ending. Getting building supplies in that way would be next to impossible. As for removing the walls of an upstairs office once it had been taken down . . .

'Does Your Excellency . . .'

'On Rue Sherif,' said Raf. 'Bricked up.'

Five minutes later, the foreman came back with two workmen who looked even younger. Each carried nothing more sophisticated than a crowbar.

Next to arrive were the police. Two officers came at dawn. Stepping over rubble to pass through the freshly opened front door. No one had reported noise or called in with suspicions about a truck parked on Rue Sherif. And they didn't come to check that builders were meant to be ripping out a wall to make space to remove bits of a crime scene. They came for Raf. And it was a measure of Felix's fury that he didn't come himself.

Five minutes after the two officers appeared, Madame Mila arrived in a long blue Mercedes, with tinted windows. The kind of car that screamed *important government official*. Raf could put the sequence together in his head. Hamzah had turned up at the precinct with his lawyer, quoting Raf as his reason for being there. Hamzah had left the precinct. In a fury, Felix had woken the Minister to get permission to bring in Raf.

The only thing Raf didn't understand was why the Minister had immediately called Madame Mila or what Madame Mila could want from him. It turned out to be his signature.

'Sign here.' The woman thrust out a notepad and a stylus.

Raf glanced at the screen and shook his head. 'Not without knowing what it says . . .'

'You can't read?' The woman's voice was incredulous.

'Not Arabic,' said Raf, 'though I can speak it . . . How well do you speak English?'

The woman said nothing.

'Well, then . . .' He reached for the pad and passed it to Hani. 'You tell me,' he said. 'What does it say?'

The girl skimmed the swirls of Arabic, then read them again slowly, her lips twisting as she mouthed the words to herself. 'I don't want this,' she said to Raf, her eyes suddenly enormous with fear.

'Why not?' he demanded. 'What does it say?'

It was Madame Mila who answered. 'An order is being issued for Hani to be made a ward of my office and given into protective custody.'

'*An orphanage?*'

The coroner-magistrate looked at him as if he was mad. 'Lady Jalila has offered to stand guardian to this child.' She glanced at Hani. 'You are a very lucky young lady.'

'If that's a court order,' Raf said slowly, 'why do you need my signature?'

'A formality,' said the woman.

'And without my signature . . . ?'

'The girl will still be taken.'

'Just not yet,' said Raf, nodding to himself. He handed her back the pad. 'I'm afraid I can't sign this . . . The child will stay here with her nanny.' He pointed to where Donna hovered in a courtyard doorway, scowling at the noise. The old woman was cook, housekeeper and mopper-up after Ali-Din. Being the child's official nanny should add no extra burden.

'So,' said Raf. 'Am I under arrest?' He fired off his question at the elder of the two police officers. 'Well?'

'Of course not, Your Excellency, but we have been told to bring you in for questioning.'

'In that case,' Raf said. 'I'll be with you as soon as we've all had breakfast.' He paused, to look at their doubtful faces. 'Don't worry,' he said. 'You can get on the blower and tell Felix I'm not going anywhere.'

The meal Donna provided was simple. *'aish shamsi* bread warmed on an oil-fired range in the kitchen, which was where they ate. It was served with a thin dribble of sweet butter and a large mug of chocolate dusted with cinnamon. Donna also made chocolate and warm bread for the builders, then carried another tray out to the waiting police car.

'Woman's gone,' Hani told Raf, translating from Donna's Portuguese without missing a bite. The child looked less frightened now that daylight had arrived and she had a plate of warm food in front of her, but she was still obviously worried. 'Do you really have to go?'

Raf nodded.

'But you'll come back?'

'Of course,' Raf said firmly. 'They probably just want to talk about the stuff I did in America.'

'When you were an assassin . . . ?'

'I wasn't an assassin.'

Hani actually smiled. A faint flicker as if she was the only one to get the punchline to a particularly obscure joke. 'Of course not,' she said. Grabbing a whole slab of *'aish shamsi*, Hani started peeling off strips. 'I'm off to feed Ali-Din,' she announced and slipped from the table. Seconds later, Raf heard Hani's feet clattering on the stairs up to the *qaa*. It was the first time she'd stepped inside the house since her aunt was murdered.

Raf was distraught, apparently . . . Having missed out on Tuesday's murder *and* Wednesday's autopsy plus funeral, Thursday's tabloids had decided to make up for missing time by running the killing, autopsy and funeral as one breathless story, with endless sidebars of comment and very few facts. Actually, it was mostly comment or conjecture, with little blind URLs at the end of each paragraph to remind readers that they could always download more of the same.

He was also desolate, missing and strangely unmoved, Raf discovered. A little-known figure in Iskandryian society, rumour now had him as one of the most-influential fixers in North Africa. His work in America was so secret that every justified request to the Minister of Police for official information had been met with an impenetrable wall of silence.

There was a long-lens grab of him sitting on the gravel next to Hani outside the al-Mansur mausoleum and a standing shot taken at such an extreme angle it had to have been lifted from a spysat.

'Lies,' snarled Felix, sweeping the papers from a table. 'Like most of the crap you've told me.' Felix jerked his head at the officer standing beside Raf and the man stepped backwards, looking doubtful. So Felix jerked his head again and the officer scuttled from the room.

That left Felix and Raf together in a cell no more than ten paces by ten paces. All the light was artificial, glaring down from a single strip crudely screwed to a filthy ceiling. Blood – or what looked like blood – was splattered up one wall and around the chair in which Raf sat. A relic of earlier encounters.

The fat man's bunched fists were shaking with anger.

Raf stood up and stepped away from the table.

'Oh, don't worry,' Felix said bitterly, 'No one would dare get heavy on *your* ass. We're not that stupid.' He slammed a file on the table and nodded to Raf to open it. Inside was a single sheet of A4 paper. At the top was a pixelated mugshot of Raf, still wearing dreadlocks and beard.

'We received this while you were on your way in,' said Felix. 'Only it was crypted so we couldn't immediately get it open. But that was okay, because five minutes after you arrived we got sent a neat little 4096-bit key. Nothing too complicated, right? Because we're police and we're stupid . . .'

The fat man pulled a packet of Cleopatra from his pocket and tapped loose a cigarette. Ignoring the 'No Smoking' sign glued to the door, Felix lit up with an old 7th Cavalry Zippo and dragged carcinogenics deep into his lungs. 'You know, it's hard to believe anyone of twenty-five could have built up this kind of record.'

Raf ran his eyes down the sheet with rising disbelief. It was hard to imagine how anyone could have that record, full stop . . . Personal envoy from the Sultan in Istanbul. Weapons training at Sandhurst. A spell in Paris, counter-intelligence at Les Halles. A level of security clearance so high its name was blanked out because no one at the precinct had authority to know it existed. Throw in genius-level IQ, eidetic memory, weapons-grade negative capability and it read like a biofile straight out of . . .

'Yeah,' said Raf, 'I find it hard to believe myself.' Every year of his life was covered, from leaving school to arriving in Iskandryia: he just didn't recognize any of it.

'Mind telling me why you warned Hamzah?' Felix ground his cigarette butt out on the table top and promptly lit another one, inhaling hard. His jacket stank of cigarettes, whisky and disappointment. 'Unless, of course, it's a secret.'

'No secret,' said Raf. 'He just didn't do it.'

'And you know who did?'

'No.' Raf shook his head. But he did know it wasn't Hamzah.

'Let me see,' said Felix. 'Your aunt arranges a marriage that

comes apart before it happens. Hamzah threatens to kill her.
She dies. We decide to bring him in for questioning. With me
so far . . . ?'

Yeah, he was.

'And then, very strangely, you tip him off and a few hours
later his boys are demolishing large chunks of the al-Mansur
madersa. Conveniently destroying a crime site in the process.'

'It gets worse,' said Raf. 'My aunt took Hamzah for $2,500,000
in commission on that deal. It's missing.'

'Sweet fuck.' The fat man's cigarette went head first into the
table, dying in a shower of sparks, and out came a hip flask.
Felix examined the thing as if he'd never seen one before and
thrust it angrily back in his pocket. 'You wanna coffee?'

An old Otis hauled them up to ground level and they left
together, walking under the oppressive grandeur of the precinct's entrance portal. On their way through, every officer at
the front desk stared at Raf until he stared back and ten people
looked away at once. 'Get used to it,' said Felix. 'Where do you
want to go?'

'Le Trianon.'

'Should have guessed,' said Felix and clicked his fingers for
a taxi. It was only 9.30 in the morning, but the fat man still
recognized when he was right over the limit.

Raf was shown to his table only seconds after two Americans
were ejected to make space. The New Yorkers stood on the other
side of the red silk rope, glaring and muttering until Felix went
to talk to them. They left quickly after that.

'What did you say?'

'Me . . . ?' Felix waited until the maître d' had finished arranging his plate so one octagonal edge exactly aligned with the
table.

'Which one would Sir like?' The man asked, nodding to a
trolley filled with pastries.

'All of them,' Felix said bluntly. 'But I'll take those three.'
He pointed out three pieces of baklava dusted with crushed
almonds. 'And bring me a proper-sized cup of coffee . . .'

'Well?' Raf asked.

Felix looked down the street as if he might still see the departing New Yorkers through the press of bodies filling the sidewalk. 'Said you were the Khedive's personal hit man and they'd been hogging your table . . . You're not, are you?' Before Raf could answer, Felix flipped up his hand. 'Don't feel you have to answer that, obviously.'

Huntsville had been simple. Raf had understood the rules. Most of which he'd kept and a few of which he'd broken. He'd taken who he'd become on remand and kept the identity, because it worked. The freaky hair and biker beard had been good protective camouflage. But trying to understand his new life was like pushing water up a hill. Every time he got near the top the fox curled up inside his head warned him it was the wrong hill or the water was gone. Raf was tired, more scared than he dared admit and he was alone in a city that got more, not less weird the more he knew about it. And then there was Hani . . .

'Look,' said Raf, 'can I tell you something?'

Felix bit off another chunk of baklava and Raf took this for assent.

'That piece of paper,' said Raf, 'it's crap, all of it. I don't have weapons training. I'm not in the Sultan's employ. I've never even been to Stambul . . .'

'Yeah, right.' Felix asked, swallowing his mouthful. 'So what *were* you doing in America?'

Raf didn't answer. He couldn't.

Felix sighed, but whatever he wanted to say was cut dead by a sudden buzz from his watch. 'You'd better get home,' he told Raf as he tapped the *off* button. 'Madame Mila's turned up again.'

'*She* called *you?*' It sounded unlikely even as Raf said it.

'No, that was Hani.'

'How did she know I was with you?' Raf asked.

The fat man scooped up the last sticky crumbs of baklava and stuffed them into his open mouth. 'More to the point,' he said, 'how did the kid get my number?'

Chapter Thirty-one

Seattle

'And where do you think you're going?'

ZeeZee paused on the steps while a doorman raked him with the gaze that hotel staff everywhere reserve for tramps, hawkers and delivery boys who've come to the wrong entrance.

'Got this.' ZeeZee lifted the cardboard crate a little higher and waited. What people expected to see was usually what they saw: it cut down on thinking time. ZeeZee had been about five when he'd worked that out. The doorman expected elegant diners and the occasional delivery boy too idiotic or ignorant to find his own way to the service entrance at the rear.

Which was what ZeeZee gave him.

'Where do you want it?' ZeeZee might sound stupid but he was being intelligent, more than intelligent . . . Unintelligent people who disappointed Hu San usually ended up having accidents. While people intelligent enough to be disappointed in themselves mostly decided to suck on a gun barrel, to save Hu San the trouble.

ZeeZee didn't intend to do either: but nor was he stupid enough to try to hightail it out of Seattle. His only route to safety was to face up to Hu San in such a way that he was both alive and forgiven when the confrontation ended. And since getting to Hu San before *Wild Boy* had been an impossibility, success depended on meeting the woman later, in a place Wild Boy didn't go.

That Hu San knew nothing about the upcoming meeting was obvious. Her evenings at SHC were private, a shrine of calm in the busy wilderness of her day, and it had never occurred to her that anyone might dare interrupt.

Getting unnoticed into SHC took a pair of overalls, a Mariners baseball cap worn back to front, bad attitude and a case of vintage Mumm. Not that ZeeZee could afford twelve bottles of champagne, but any price that saved his life was cheap.

'Round the back, idiot.' The doorman glared at ZeeZee, then stepped quickly back as a thin woman in Arctic fox climbed the steps and nodded for the doorman to start the revolving door.

'Good evening, Madame. I do hope you have a pleasant—' That was as far as the man got before ZeeZee pushed forward.

'Just tell me who gets this, okay?'

Both fox-fur and doorman turned in shock.

'Look,' said ZeeZee. 'Somebody has to sign for this crap.' He shifted the clinking box higher still, until it half blocked his face. 'Come on . . .'

The woman stared at him. She had the taut manner of a judge or maybe an upstream divorce lawyer. Someone prosperous, someone who expected lesser species like delivery boys to show her respect. 'Who do you work for?'

'Why?' ZeeZee borrowed the look he gave her straight from Wild Boy. A hard-eyed stare that ended in a deceptively gentle smile. 'What's it to you?'

The doorman was giving ZeeZee directions and a name before the boy even had time to return his attention to the uniformed flunky. 'There,' said ZeeZee, 'that wasn't too hard . . .'

Darkness, silence and cats. His three favourite things. Or maybe the three things that made him feel safest. The stink he could have done without. Scrawny grey shadows fought over an empty foie-gras tin fallen from a sodden cardboard box, pencil-thin backs crooked in anger. Along one side of the courtyard was an open loading bay, along the opposite side were trashcans, all overflowing.

Either the garbage union were on strike or SHC hadn't heard of recycling. Whichever, the courtyard stank of rotting food and cat piss. Seattle's most exclusive dining club had two faces and this was the other one.

'Elmore,' ZeeZee demanded of an elderly Hispanic sitting on the edge of the loading bay, pulling heavily on a cigarette. Dead butts littered the ground below his dangling feet like empty cases from an over-active machine-gun.

The man jerked his thumb behind him, towards darkness.

ZeeZee adjusted his eyes. The darkness was large and empty, overlooked by internal windows and stained across its scuzzy floor with food spills and scabs of old chewing gum.

Choosing a door at random, ZeeZee kicked it open and staggered down a passage past the open door to a kitchen, case clutched firmly in his hands. Heat blasted out at him, along with the stink of grilled fish. Somewhere inside the kitchen a radio was playing an ancient Daniel Lanois track, the soft rock drowned beneath a crash of plates and the clatter of table silver.

A swing door at the end of the passage flipped ZeeZee from one world to another: the back-of-house peeling green paint changing to distressed wooden panelling, as the old linoleum underfoot became carpet, not deep pile but expensive and exactly matched to the pale colours that swirled down the room's long hand-made curtains. He was staring across a foyer and through a revolving door, straight at the back of the uniformed doorman.

It was time to change identities.

Dumping his overalls in a swing-top bin next to old-fashioned porcelain urinals, ZeeZee crammed his champagne crate in an under-sink cupboard beneath the powder room's row of stone basins. Of course, he had to flip the cupboard's brass lock with the blade of his pocket knife, but the damage was minimal and a twist of torn-off paper jammed the door shut again.

The figure that straightened up in the mirror was smart. Unquestionably young but neatly dressed in white shirt and Hermès tie bought for the occasion. His blond hair was just slightly too long but combing was enough to turn the look from unacceptable to merely louche. A fat cigar was all it took to finish the part of rich boy about town . . .

'I'm sorry to trouble you, Madame.'

Hu San looked up from her notebook to see an Armani-clad barman hovering nervously at her elbow.

'One of our new members is most insistent about joining you.' The Turkish boy's nod was discreet, but there was no mistaking he meant the young man who stood at the bar, smoke spiralling up from a Romeo y Julieta held tightly between the fingers of one hand.

Dark eyes locked onto ZeeZee's face. There was no shock or outrage, barely even surprise. It was, thought Raf, like looking into a deep well and not even knowing if there was water at the bottom. 'Send him over,' said Hu San. 'But tell him to lose that cigar first . . .'

Around the edge of the room, on black leather banquettes, slouched Seattle's wealthy. Tall and blond or dark, handsome and unfortunately not tall at all, elegantly dressed or expensively dishevelled, both women and men talked intently or stood to shake hands and air-kiss briefly. The Brownian motion of money.

The woman with the fox fur was repeating her story of meeting a horrible delivery boy on the way in. She was telling it for the third time and her partner was still pretending to be shocked.

Only a few of those in the room showed their age in a surgical tightness around the eyes, the regrettable side effects of having reached middle age before the start of nanetic surgery. The rest had that youthful permanence which came from being able to afford faces that were constantly rebuilt from the inside.

Hu San sat in the middle of the room, in her own exclusion zone. Expensive hair, simple jewellery. Anyone who was close enough to her table to smell her scent or see the tiny silk characters embroidered on her black jacket was too close. And getting too close to Hu San was dangerous. Only, in ZeeZee's case, staying away was more dangerous still. She was vaguely impressed that the boy had been able to work this out for himself.

'What will you drink?' Hu San demanded.

'A Budweiser.'

'Green tea,' she told the waiter, 'and bring a glass of house white for our newest member.'

'So, tell me why you're here,' said the Chinese woman once the drinks had arrived and ZeeZee had pulled up a chair of his own.

Very carefully, the English boy placed his long-stemmed glass onto the white tablecloth between them and – despite being seated – put his hands together, bowing as best he could. 'I wish to apologize,' ZeeZee told Hu San. 'Haruki has told me how badly I have disappointed you.' He used Wild Boy's real name when talking to Hu San, but then, everybody always did. 'I am truly sorry.'

Hu San nodded. 'Drink your wine,' she said. 'I'm going to make a call.'

No mobiles allowed, not even in the bar. ZeeZee could understand that, especially in a dining club that thought stone basins were smart and didn't serve beer. And that was the last thing he bothered to think until her return was signalled by a hand resting lightly on his shoulder, the merest brush. Probably no more significant than reaching out to pat a stray.

'I've booked us a table for supper . . .' said Hu San. 'A waiter will bring your drink.' And she nodded to the Turkish boy behind the bar who watched them go. Not openly but almost proprietorially, as if noting, with slight bemusement, that two rather disparate people had made friends in his bar.

'Wow,' said ZeeZee, stopping in the doorway of the dining room. A low ceiling was hung with swathes of cream silk that made it look lower still. The floor was blond wood, probably beech, the gold walls anything but straight, rippling round the large room in soft, almost Gaudiesque curves. The effect was of dining within a vast, impossibly expensive tent.

Hu San smiled. 'I own both this club and the hotel,' she said, answering a question ZeeZee hadn't asked. 'The city may not like me, but without my money this place would have shut years ago.' She nodded towards a window and the dark glittering water of the harbour beyond it. 'Five floors, *original building, right on the waterfront, less than two hundred members . . . It costs me over a million a year in lost revenue.'*

'So why do you do it?'

'Work it out.' Hu San's smile went cold.

'Influential people, increasingly valuable location . . .' The boy stood just inside the door and watched money rise off the other diners like steam. 'And inside information,' he added finally, afraid that Hu San would be angry. Instead the Chinese woman just nodded.

'Good,' she said, 'Not just a pretty face after all. Now,' she clicked her fingers lightly, 'let's eat . . .'

Hu San ordered for both of them. Anorexic food for anorexic appetites. It certainly wasn't what got served in the cafés and bars he used. The soup was Savoy cabbage, a teaspoon of sour cream swirled into a tablespoon's worth of lightly puréed cabbage, the whole thing covered with fine shavings of black truffle. It came in a large white bowl that appeared badly chipped round the rim but was probably meant to look like that. After the soup came a sandwich, except that Hu San ate hers with a fork, so ZeeZee did the same.

Mimic, reflect, replace – if nothing else he knew his own strengths. Mind you, that was because he'd seen them laid out – boxed off and numbered – in a guarantee the fox had shown him. It was all there, zipped up tight inside his own head. And, given his mother's belief in the purity of nature, he was lucky she hadn't gone for high design, or he'd probably have had bug eyes. Except that all his augmentations seemed to be mammalian. Well, almost all of them . . .

'Eat,' said Hu San, spearing a sliver of warm pork that had been hidden under a paper-thin square of bread slow cooked until it was dry enough to crumble at the touch. Holding together the pork and bread like glue was a mustard mayonnaise mixed with shredded rocket.

Hu San drank a Californian Chardonnay with the Savoy cabbage, switched to an Australian Shiraz for the pork and finished with a chilled '38 Sauternes, which she used to wash down a tiny vanilla cream baked with armagnac prunes. She drank one half glass from each bottle and left the rest, without offering any to the boy who sat opposite and nursed his house white until its contents were blood-heat.

Occasionally she'd look at him and smile. And at the end she leaned forward and brushed his hair out of his eyes with a single finger. 'It's time for you to go,' she said. 'Remember to leave the way you came in . . .'

They were waiting for him in the loading bay. Which he could have guessed, had he bothered to think about it.

They were fast, efficient and professional. But then, that was their job. ZeeZee didn't get in even one blow, one kick . . . He was too busy fighting the length of wire that had been flipped over his shoulders from behind and now held his arms helpless at his side.

'Fuckwit.'

Until a punch caught him in the stomach, ZeeZee had assumed the person holding the wire was Wild Boy. But Wild Boy was working the gloves. Stepping out of the shadows in best street-punk fashion, his leather collar turned up against the night wind, his hair elegantly dishevelled. Both fists wrapped in neoprene gloves that were weighted along the knuckles with lead shot.

'Wrong place, wrong time . . .' Wild Boy took ZeeZee's face between thumb and finger and squeezed, gouging the pressure points. 'You know what you did? Wrong, wrong, wrong.' The first two punches caught ZeeZee in the stomach, the third slid between the English boy's rib cage and hip, causing a blood-red poppy of pain to flare inside ZeeZee's head and then wilt slowly, from the petals inwards. Only the wire kept him on his feet.

'Bastard.'

'Aren't I?' Wild Boy drew back his fist and grinned.

'Not the face,' snapped the man holding ZeeZee upright. Fear was behind the sudden anger in his voice. 'You know what she said. Not the face.'

'Shame,' complained Wild Boy, stepping up to ZeeZee to knee him through a breaking scream into . . .

In the beginning there was darkness and the fox comprehended it not. So it ran some diagnostics and the darkness was revealed as syncope, relating to abrupt cerebral hypoperfusion. A quick and dirty check on syncope and hypoperfusion convinced the fox that the problem was both local and diminishing, so it shut down again to save energy. The fox fed off neon mostly, because its nine other power options had failed.

Of course it featured telemetry, self-check integrity and various other measures designed to ensure permanence (with five intra-optic LEDs to warn the carrier in case of a system fault) but these had also failed. But then the Seimens-Oakley was a very early model and only intended to run for seven years in the first place.

So now it worked in the background on a need-to-know basis. If the host needed to know, it popped up, otherwise it could run silent for months, even years. The fox lived in ZeeZee's skull. Not his brain but his actual skull, housed in a compact ceramic case because ceramic allowed uninterrupted transmission and had high mechanical strength and identical hardness to the surrounding bone.

It had numerous functions, expressed in its own guarantee as a complicated menu of sets and subsets. But its primary function was obvious. The fox existed to keep its host alive. 'Well balanced' and 'happy' hadn't been options on the early models. And anyway, the marker for genius doubled as a marker for dysfunction: that had always been made quite clear.

ZeeZee took a shower, long and hot enough to bring out the bruises, then walked over to the mirror to take a look at the damage. He had a flowering of broken skin over his ribs and above one hip. His balls felt the size of oranges, though they looked no worse than dark and swollen plums. And dark weals circled his upper arms where the wire had held him tight.

What interested him most, though, was a raw, weeping graze down one cheek of his depressingly adolescent face. A surface wound only, probably from where he had hit the filthy concrete floor on blacking out. That seemed most likely. But wherever the injury had come from, it was bleeding – which was a start.

The tub of ibuprofen in his bathroom cabinet suggested one 200 mg tablet, increased to two if the pain didn't go. ZeeZee gulped four, washed them down with a couple of bottles of cold Bud from the fridge and waited impatiently for both beer and analgesic to bite on his vomit-emptied stomach. He wasn't brave enough to beat himself up while sober.

The first blow ZeeZee threw did no more than make his eyes water, which was less than useless, so he went back to the fridge. Maybe you had to be furious or drunk to be able to hurt yourself properly.

As a fourth Bud followed the third down the boy's gullet and the alcohol finally began to flood his veins, ZeeZee found the courage to punch his own face. Or maybe it was the idiocy. Whichever, he slammed his face down into an upcoming punch and felt an eyebrow split.

When he stopped swearing and crying, he watched the eye socket beneath the split brow close up in front of him, as he looked into a wall mirror, seeing a naked boy squint hazily back. Now was the time to wrap ice in a dishcloth or use a packet of frozen peas. But ZeeZee did neither. Instead, he took an old Opinel knife out of a kitchen drawer and yanked open the blade. Without giving himself time to think, ZeeZee lifted the knife to his face and slashed across his chin, opening a two-inch long cut that curved under his jaw.

All he needed now was a plaster and sleep . . .

Winter rain against the window of ZeeZee's bedroom woke him with a steady roll of sound, too fast to be defined as drumming. Occasionally the clatter rose as gusting wind hurled droplets like gravel straight against the glass. The temperature inside his apartment was cold enough to make even him huddle under a fourteen-tog quilt.

It was partly that his only radiator was broken but mostly the cold came from an open window. He had his years at Scottish boarding school to thank for that. In Switzerland there had been individual rooms, shower cubicles and underfloor heating. None of his Scottish dormitories had even been heated and all the windows were forever open, even when snow was falling. Fresh air and healthy living were the reasons given. Neither was true. Shut the windows and the stink of fifteen adolescents became unbearable; made worse by clouds of cheap deodorants and too much aftershave. Open windows made up for lack of washing and a once-weekly bath.

Rolling slowly out of bed, ZeeZee pulled back the curtains to give himself light and white walls that had been lost in darkness washed yellow, in the sudden sodium glare of the wet city outside. All he needed was enough light to piss — that, and another dose of analgesics. One day, of course, he'd get a real life. Probably around the time he got measured for a coffin.

Underneath its plaster, his cut had joined cleanly, the edges already lightly bound together by insoluble threads of fibrin. And now that his hands were steadier ZeeZee took time to cut and apply the neatest possible butterfly plasters. Hu San liked neat so that's what he'd give her. As promised on the box, the plasters slowly took on the colour of his skin until they were almost invisible. All the boy could now see was a clean, neat edge to the cut beneath.

Better than perfect.

What came next? Ribs, transport and clothes. Winding a long crêpe bandage round fractured ribs wasn't something he recommended. Mostly the pain just froze his lungs but sometimes, as ZeeZee reached for the unravelling roll of bandage, neural lightning caught at his heart as well. By the end, pinpricks of sweat prickled his hairline and his whole upper body felt as if it had been bound into a nettle corset. So he chewed yet more ibuprofen, though this time round he passed on the iced beer.

Usually ZeeZee had no trouble with stuff like which clothes to wear: he bought five of everything and rotated it. But today was different. Hu San wouldn't be expecting him at the breakfast meeting and, even if she was, she'd expect him to turn up in the usual dark suit, white shirt and red tie like he always did. Well, he was going to borrow a few of Wild Boy's feathers.

'Seattle Taxi Service,' said a woman after he punched nine digits on his home phone from memory. 'How can we improve your day . . . ?'

'A cab from here to the Seattle Harbour Hotel,' said ZeeZee. Then told the woman where he was and when he wanted the car, which was right then.

The line went silent. ''Yeah, we can do that. You going to let me see you?' This was a sight check, to see if he looked like some dustout or merely sounded like one.

'Sure.' He hit visual on his phone and the woman yelped.

'You're naked.'

'Yeah,' agreed ZeeZee. 'But I'll be dressed by the time the cab arrives.'

Her laugh was abrupt but not really unkind. 'You'd better be. Five minutes max . . .'

Which was what he needed, ZeeZee told himself. A countdown. He skipped on shaving because one, it would hurt and two, Hu San was obviously into rough trade. All the same, he took a razor to his jaw line. Black jacket, because that was the only colour he wore. A PaulSmith leather job, tailored but not tight. From right at the back of his small cupboard, he pulled a slate-grey silk shirt he'd bought but never worn and matched it to a pair of deep red trousers some Polish girl had given him two weeks before they split. She'd also been responsible for the silk shirt. He couldn't recall her name but he remembered the snakeskin bag he'd bought her, the by-product of one of his random attacks of senseless guilt.

Black shoes, black tie, and finally a pair of Armani shades with smoke-grey lenses that he'd found left forgotten on a café table near Hu San's shop. ZeeZee was dressed before the taxi arrived.

A porter rushed to open his taxi door and ZeeZee slipped the man $10. Maybe it was meant to be more, but that was what he had and it seemed quite enough to do the trick.

'HS Export,' he told the girl at the desk.

'They've already started,' said an older man, materializing behind her from some cubbyhole where assistant desk managers lived. He was trying hard not to stare at the cut on ZeeZee's face and not doing a good job.

'No problem,' said ZeeZee lightly. 'Have they actually started breakfast yet?'

The man looked at the girl who picked up an old-fashioned desk phone. 'Yes,' she said, 'I'm afraid so.' She nodded as she spoke, emphasizing the fact.

'Then perhaps you could order me Earl Grey and toast and have it brought straight in . . .' ZeeZee smiled before turning away. He knew which door to head for because there was a sign on it saying HS Export – meeting in progress and, besides, it was the same conference room every week . . .

'My apologies.'

Hu San looked up, saw the English boy standing stiffly in the open door and almost smiled. Saving face was something she understood.

Safe behind his shades, ZeeZee skimmed the room, editing out Victorian landscapes, Persian rugs, a large silver samovar and other examples of instant antiquity, probably bought by the yard. What ZeeZee was interested in was his audience. The one he was about to wow by doing precisely nothing.

Mostly they were suits. A couple of enforcers. Plus Wild Boy and Hu San. All sitting round a table in front of their almost-finished breakfast. Same as it ever was.

'You're late . . .'

'I overslept,' ZeeZee's voice was languid. The kind of drawl for which he used to beat up kids at school.

'Overslept?' Hu San did smile at that. 'Sit down,' she told ZeeZee shortly and he did, taking the only place still free. At the other end of the long walnut table, directly opposite her.

Timing was everything in life, so the fox once said. ZeeZee

waited until Hu San was in mid flow, running down a list of recent successes and the very occasional failure, pulling facts and figures alike out of her head, and then he slowly and silently took off his shades and watched her words slow, falter and finally dry up.

When she spoke her face was utterly impassive. That was how everyone sitting round the table instantly knew she was furious, though most of them still assumed it was with ZeeZee.

'What happened to your face?'

'My face?' ZeeZee's fingers came up to caress the slight graze on his cheek, the understated scar across his chin and the dark and swollen eye that removing his shades had suddenly revealed. 'I came off my bike.'

'Did you?' Hu San stood up and walked the length of the table. She didn't even make the boy come to her. Gripping ZeeZee's chin between her first finger and thumb, she twisted his face towards the light, only to drop her hand as pearls of blood oozed between the butterflies.

'You came off your bike?'

The boy nodded. 'Sure. I had supper with a friend, drank too much and slid the Suzuki on my way home. These things happen . . .'

'Is the bike damaged?'

'No.' ZeeZee shook his head. 'Like me, there's hardly a scratch.'

Hu San opened her mouth to answer but whatever she intended to say was stopped by a knock on the door.

'What . . .'

A waitress stuck her head nervously round the doorway. Her cheeks had gone red before she'd even stepped into the crowded room. In her hands was a tray. 'I'm sorry, Madame. It's the tea and toast that—'

'Over here,' indicated ZeeZee, flipping up one hand.

The girl walked over to where ZeeZee sat at one end of the table and silently put down the tray, leaving just as quietly. ZeeZee knew that everyone was watching him, especially Hu San. That was why he made sure his fingers didn't shake as *he carefully poured the tiniest splash of milk into his cup and followed it with Earl Grey. Then, very slowly, he started to butter his toast.*

The Japanese weren't the only people who could conduct a tea ceremony.

Chapter Thirty-two

8th July

'Okay,' promised Raf. 'Everything's okay.'

'No,' said Hani crossly. 'It's not. How can it be?'

It was true that Madame Mila had finally gone, taking with her two uniformed policewomen and the court order she'd been trying to wave in Raf's face. But it had taken threats to get rid of her, even if they were largely unspoken and involved not her life but her career.

'You can't win,' Raf had said as he'd entered the courtyard and stepped between a furious Madame Mila and Hamzah's Taureg foreman who was resolutely blocking her way.

'Can't I?'

'No,' said Raf. 'You can't.' Leaning forward, he lifted the RayBans from her nose and smiled as the magistrate-coroner blinked in the sudden glare. 'And before you try you should make sure you understand who you're dealing with.'

'Yes. I know,' she said. 'You're a pashazade.' The anger in her voice was cut with contempt that Raf could pull rank quite that crudely.

'No,' said Raf, thinking of the fox. 'I mean . . . Who am I? What do I do? Why am I here . . . ?' He paused. 'I suggest you have one of your pet policewomen call the precinct to find out.'

At a nod from her boss, the nearest officer flicked a switch on her belt and tapped a throat mike twice with her finger. Raf didn't hear the question or answer but he saw the woman's mouth tighten. Then she leaned across to whisper bad news into Madame Mila's ear.

By now half the precinct would be claiming they'd known he was special forces all along. While a couple of the more out-and-out fantasists would be remembering when they'd met him before. Their lies turned to truth by simple unquestioning repetition. Of course, it just meant if someone did decide to come after him they'd come carrying heavier guns . . .

After Madame Mila left, Raf rode the lift up to the haremlek, intending to ask Hani where she wanted to live, since she didn't want to live with Lady Jalila and her other aunt was dead. He also intended to suggest that Donna went with Hani to wherever it was. He'd keep Khartoum on to run the madersa. The old man knew which souk sold what and, besides, Raf needed someone else around. The ramshackle building was far too big for one man to live in on his own, even someone as antisocial as Raf.

By the time Raf reached Hani's door he'd amended his plan to asking Lady Jalila for advice on good schools. There were worse places to live than away from home; and, in Hani's case, boarding was probably her best option. Particularly as the only realistic alternative Raf could think of involved sending her to his father in Tunis or trying to find her a foster home.

'And the Djinn who was of the Only True Faith looked closely at the child asleep on the golden bed and marvelled at the loveliness of her hair that was like midnight spun into thread. And the cloth on which she lay was embroidered with pearls like tears and her nightdress was as white as moonlit clouds.'

Hani hiccuped and her screen stopped recording. Carbon dioxide cured hiccups, or so Hani had been told, so she exhaled into her cupped hands and breathed in again, inhaling cinnamon-scented breath. She didn't really want to tell Ali-Din a story but she'd finished *Golden Road III* for the second time and she was bored. Or rather, the afternoon dragged more slowly than ever if she left it unfilled. And talking to herself kept the hurt at bay, mostly.

Hani clapped to get the computer's attention.

'And when the Djinn saw her, he unfolded his mighty wings, saying "Glory to the True God. This is a creature from paradise." And he flew heavenwards until he met the Ifritah and said, "Marvel at the poor child who sleeps here in innocence. For you will see none more brave . . ."'

On the plate beside Hani's screen were a few cake crumbs, not really enough to bother with but Hani scooped them up crossly, squeezed them into a sticky mass and then pushed them into her mouth. She had heard the lift whine noisily as its wire dragged over the ungreased wheel at the top of the shaft. Aunt Nafisa had promised to get the lifts serviced. That was another thing which wouldn't come true.

'And the Ifritah spiralled down from the star-studded firmament, alighting on the balcony of a marble palace in old Cairo and did as the Djinn bade. And, Glory to the True God, the child who slept in innocence in the golden bed was every bit as beautiful in loveliness as the tattered beggar boy asleep in the old graveyard by the grave of his father . . .'

Hani knew he was there, but she didn't stop telling her story and she didn't look round. To do so would be to admit that a man had entered the haremlek. And that was something that never happened. So, instead, she kept telling her story to Ali-Din and the puppy told it secretly to her screen, which wrote it down in flowing letters, with ornate calligraphy for the names of God and less ornate but still beautiful capitals for the names of humans, locations, ifrits and djinns. She'd chosen the lettering herself from a database at the Library. Accessing the script had been easy; she'd just pretended to be a professor of literature from Cairo University. Cairo was Hani's favourite city. She'd never been there, but in *The Arabian Nights* that was where the most beautiful girl ever born was discovered, sleeping, by a djinn.

Lady Nafisa hadn't liked Ali-Din and she hadn't liked *The Arabian Nights*. But then, Lady Nafisa was dead. So that showed what *she* knew.

'Hani.'

Raf could have told her a story of his own. Maybe he would, one day. Maybe soon. On the red-tiled floor, beside the girl's small chair, a robot dog sat in what looked like a puddle of spilt tea. The dog was silver, leather and tattered felt, with floppy plastic ears and a long tail that ended in a blue glass button. Instead of eyes the dog had a black plate stretched over the top third of its head like a motorbike visor, behind which were twin video cameras.

What the dog saw she saw, in a tiny window open on one corner of her screen.

'Ali-Din's made another mess,' Raf said quietly.

Hani's eyes slid to the rag dog and she nodded doubtfully. 'He's not real.'

'I can see that,' said Raf. 'But then, nor is my fox.'

The glance Hani flicked at her screen was to check she wasn't dealing with a complete madman. *Been there*, thought Raf. *Felt that* . . . 'We need to talk,' he said apologetically.

It took an effort, but Hani made herself turn round; made herself wait until she had Raf's whole attention; made herself ask the question, even though she already knew the answer . . . 'You're going to send me away, aren't you?' Her words were little more than a whisper.

'Hani, I can't . . .'

'Knew it.' She almost stamped in frustration. 'I can help here. I won't get in the way.'

'It's not about—'

The girl didn't let him finish that sentence, either. She wasn't interested in his reasons any more than Raf would have been if he'd been her: adults could excuse anything. Even things they didn't really believe in. They both knew that.

'Why, then?'

'Because . . .' He didn't have a *because*. Or, rather, he had dozens, from local tradition to his own convenience, all of which he could justify, in none of which he actually believed. But then, believing in things got you hurt. And if the thing you believed in was a person, that could land you in jail.

'We'll talk about it later,' he said. Remembering that that was what adults had said to him.

Next morning was Friday and the city was shut. Gathered together in the early-morning cool of the kitchen, Khartoum, Raf, Donna and Hani ate breakfast, before Raf and Hani started work cleaning up the rubble that Hamzah's builders had left

behind. Hani insisted on cooking and gave Raf a plate piled
high with flat bread and sticky chunks of comb honey. Her
own she left empty except for a peach and a handful of
grapes.

Only when Raf had finished did Hani pile up the dishes
in the sink. After that, she made a second bodun of java,
even though Khartoum and Donna drank only mint tea and
Raf insisted he was wired enough already. Then she went to
fetch a broom, the room echoing to her footsteps.

Outside the kitchen window Rue Sherif was almost empty,
missing its usual heavy grind of traffic. And the few taxis that
travelled moved unhindered along almost deserted roads that
saw the trams stilled and most shops locked tight. Loud-
speakers everywhere were calling the faithful to prayer, from
minarets dotted like spindly rockets across the humid city. Raf
ignored them.

'Isk wasn't always this quiet,' said Hani. She spoke with the
absolute certainty of someone aged nine. 'But it all changed last
year. Now you aren't allowed to drive unless you're going to the
mosque.' She carefully swept a pile of crumbs from under the
table into a plastic dustpan and, just as carefully, tipped the pan
into a metal dustbin. Which was fine, except that blowback sent
a swirl of dust and crumbs up into the girl's face and started her
sneezing. 'Not funny,' she said fiercely.

All of the major rubble from the hall had already been
removed by Hamzah's men who'd left behind only dust, grit,
fist-sized chunks of brick and the fine white bones of dead
mice and an unlucky kitten. No treasure, but Hani was getting
to grips with her disappointment.

The wooden double door on Rue Sherif now opened onto a
newly revealed entrance area, tiled in black. To right and left,
running round the edge of the hall, an elegant split staircase
hugged the wall, alabaster balustrades rising around its edge,
the ever-increasing gap between floor and stairs filled in with
what looked like a smooth fall of ice that turned out to be white
marble.

The actual walls were bare, stripped of whatever paintings,

tapestries and hangings had originally cut the monochrome severity of the black floor and white staircase.

The style was Third Empire, which was undoubtedly one of the reasons why it had been bricked away. At a time when Iskandryia's Nazrani contingent had been building ornate villas in the High Moorish style, Ottoman families were having their own ancient houses demolished to be replaced with buildings better suited to Faubourg St Germain. Two hundred years later both communities were still embarrassed by their earlier enthusiasm. The hall might be the only part of the Madersa al-Mansur to be reworked in Third Empire style, but its European influences would have been enough of an embarrassment to Lady Nafisa for her to have it bricked away. But then, this was a woman whose outward acceptance of *inshallah*, the surrender to God's command had been such that she avoided using the future tense in public, because it presumed on the will of God . . .

At the top of the marble stairs, Hamzah's builders had unbricked another archway, one that led to an alcove. Without being asked, they'd demolished a wall between that alcove and the *qaa*. Of Lady Nafisa's smoked-glass office nothing remained but a bad memory.

Just how Hamzah's team had done the work they had in the brief time they'd taken was beyond Raf. All the same he was grateful, and looking round at the new entrance, the rebuilt *qaa* and the replacement mashrabiya he felt more at home than he'd felt . . .

For ever was the answer, if he was honest. And Raf kept on feeling right at home, even when someone rapped with a cane on his new front door and a tall, instantly recognizable man strode in. Or, at least, strode as much as anyone could with a damaged leg and a walking stick. The resurrected hall was swallowed in a single ironic glance.

'You've wasted no time.'

Behind General Saeed Koenig Pasha walked Lady Jalila, a scarf wrapped demurely round her hair. Then came two bodyguards from the General's personal cadre who silently took up positions either side of the front door. The General's face had that stony-eyed glare usually found only on statues. His skin was dark, not from the sun but from heritability and his cheeks were hollowed out with age and lack of sleep. Piercing eyes examined Raf from under heavy brows.

'You and I need to talk,' he told Raf, his gaze sweeping the hall until it reached Khartoum. 'Leave us,' the General ordered. 'And take the child with you.'

He pivoted round to face Raf, malacca cane thrust hard on the floor. 'I take it this is the way up?' The tiles were crossed in a clicking of walking stick and boot-heels before Raf even had time to answer.

Lady Jalila followed, demurely.

Walking directly behind Lady Jalila, Raf got the full benefit of the sight of her buttocks as they flexed with each step she took, sliding beneath the shot silk of a sand-coloured suit. If she wore underwear it was only a thong: he knew that because the afternoon's heat and humidity made her skirt fit tighter than any second skin.

The woman climbed the stairs slowly, one at a time, in a stride that almost let Raf catch a flash of inner thigh and waiting darkness. There was a sleekness to her legs and bottom that spoke of personal trainers and whole days spent working out in some exclusive gym of which he'd undoubtedly never even heard.

At the top, General Koenig Pasha walked through the spot where Lady Nafisa's office had been and clattered his way to the balcony to stare at the darkening sky. A storm was coming in, but not fast enough for his satisfaction. It was left to a slyly smiling Lady Jalila to do the social chit chat.

'So,' she said, 'how are you?' With a practised sweep, she pulled the scarf from her head and shook out her blonde hair, then casually smoothed the front of her jacket, full breasts briefly obvious beneath thin silk. She was watching Raf watching her and her smile faded the moment she realized it wasn't being returned. The unspoken offer, if that was what it had been, came and went before Koenig Pasha even had time to turn round.

'I thought we should talk about your niece,' said the General.

'Hani?'

'You have others . . . ?'

Not that he knew about.

'You see,' said the General. 'There's a problem. It seems Lady Jalila and your aunt had an agreement. If anything should happen to Lady Nafisa, then her cousin was to look after Hani. In fact, I gather the Minister and Lady Jalila had actually promised to adopt the child.'

'And Lady Jalila has this in writing . . . ?' Raf's voice was polite.

He could have spat in her face and her disgust would have been less. 'No,' said Lady Jalila tightly. 'I don't have it in writing. Neither of us imagined a situation where that might be necessary. Of course, I didn't know about you then . . .'

'Or I about you . . .' Raf said simply and watched her hesitate.

'Hani will be better off with Lady Jalila,' said the General. 'A country estate, the best schools . . . And, of course, she's known Hani all her life.'

Whereas Raf barely even knew himself. Okay, so only he knew that . . . but a country estate? 'I thought Lady Jalila lived in the *Quartier Greque*?' Raf said contemptously, naming an overpriced area of mercantile houses near Shallalat Gardens. Vast and ornate, the houses had gone from fashionable to slum tenements and back again in a century. Leave anything long enough in Isk and eventually its time would come round again – that seemed to be the rule, anyway.

'We're selling the house,' Lady Jalila said crossly. 'I've got an architect drawing up plans for a summer villa out beyond Aboukir. I'm sick of the city in this heat.'

'And the Minister?' Raf asked politely. 'Is the Minister of Police for Iskandryia really planning to live in the suburbs?'

'He's got his flat over the precinct. Next to your fat American friend. And I've already got my eye on a new winter house, though I'm not sure what business it is of yours . . .'

Raf stood up, just as Donna brought in a tea tray. One look at the old woman was enough to confirm how terrified she was to be in the presence of the General. Raf didn't feel too special about making matters worse. 'I'm sorry,' he told the old woman. 'But you'd better take it back. Lady Jalila is just leaving.'

And the most feared man in North Africa who, as a young military commander, had shot his own brother for disobeying an order to retreat, raised one heavy eyebrow and padded silent as a leopard after the furious woman. He nodded once at Raf and then again to Donna, scaring the old Portuguese maid almost witless. The famed anger that Raf had expected to see break like thunder across his patrician face was entirely absent. If anything, Koenig Pasha seemed almost amused.

'Felix called,' said Hani, as soon as Lady Jalila had gone. 'He wanted to talk to you so I told him you were with her . . .'

'What did he say?'

'Something very rude.' Hani grinned. 'I don't think he likes her. Mind you, I don't think anyone likes her.'

'So you definitely don't want to live with Lady Jalila?'

Raf regretted his suggestion the moment it was spoken. Hani's answer was a rising babble of outrage that died only when he grabbed the child and scooped her up, ignoring the fists that tried to hammer at his head. When Raf looked round, Khartoum was standing in the doorway, glaring.

He had his answer.

'I had to ask,' Raf said gently.

'Never.' Hani's voice was fierce, her chin held high. 'I'd run away first.'

'But she was Aunt Nafisa's best friend . . . ?'

'That's not my fault,' Hani said crossly.

Chapter Thirty-three

Seattle

'Sorry to trouble you.' The voice was scrupulously polite, the accent so floppy haired that Hu San knew immediately who was on the other end before the boy had even announced his name.

It was late and an ice-cold wind blew in off the Sound, throwing white spray against the harbour walls. Up in her penthouse, Hu San sat listening to Nyman's Piano Concerto and drinking jasmine tea. The rain outside and the churning sea below didn't bother her. Weather only made Hu San feel more real.

Though ZeeZee had never called her before, at home or at her office, which was how she still thought of her small waterfront shop, Hu San had been expecting this phone call. She'd been expecting it for three days, during which the English boy had gone calmly about his work, serving court orders and reporting back any information that he thought the Five Winds Brotherhood might find useful.

Now he would want to complain about Wild Boy. She knew her staff called Haruki 'Wild Boy' behind her back. What they didn't know was that it had been she who first came up with that name, back in the days when Wild Boy was a scruffy street kid who trawled the strip with a gravity knife in one back pocket and a tube of KY in the other. It had been an easy trade. She liked his looks and he liked her money. Besides, any scraps she could offer him from her life were better than the one Haruki already had.

'I hope you're not about to give me a problem,' Hu San said shortly.

'I don't think so. I was hoping for an address for Haruki?'

Half question, half request . . . Still, it threw Hu San off guard.

'What?'

'I owe him an apology.'

For what, exactly? Hu San wondered. Maybe the English boy had heard about her anger with Wild Boy and held himself responsible. If so, the boy was right: he was responsible for Wild Boy's current disgrace. But that still didn't mean it was his fault. Hu San clearly remembered saying Not the face. Wild Boy hadn't listened and she couldn't accept that.

Wild Boy was on ice until he grovelled properly. Screaming fits and protests wouldn't do, and nor would sulking. And yes, sex complicated things, no one could deny that. All the same, she expected obedience, even from the boy who sometimes spread her legs.

'Tell him to quit sulking,' said Hu San and rattled off the address for an apartment block two streets back from the harbour. She paid the rent, she paid his bills and she paid the woman who went in once a week and cleaned up. In fact, she paid the woman double, once to do the job, and once again to ignore the discarded roaches and the gun Haruki could never remember to hide away in a locked drawer.

Let them make friends, thought Hu San tiredly. Or she'd get rid of both of them. Besides, both their sets of bruises should have started to fade by now. And anger faded like bruises, or it did in people wise enough not to nurse it. As to whether Haruki was as wise as the English boy obviously was, that was something Hu San reckoned she was about to find out.

Payback time.

ZeeZee blipped his bike into life, let out the clutch and felt his tyres squeal on the wet tarmac. Rain had cleared the harbour road of everything except a delivery truck, a police car and him. Spray from his back wheel rose behind the Suzuki like a wave. And by the time he reach Wild Boy's apartment, rain was vaporizing off his single exhaust to add its own fog trail *to the spray. It was cold and undeniably wet but ZeeZee was seriously enjoying himself.*

Hidden strips lit the foyer inside Wild Boy's building. A wall of glass separating the warmth of the foyer from the dark and rain of the sidewalk where ZeeZee had left his bike.

'Going all the way,' he told the clerk behind the desk, pointing his finger at the ceiling. Inside a lift, he checked his gun. Full load, seven shots. Flipping out the cylinder and then flipping it back. Only then did he realize a video camera was positioned in the top right corner of the lift. Too bad. Besides, he had a license for the gun, because delivering court orders meant not everyone liked to see him coming.

ZeeZee counted off the floors as each number lit and the lift shot past, headed for the penthouse. What was it Wild Boy always used to say? It ain't over till the fat lady pings . . . The English boy took a fold of paper from his pocket and looked at it. Wild Boy lived on this stuff – that, and Mexican red. Hu San – he wasn't too sure what she used, but something more than just life regularly reduced her eyes to dark pinpricks. He, on the other hand, didn't even smoke. The fox didn't approve.

Not usually.

Weighing the twist in his hand, as if it might actually have a weight rather than being too light to feel, ZeeZee shrugged and carefully unwrapped the chemical origami to reveal the grey, salt-sized crystals inside.

'Have a great evening,' said the lift.

'Thanks,' said ZeeZee as he put his nose to the paper and inhaled, hitting it with both barrels. 'I intend to . . .'

A creak of the apartment door tugged Haruki away from his dreams. Far away – in the world inside his head, which was less safe even than the world outside – he registered first the click of a lock recessing itself and then a door creaking open on hinges that needed oiling.

The next click was closer and dispelled his dreams like wind through smoke. It came a microsecond ahead of the cold kiss of metal on his forehead. Revolvers that operated on double-hammer action were increasingly rare but Haruki knew of at least one person who owned a model like that. The cold-eyed English boy who walked alone and mostly talked to himself.

'Get up.'

Haruki opened one eye. His other was still too badly bruised to open. Around the eye he could, there were distinct bruises, left by a bony knuckle.

'Out of bed.'

Slowly, very carefully, Haruki eased his feet out from under the covers, toes feeling for the floor. The cold made him reach instinctively for his silk dressing gown.

'You won't need that.' A hand flicked Haruki's fingers aside before they could touch fabric. 'Walk over to the window.'

Haruki did what he was told, trying to ignore both the cold and his own nakedness. Most of all, he tried to ignore the revolver and a rising fear brought on by questions he suspected it would be stupid to want answered.

'Open the curtains.'

He did that, too. Seeing the pinprick lights of Seattle flicker in the falling rain. The carpet felt sticky under his bare feet and the room stank of incense, empty beer cans and half-finished Singapore noodles. The sheets were dirty and his Toshiba wall screen was running nothing except static, but the view out over the harbour was heart-stopping. So beautiful it almost made up for dying surrounded by his own squalor.

'Now open the window.'

The glass slid back silently and a sudden gust of cold raised goose bumps on Haruki's naked skin. 'Why are you doing this?' Wild Boy asked. His voice sounded small, even to him. 'We didn't touch your face.'

The English boy shrugged. 'Did I ever say you did?'

'You let Hu San think so . . .' Wild Boy's hand went up to touch the bruise below his eye and his fingers came away wet.

'How sweet,' said ZeeZee. 'You're crying.' He raised the gun and sighted along the top, seeing a naked Japanese boy no older than he was. 'Any last requests?'

Haruki just looked out from under his fringe.

ZeeZee sighed. The fox was right and he was wrong.

'I don't know about you,' ZeeZee said as he lowered his gun. 'But I'm not finding this nearly as much fun as I thought.' Stepping back towards the bed, he threw Haruki a dressing gown.

'You don't love her,' Wild Boy said fiercely.

'And you do?'

Haruki nodded, sliding first one, then another arm into the gown and knotting the belt loosely round his narrow waist. 'And she loves me.'

'Not any more,' said ZeeZee.

He closed the apartment door behind him and left Wild Boy to lock up the window and call Hu San, if he was that stupid. Not that he would – call Hu San, that was . . . ZeeZee knew Wild Boy. Shame would prevent him.

Haruki was right about one thing, though. ZeeZee didn't want a lover, certainly not a Chinese gangster in her late thirties. A mother – now, that was something different. But that was one place even Wild Boy couldn't make him go.

Shoving his gun back into its holster, ZeeZee zipped up his black biker jacket and hit a button to call the lift. He didn't know how well Wild Boy would sleep but as soon as he got back to his own room he intended to crash out like the proverbial log, cooking sulphate or not. And then, first thing tomorrow he planned to get up and go visit Micky O'Brian. Hu San wanted a small package delivered. Something by way of apology for the recent misunderstanding . . .

Sitting on the edge of his bed, knife in hand, Haruki remained awake for the best part of five hours while he went over what had happened. What he'd said, what had been said to him. It was as if black and white had suddenly reversed. Maybe he could have handled matters differently. Perhaps he really should have launched himself at the English boy and not even thought about the gun.

Except that if life had taught Haruki anything it was when to lose fights. Most times he fought hard and won but occasionally he knew to give in. That knowledge had saved his life as a kid.

He wasn't proud of how he'd made his living before he met Hu San but never once had she shown anything but sympathy. Until now . . .

Sadly, Haruki put his hand to his swollen eye and then touched the edge of the blade to his throat. No use, he didn't feel brave enough for really grand gestures. Reversing his grip, so that he held the blade securely, Haruki dragged its point across his wrist, feeling sick. The wound should have been deeper but two glistening sinews blocked his way.

The tears that started up ran unchecked down his face as he sat there on his bed, his one good hand wrapped tight round his damaged wrist, trying to hold the edges of the cut together. For all his front, it seemed he couldn't even kill himself properly. Haruki had a decision to make without being sure how much time he had left in which to make it . . . In the end, shame or not, Haruki ordered his mobile to call Hu San and keep calling until it got through. He wanted to apologize or say goodbye, whichever seemed appropriate.

Chapter Thirty-four

10–11th July

Saturday began hot, the early-morning sun turning the Corniche to a burning silver strip that flared along the shore and separated the city from its beaches and low-lying headlands. But even early, with the sun hanging low over Glymenapoulo to the east, the air was too heavy and too sticky for blue sky to last.

A headache settled over the city, dogs growing restless and feral cats slinking from the shade of one shabby tenement to another. Policemen pulled at their high collars as they tried to relieve the itch, women scratched discreetly and men at café tables casually adjusted their balls. Through endless shuttered windows came the sound of toddlers whining, being slapped and whining louder still.

Under their glass roofs the souks overheated, peaches turned bruised and rancid in the open markets and at the taxi rank on Place Orabi a driver killed two passengers in an argument over his tip.

The storm came in at noon, as muezzin were calling the faithful to prayer. It fell on Iskandryia in a rolling landslide of dark clouds that slid down the coast, vast and soot-hued, banked so high that the outer edge of each cloud turned back on itself and still kept climbing. Looking up was like staring down into a bottomless canyon.

And with the clouds came a chill that cooled the air until the only heat was latent, radiating back from alley walls and parked cars. But Hani didn't notice the sudden chill at the time because she was too busy in the haremlek throwing 'rubbish' clothes into a black plastic bag . . . Rubbish meant anything neat, anything fussy, anything that Hani's aunt had made her wear . . .

Now they were up in the attic, rubbishing that without quite saying so, Raf had decided to get the al-Mansur madersa swept clean of ghosts and rearranged by the close of the weekend. Some ghosts need exorcism. Some die, shrivel in the daylight or let time brick them off into the little-visited rooms of memory.

His own were mostly sterilized and labelled, neatly hidden away by the fox or secure behind emotional safety glass as the regime at Huntsville had demanded. But Hani's ghosts . . . Raf intended to kill those with a bucket and mop, black bin liners and the scrape of clumsily moved furniture.

'It's dark . . .'

'I know,' said Raf, glancing round. 'The electricity's out again.'

'No.' Hani stood in a doorway, holding a torch. 'I mean it's dark outside. The whole sky's gone black . . . Come and see.'

'Let me just finish this,' said Raf, picking up a chair. He was sorting through an attic, which led out onto a flat roof. A room stuffed with ancient china, wall hangings, carpets and old chairs, domestic detritus to which people had been too attached or too lazy to discard. The space was also home to a wasps' nest, high in one corner, and a tribe of mice that left markers in a spread of oily seed-like droppings.

They'd gone up there to find new furniture for the *qaa*, after Hani had rejected the original stuff on the basis that Aunt Nafisa liked it. Raf had seconded her opinion on the grounds that the silver chairs, at least, were unbelievably uncomfortable.

There were undoubtedly very good reasons why it was a psychologically bad move to let Hani discard her smart clothes and the *qaa* chairs on the sole basis that they had been liked by an aunt whose death she should have been mourning. And no doubt any child psychologist could have told Raf exactly what those reasons were but, since he'd had enough of psychologists as a child to last both of them a lifetime, he didn't care.

As Hani waited, the first heavy droplets of rain hit the flat roof outside. 'It's beginning,' she announced and then she was gone, stepping though a sudden steel-grey sheet of rain that closed off the open doorway like a bead curtain.

'Hani!'

He was too late. By the time Raf reached the door, Hani's hair was plastered to her face and her green tee-shirt had turned dark and heavy with rain. She was laughing.

'Come on.'

The water was warm and the drops huge, falling so heavily that they bounced off the tiles until the guttering that drained the roof could no longer cope and a skim of water built up across the surface of the roof to swallow the rain.

'Does this happen often?' Raf had to shout to make himself heard above the noise.

Hani grinned. 'Not like this.' She spread her arms wide, welcoming the torrent. 'This is wild.' And it was.

Walking to the edge, she leant over the parapet to watch rain racing through a storm pipe at her feet and fall in a heavy stream on Rue Cif below. Waves of racing water drove down the middle of the road, sweeping rubbish before it.

'The carpets,' said Raf, suddenly. 'Come on.'

With Hani's help, he dragged a heavy roll of cloth out onto the flooded flat roof of the madersa, discarding his shoes and socks to trample back and forth across the unrolled bokhara until grey water seeped between his toes and was washed away by rain. By the time he'd dragged out his second rug, Hani had ripped off the Nikes he'd bought her the day before and was trampling hell out of a small carpet of her own.

It rained . . . and then it rained some more. Fresh clouds rolling in over Iskandryia to replace those that were empty. Until they too were spent. By the time the storm had burnt itself out, four carpets were clean and two wall hangings were refreshed enough for the dark smudges across their middle to be revealed as mounted archers chasing what might have been antelope.

'It's over,' Hani said, looking up at the clearing sky.

Raf nodded. The air was cool – and smelt completely clean for the first time since he'd arrived in El Iskandryia. The pressure was gone, too, the city's headache lifting, with the storm clouds. Above the street swallows swooped, nymphing on newly hatched insects. Coming in low and fast, flying in formation, their shrill cries rising and falling as they swept by.

Felix rolled up the next evening in his Cadillac and dumped the car with its keys in the ignition, two wheels on the road and two on the sidewalk.

'You trying to get it stolen?' Raf demanded, opening the new front door to greet the fat man.

Felix glared at the nearest fellaheen who stepped into the road rather than try to push past the fat man or his car. 'No one would dare,' he said. It took Raf a moment to realize Felix wasn't joking.

'We've got a problem,' said Felix. He dug his hand into a pocket and pulled out a black G-Shock special, the kind people bought on planes. 'This yours?'

Raf nodded. Anything else seemed pointless.

'Thought it was hideous enough. Want to tell me when and where you lost it?

'I didn't even . . .'

'. . . Know it was gone. So I take it you don't admit to making a quick trip to my HQ in the last twenty-four hours?'

Raf just looked at him.

'We've lost some plastique,' Felix said flatly. 'It happens. Someone at the precinct cuts a block in half, amends the evidence docket and usually sells it back to one of the crime families. Or to someone with a grudge . . .'

He was speaking openly, Raf realized, because the reality of who Felix saw was obscured by a fantasy CV that let the fat man treat Raf as more than equal.

'The problem is the plastique was lifted from Mushin Bey's office.' Felix paused, long enough to let that sink in. 'And your watch was found in the corridor outside.'

'Shit.'

'Oh, it gets worse,' said the fat man as he pushed past Raf and started up the recently uncovered stairs. Raf was still wondering how everyone who came in knew exactly where to go when the answer hit him in the face. All large houses of a certain period followed a rigidly defined floor plan. There was nowhere else those stairs could go.

'Coffee?'

Felix grunted, which Raf took for *How kind. Yes, please* . . .

'Got any cake?' Felix demanded when Raf put a tray in front of him. By the time Raf had returned with baklava, Felix was emptying the last drop from his biggest flask direct into the brass coffee pot.

'You're going to need it,' he said, seeing the look on Raf's face. 'You're officially off the hook regarding this.' He tossed the G-Shock onto a table. 'Though privately General Koenig Pasha himself says tell you not to be so bloody careless. And to listen very carefully to what I've got to say before you go take a private pop at the *RenSchmiss* brigade . . .'

Raf sighed.

'You remember the broken mashrabiya?' Felix said.

Yeah, he remembered it.

'We took a couple of bits off Hamzah's boys and ran them under an electron microscope. The carving was ripped apart from inside. Not smashed from the outside. You understand what that means?'

Raf had a pretty good idea, and he didn't like it one little bit. 'That I'm back to being the main suspect?'

'No,' the fat man shook his head. 'Not with polygraph readouts as flat as a boy's tits . . .' He pulled out a leather-bound notebook and flicked it on, buying himself time as he pretended to read off the results. He could actually recite them from memory and had, in fact, only just done exactly that over his mobile to the Minister for Police.

'The mashrabiya was destroyed from inside. There were no fingerprints other than Lady Nafisa's on the pen. The scrapings from under her nails contain skin, but it's her own, and that bruise on the palm of her hand . . .'

'Matches the missing top for that make of pen.'

Felix nodded.

'And the stigmata on the other palm?'

'Is an impression left by the diamond ring on her other hand.'

Raf lifted his right hand and put it over his chest, then placed his left hand over the top of that, trying to imagine jerking down so hard that the sharp edge of a ring on his right hand sliced into the hand above as he drove a pointed object into his own heart. He couldn't.

'And I know there were no hesitation cuts,' added Felix. 'But there were no defensive cuts, either – no stabs into her hands, no slashes between thumb and fingers. And her shirt was open . . .'

'Which means what, exactly?'

'Murderers usually stab through cloth. Suicides don't . . . I'm really sorry.' Felix looked from the coffee cup in his hand to the newly cleaned *qaa*. There was a freshly washed carpet on the wall. A recently polished leather Ottoman in one corner. Donna had even put a vase of wild roses on a marble side table. He could recognize an exorcism when he saw one. Even when it was all for nothing.

'I don't know how to say this . . . But in Iskandryia suicide is a crime. One with severe penalties.'

'She's already dead,' Raf said flatly.

'I know,' said Felix. 'By her own hand. And that means her entire estate becomes forfeit. This house now belongs to the Khedive. By law, you have thirty days to make other living arrangements.'

'No,' Raf said.

'That's the law. But I've discussed it with the Minister and the Minister's discussed it with the General. We're prepared to say it wasn't suicide if you're willing to back up an announcement that your aunt's will names the Khedive as sole heir.'

'I mean, no, she didn't kill herself.' Raf knew his voice was shaking but, try as he might, it was impossible to keep it steady. 'She didn't kill herself . . . She wouldn't . . . Why break the mashrabiya, why use a pen?' More to the point, why bring him over from Seattle if she planned all along to kill herself?

'Distraction, maybe?' Felix shrugged apologetically. 'Someone decides to off themselves, who knows what goes through their mind?'

'She was murdered,' Raf said firmly. 'You tell your Minister that.'

'That's what Mushin Bey told me you'd say,' Felix muttered. He hated it when his boss was right.

'Yeah? Well, you tell him I'll nail the killer . . .'

Felix looked deeply unhappy.

'He said you'd say that as well.'

Part Two

Chapter Thirty-five

28th July

Club CdH was hidden at the bottom of a well.

And on clubnite its crowded spiral staircase stank of cheap lager, expensive scent and musty groundwater. This last was because the shaft fed down to a vast cistern strung with steel walkways and ratchet joists, with a bar and JVC sound system at one end, both on a raised area where half the water-filled cistern had been paved over centuries before with stone slabs.

Underwater lights, sunk to the bottom of the cistern, up-lit swimmers so that they cast huge black shadows onto the vaulted ceiling overhead. Only a few clubhards swam naked. They went naked not because it was that kind of club but because public nudity was banned in Ottoman Africa and even being at CdH made a political statement.

That, at least, was how Zara justified it, if asked. Besides, everyone knew $E=MC^2$ was a cuddle clone. It made danceheads love each other. It also made them way too chilled to be able to do anything about it . . .

The electrics were working, the bar was stocked with Star, memory on the sound system had been loaded for tonight's mix. Come midnight the place would be rammed to the rafters, the crowd split unevenly between the majority on the dance floor and those, like her, who would be swimming. Zara grinned and adjusted an earbead, scanning bands until she found the voice for which she'd been searching.

Av was out there, spreading the good word.

'That was Vertigo Voudun, the Blue Ice mix. And don't forget tonight – CdH goes naked.' He spoke through a button mike slicked to his throat. Inside his helmet Avatar had true quadsound, aural grooves cut into the lining to channel music to his ears. Stacked into one of the drag-resistant side panniers on his cut-down Yamaha WildStar was a hit-and-run sound system. The other pannier held kit that uploaded to a pirate satellite channel.

It was an old Balearic cliché to wire the bpm of a mix to the DJ's heart rate but Av didn't do cliché or tradition. He had the bpm wired direct to the engine of his bike. Every blip of the throttle upped tempo, every increase in tempo upped speed. And hard/Trance didn't even kick in until his speeds were strictly illegal.

'This is LuxPerpetua with *Escape Velocity*, the FNM 90–2 mix . . . And remember, naked at CdH . . . Enjoy.' Avatar slammed opened his throttle and blasted the WildStar and himself clear over the red line.

Zara locked the door behind her. *Danger* read a rusted sign. *40,000 volts. Keep out.* Avatar had lifted it off a substation at the North End of Rue Ras el Tin and Zara had epoxied it to the door hiding the way into the well. So far, no one from the city's electricity board had turned up and tried to read their meter.

Known as *CdH*, the *Club des Hachichins* could only be reached by the red spiral behind that door. The staircase was six months old and ceramic, bolted together with green screws, each one the size of someone's finger. Rumour said Av had stolen it from a hotel in Shatby that was looking for it still.

Zara had no idea of the age of the stone-lined shaft behind that door but she assumed it was at least five hundred years. Anything younger than this in Isk was regarded as almost new. Besides, newer than that and she'd have been able to find it on the city maps at the Library.

Zara was the club's promoter, organizer and owner. That was, she owned it if anyone did, inasmuch as the medieval cistern was below a multi-storey car park owned by HZ International – which was her father by another name.

Once there had been hundreds of cisterns below the city, with arched roofs and stone-lined holding tanks. Every important family, every mosque or madersa had had one. Sometimes they had even been owned by individual streets or one of the souks. Most had dried up, collapsed or been forgotten. Of those that were known still to exist, twelve were mentioned in Fodors. CdH occupied the thirteenth.

She'd found the cistern before she went to the US but she'd only started up CdH on her return. And already Avatar and a posse of doormen were having to turn punters away. Clubnite ran one day each month, the date chosen at random by software on Zara's notebook. All clubs went out of business eventually, but she and Avatar were doing their best to lower the odds against theirs doing the same.

And though Av was pretty freaked about not being followed, Zara knew that was just kiddie shit. Meanwhile, tonight was another clubnite and it was her job to go collect the brain candy.

Chapter Thirty-six

28th July

'Find the man. Deliver the package. Do it on time . . .'

This was his first day in the job and Edouard wanted to get things exactly right: because that way he'd have a better chance of getting chosen again tomorrow. Employment in Iskandryia was difficult. Upset one man and ten potential employers could slam their doors in your face. Edouard spent a lot of his life trying not to upset important people who might one day employ him. And the important person he'd visited this morning ran a courier service out of an office above a haberdasher's at the back of the tram station on Place Orabi.

Now Edouard had a day's work, with the chance of more work tomorrow if he was efficient. And he hadn't even had to do this first day for nothing to show he was adaptable.

What he had to do was deliver a package, but not until 11.30 a.m. Edouard pulled his old Vespa back onto its stand and waited. He'd found the right café, on the edge of Place Gumhuriya just as he'd been told, and had spotted the man in the photograph. Now he just had to wait for the right time . . .

'And that was LuxPerpetua and this is Isk's own Ahmed Shaabi with *Jules&Jeel* . . .' Slap bass began to stumble in and out of a drum track that sounded more Bedouin than anything else. To Raf it was just weird-shit music from a radio taped to the seat of some scooter parked up at the lights. Three weeks had passed since his aunt had been found dead and in one week's time he would have to move himself, Hani, Donna and Khartoum out of the madersa.

He was doing his best to think about something else.

On the notebook in front of him was a list of names. The

notebook was the old-fashioned kind with paper pages because that was safe. Short of looking over his shoulder or using a seriously hiRez satellite, no one could see what he was writing and he was secure in the knowledge that no pet geek of the Minister's was sitting five tables away with a hidden Van Eck phreaker, recording everything he put up on screen.

Most of the names were crossed out, but half of them had then been written in again. In the centre was his aunt, circled heavily. Radiating out from Lady Nafisa were lines leading to Hamzah, Jalila, the General, Mushin Bey, Zara . . . Lines from these names led to other names until the page was a matrix of connections – all leading nowhere.

What he had was a diagram as hermetic as any kabbalistic chart and about as informative. Because, when it actually came down to it, Raf had to admit what he'd been avoiding admitting even to himself: he couldn't prove for certain it was murder. And even if it was, what chance was there that he could solve a crime from scratch and with no obvious clues.

He'd followed them all except the General, who hadn't left his house in weeks. Bought himself a digital scanner he couldn't really afford in Radio Shack and fed it Zara's number and then, in desperation, the number of the Minister and finally of Felix. The Minister hid his calls behind heavyweight crypt, Felix seemed to leave his mobile off most of the time and from Zara, once his scanner had cracked the crypt, he'd learned only that she ran a club and the GSP coordinates she gave out to selected punters indicated it was in a multi-storey garage. Which was vaguely interesting, if not helpful.

It was Wednesday, 28 July, 10.48 a.m. and his heartbeat, blood pressure and alpha count were almost normal, if maybe a little on the high side. No one at the office had yet tried to call him and he'd sat outside the Gumhuriya café for thirty-five minutes – which, in direct sunlight, was thirty-five minutes too long for his genetic make-up. The heat was thirty-four degrees and for once humidity was low. All this he read off from the face of his watch. None of it really interested him.

Missing from the report was a record of the complex organic

molecules gating through myriad alveoli in his lungs, flooding his blood system each time he sucked the plastic mouth piece of a small sheesha.

Tetrahydrocannabinol

The brass water pipe had bright edges. As if someone had traced neatly round its undulating body with light. The trunk of a eucalyptus, in whose shade Raf sat, was split in two at head height, then split again and again, time branching, until it ended as a luminous three-dimensional schematic, the answer to some important question no one had ever remembered to ask. He had a feeling the 'no one' might have been him.

Raf wasn't sure if he should have accepted the water pipe or not.

'Fuck it.'

A minute or so later, Raf repeated himself.

Later still, he rested the sheesha's purple tube and mouthpiece on the café table in front of him and checked his wrist. Not as much time had passed as should have done.

Swirled a glass of cooling tea with a spoon, Raf watching its brief vortex slow and die. Entropy. He was hot, his shirt was sticky and a thumb print smeared the lenses of the shades that kept the city at bay.

He was breakfasting at a felah café on Place GH, incongruous among thickset moustachioed men wearing striped shirts or long jellabas. Everybody in the place was male, apart from an elderly Tunisian woman in black who appeared every few minutes carrying plates from the kitchen, which she left at one end of the counter for a waiter to deliver. It was a face of the city he hadn't seen, where full breakfast cost half the price of a croissant at Le Trianon and the first sheesha came free.

The only reason they accepted Raf at all was because of what he wore. Though it had taken him several mornings to understand that. The jacket was long and black, and it came from the back of a cupboard on the men's floor at the madersa. It was old and had a collar of the kind that turned up rather than folded down. People glanced at him oddly in the street whenever he went out, but they still moved politely out of the way.

New clothes. The thought was random but true. However, thinking it and achieving it were different matters, because his credit card had expired along with his aunt. A fact he'd only discovered when he had tried to use it in the French boutique near Place Orabi. What little money he had was borrowed against his salary from the Third Circle, which was looking more token by the day. Apparently working for S3 was an honour; it was just a pity it wasn't one Raf could afford.

Of course, he could always ask Hamzah for a job.

Or not.

The kif in his pipe tasted sour, even though it had been cured in honey. *But that's just me*, thought Raf. The whole of life had turned sour the moment Felix barged into the madersa more than a fortnight back, dropped his bombshell and then gone, leaving Raf with the job of telling Hani she'd lost her aunt and now she was losing her house. Which wasn't a good thought, because it just made Raf remember that he still hadn't told her. And he really should have done.

God help her.

He couldn't eat for worrying and he didn't want to drink, no matter that spirits could probably be found in half a dozen illicit bars within five minutes' walk of somewhere like Le Trianon. As for drugs . . . Leaf cured with molasses or honey was hard to avoid in this part of the city. Kif was sold ready-rolled by hawkers on every street corner and as huge, wood-stamped blocks in the *suqs* around el Magharba. But despite today's sheesha, dope had never really been his style and when he did break with the fox's good intentions, he used amphetamines. The basic kind cooked up in basements. Speed made him feel the fox more strongly.

But Isk ran at the wrong speed for sulphate. And while coke could undoubtedly be found behind the black glass doors of expensive nightclubs, just as dance drugs could be had in the tourist haunts, which filled nightly with German kids whacked out on substances a mere molecule away from MDMA, finding fuel to feel the fox had proved more difficult.

Besides, the fox was dying. Raf was pretty sure of that. It

spoke less and less often and mostly after dark. It didn't talk to him the way it used to and it had offered no advice on how to find his aunt's killers, not even bad advice. Most of the time, when Raf went looking inside his head for the animal, he found only flickering facts and an emptiness where the voice used to be. And all taking the sheesha had done was add an echo to that emptiness. An echo of silence at odds with the street noise around him.

To Raf's right was the neo-baroque monstrosity of Misr Station, terminus for the A/C turnini that ran through from Cairo. From above, the tracks looked toylike and the dusty square seemed small, crowded and dirty, set between an overflowing taxi rank and a sprawl of flat roofs broken occasionally by the spiky minaret of a mosque, the breastlike dome of a Coptic basilica or the spire of a Catholic church.

Higher still, the individual buildings blurred into a street plan that revealed only roads and blocks of solidified city life. The darker alleys, where the sun daily lost its battle against shadow, faded out until even el-Anfushi's widest streets showed only as hairline cracks that finally blurred and vanished. Raf's throat was too tight and getting tighter as he fought against the thinness of atmosphere, fought for breath.

'Your Excellency?'

The city span up to hit him, hard and fast. And Raf had to slam one hand on top of the other to stop both from shaking. He didn't feel very excellent about anything.

'You all right?' The boy's voice faltered as Raf glanced up. 'I'm sorry, sir. I mean, can I get you anything else?'

A new life, a proper childhood, the answer to who really killed his aunt because, sure as fuck, she *didn't* do it herself . . .

'Felix,' Raf told his watch, popping in an earbead in time to hear the number being dialled. There were things they needed to talk about. Like the fact Raf had recently warned Mushin Bey that Lady Jalila and he would have to take Raf to court before they could get their hands on Hani.

'Get me some fresh tea,' said Raf, peering at the waiter. 'And take this away.' He pointed to the sheesha, now growing cold on the table in front of him.

Felix arrived just after the tea. Running his pink convertible up onto the sidewalk and stepping straight out to stand beside Raf's table. 'You look like shit,' he said, as he yanked out a chair. 'But I imagine you know that.'

Without asking permission, he lifted the notebook out of Raf's hand and snorted at the chart. 'Very pretty,' he said, about to hand it back. Then he paused, and jabbed his finger at one of the names. 'We're raiding her dance club tonight,' he added as an afterthought. 'You might want to come . . .' The gravel in his voice was a legacy of too many cigarettes, years of alcohol and the fact Felix regarded anything before noon as early morning.

The fat man ordered hot chocolate with whipped cream and two almond croissants. 'Falafel or cakes,' he said to Raf in disgust, when the waiter had gone. 'No one in this godforsaken pit knows how to cook proper food.'

'Why stay, then?'

Felix looked surprised. 'You think anyone else is going to employ me on that salary?' he asked. 'Anyway, I'm too old for Los Angeles and too high-rent for some burb. And besides . . .' The fat man paused, chosing his words with care. 'There's fuck all real crime here.'

Raf wanted to laugh. Or maybe cry. Or just go to sleep . . . He wasn't certain which. Maybe all three.

No crime . . .

'Oh, sure,' said Felix. 'Twice a year the winds come and the murder rate doubles, but that's keep-it-in-the-family stuff. The odd drunken Russian gets rolled, but only occasionally and then only if he's stupid. There's rape, but no more than anywhere else, the occasional mugging, the odd drugstore heist, predictable low-level stuff. But the real shit? Forget it.'

'Gangs,' said Raf. 'Drugs running, organized crime . . .'

'What about it?'

'. . . It must exist . . .'

Felix smiled. 'You want to know what my boss does about organized crime? He invites the heads of each family to dinner once a year and reminds them – politely – to keep paying the General their taxes.'

The fat man shut up after that, but only because his chocolate had arrived in a cup the size of a bowl. When Felix resurfaced, the bowl was empty and cream ran across his upper lip in a tide mark.

'Message direct from the General,' he said. He picked up a croissant, looked at it and then put it down again, carefully dusting sugar from his fingers. 'He thinks it would be nice if you gave back the plastique.'

'Didn't . . .' said Raf, '. . . take any explosive.'

'Then who did?'

'How the . . .' Raf couldn't remember the rest of that sentence so he finished the next one instead. 'Who . . . stole . . . my, . . . watch?'

Who . . . stole . . . my . . . ? Felix leant in close and lifted the dark glasses from Raf's face. Swearing in disgust when the bey threw up one hand to protect his eyes from the sudden light. The pupils gazing back at him were vast and empty, black as dead stars.

Fucking terrific: he was Chief of Detectives. He was meant to notice these things. 'Get trashed, why don't you . . .' Flipping open his briefcase, Felix reached inside for a Bayer-Rochelle inhaler and went back to swearing. His police issue THC inhibitor was almost empty.

'Use the rest of this,' the fat man told Raf. 'And then go to the pharmacy . . .' He pointed across the square to a neon green cross. 'And buy another. Then we'll talk.' He tossed Raf the empty inhaler, sighing as Raf fumbled the catch.

'A package for Ashraf Bey.' Edouard stood at the fat man's elbow, shuffling nervously. Despite the heat he was dressed in a cheap Kevlar one-piece and wore a smog mask. His one-piece had *atlas cares* scrawled across the shoulders in a kind of casual, outdated corporate scrawl that fifteen years earlier had probably taken some account exec three breakdowns and most of a week just to brief.

Edouard was worried. He'd been told to follow his instructions exactly. And it was unquestionably noon, because the square echoed with the cry of a muezzin, and he definitely had the right café – but now the right man wasn't here any longer. Edouard had decided he'd better deliver the package to the right place at the set time and then wait for the right person to return.

'I'll take it,' said Felix.

Edouard was about to protest when Felix flicked open his wallet and flashed his gold shield. 'I said, I'll take it . . .'

'You'll still have to sign.'

The fat man scrawled his signature across a pad and reached for the fat envelope. 'Go,' he said and Edouard went. Unhappy but resigned. A second day's work looked increasingly less likely every time he ran what had just happened through his head.

Glancing across the square to the apothecary, Felix checked Raf was still out of sight and gently shook the envelope which was brown, padded and looked very much like government issue. From habit, the fat man held the envelope by its edges, so as not to leave fingerprints. The only obvious anomaly he could see was that its flap was tucked in rather than glued, as if the sender had been too lazy to gum the thing shut.

'What the hell.' Felix rattled the package until a flat box slid out into the table. It wasn't like he'd actually opened the thing. What he got was a chocolate box, the expensive kind. Charbonel & Walker. Stuck to the top was a small white card with kittens on the front and a lazer-printed message.

'If you get this, I'm already dead – Aunt Nafisa.'

Which wasn't what Felix had expected the card to say. For a split second he almost slipped the chocolate box back into its envelope. That way he could watch Raf's face for surprise or horror, for any clue at all as to what was going on. Because, as far as Felix was concerned, liking Raf and trusting the guy were two separate things entirely.

But not even taking one peek was asking too much and, besides, knowing exactly what was inside put Felix in a still stronger position. Particularly if it was letters, maybe a diary, even photographs . . .

Felix lifted the lid and a sweet smell grew. Not flowers, chocolate or marzipan. Something he knew so well the stray hairs had risen on the back of his neck before his brain even made the connection. RDX/C3. High-brisance *plastique* explos—

Glass into diamonds, shattering.

But by then a hundred eight-millimetre ball-bearings had already taken off half of the fat man's face and removed his right arm at the shoulder, though Felix hadn't yet grasped that. Where his cheek had been was living skull, yellow and glistening, one eye socket a smear of beaten egg white. A fist-sized hole in his temple exposed his brain and across his upper chest wounds had blossomed like blood-red poppies. The blast area was both precise and limited: the chocolate box little more than housing for a simple claymore.

Fractured jaw opened impossibly wide, the fat man began to scream silently at the world. He tried to stand, found his leg was broken and crashed sideways, taking the table down with him.

And still no one moved until Raf came running through shock-stopped traffic. Doing the fat man's screaming for him.

Sightless and almost deaf, gravity dragging the last shreds of identity out of his shattered skull in a heap of folded jelly, Felix still managed to make it to his knees, then spasmed and fell forward, grit sticking to flayed flesh.

It was pointless even trying to talk to a man whose throat was ripped open, whose cerebral fluid oozed from an open skull and whose pumping blood was creating tiny cascades that branched left and right down cracks in the sidewalk, taking the shortest route to the gutter. Yet the pointlessness didn't stop Raf shaking Felix. Shouting at him.

In the distance the wail of an ambulance fought the siren of a racing police car. But the ambulance, at least, would be too late. The fat man was a corpse, his body just didn't know it yet.

'*Do it.*' The words came suddenly, cold and clear.

Raf wanted to ignore them. To pretend he hadn't heard. *'Do it,'* said the fox, who never usually woke in daylight. So Raf did.

Unclipping the holster from the fat man's belt – badge, spare clip and all – Raf slid free Felix's Taurus and checked the cylinder. It was loaded with ceramic-jacket hollow-point.

'Back,' he ordered. And, watched by a retreating crowd, he untangled the fat man's coat from a broken chair and wadded it into a bundle to act as a pillow for Felix. Then, rolling Felix on to his front almost as if for sleep, Raf put the muzzle to the point where the fat man's skull met his neck and softly squeezed. What was left of Felix's head exploded, along with a chunk of pavement below. It was only luck that stopped ricocheting fragments taking out Raf's own eye.

Friendship came with a price that both of them had just paid.

Sirens split the shocked silence that followed. Jellaba-clad gawpers scattered suddenly as a cruiser slid to a halt kitty-corner to Place Gumhoriya. Out of its doors came two armed officers in flak jackets, assault rifles at the ready. But by then Raf was already gone: retreating through the crowd, the fat man's gun thrust into one pocket.

He jumped a tram, standing at the back on its open wooden platform, slipping off at a crossing to cut through a narrow alley full of empty shops and boarded-up houses. A builder's board promised total redevelopment. The completion date for the project was two years before Raf had arrived in Isk.

The smell of urine and damp earth filled his nostrils, coming from houses that had fallen in on themselves to become gardens kept lush by sewage leaking from a shattered pipe. The area was full of blind alleys and cluttered yards. Sometimes two blocks was all it took to slide from comfort to abject poverty – or vice versa. Money clung to the boulevards and the coast. Cut back from those and the city of the poor was always there. The cities of darkness, of brothels and lies. Old beyond meaning or memory, desolately grand and running by unspoken rules.

Raf was beginning to feel horribly at home.

He stepped through an open door into a deserted house and

kept going until he reached a locked door at the rear. One kick opened it and Raf found himself watched by an old woman as he crossed her courtyard and stepped out into a crowded street.

It was only when Raf stopped, looked round and tasted the sweetness of blood at the corner of his mouth that he realized a sliver of pavement had opened his cheek clean as a blade.

RenSchmiss

Chapter Thirty-seven

28th July

The water lights were off, the house lasers down. Somewhere at the other end of the vaulted room, a band was tuning up. And here, where tiny waves splashed against the rough stone of a cistern wall, Zara had wrapped herself in the darkness. Below her feet had to be the bottom of the cistern but she had only a sense of hanging over emptiness.

Three months before, a stoned-cold immaculate Danish boy had gripped tight to a rock and let the water close over him. Only to drop his ballast and kick upwards. He claimed to have seen a skeleton on the bottom, arms crossed over its chest. And people did disappear in Isk. Disappear completely. But Zara didn't really believe the story of the skeleton. Something had gone wrong with a batch of E/equals that month.

All the same, she did believe the darkness was occupied. Because whenever she left other swimmers behind and slid herself into a dark corner far away from the safety of the steps leading up to the dance floor, she could sense that something down there was aware she was there, hanging in the water above whatever it was.

Though maybe that was just E/equals too, from way back . . .

Now was chill-out time. Av's decks were deserted. The huge bank of smart lights rippled rather than throbbed, stilled by the lack of strong beat to catch and follow. Up on stage, out of her sight, four elderly black guys were coming to the end of an acoustic set – well, mostly . . . Something intrinsically West Coast ethnic that mixed Cape Verde with Mbalax and Soukous. A click track hiccuped from a child's beatbox, almost lost beneath balafon and sabar.

And the fit sounded loose but was actually tight and Zara felt relaxed for the first time in weeks, though that could have been from mixing Mexican with Moroccan.

Zara sighed. And kept sighing until the water closed over her again and bubbles like large pearls rose from her lips as she raised her arms and slid deeper. She would have gone deeper still but the pearls were gone. So she kicked once and glided to the surface.

'Going down, floating up . . . Guess you could call that an Ophelia complex,' said a voice right beside her. 'Oh no,' it countered, 'because then you'd be wearing some clothes . . .'

Instinct made Zara cover her breasts, and water made her choke as her head bobbed below the surface. When she'd finished coughing, she concentrated on swearing. She knew who it was.

What she didn't recognize was the voice of whoever spoke next.

'That was rude.'

Arms splashed up to snake round Zara's neck and Hani was suddenly glued fast like a limpet. She was grinning in the darkness. Breathing hard, though at first Zara thought that was from the swim. Then she realized the child was excited, dangerously excited.

'He hit a big man at the door,' said Hani. There was a horrified fascination in her voice.

'He wouldn't let us in,' Raf said apologetically.

Zara snorted, her face hidden in shadow until Raf adjusted his eyes and she came into view as cleanly as if someone had toggled the brightness on a screen.

'He didn't get up,' Hani added.

'Unconscious,' insisted Raf hastily, 'nothing worse. I had to see you . . .'

'Why?'

Of all questions it was the simplest to ask and the hardest to answer. Had Raf been thinking clearly, or even at all, he might have known he was in shock from Felix: seeing someone killed did that to you. But he wasn't supposed to do shock, at least not according to the wretched genetic-heritability guarantee. And anyway, he had more than one reply to her question.

Club. Felix. Hani . . . which came first?

Raf had to remind himself that Zara couldn't see in the dark, that her hearing was probably only average. So she might have missed the thud of heavy boots as bouncers criss-crossed the club searching for him. Pretty soon one of the bone clones would engage his brain and decide to fire up the water lights.

Except that they were about to be cornered themselves, if the distant clang of a door and abrupt trill of sirens at the high edge of his range was any clue.

'You're being raided,' Raf told Zara.

'Shit . . .' She sounded almost grateful. 'That's what you came to tell me?'

No, he'd come to beg her to look after Hani and to tell her was Felix was dead. Just like his aunt was dead. This city was turning into a personal war-zone and he was still busy trying to spot the enemy.

Raf shook his head, remembered she couldn't see him and opened his mouth to speak. But it was already too late. Up on the spiral, a riot cop using a throat mike attached to the kind of bass-heavy public hailer that turns your guts to water and dribbles them round your feet was demanding that *Someone Turn On The Lights. NOW* . . .

'How many ways in?' Raf felt an adrenalin rush kick-in with a vengeance. The fox was back on line.

'One,' said Zara.

Even Hani groaned.

'Two,' Zara amended, then corrected herself again. 'Three . . . Do storm drains count?'

Hani grabbed her tee-shirt from a corner where she'd left it and scooped up Ali-Din while Zara went looking for her clothes, which should have been folded neatly beneath a bench. Raf's own suit was sodden but at least he was wearing it.

'You need new clothes,' Raf ordered.

Zara opened her mouth to protest but Raf was gone, sliding

off in a different direction towards a blonde girl in spray tights, a snakeskin waistcoat that might once have slithered and a long trench coat cut from wafer-thin *faux* ocelot. Zara couldn't hear what Raf said but the girl handed over her coat without comment.

'Use this.' He stood between Zara and the worst of the crowd while she struggled into the coat. Searchlights were in use but the house system seemed down. If Avatar had any sense, thought Zara, he'd have pulled the fuses.

'Over there . . .' Zara said, nodding to a wall that lit and vanished as a hand-held hiLux hit the stonework and then swept back over the restless crowd. The crash squad were still looking for the main switch.

'. . . We need to get over there.'

Covering part of the wall was a swirl curtain that shimmered with an infinitely ridiculous number of infinitesimally small fluorescent beads trapped between its warp and weft. Raf didn't really have time to admire the effect. His brain was rich with theta waves that rolled across his cortex, firing neurones. Behind his eyes was a memory of Zara naked, soft hips and no body hair. Her legs long, her stomach almost flat. Water rolling in droplets between full breasts.

Sweet memories that stopped him remembering ugly things. Like blood turning black in a gutter or a breeze-blown fragment of ribbon fluttering across the road towards him.

'He wasn't listening,' Hani said.

Zara sucked her teeth, crossly. 'This way,' she ordered and ducked under the curtain. Her fingers twisted and fluorescence blossomed from a broken trance tube. They were inside a packed alcove that was arched over with crumbling red brick, and around them was rubbish, mostly broken beer boxes or empty industrial-size containers of still mineral water. Someone's knickers lay discarded on the floor.

Beyond the alcove was a gap where a storm drain fed into the cistern from the street. Clearly visible on the wall were crumbling iron handholds, rusted with age.

'You first,' Zara told Hani, 'Me next, Ashraf last . . .'

That was the order in which they went and that was the order in which the *morales* arrested them in the narrow side street where the drain began. With Raf climbing out to find Hani silenced by a hand over her mouth, while Zara stared furiously at a *gendarme officer* with skin the colour of pure chocolate and a bottle-green uniform so immaculate it must have come straight out of a box.

Overhead an ex-Soviet copter, with a searchlight now fixed to the side of its gun bubble, pinned Raf in its beam then flicked its attention to another street as soon as the officer moved in, Colt held tightly in her hand.

'*Ashraf Bey,*' she said, looking in shock at Raf's still-dripping suit.

'Yeah,' said Raf. 'Me.'

Behind the officer were two privates and at the end of the narrow street was a green van the same colour as the woman's uniform. Its rear doors were open and waiting.

Been here, thought Raf, *done that. Not doing it again.*

There were three ways it could go. She could let him walk, try to arrest him or call for advice and back-up. Only the first was any good to him and Raf didn't see it happening. Not if the screen-splash he'd caught at the madersa had been right and the IPD were busy nailing Felix to his forehead like the mark of Cain.

Crunch time came as the officer lifted her wrist to her face, ready to call HQ.

'Don't even think about it.' Raf had the fat man's gun out of his sodden pocket and in his hand before she had time to do much more than flinch. Her own weapon still pointed lazily at the ground. She'd got the uniform all right, she just hadn't got the moves.

'Fuck up and I'll kill her,' Raf told the two privates. 'Understood?' The gun wasn't the only thing he'd borrowed from Felix. The sudden hard-ass drawl also belonged to the fat man.

'Your watch,' Raf demanded.

Bottle-green handed it over with a scowl that turned to

distilled hatred as Raf tossed her elegant mobile straight down the storm drain. Now her HQ could pinpoint it all they liked.

'Going to shoot *me* too?' The woman's voice was cold, her contempt unchecked. Raf didn't know quite what she saw when she looked at him but it was something she hated. He wasn't too sure he liked it that much himself.

'Felix was dying,' Raf said shortly. Which was true. Half of the fat man's skull was gone, his brain a fat slug that gravity enticed towards the pavement.

'This man murdered Felix Bey.'

For all the attention the officer gave the gun in his hand, Raf might as well have been unarmed. Except then, of course, he'd have been under arrest already.

'There was a bomb,' said Raf, seeing shock explode in Zara's eyes. 'Felix took the full blast.'

Zara pushed hair out of her face and stared at Raf. 'You finished him off?'

'Yeah.' Raf nodded. 'What was my option? Let him exist on life support, wired up and quadriplegic, surviving on sugar-water and vitamins?'

With definitely no alcohol, no illegal porn channels and no working gearstick to engage even if he did. 'He'd have hated it.'

'So you got to play God?' That was the officer.

'Someone has to . . .' Raf spun the Colt round his finger, stepped in close and jammed the gun under bottle-green's chin.

'Ashraf . . .' Zara's voice shook. 'Don't . . .'

'I didn't kill Lady Nafisa,' Raf said slowly. 'And I didn't murder Felix.' He was talking to the officer, but Zara was listening and so was the kid; so really he was talking to them too. 'But I'm sure as hell going to hunt down whoever did. And I'll shoot anyone who gets in my way. You make sure everyone gets that message.'

Lifting the gendarme's Colt from her lifeless fingers, Raf tossed it after the watch and then walked her to the rear of her van, with the two squaddies following meekly behind. She climbed into the riot van without being asked.

'Now you,' he ordered and the squaddies scrambled inside, jostling each other in their haste. They stank of sweat, fear and kif. Which was what you got if you conscripted *fellah* who just didn't want the job. Still smiling, Raf slammed the rear doors, locked them and dropped their electronic key through the grille of a storm drain.

'Coming . . . ?'

Watchful and unhappy, Zara shook her head. 'No,' she said. 'Running away only makes things worse.'

Raf's laugh was sardonic. 'You obviously never tried it.'

Chapter Thirty-eight

29th July

Sudden and abrupt, Raf's kick echoed off the side of a derelict Customs shed, booming out over rusty tracks to the night-time emptiness of the docks beyond. No lights came on anywhere, no security guard ambled out of the darkness to find out what was going on.

The stretch of crumbling tenement south of Maritime Station was that kind of area. Low concrete housing with rusted bars for shutters and blank squares of chipboard where glass should be. Cancerous enough to make every project block Raf had ever seen look suddenly rich

'For me . . .' Raf announced, as he kicked again at the steel door of the deserted warehouse, under a peeling signboard that read *Pascarli & Co, Cotton Shippers*, '. . . her timing makes no sense. That's the problem.'

He'd talked his way through the first two diagrams in his notebook, skipped the autopsy data as being much too upsetting for Hani, and was back to chasing timescale round in his head. Who was where, when?

He was talking to Hani because it beat bouncing ideas off thin air and the fox was back in hiding, or dead. Or both. At least the kid had Ali-Din to talk to, not that she spoke much to her rag dog either these days.

Hani was worried about something but asking her directly about it hadn't worked. Though he'd tried that several times, starting when he'd got back to the madersa after Felix flatlined. All he'd got in return was sullen silence.

Back then, Raf hadn't told the small girl the fat man was dead: any more than he'd told her they had to leave the house.

Just asked his question and regretted getting no answers. But scaring kids wasn't his style. And besides, Raf could remember a time when he too had shut right down, until the adults round him began to say his lights were on but no one was home. And he *had* been home, of course – he just wasn't answering the door . . .

'You see,' Raf said. 'Aunt Nafisa went to a committee meeting at C&C at 10 a.m.' He used *a.m.* because that was what Hani knew. Lady Nafisa had thought the 24-hour clock vulgar. 'She left her meeting at eleven, but didn't get home until one. So where was she . . . ?

'Now,' said Raf, answering his own question. 'She could have been shopping.' He kicked one last time at the door and it flew back to reveal damp-smelling darkness. 'But then, what happened to her parcels?'

But it wasn't shopping, because Lady Nafisa didn't buy things when other people were about. She made stores open for her specially, at night, when she could count on the manager's full attention.

'Through here,' Raf told the girl and stepped into a musty darkness, nudging the door shut with his heel. Her fingers in his hand felt as fragile as twigs and almost as dry. She hadn't yet asked Raf why he'd really shot the fat man. But as she'd trotted through the night towards the docks, the child had tossed possible answers around in her head and not liked most of them.

It had been Ali-Din's job to find the warehouse. And the way it worked was that every time a crossroads appeared, Hani would stare at the eyes of her rag dog and then nod left or right depending on which eye blinked. If neither lit then the route was straight ahead. The puppy ran on some kind of satellite positioning system matched to a template of Iskandryia.

Hani's slight thaw had lasted until they reached the end of Fuad Premier, where a narrowing boulevard intersected with Rue Ibrahim and rattling midnight trams ran south-west from Place Orabi towards a rail terminus and the Midas Refinery stockyard.

The address Zara had given Raf was on the far side of the tramline, in an area where ramshackle souks gave way to near-derelict tenements before ending in a stink of sewage, rotting fish and diesel that leached from rusting dockside cranes dotting a cancerous concrete wilderness at the south-east end of Western Harbour.

It was dog-shit city.

A whole area of festering poverty that the *Rough Guide* didn't mention, other than to suggest that visitors should keep to the main routes during the day and avoid the place altogether at night. The official city guide omitted any mention of the area.

And, in a sense, the tenements and sprawl of empty warehouses *didn't* exist for most people in Iskandryia: for them, the slums were invisible and unnoticed, except by *felaleen* who didn't vote or would only have voted the wrong way if they did. America might stack its urban poor one family on top of another in high-rise blocks but in North Africa the poor were marginalized in a more literal sense . . . They lived at the barren edges of its cities or in occupied unwanted spaces like this one – which existed between a tramline and the dockside railway, was edged along its third side by a canal and slid, on its one good side, from squalor through poverty to the almost picturesque as it finally meshed with the souks of the El Gomruk . . .

'Up here,' said Raf, reaching a ladder. His voice echoed inside the empty warehouse the way kicking down its door had echoed off derelict buildings outside.

Above was a prefabricated office, slung between two steel girders originally added to strengthen the brick walls of the warehouse. The spiral staircase that should have led up to it was missing, so maybe Zara's tale of an upset hotel was untrue.

'Can't see,' Hani protested. She sounded cross and upset, but at least she'd started talking.

'I can,' said Raf. 'I'll go first and you follow after.' Part of him wanted to do it the other way round – so that he could catch Hani in case she slipped – but it was impossible to know what he might find in the office, so he went first. He could have made her stay below, of course, but he knew the child would like that even less.

'How can you see?' Hani asked scornfully. 'It's dark.'

'Ali-Din can see in the dark.'

'That's different.'

'Why?'

'Because Ali-Din is only . . .'

Her voice trailed away and Raf started climbing. Left hand pulling him up the ladder, his right tightly gripping the fat man's revolver.

The prefab was empty of people and full of kit. Each wall was smothered with cheap Ikea shelving, the bolt-together kind. Metal tables were pushed hard against the shelves. The only gap on the walls was a window, that would have looked north along the dockside towards Maritime Station if someone hadn't covered it over with tar paper and taped along all the edges. There was a sourly mechanical, almost chemical stink to the place, underlaid with stale tobacco.

Most of the kit in the room was instantly recognizable, like two stand-alone Median PCs and an Apple laptop with a fold-out satellite dish, which was definitely illegal. Plus a stack of vinyl piled next to a Blaupunkt mixing desk. The rest of the apparatus was far weirder. Starting with a full scuba suit, matching quadruple oxygen bottles and a shrink-wrapped box of sterile 1000ml beakers stacked next to the entrance hatch.

And someone had gone to the trouble of dragging plastic drums of distilled water up to the office. But that was the least of it. In one corner was a Braun freezer, wired to a bank of car batteries. In the opposite corner, a cupboard made of glass had an extractor hood taped and double-taped to its top, with a duct leading straight out through an outside wall.

On a table by the cupboard a long glass spiral of tubes fed down to a sealed beaker and every ring in the spiral was joined to the next with a ground-glass joint. Jammed between two of the rings was a half-smoked packet of untipped Cleopatra, while a battered paperback copy of *Uncle Fester's Organic*

Chemistry leaned against the beaker. The *Fester's* was the edition with a skull on its cover.

Inside a medical chest placed on the floor next to the table were bandages, burn salve, spray skin, surgical glue, a small canister of Japanese oxygen and a box of surgical gloves. There were also a dozen more packets of untipped Cleopatra.

'What have you found?' Hani demanded.

'A kitchen,' said Raf as he returned to the trap door and put out a hand to help her up, 'but not the kind you know.' He tried not to mind that the child flinched away from his grip.

'*Wake up*,' said Hani.

Raf came to on his feet. Banging into shelving as he spun, hand going for his shoulder holster before he remembered he didn't wear one these days and the gun was in his pocket.

Instinctively, he checked the fat man's revolver, fast-flipping the cylinder. Out and in. The weapon was one shot light – as if he could forget.

Still, with luck, whoever Ali-Din said was coming wouldn't know that.

'*Ali-Din . . . ?*'

Raf stopped.

'How does Ali-Din know someone's coming?

In answer, Hani put her puppy on a table by the taped-over window. The rag dog shuffled round and swung its large head until its eyes stared at where the tenements would be visible in the early-morning daylight, if only plyboard and tar paper hadn't replaced the glass. When its head stopped swaying, its blue-buttoned tail started to wag, like a faulty metronome.

'Don't tell me,' Raf said. 'The nearer the person, the faster the wag?'

Hani nodded.

'So it's a friend?'

Hani's eyes went wide, impressed at his grasp.

'A friend?' Raf stressed, even though he already knew the answer.

Whoever had given the toy to Hani had chosen an expensive

model. Though the mechanics couldn't be that difficult. To greet or growl the unit wouldn't even need satellite tracking – not the visual kind, anyway. Simple band scanning could check numbers on a mobile against basic visual recognition software and have the wag or growl defined either by how the child had reacted visually to that person before, or else, if the unit was really expensive, by reading off stress levels or beta waves.

There'd be a time lag of a few seconds but nothing too difficult to hide.

'Tell me,' said Raf, as he pocketed the revolver and headed for the trapdoor. 'Wag or growl? Which did Ali-Din do when he saw Aunt Nafisa?' Hani still hadn't answered when he reached the bottom of the ladder . . .

'Sweet fuck.' Raf forgot all about saying hello to Zara. Instead he stepped out into the morning glare, scrabbling for his dark glasses. He still couldn't get used to the North African sun, not after the grey skies of Seattle and the equally soft skies of Switzerland and Scotland before that.

Zara was dressed in tight black jeans, matched with a white silk shirt with long sleeves, no bra and only flip-flops on her feet. But it was her split lip he noticed.

'Leave it,' she said, when he tried to check the swelling. She stopped outside the warehouse door, refusing to go any further. 'I want to know why you shot Felix . . .'

'He was already dying. I just speeded it up.'

Zara sighed. 'How very macho.' She pulled a print of *Iskandryia Today* from under her arm. 'You sure it wasn't because he told the truth about Lady Nafisa's suicide?'

'How do you . . . ?' Raf demanded.

'The whole city knows,' said Zara and shoved the front page in his face. Felix stared out, looking fifteen years younger and a hundred pounds thinner than when Raf had last seen him. There was no picture of Raf, though the words *Suicide, Lady Nafisa*, and *Ashraf Bey* made cross-heads down two columns on the right.

'Nafisa didn't commit suicide,' Raf said flatly. 'She was too devout, too *respectable*.' He put heavy stress on the last word, and knew it to be true. Delete and discard were functions his unconscious had never had to master. He could actually *see* Lady Nafisa, alive inside his head, retiring to her room five times a day for prayers. See her reprimanding Hani for playing with Ali-Din that first Friday when the child should have been reading quietly or practising needlework.

Suicide was a sin.

Besides, she was too selfish, too in love with who she was to throw over worldly grandeur without a fight. Lady Nafisa didn't cast herself into darkness. Someone forced her through that door . . .

'There's been a couple of people on the radio who agree it wasn't suicide,' said Zara. 'They say it was you.'

'Me?' Raf stopped, shook his head and stared at the picture of Felix. He hadn't murdered the fat man and he hadn't killed his aunt. And Raf didn't need to stake his life on it, because he already had.

The raid on CdH also made the front page, but much smaller. And the picture of Zara was a paparazzi shot, snatched outside the Precinct as she clambered from the back of a riot van.

The copy didn't actually need to say she'd been naked beneath her coat when arrested, because the valley of shadow just above where the *faux* ocelot buttoned told its own story. Which hadn't stopped the paper stressing her nakedness three times in three paragraphs.

'What did they do to you?' Stepping forward, Raf took Zara's chin gently between first finger and thumb and turned her cheek to the light. A heavy bruise could just be seen beneath carefully applied concealer. One eye was also bruised and bloodshot, though Zara hadn't bothered with belladonna drops. No amount of eye brightener would be enough to hide her puffy eyelids or the redness where tears had dried.

Without thinking, Raf put an arm round her shoulder to help Zara into the warehouse, and felt rather than just heard her intake of breath and sudden hiss of pain.

'Forget it,' said Zara, brushing his apology away with a sour smile. 'No one else seems to think it's important. So what do you think of the place?' She stepped past him and into the warehouse. 'The collective use it. I just pay the rent.'

'The collective?'

'Friends . . .'

'But you all share the profits?'

Zara shook her head. 'I let them sell stuff at the club, at their own risk. CdH takes nothing off the top . . . Took,' she corrected herself. 'We *took* nothing off the top.'

'Doesn't look like that made a difference,' said Raf, one finger tracing a raw welt that ran round the side of her neck. Its edges were puffy and pinpricked with blood. This time Zara didn't flinch.

'Bastards,' said Raf.

Zara laughed. 'You think the police did this?' There was a slow-burn anger in her voice, like slightly damp black power getting itself ready to hiss and flare. 'The *morales* were politeness itself. Even drove me back to Villa Hamzah in an unmarked car. This is my mother's handiwork.'

'Because you were arrested?'

'Because I was naked. Because I was with you. Because no one worth anything will ever marry me now . . . How many fucking reasons do you think she needs?' Zara took a deep breath, steadying herself. 'Why do you think I was so desperate to get away to New York?'

There was no answer to that.

Raf eyed the ladder doubtfully. Seeing Hani crouched at the top, watching them with a blind intensity.

'I'm up here,' she told Zara. 'Do you want me to come down?'

By way of reply, Zara began to pull herself up the ladder, wincing at every new rung. By the time she reached the top, pain had her breathing only through her mouth, though she tried to hide the trembling in her hands.

'Antiseptic,' Hani told Raf, 'and cotton wool.' She put them into his hands and returned with a spray that read *plastic skin*, another of analgesic and a small bottle of mineral water . . . Ripping a stained blanket off a lopsided camp bed, she nodded for Zara to lie down, which the young woman did, being too tired to disagree.

'This will hurt,' said Hani, her voice serious.

'Really,' Zara said dryly. 'What a surprise.' For the first time in hours the child almost cracked a smile. But that vanished the moment Zara tried to take off her shirt and found it was stuck to her back.

Hani proved to be more than adept when it came to dressing the wounds, which she did with minimum fuss and maximum patience, stopping every time Zara swore or jerked under her touch. When one blast of analgesic proved not enough, Hani resprayed Zara's bare back and counted up to fifteen before she began again to lift off dried blood with wet cotton wool.

Though Hani's proficiency wasn't what held Raf's attention. What gripped it – so tightly he had to remind himself he'd actually seen Zara naked, not just without her shirt – was the curve of one full breast as it pressed out at the side, as she lay face down on that rickety camp bed. He'd seen his share of naked women, although none of them quite that beautiful; but this was heartbreakingly different, and he felt the breast's shape in his head like a shiver.

Somewhere in his psycho-profile files at Huntsville there was probably an explanation. Which, no doubt, Dr Millbank would have been happy to expound. Back there sex was something to be talked about, analysed and discussed, preferably in open meetings. In return, Huntsville ran 'access weekends' in a block of log cabins that looked like a bad lakeside motel. Every window had red checked curtains, little beds of nasturtiums prettied up both sides of the front door and books stood in neat rows on shelves inside, along with framed prints of snow-capped mountains and a fridge full of Miller Lite and that pale Mexican beer. The low-rent kind that made it hard to get drunk.

But the *normalizing* touches were irrelevant. All anyone was really interested in were the big Shaker beds with their disposable sheets that got replaced each morning.

It hadn't mattered that Raf had no one to come visiting. At the end of his first month Dr Millbank signed him off as in need of ongoing psychosexual therapy. His designated therapist was a blond academic in her early thirties who was writing a thesis on *regressive institutionalization*. One weekend the academic didn't arrive and a dark-haired serious Canadian student of hers turned up instead. All the Canadian wanted to do was heavy pet and then take breaks to make notes. It was from the student that Raf learned his therapist had been working on the same paper for eleven years. Which sounded pretty institutionalized to him . . .

When Zara's welts were clean, Hani sterilized the area with antiseptic, waited for it to dry and then graffitied over each one with a thick line of plastic skin; and all the while the child's face was frozen into a mask, seconds away from dissolving into tears.

'Hey, it's okay,' Zara insisted. 'It just stung a bit, you know?'

Slowly, Hani nodded. And the movement was all it took to tip the drops from her eyes and spill them down her cheeks: rendering Raf instantly irrelevant, though he didn't know why.

The two girls looked at each other, then back at Raf.

'South of here,' said Zara, 'you'll find a boat, just before the railway jetty.' She pushed herself up on one elbow, revealing a flash of breast as she dipped one hand into her jeans pocket. 'You'll need this,' she said firmly. The card she gave him was grey, scratched and dull with age. It was blank on either side. 'We won't be long.'

'What about . . .'

'Hani's going to clean up my face, aren't you, honey? And then we're going to talk, in private. Then we'll do our prayers. After that, we'll come and find you . . .'

The first vessel Raf came to stank of oil and rested so low in the water that any half-decent wave could lap over its side and finish the job of sinking it. The next two were small tunny boats, battered red hulls and peeling oak decks warped and split with heat. Old-fashioned steel padlocks locked tight their cabin doors.

After that was a long gap of jetty where rusting bollards waited vainly for bow ropes from container ships that would never come back. The new boats docked in the deeper waters behind him. Ferries and cargo vessels from Marseilles and Syracuse, roped fast to the jetty of Maritime Station. And beyond those were, anchored sleek grey cruisers and an elderly aircraft hangar that stood off from the entrance to the naval base at Ras el-Tin. The General was rumoured to keep certain prisoners aboard the *Ali Pasha*, held below decks in conditions of both sumptuous luxury and restraint.

Ahead of Raf, where shallows condemned the water to near-emptiness, the main dock came to an abrupt halt as the dockside jerked back onto itself to become a long jetty which angled out towards the middle of the harbour. The glint of wheel-hammered tracks confirmed that the spur was still in use. Probably to shunt containers out to Soviet cargo carriers too vast even to dock alongside Maritime Station.

Raf was still looking for the right boat when he realized he'd been staring at it for the last ten seconds without registering the fact. It was there, all right, in a vee of greasy water where the dockside folded back to become the jetty. Only what Raf first saw as dead water beyond the boat turned out to be the mouth of Mahmoudiya Canal, feeding from a large hole in the side of the dock.

Two centuries before, twenty thousand *felaheen* had died in three years digging the fifty miles of waterway that now linked El Iskandryia to the capital. The canal was built on the orders of the khedive, so goods could flow from Cairo to North Africa's greatest port, while fresh water from Iskandryia could be diverted to irrigate the hinterland. First started in 1817 on the orders of Mohammed Ali, it was built by a French architect – as was much of Iskandryia from that period.

For the first hundred years the canal, or at least the bit that circled the city, was lined by some of Isk's grandest houses, each with a luxuriant garden leading down to the water's edge. But the houses crumbled and the rich left. The clear water clogged with madder rose, effluent and finally bodies as Spanish Influenza hit the city and, for ten weeks or so, Iskandryia emptied of the living, leaving only the dead.

Now Zara's black boat rested in the shadow of that canal mouth, lying so low in the water it too might have been slowly sinking; except this vessel was designed to ride almost level with the waves. Fifty feet long, ten wide at the stern once its chisel-edged prow had finally flared out, the boat was an ex-UN-issue combat craft. Stealth-sheeted and proof against infrared sensors.

Its retractable glass antenna was just visible at the rear. Turned off, the antenna was transparent to radar. Only in the brief periods when it was broadcasting or receiving did the inside of the hollow glass whip turn to plasma, as a single metal electrode at its base stripped electrons from gas.

The last time Raf had seen a VSV had been ten years before on CNN when one of the 15,000bhp craft had been in the middle of being freighted aboard a McDonnell Globemaster V to be air-lifted to some emergency in Indonesia. If he remembered correctly – and, as always, he did – out of the water it looked like a cigar tube that someone had pinched flat at the front end. That, and the fact it had once been the fastest ocean-going vessel in the world.

'Well . . .' Raf glanced from the old VSV to the grey card in his hand. 'Why not?' There was a lot about Zara he didn't know. In fact, he suspected that there was a lot about her that a lot of people didn't know, starting with her parents.

A slot next to a small door at the rear of the long cockpit swallowed the card and then spat it out again. Without any sound, without a single diode lighting or any other clue that the VSV's computer even knew he was aboard, the door frame scanned Raf for weapons and confirmed the card was real. The multiple check-sums matched those in memory and Felix's revolver was judged not hazardous.

A lock clicked and the door opened outwards. The cabin inside was as clean as the boat's outside was filthy and Raf realized the litter on the decks, the tide marks and oil smears were intentional. Someone had ripped out the original bucket seats that had run down both sides of the cabin and replaced them with two metal beds, a small fridge, a bank of comms kit and, most bizarre of all, a shower cubicle.

The only other thing in the stripped-bare cabin was a white telephone, the old-fashioned kind with a handset that needed to be picked up. The phone was busy taking a message and a read-out on its base announced that its memory was already backed up with ten others. Probably all from the same man by the sound of it . . .

'Zara.' Anger fought worry in the caller's voice, worry winning. 'Your mobile's turned off and I've tried everywhere else. If you're there, pick up . . .'

'Zara, are you there? *Zara* . . .'

For a second, Raf was tempted to leave the receiver in its cradle and let Zara deal with her father when she finally turned up: always assuming she did and that sending him ahead wasn't her ploy to get Hani away from a dangerous maniac. But there was something approaching desolation in Hamzah's gruff voice. His fury a flip side to a love he'd probably never put into words but which was there all the same.

Raf lifted the receiver. 'She's not here.'

'*Not* . . .' Hamzah sounded stunned. 'Who is . . . ?'

Realization hit him a second later.

Zara refused to use the word *beat*. Grown-ups either hit children or they didn't, in her opinion. Calling it something else might soothe an adult conscience but it made little difference to the child.

'It's okay, honey. You're allowed to tell me.'

Hani didn't answer. Partly because she'd never really seen another person naked and she was looking at Zara with the disturbed fascination of someone who knew that, one day, strange things would happen to her body too. And partly it was because Hani didn't know the right answer.

Hani tried very hard to give only right answers, even if other people thought that wasn't true. *Other people* had always been Aunt Nafisa and Donna, but now her aunt was dead and Donna was still at the madersa and *other people* were Ashraf and the woman standing in front of her, struggling to get into her filthy shirt without letting the cloth scrape her back.

'Do you want me to do that?' Hani asked.

Zara nodded, and sat back on the edge of the camp bed.

'This arm first,' Hani said.

Obediently Zara threaded one arm through the offered sleeve.

'Now this one . . .'

'Did she?' Zara asked, gently moving Hani round so the child stood facing her. The child blushed, though at what Zara wasn't certain.

'She did, didn't she?'

Very slowly Hani nodded.

'Often?'

'Sometimes.' By now the child was gazing anywhere but at the young woman in front of her.

Zara didn't need to ask if the blows were hard. She'd faced that question for herself and could answer as a child. All blows were hard when it was someone who was meant to love you and someone you were meant to love – did love – until you finally taught yourself not to . . .

'Something happened, didn't it?' Zara said gently.

Hani shook her head.

'Yes,' said Zara. 'When Lady Nafisa came home . . . You saw her come in and something happened. Was she angry?'

'No,' Hani said, nodding. The answer was there on her tongue but her mouth was closed into a bitter, troubled trap, holding in secrets too heavy to speak.

'Tell me,' Zara said. 'She came home and you were where . . . ?'

'In her study,' Hani's voice was a whisper. 'She'd taken Ali-Din.' Hani clutched the rag dog tight, as if someone might be about to confiscate the toy again.

'So she hit you . . .' Zara could understand the child's hurt. She'd inhabited that world until first thing this morning. Now her world would be different.

'No,' said Hani. 'She missed. So I ran away.'

'She missed?'

Hani nodded. She was thinking. Remembering, but not quite understanding. 'Aunt Nafisa was falling over. She shouted at me because her head hurt.'

'What?' Zara asked quickly. 'What did she shout?'

'To get a doctor – and to leave her alone.'

'So what did you do?'

Wide eyes regarded Zara. 'I shut the door and locked it . . . She was drunk. It's wrong to be drunk.' Hani nodded intently, reassuring herself. 'When Donna got drunk Aunt Nafisa slapped her and said next time she'd call the police . . .'

So you didn't call a doctor, thought Zara, *because you didn't want the police to come. And then your aunt was killed and the police came anyway. No wonder you're traumatised.*

'Honey,' said Zara as she stroked Hani's cheek, 'it's okay. You did right. And I promise we won't let anyone know she'd been drinking.'

The anger coming down the line was almost palpable. Hamzah's fear finally finding a target it could hate. 'I will kill you if you've hurt her . . . Do you understand?'

'Me, hurt Zara? I thought that was your wife's job.'

That earned Raf stunned silence. Raf could do misdirected hatred too, better than most. Raf and Hamzah were two minutes into what passed for a conversation and were already headed for a brick wall.

'You shot Felix Bey,' Hamzah said finally. As if that was proof Raf intended to slaughter his daughter as well.

'News travels . . .' So did a memory, sliding out of the past. Felix discussing the General. Felix bad-mouthing the Minister. Felix talking about skimming his percentage off men like Hamzah, but still not looking the other way. In a city like Iskandryia anyone could have sent that bomb.

Raf ran tired fingers across his scalp, feeling stubble. It needed washing along with the rest of him. He felt old and tired, centuries older than when he had first arrived in the city. His face was narrower, his dark blond beard made his lips look thinner and chin more pointed. There was a vulpine cruelty to his own face that Raf didn't recognize.

The prince must make himself feared in such a way that, if he not be loved, at least he escapes being hated.

An old memory.

Well, okay, if the fox said so.

'Let me tell you about Felix,' said Raf angrily. 'He had cancer of both lungs and a liver with more holes than a sponge. He drank a bottle of whisky a day and had a daughter he hadn't seen in years. What he didn't have, when I last saw him, was medical insurance covering lifestyle choices or losing half his head . . .'

The words were ice-cold, burning with blue fire. Raf didn't really know the person who spoke them or recognize the anger that shot them out of his mouth and down the line to the suddenly silent industrialist. He only knew that, this time, that person was him.

'He told me he was the only really honest cop in that place and I believed him. And, yes, I shot him,' said Raf. 'I put a gun to what was left of his head and pulled the trigger. And I'd do it again. Right now, tomorrow, next year, whenever . . . He was the closest thing I'd found to a partner in this stinking sewer of a city and I owed him. What part of all this don't you understand?'

The man on the other end broke the connection quietly. Seconds later the windows darkened to an impenetrable black, the interior of the boat brightened as bulkhead lights came on and the dashboard lit with a dozen different read-outs. Over on one wall a window came to life, revealing a rolling news programme. *Ashraf Bey trapped.* Below it, a wall-mounted keyboard beeped once to show it was live.

A tiny voice from the VSV's console announced the craft was shielded, operating fooler loops and running overlapping stealth routines. It also told Raf that he had visitors.

'Well, now,' Zara said, as he opened the door to her and she saw the live array of the console beyond. 'You want to tell me exactly how you managed that?'

Chapter Thirty-nine

30th July

The aged *felah* behind the make-shift counter looked as old as a twisted olive tree until one noticed his eyes. Then it became obvious that although hot summers and wild winter storms had beaten his face to the colour and consistency of cheap leather, the man's eyes revealed his true age: which was still old enough to have seen almost everything the city could offer, except the sight of police openly surrounding the madersa of a bey.

And he knew it was Friday afternoon and his street licence banned working but the crowds were out – and when the crowds were out they needed feeding.

'*Taamiya . . .*' Falafel. On the cart in front of him was a stack of aluminium bowls, three wine bottles now filled with some kind of sauce and a ladle. The wide neck of a metal jar stuck through the flat top of his cart. Inside the jar, already-cooked falafel were slowly cooling.

On a separate cart, in a huge metal container of bubbling oil, bobbed more taamiya ready to be scooped out and transferred to the main cart. Next to the bobbing taamiya was a smaller bowl of beaten egg into which they'd been dipped, before being rolled in bread crumbs ready to fry. Here too were kept piles of pitta, which a slash of the knife converted from simple flat bread into a pocket waiting to be filled with taamiya, chopped salad and sauce.

The younger man took the food he'd asked for and gave the cart owner a handful of change, half of it adorned with the profile of the Khedive, the rest featuring His Imperial Majesty. Only the poor still used small change and it didn't matter to them whose head was on the coins, so long as agreement

244

existed how much each little circle of metal was actually worth.

'La.' Raf waved away an even smaller coin the falafel seller offered as change and bit into his warm pitta bread, tasting fresh coriander and feeling oil run into his beard. He hadn't felt hungry when he ordered the pitta, had merely needed something extra to help him blend with the restless crowd gathered around the taped-off entrance of Rue Cif. But now, with his striped and tattered jellaba – that cloak of invisibility worn the length of the North African littoral by the dispossessed – and taamiya in his hands, Raf felt ready to begin fighting his way through the crush.

There was a knot in his stomach and it wasn't all hunger. Although more than twenty-four hours had gone by since he'd last eaten, maybe longer. Raf wasn't sure, because he wasn't wearing a watch, and that was part of blending in too. If he could find a street stall he'd pick up a *faux* Rolex, something obviously cheap and not real.

What he needed was something suitable for a jellaba-wearing felah, like a cheap Thai fake or the kind of flamboyant G'Schlock copies garages gave free with gas . . . Just as he'd needed the budget wraprounds he'd picked up from a 24/Seven in Place Orabi which made the people he was pushing through look amber and ghostly. Some of the crowd had been brought here, like him, by newsfeeds or radio. Most had just followed neighbours or stopped off on their way back from a mosque.

'What the fuck happened?' Raf asked, offering a tiny coin to a woman hawking plums from a woven satchel. 'An accident?' For all he knew the felaheen used ornate politeness when talking amongst themselves but, if so, the woman didn't seem to notice. And if she looked at the stranger with the torn jellaba in surprise it was at the fact he even had to ask.

'They're searching Ashraf Bey's house.'

'He won't be there . . .'

The woman spat. 'Of course he won't. He's under arrest. They're looking for proof the pig killed his aunt for the money . . .'

'What money?'

'There was money,' she said shortly. 'And there's a reward for information. That's what I heard.' The next time Raf looked, the woman was shuffling towards a uniformed officer, ignoring outstretched arms that offered coins for her remaining fruit.

'Out of there.'

Raf was moving in the opposite direction before he realized what the fox had ordered his body to do. *Too fast*, the fox told him, its voice faint. And Raf halted his panic-driven trot to a slow stroll, pushing his way to the front of the crowd. He was helping kill off the fox, by making it appear in daylight. They both knew that. But the fox had never said anything about it, never criticized.

'Head for Mushin.'

The man he'd come looking for stood like a poisoned dwarf just inside Rue Cif, staring hard at the rear door to the madersa. What did the man hope to find? Raf had no idea. Unless the Minister was just there to be seen by the news 'copters overhead and the ground crews.

'Shield,' whispered the voice in his head and then it was gone, fading to static that fizzled and died. Raf was alone again.

Tossing his half-finished pitta into the dirt, Raf flashed Felix's gold shield at a surprised police sergeant and stepped over the tape before the man had a chance to check the name or protest. The fact that Raf headed straight for Mushin Bey was enough to make the sergeant step back, muttering bitterly about plain-clothed shitheads.

'Hey, you,' said the Minister. 'Back behind the line.' The small man didn't just look like a cinema usher, he sounded like one too.

Raf grinned and flipped open Felix's pass to show the shield and then as the Minister's eyes widened, rammed the barrel of the fat man's revolver hard into the small man's thigh. 'I've got his gun, too,' said Raf, relying on their distance from the crowd and the long sleeve of his own jellaba to keep the revolver hidden.

'You won't . . .'

'I just did,' said Raf. He nodded towards the middle of Rue Cif, where the closed-off street stood dark and empty and the crowd and police looked very far away. 'Take a walk.'

Mushin Bey wanted to complain, to threaten, to promise Raf that he'd be hunted down like a dog – but one look at the hard edge to the young bey's face told him not to waste his breath. This man would kill him if necessary. And all that Raf knew about the Minister, he read written in fear on a weasel face and deduced from panic rising from the man's skin, unsweetened by courage.

He was no more a real head of police than Raf was a real bey. Mushin Bey was a politician, which put him off the list where killing Felix was concerned. The man had needed Felix, rotted liver and all.

'Okay,' said Raf. 'It's murder now you think you can pin Nafisa on me, but it was suicide when you couldn't. So tell me, who are you protecting?'

'No one,' said the Minister. 'As you well know.' He sounded like he believed it. And he tried to stare back, but his pale eyes slid away from the wraparounds bisecting Raf's face, fear subverting any real anger.

It was a feeling Raf suddenly recognised. Already there was a fragment of worry inside his head telling him to put down the gun and surrender. To give himself up to authority as he always did eventually, once the brief flare of anger had burned out to leave only the taste of failure in his mouth. A death penalty existed in Iskandryia as it did in all Ottoman cities, even the free ones, but he could cut a deal. He didn't doubt that . . .

'We know about Felix fixing the autopsy,' the Minister said flatly. 'What did you have on him? Little girls, drugs, pay-offs . . . ?'

'No one fixed that autopsy,' Raf said crossly, jostling the Minister further back towards an empty area of the street. 'Unless it was you?'

Without intending to, Mushin Bey answered with an instinctive shake of his head so minute it was almost subliminal. Raf believed him. What he found impossible to believe was that the man wasn't covering up for someone else.

'Tell me,' said Raf, 'when did you switch from being certain it was suicide to being certain it wasn't?'

'When you had Felix killed. I assume you suddenly realized he'd stuffed you up with that suicide verdict.'

'When I . . . ? He was dying,' said Raf. 'It was a *coup de grâce.*'

And then the Minister explained something that stood Raf's day on its head and made a mockery of the scribbled and intricate chart of connections carried deep in Raf's pocket. Mushin Bey wasn't talking about the shooting. He meant the bomb. They'd found the man who'd delivered it and he was happy to help. The Minister paused for a second and amended that to *very* happy to help. And what really impressed the Minister, and he was prepared to admit this, was Raf's idea of arranging for the bomb to be delivered to himself. What better way to divert guilt . . .

'It was meant for me?'

'Don't . . .' The Minister didn't get to the next word because by then Raf was bringing up his gun.

'You know what I think?' Raf said as he flicked back the hammer and positioned the muzzle carefully under the Minister's chin so any bullet fired would be guaranteed to remove most of the back of the man's skull. 'I think you know who killed Lady Nafisa.'

'Me?' Anxiety shrivelled Mushin Bey's face. Panic blossoming until it was only a matter of seconds before the Minister either soiled himself or else started pleading for his own life. And every emotion inside the man was stripped naked except for the one that Raf actually sought.

Guilt would have been enough to make him pull the trigger.

'I didn't murder Felix and I certainly didn't murder Lady Nafisa.' Raf's voice was hard. 'I'm not so sure you didn't, but you get the benefit of my doubt . . .' That was the kind of crap Dr Millbank used to speak all the time. 'But *someone* killed them, and if that turns out to be you . . .

'Remember,' Raf told the man, 'I trained in places that wouldn't even let you through the fucking door.' And with that, he leaned forward and dropped something soft into the Minister's pocket, smoothing the jacket neatly into place.

'The remains of that plastique I didn't take,' Raf said simply. 'Take you off at the hips, no question.' He thrust one hand into his own pocket and kept it there, closing his fingers round a tube with a spring-loaded button on top. 'I'm going to walk out of here. You cause me *any* problems and I'll leave you as chopped steak all over the street. You understand me?'

The minister did.

Idly clicking the button on a breath-mint dispenser as he walked away, Raf wondered how long it would take Mushin Bey to discover that the object burning a hole in his pocket was actually one uneaten plum.

'Yes, I shot him . . .'

Two wheels bit and the bike was flying. Hot summer wind rammed its way through ventilation ducts cut into the bike's aerodynamically perfect fairing, cooling the Japanese v-twin as DJ Avatar red-lined his whole way down the sweep of the Corniche.

'And I'd do it again.'

He was too fired up on the mix, too wired to check his profile in the smoked windows of expensive cafés lining the final stretch of road.

'Right now, tomorrow, next year, whenever.'

Av didn't recognize the man's voice – because they'd never spoken – but he knew who it was. Just as he knew for sure it had to be Zara who'd dumped the file into his postbox. Her way of apologizing for who the *morales* drove home and who they kept locked up in a basement for forty-eight hours with a pisspot for company. Though where a murderer and his half-sister fitted together . . . Well, that was some place he definitely didn't plan to go for too long.

All the same, the mix was sweet and its message sweeter still. Pure and illegal as the fragments of meth still burning the back of his throat. The police had cracked the club but this was his revenge.

Simple bass went nowhere slowly. The synth line looped colder than liquid nitrogen, crackling with static.

'Believe it. This is DJ Avatar and that was *the Bey*. Coming at you from the wrong side of the mirror . . .' The boy hit a button on his handlebar: manic laughter drowning out the track and then it was back, sucking its way inside his brain and the brain of everybody else listening, which by now was most of the city.

'Enjoy . . .' The bass dropped out to be replaced by a double heartbeat and the sound of pure anger, expertly mixed.

'Let me tell you about Felix . . .'

Chapter Forty

31st July

A wave rolled over Raf's shoulder, leaving droplets that shone like opals in the noon sun, their salt still prickling his factor 40-coated skin. *Let me tell you about . . .*

He couldn't get Av's mix out of his skull but had moved beyond minding.

Behind him, the moored VSV operated at half stealth, which gave it the radar profile of a small fishing boat. Raf didn't even know where he was, only that the vessel was nestling between two rocky headlands off a low island that lacked any fresh water. And that didn't matter: Zara had brought her own supply and, anyway, VSVs carried small desalination units at the stern.

The sea was wine-dark, the sky a blue so impossible that, even through shades, it looked as if some unseen hand had ditched the presets and started messing with both saturation and brightness. Umber-hued shrubs lined the lower reaches of a stunted hill, their gnarled roots clawed into the thin dirt that had collected between huge rocks – and Raf could smell the scent of lavender blowing towards him on a warm wind.

They were there because Zara had announced that going there would be a good idea. And, without being told, Raf got the feeling that she'd visited the island many times before, though with whom she didn't say. All Raf knew about her island was that it was three hours from Iskandryia – three hours, that was, if one travelled in a boat that cut through waves the way light skewered darkness.

'Hey, look at me.'

Raf watched as Hani launched herself, head first, off the side of the boat to sink below the waves in a stream of bubbles. She was diving, if it counted as diving to sit on the very edge of the deck and bend forward so far that her arms almost touched the waves.

'Did you see?'

Raf nodded and trod water as Hani splashed her way towards him with clumsy strokes. 'Got you,' she said, her arms coming up round his neck: so that Raf was suddenly carrying her slight weight. The child's hair spread in rat's tails across a face that was suddenly split by a knowing grin. 'Are we running away?'

'Only for today.'

Hani nodded thoughtfully. 'Better do some more dives, then.'

From the deck of the VSV, Zara smiled as the child unhooked her arms and paddled back towards the boat. Her father, now – he ran in the opposite direction from responsibility and called it work.

Watching Raf with Hani was like seeing storm clouds clear. Zara knew exactly what had burnt out the storm, because she'd orchestrated it. Well, sort of . . . It began when Raf was out, checking exactly what was happening at the madersa and she'd started going over all the men she'd known, which wasn't many. Whatever his reasons, her father had little to do with his brother and so she'd never met her cousins on that side. And her mother was an only child, as if that wasn't obvious.

Boyfriends: there'd been two in New York. She'd chucked one of them and one had chucked her, but both times it had been over the same thing. Speaking to her friends in student halls, Zara had taken to referring euphemistically to the reason as *cultural differences.*

Both boys had been white, both Protestant, both uptight and angry but too repressed to discuss it, do anything about it, except glower or sulk. She saw the same repression in Raf, for all that he was meant to be half Berber. He could undoubtedly do both in-your-face or reserved – violence being the flip side of stepped-back – but a straight-out raise-your-voice hand-waving argument? Zara didn't think so. Which was why, after he finally got back from talking to Mushin Bey the previous night, she hadn't given him any option . . .

And for a while she hadn't been sure she was right.

Sitting on the floor of the VSV, darkness falling over the Western Harbour outside, Raf had rubbed one hand tiredly across the back of his neck and asked the kind of question you ask when your anger has been coming out of every radio in every cab in the city. And when getting home means walking unnoticed and unknown past slum kids chanting your words in the street.

It was too late to stop Avatar's mix burrowing worm-like into the city, because *InnerSense/Fight Bac* was racking up heavy rotation, roughly every fourth play. But Raf still wanted to know one thing:

'How the hell did he get it?'

Zara swept the hair out of her eyes and hugged Hani closer. The child was curled up into a little ball, her head on Zara's knee and the rag dog clutched between sleeping hands.

'Own the streets,' said Zara, quoting a liberation theosophist currently serving twenty-five years solitary in Stambul, 'and you've got the city . . . He does it from the back of a bike, you know. Doesn't need to, that's just the way it's developed.'

'Who does?'

'Avatar. My brother . . .' Zara made it a point of principle never to add the *half*.

'Your . . . ?'

Zara nodded, 'Yes,' she said. 'Av. You met him on the tram. I gave him the sound file.'

'You what?'

Their argument went from there. And at the point when Hani scrambled off Zara's lap to cower against the bulkhead, her thin legs tucked up to her chin and her eyes wide with fright, having everything out in the open no longer seemed such a good idea to Zara and the damage looked done.

Zara had just finished accusing Raf of being an arrogant, over-bred, emotionally retarded inadequate and Raf was explaining to Zara in over-simple words why it wasn't his fault if she was some spoilt little rich bitch who'd got done for stripping off at an illegal club.

As for marrying her . . .

'*Stop it.*' Hani's voice was fierce, her chin jutting forward and her mouth set in a determined line. She was way too cross even to acknowledge the tears that rolled down her face. '*Stop it.*'

The small cabin was loud with their sudden silence.

'I'm sorry,' Raf said quietly and he got up to leave the VSV.

'Don't go far,' Hani ordered. 'You'll only get lost.'

Darkness he liked, and silence. Both of which he got, staring out over the shimmering black expanse of the Western Harbour. There had been drunken shouting from Maritime Station as a party of Soviet sailors were escorted back to a destroyer by police: and Customs boats were making great play of criss-crossing the water at high speed, their searchlights cutting across the waves. Only, the sailors had got safely back on board and the cutters had given up sweeping the waters on the dot of midnight and returned to base, leaving the way clear for small, unlit boats to sneak out of the harbour mouth.

'That's the thing about night-time,' Zara said behind him. 'It makes even something as ugly as Maritime Station look beautiful.' She put a chilled beer into his hand and Raf was glad he'd pretended not to hear the door open.

'You know,' said Raf, 'I've probably got a head full of hard-ware I didn't ask for and, yeah, I can see in the dark but I don't think I'm over-bred, though I'll agree the emotional stuff . . .'

By way of answer, Zara ripped the top off her beer. As apologies went it raised more questions than it answered, but it was still better than she expected.

'I'm pretty sure I'm not even a real bey,' said Raf. 'I don't have finely honed battle skills and I wasn't working for the Seattle Consulate when it got bombed or even before that . . .'

She held out her beer and, after a second, Raf realized he was meant to take it. Then she waited, while he worked out he was meant to give Zara his unopened can in return. The beer felt melt-water cold and tasted clean and slightly sweet.

So he concentrated on tasting it, not taking a second mouthful until he'd properly savoured the first.

'What were you doing in America?'

'I've been in prison,' Raf said simply. 'Outside Seattle. I was there for a while.'

'Why?' Zara demanded.

'I was charged with murder.'

'Don't tell me . . .'

'I didn't do it.'

Zara felt her lips twist into something that was almost a smile. 'But they arrested you anyway.'

Raf nodded. 'The thing is,' he said, 'I don't really know what I'm doing here. And there's something else. Why are you . . . ?'

'Why am I helping you? Let me see,' said Zara, counting off the points. 'You jilt me publicly, you shoot the fat policeman, I'm not wearing any clothes when I'm arrested and you're accused of murdering your aunt for money . . . I don't know, you tell me.' She looked at him, then looked again when she realized he really *didn't* understand.

'I'm tainted,' she said flatly. 'No one will marry me. I probably don't even have my old job any more. I need you to be innocent . . .'

'And you came out to tell me this?'

'No,' Zara shook her head. 'I came to tell you that Hani wants to say something.'

What Hani wanted to tell him was that Aunt Nafisa had had a big argument on the phone months before Raf even arrived. And Hani knew who with because her aunt spent a lot of time calling the man *Your Excellency* and *General.*

'So,' Zara kept her voice low. 'What do you think the argument was about?'

Raf shrugged. They'd been talking about it all day, whenever they got a second to themselves. And the only idea he'd come up with was too ludicrous to share.

'Well,' said Zara, 'tell me this. Do you think she was drunk?'

The VSV was on its way back from the island, steering itself and running every routine in its armoury. This time round, it was Zara who leant against Raf's shoulder, while Hani slept on the bed opposite, a sarong pulled tight round her like a sheet.

Did he think his aunt drank? No, even though the child had seen her staggering round the house. And Raf was sure narcotics were out, but equally he didn't believe it was suicide. Which brought him back to murder. And if the *Thiergarten* were left out of the equation, and Raf really didn't believe she'd been assassinated on orders from the khedive's advisers, then nobody seemed to have a motive, unless it was hothead students at the German School in Iskandryia, and Raf didn't believe even they'd be that stupid.

General Koenig Pasha might be half Prussian but, from what Felix had said, the General tolerated *Thiergarten* activity and that was all. And the students at the German School were unpopular, as young men with no real cares and excess money usually are: they knew full well the debt they owed Koenig Pasha for their protection.

'Drunk?' Raf said. 'I don't know . . . I'm losing the thread.'

'Assuming there is one.'

In less than two hours' time they were due to enter Isk's western harbour by running parallel up the coast, sliding between the shore and a breakwater, using a route firmly fixed in the boat's memory. And thought Zara, chances were they'd still be going round in circles discussing Nafisa.

The VSV would take a route close to the rocky shore, running low in the water and silent, staying well away from the naval base at Ras el Tin. And yet the naval base would still see them on screen.

But it wouldn't matter.

Because, as she'd already told Raf, the boat belonged to her father who had an understanding in place with the General himself. A dozen passenger liners a day might dock at Maritime Station and still the western harbour's single biggest commercial activity was smuggling. Hashish, vodka, Lucky Strike, Nubian girls . . . It didn't matter. Cargo passed in and out through Western Harbour and the General's men took his ten per cent off the top of the lot. To simplify life, boat profiles were logged at Ras el Tin and somewhere in a subset of a subset of the Navy's housekeeping routines was a constantly updated record of how many runs each boat made.

It kept everybody honest.

'Want to tell me about that hardware in your skull?' She asked Raf.

'No,' he shook his head slowly. 'I don't think so.'

Some days he wasn't even sure the fox was real. Although the malfunctioning hardware was, obviously. And somewhere in the soft stuff he had filed away a perfect memory of promises from a genome sub-contractor in Baja California that went belly-up two years after he was born. Infrared sight, ultraviolet, seven colours, nictitating eyelids – the 8,000-line policy said plenty about effective night vision and very little about retinal intolerance to sunlight.

Originally humans possessed four colour-receptors, only they weren't human then, or even mammal. The fox had once explained it all, sounding almost proud. Most primates now had three receptors only, which was still a receptor up on the two that early mammals originally had, being nocturnal. Raf had a guaranteed four, with his fourth in ultra-violet. Something he had in common with starlings, chameleons and goldfish.

Later clauses dealt with extra ribs to protect soft organs and small muscles that let him close his ears. Only now probably wasn't a good time to mention that.

Idly, Raf kissed Zara's hair and smiled when she gently pushed him away . . . If she really wanted him to stop she'd say so. Her forehead tasted of salt and so did her bruised lips when she finally raised them, her mouth opening until he could taste the olives and alcohol on her breath.

'Wait,' she said.

When Zara had finished tucking in Hani, the thin sarong completely covered the sleeping child, resting lightly over Hani's face so that it quivered with each breath like the wing of a butterfly. 'That's better,' said Zara.

'Lights lowest,' she added and the cabin dimmed.

The next time they kissed it lasted until he moved Zara gently backwards and she winced. 'God, sorry.' Raf had seen the bruises again when Zara swam briefly, letting salt water sterilize the whip marks.

She shrugged. There had been worse. 'Guess what?' Zara said lightly. 'You're the oldest man I've dated.'

'I'm twenty-five!'

'You look older.'

'I don't feel it,' said Raf, 'except on the days I'm a thousand.'

She wore no bra that he could feel and, when his hand finally found them, her breasts beneath her shirt were fuller than he remembered, tipped with soft nipples that promptly puckered against the cloth.

Raf kissed her lips, as if kissing might take her attention off where his hand had strayed, and when her lips melted he risked smoothing his palm softly up over a hidden nipple, his touch feather-light.

'How long before we're back?'

Zara smiled. 'Not that long.'

He wasn't sure which question Zara thought she was answering; but reckoned this was the point where those *cultural differences* came in. Except her fingers were already undoing enough pearl buttons for him to slide back the sides of her shirt and reveal one full breast.

It tasted of the sea, so Raf's tongue traced the taste in a salt circle around her nipple, feeling her flesh pucker and harden, then turn soft as his tongue lapped wave-like over the top.

Zara shivered.

So Raf undid a few more buttons for himself, bringing up both hands to grip her newly freed breasts. His balls ached, his brain swam with alcohol, cheap drugs and cheaper memories but he knew that on this boat, with this person, he'd finally discovered where he belonged, where he always wanted to be.

'Let me try this,' said Zara and she shuffled him sideways, off the long seat until Raf was kneeling between her open knees with his hip pressed hard into her. Her knees locked and she wrapped both arms around Raf's hips to pull him tighter still. Her movements were deliberate, intense and shockingly private: as if, despite the fact Raf was kneeling in front of her, his hand gripping one breast, she was somewhere else, alone.

He couldn't see her in her eyes. And yet Zara wasn't totally in that urgent, rocking darkness between her knees. A darkness so intense he could taste a different salt rising to drug him. She was rocking, pushing herself forward and grinding hard against him. Each movement faster and harder than the one before. Breath hissed between her teeth like pain as she muttered something over and over. Some command or order that finally spilled her over the edge into a sudden gasp that she swallowed, muting it to a low moan that died as the rocking ceased and she pushed him away.

She was crying.

Chapter Forty-one

1st August

The Sunday-morning air held more smells than a spice market
– baking bread, an open drain, wood smoke from a *hamman*,
turmeric from a locked warehouse . . .

All the scents mixed in her nostrils as Zara ploughed her
way across the city, down starved alleys that turned right,
then left, then right again. She was walking the bottom of a
dark crevasse. Guided not by daylight, which was confined to
those brief patches of sky visible between roof edge and a forest
of satellite dishes or aerials, but by her inbuilt, almost perfect
sense of direction. Not to mention anger, barely restrained
irritation and killer PMS.

There were 150 districts in Iskandryia. Cities within the city,
villages within towns. Some were rich and some crowded, a
few almost deserted, backdrops to a play with no characters.
Rotting houses and crumbling souks emptied of the living by
the Influenza attack of '28. Her grandmother had died in the
epidemic and so had an aunt. That so few members of her
family had been taken, and those old and ill, was regarded by
her father as a kindness from God.

Other districts were too poor to have been mapped. They
went untaxed as well, because no one earned enough to make
taking direct taxes worth the trouble. Where that happened,
other groups levied tariffs instead, in the name of religion,
protection or some banned nationalist ideal kept alive by
crowded housing, open sewers, infrequent water and non-
existent medicare.

These groups paid protection in their turn. And those they
paid had their own dues to pay. And somewhere high above

them, like a hawk looking down disdainfully at vermin on the ground, hung the shadow of her father . . .

Ashraf Bey knew nothing of this city. He thought he did because he knew Place Zaghloul from Place Orabi and could walk from Le Trianon to Rue Cif without consulting a map or needing to stick to the grand boulevards. He believed Isk was a European city lodged on the edge of North Africa.

Anyone who knew anything knew that this was at least as untrue as it was correct. There *was* an elegant European city of red-brick apartment blocks, stuccoed villas and vast palazzos. But it made up only one layer and that was mostly confined to the sweep of the Corniche, the apartment blocks both sides of boulevards like Fuad Premier and an area around Shallat Gardens where irrigation kept manicured lawns preternaturally green.

The *real* El Iskandryia had more layers than baklava, more layers than time itself. There was the expatriate-Greek city, the city of visiting Cairene families who appeared at the start of summer and vanished just as promptly. And the city of Jewish shops and synagogues, of rich Germans and infinitely less rich Soviets. And below all that the invisible, the Arab city from which her father hoped to remove her and his family. . . Money could do that, if it was used well. Take you from *felaheen* to *effendi* in three generations.

The city moved across time as well as cultures. A single turn from one alley into another could throw you back a century, to spice markets and dark warehouses where herbs hung from wooden poles, drying in the hot breeze. Another turn, a different alley and the present receded further, as the scent of herbs changed to the rawness of uric acid, of dressed hides hanging in a tannery while raw skins were trampled underfoot in urine-filled vats by men with jellabas pulled up round their hips.

She loved El Iskandryia, its uncertainties and contradictions. Its outward self-assurance and inner darkness. It was the politics Zara didn't like. But then some things in life were beyond change: that was what her father said. She still hoped to prove him wrong.

Zara shook her head, still troubled. She believed Ashraf Bey when he said he'd been in prison rather than working at the Consulate; at least, she did most of the time. What she didn't believe was that the Emir wasn't his father. And she knew that was a double negative but didn't care. She needed to see her father and, since she couldn't go home, she was on her way to meet him at Hamzah Plaza, though he didn't yet know that.

Her hair was perfect. Her make up so immaculate that no bruises were visible. Even her lip looked normal.

Straightening her shoulders, Zara adjusted the lapels of a dark Dior suit she'd just carded at Marshall & Snellgrove – having woken a personal buyer to get the relevant boutique opened early – and stalked across the square towards a building she'd never before bothered to visit, her father's HQ.

The building she approached was black, with the pillars of white marble and a three-storey entrance carved from red sandstone and modelled on a horseshoe arch in M'dina. Her father was very proud of his building. The architectural critics had been less kind. *Ersatz Moorish* was one of their gentler comments.

What sounded like rain turned out to be an alabaster fountain set in the middle of a sunken garden. A thing of elegant lines and stunning simplicity, the fountain had been carved a millennium before for one of the princelings of Granada. Her father had never mentioned its purchase, far less what it might have cost.

Zara swept past the fountain and in through a revolving door that began to spin just before she reached it. Ahead of her waited a bank of elevators with glistening mahogany surrounds and brass doors polished to a shine. Any one of them would take her up to the top floor.

'Miss . . .' A rapidly approaching security guard almost but not quite raised his voice as he glided across the foyer, intent on stopping her reaching the lifts. In his face politeness battled with exasperation. Politeness won. His eyes had already priced her suit and noted her air of confidence but he allowed himself a second glance as he got closer, to confirm what he already suspected . . . He didn't recognize her.

Zara stopped.

'Visitors have to sign in.' He motioned towards a distant reception area where a young woman stood watching them. 'You do have an appointment?'

'No,' said Zara, 'I haven't. But my father will see me.'

She punched the button on a lift and watched the doors slide open, almost silently. The security guard was still looking suitably appalled when she stepped inside. He probably had a kid, Zara reminded herself, plus a wife who was bound to be pregnant, a mortgage . . . He needed the job she was busy losing him.

'Ring my father,' said Zara. 'Tell him I'm on my way up. Say you couldn't stop me.'

The man nodded and stood back, instantly relieved. He'd remember her kindness and not the arrogance that had let her walk through him, Zara knew that. And he wouldn't realize what he'd just told her – that her father was already in . . .

Which meant he'd had an argument with her mother. Zara smiled. Her father only ever came in early on days following an argument. Some weeks he forgot about going to the office at all. Why should he, when anyone he needed to see could be ordered to come to him? His office on the top floor existed mainly to remind people who was in charge.

Hamzah didn't do lunch with visiting foreigners – he had staff to do that for him – and he didn't take taxis or even use his chauffeured stretch much. He walked, because money bought time and that created space for him to walk if he wanted to, which he invariably did. More people saw him that way. Remembered he'd begun as one of their own.

She loved him, of course. Feared him, too. More than she feared her mother, if she was honest. Checking her hair in a mirror, Zara brushed one sleeve to remove dust from where she had touched an alley wall and stepped out, head high, when the lift reached its destination and the doors opened. She expected to see her father waiting at the top but he wasn't.

Instead she got a small woman with tightly cropped grey hair and large amber beads.

'Miss Zara?'

'Olga Kaminsky?'

The woman's eyes widened and Zara smiled her best smile. 'My father mentions you,' she said lightly. 'Always compliments.' Zara could almost see the woman reassess her, as she took in Zara's suit, her immaculate hair, the discreet and appropriate jewellery and the folded newspaper tucked under one arm. She didn't look like a spoilt brat who got herself on the news for being in trouble with the *morales*. Which was precisely the point.

'I'm sorry to turn up unannounced, but I was hoping to see my father.'

Olga Kaminsky nodded. 'He's expecting you.'

The door to her father's office was ebony carved into arabesques and inlaid with leaves of pink or pale blue marble. Olga knocked once and went in without waiting to be invited.

'Miss Zara,' she announced, stopping in front of a huge desk.

Duty done, Olga Kaminsky turned to Zara and smiled. 'How about some coffee? And maybe a croissant . . . ?'

'Well,' said Hamzah as the door shut. 'Coffee *and* croissant – and I'd always been under the impression that Olga didn't approve of you.'

'How could she not approve?' Zara said. 'She hadn't even met me . . .'

Hamzah laughed. Neither of them mentioned the fact that Zara hadn't been home for thirty-six hours. Or why. All the same, he saw how carefully his daughter carried herself as she sat back in a large leather chair without being invited.

'Nice place.'

His office was everything Zara expected. Huge, with windows along two walls, the longest looking north over the Corniche and a blue splash of the Mediterranean beyond. The other looked out over the red-brick edifice of St Mark's College, where Hamzah had swept floors when he first arrived in Iskandryia.

A mountain of printouts balanced on one of the leather chairs, while an old Toshiba notepad sat open on the sofa. On the wall behind his desk an out-dated assault rifle balanced on two nails. It was old, rusty, stamped out from cheap, sheet steel. A Kalashnikov AK49. Like the fountain outside the office, Zara had never seen it before.

The whole room was a mess, which didn't surprise her. His study at Glymenapoulo was the only room her mother wasn't allowed to have cleaned. Here, he didn't even have someone to nag him about the mess – unless that was Olga's job.

'Coffee . . .' The door opened ahead of the knock and his PA walked in holding a tray. 'Your Excellency . . .' Olga served Hamzah his tiny cup of Turkish coffee and beside it she put a plate of rosewater Turkish Delight, studded with almonds. 'And here's yours,' said Olga. Zara got a long cappuccino and a croissant, along with a linen napkin.

As the woman turned to go, Zara realized her father was blushing. For a horrified second she considered that there might be something between Olga and him and then realized that it was the honorific. He'd wanted *Your Excellency* so badly and now it made him blush. Zara smiled. Her father would get used to *effendi*, just as he'd got used to living in a villa surrounded by European antiques. And once he was used to it he'd start to enjoy it. That was his way.

'I suppose you've come to tell me you're not coming home?'

'No,' said Zara. 'I've come to ask for your help . . . But you're right,' she added, recognizing the truth in what he said. 'I'm not.'

'Do you want to return to your friends in America?'

'No.' Zara shook her head. 'I'm not going to run away. Not even if that's what you want . . . This is my city too.'

Hamzah's nod was approving. 'It's not easy, an unmarried woman living alone. You'll need an apartment, a driver. I can supply those.'

'Let's talk about that later,' said Zara, in a voice Hamzah knew meant she would do anything but. 'Right now I want to talk about Ashraf Bey.'

Hamzah thought about mentioning his daughter's face had suddenly gone red and decided against it. The picture of her on the news in that idiotic coat was too clear in his head. Instead, he glanced out of a window, then reached for his cup. The coffee was too hot but he drank it anyway, chasing away its mudlike bitterness with a piece of Turkish delight. 'Eat your croissant,' he said, 'or Olga will be upset . . .'

They were negotiating, silently and without words: he knew that. Even in El Iskandryia the gap between what could and what couldn't be said was vast, and Isk was the most relaxed of the Ottoman cities. A free port and a micro-state. The personal fief of its owner the Khedive – unlike Cairo, which the Khedive held in trust for the Sultan in Stambul.

But freedom was relative. And the gap between father and daughter still wide. In many families it was unbridgeable. The woman he sat opposite knew less about him than he actually knew about her, which was almost nothing.

He feared she'd taken at least one lover while in New York. But the only real thing he knew about her was what she'd told him the night before she flew, when they were talking obliquely about the three months she'd just spent in a Swiss clinic. Which was that she wasn't proud of everything she'd done, but she was ashamed of very little.

'I can give him money,' Hamzah said simply. 'A route out of Iskandryia if that will help. But I can't protect him . . .' He wanted to say more, to ask obvious questions, but for Zara the only question that mattered was the one she asked.

'Why do the police insist he killed his aunt?'

'Maybe he did,' said Hamzah, chewing the edges off a cube of Turkish Delight. He smiled sadly when Zara handed him her napkin. 'Have you thought of that?'

'He swears he didn't.'

'And you believe him?'

Zara bit her lip and nodded, not trusting herself to speak – which her father found more worrying than anything else.

'Olga.' He punched a button on his desk. 'Tell legal to call me.' Seconds later a screen beeped and the face of a small bald man squinted out at Hamzah. 'Excellency?' The voice was reedy, the accent cut-glass Cairene.

'Beys,' said Hamzah. 'They have complete *carte blanche*. I'm right, aren't I . . . they can't be arrested?'

The elderly lawyer hesitated. 'Up to a point, Excellency . . .'

A small smile lit Hamzah's face and he jerked his chin towards the screen to indicate to Zara that she should listen carefully. 'What are the exceptions?'

'Two types of murder – of a mullah or a family member – gross blasphemy before two reputable witnesses, and gross outrage of a minor, witnesses ditto.'

'So Ashraf al-Mansur can be arrested?'

'Given that he murdered his aunt, yes . . .'

Hamzah held up his hand to still Zara's protest and she suddenly realized she was out of the screen's line of sight. The lawyer couldn't see her and so didn't know she was there.

'Thank you.' Hamzah blanked the screen. 'My first question,' he said to Zara, 'is why do they *really* want Ashraf al-Mansur? And my second is, who exactly is *they* . . . any ideas?'

He sat back in his chair. 'No? Then I suggest you find out or I suggest your friend does . . .'

The meeting was over, Zara realized. And what was more staggering than her father treating her as an adult was him treating her as an equal. She'd asked him a question and he'd given her two relevant questions in reply. Either one of which might be the key. Going to America had been a good move, whatever work friends might say. And returning had been the right move too, whatever Zara might sometimes think herself.

'What do I tell your mother about why you're not coming home?' Hamzah's voice was neutral. But his eyes widened as Zara pulled off her silk scarf, to reveal that she wore no shirt beneath her Dior jacket, and began to undo her jacket's black glass buttons. At the last minute, she turned her back on her father and slid the silk jacket down over her shoulders, revealing the marks.

'Tell her what you like.'

Ten minutes after Zara left her father's office and headed on foot towards the General's mansion, Hani crawled out of her bed, looked round and went to shake Raf. 'Zara's gone,' she said.

'Has she?' Raf sat up, groaned and slid his legs over the edge of the couch. He did his best to sound unconcerned but he needn't have bothered. Hani was too busy pointing at his feet.

'You're wearing shoes,' she said.

Yeah, he was. Both of them fully dressed was one of Zara's conditions for sharing the VSV's narrow bed, though even being dressed wouldn't make a difference if Hani told someone he and Zara had shared a mattress. Zara was under twenty-one and behaviour likely to corrupt a minor would be the least of it.

'After I went to sleep,' asked Hani, 'did you argue?'

'No,' said Raf, 'we talked.' *And got nowhere*, he added silently. At least he didn't think they'd got anywhere. It was hard to remember with his mind full of Zara's breasts and the taste of her in his mouth. Maybe she'd believed Nafisa's death really wasn't his responsibility. Maybe not. He'd try to work it out when his hangover took a holiday.

Where Zara had gone was solved by a brisk call from Hamzah. 'Zara dropped by,' he said, sounding amused. 'She said I should give you this.' Hamzah reeled off a string of numbers that became letters towards the end. 'Your aunt's bank details,' he added, seeing the blank look on Raf's face, 'From when I paid Nafisa's commission . . .'

'Where's Zara now?'

'I don't know,' said Hamzah, 'not officially. But unofficially I gather she's headed in the direction of Shallalat Gardens and the General's house.' He clicked his fingers and the screen went blank.

Raf groaned. 'Coffee,' he begged Hani.

'Tastes horrible,' she replied. But she went hunting all the same until she found tins of cappuccino stacked in a locker at the stern. Peeling back the lid on a tin, Hani took a mouthful and spat it at her feet. 'If that's what you want.' With a shrug and a sigh, she tipped the remains of the can into a saucepan and lit a small ring in the pull-down galley. When the sweet liquid was hot she poured it carefully back into the can.

'Here,' she said.

Raf drank it while she watched, her eyes alert for any hesitation. 'Perfect . . .' He sat back and put his hand behind his aching head, thinking about his aunt's bank details. 'You had a computer at the madersa, didn't you?'

'LuxorEON,' she said. 'Broadband access, running Linux.' Her voice was a dry imitation of Nafisa's at its most patronizing. Then she shrugged, bony shoulders hunching beneath her tee-shirt. 'Why?' Hani asked. 'What do you need . . . ?'

Numbers rolled up the screen so fast they made Raf feel even more hungover than he already was. These were dead accounts at Banque de Lesseps. And he had Lady Nafisa's account details scrawled on a scrap of paper but Hani wasn't interested in that. The numbers on the VSV's screen were scrambled and she had an animated on-screen helper doing something with algorithms at lightning speed as she searched for Lady Nafisa's old account.

The computer aboard the VSV was an old stand-alone, the kind that used a satellite modem and made up in sheer memory what it lacked in speed or connectivity. It had taken Hani all of two minutes to junk every default setting and come up with a configuration she actually liked. But then, as she pointed out with a surprising lack of bitterness, if you've spent nine years trapped in the same house with only a computer for company, you get good at it or you get bored.

'That one,' said Hani as a 28-digit number lit red and the screen froze. Everything else on the screen disappeared and the number shuffled itself until Hani was left with the same 8-digit/3-letter sequence Raf had scrawled in front of him. She made a couple of passes with the cursor, her thumb moving lazily over a trackball, and the number disappeared. 'Don't worry,' she told Raf, just as he started to do exactly that. 'It's checking we're legal.'

She smiled and Raf tried to smile back. He'd no idea what Hani had just done.

'Here we go,' said the child as a bank logo began to animate on screen and the account went live again. There was quiet pride in her voice and an air of competence about her that would have looked impressive on someone three times her age.

'You're good.'

Hani nodded, taking Raf's compliment as a statement of fact. Fingers dancing and thumb rolling her trackball, Hani opened and shut screens at the speed of thought, collecting passwords and opening and closing trapdoors. She rode a rhythm that drummed inside her own head until her fingers suddenly faltered and Raf could almost feel the child's confidence vanish. When Raf looked round, a photograph of Lady Nafisa stared at him from the screen, arrogant and imperious.

'I'm going to use the—'

Hani slipped out of her seat before Raf could say anything and so he sat there, trying not to listen to the child throw up her breakfast. The water in the heads ran, then ran again and she came out wiping her mouth. Neither of them said anything but the first thing Hani did when she climbed back into her seat was to make Lady Nafisa disappear.

'She said she was living on her savings,' Hani said, nodding at a seemingly endless list of red figures. 'She always did lie.'

Nothing in Nafisa's accounts made obvious sense, but Raf expected that. And he was beginning to see the pattern. His sense of self might be fucked, but he could knit connections from nothing and call it logic. Just as the madersa had rich public rooms and the private rooms had been bare even of furniture, so ran Nafisa's accounts. Money had been spent lavishly on clothes but almost nothing on food. No payments at all for Khartoum or Donna. Very little on electricity, none on Hani's broadband connection, which meant it was either illegal or someone else was footing the bill.

So far, so predictable.

The surprise was in the brackets that ran like a sour river along the bottom line. Picking 1 January as a date and flicking back year on year showed that her account had been overdrawn for at least ten years, which was as far back as Raf bothered to check. Not huge amounts in someone like Hu San's terms, but getting larger and literally in the red. Until this April.

'Shit.' Raf was talking to himself but Hani squinted at the screen as he highlighted a figure. Hamzah had lied. She hadn't taken him for $2,500,000: her commission had been double that. $5,000,000 from Banque Leventine in Cyprus. Straight in and straight out again, almost immediately, only this time in two amounts. $4,500,000 to an account in El Iskandryia and $500,000 to Havana.

'Let me . . .' Small fingers flicked over the keyboard, numbers resolving. The name that came up meant nothing to Raf.

Caja de Cuba.

'Want me to chase it?' Hani's voice was neutral.

'If you can.' Raf had no intention of asking when she'd learned to crack files – or how. He was far too worried she might stop.

'Okay.' And with that Hani squared up to the screen, smiled slightly and let her fingers loose, chasing one link after another, running searches and routines she seemed to pull out of the air. Beside her sat the rag dog, a mechanical *whirr* coming from its guts like a low growl.

'What . . .'

'Back up,' said Hani. 'The screen talks to him and Ali-Din remembers.' She sucked at her teeth to signal that Raf shouldn't ask any more questions and went back to work.

'Got it,' Hani said finally. 'Started here/ended Seattle. You want to know everywhere the $500,000 went in between?'

Raf didn't, so Hani cross-referenced the new account number to a customer bank database, which took almost no time at all because – unlike with Banque de Lesseps – the data at the Seattle end wasn't double-encrypted. This time the name meant something. Clem Burke, lately of Hunstville, registered as sole owner of Seattle's newest detective agency.

'Now the next one,' Raf told Hani. But she was already on it, leaning in close as if trying to crawl right inside the screen.

Raf was forgotten, he realized. The world outside did not exist. There was a hunger to the child's face, a intensity that reflected pure concentration. Her brows were knit, her lips clamped tight. This was the other thing in her life over which she'd had control. What she ate and what she did on screen were ring-fenced for her alone. A thin slice of a life that everybody else was parcelling up and deciding for her own good.

Ali-Din was a side issue.

'Got it,' said Hani. Numbers resolved as the screen on the VSV talked via uplink to a datacore at Banque de Lesseps and data fed back, anonymous and cold, nothing but presence and absence of electrical charge until on the other side of the screen to Hani an electron beam rastered down the glass and Hani swore.

H.E. Saeed Koenig Pasha. The General's own personal bank account. Shit indeed. Fear played inside Raf's head like a whistle off the walls of an empty courtyard, heard every day without really hearing, until one stumbled over oneself, sat cross-legged in the dust. Hani broke the connection without being asked.

Next they looked at payments that had come in. And the first and most obvious point was that until the $5,000,000 from Hamzah there had been nothing for at least nine months. Before that, going back five or six years, there had been regular payments, spaced maybe four or five months apart, starting big and getting less and less.

To Raf it looked like someone selling off the family silver and waking up one morning to find it was all gone. Maybe her outgoings would be more use.

'Try that,' he suggested, pointing to a small, fairly regular debit in Nafisa's account. The last time it had been paid was the day he'd arrived in Iskandryia.

Hani went back to her screen.

Chapter Forty-two

1st August

'You must be Zara bint-Hamzah,' said the boy who opened the door to her. Before she could ask how he knew, the boy had stepped back and was ushering her through the front door of the General's palatial mansion on Rue Riyad Pasha.

He was about her age, maybe slightly younger, dressed in a simple shirt and tan chinos. A faint – a very faint – beard could just be discerned on his face.

'This is where I ask you if you have an appointment to see the General and you say no, but it's very important . . .'

Zara nodded.

'A pity. You see, the General never receives anyone without an appointment. It's a matter of principle . . .'

'I thought anyone could petition the General?' Zara said. She didn't mean to sound as upset by his news as she did.

'Of course,' said the boy with a smile. 'Anyone can. Just write a note and leave it. In five weeks' time, when the secretariat have worked their way down the pile, someone will read your note and, if necessary, bring it to his attention.'

'What counts as "necessary"?' Zara asked.

'A threat to his life. A threat to the life of the khedive. News of an uprising . . . We got a lot of those.' He ushered her though another door into what looked like a dining room, then another, this time into a small study. On the wall was an oil painting of the old khedive and a smaller – if only slightly – portrait of the General wearing full uniform, with a curved sword hanging from his belt. The sword in question stood in the corner of the room, balanced upright like an old umbrella.

'Better not stay here too long,' said the boy. 'He doesn't really like people in his office.' From the top drawer of an ornate desk, he selected a key and used it to open French windows that led out to a garden.

'Come on,' he said, then paused. 'Have you been here before?'

Zara just looked at him until he shrugged.

'I'll take that as a *No*.'

Tall cedars rose from a lawn that was emerald green. The kind of lawn that old people talked about when they mentioned the mansions that used to line Mahmoudiya Canal, even though they'd never seen the lawns themselves and had only heard of them from their grandparents.

'Underground irrigation,' said the boy. Beds full of red and blue flowers that Zara had never seen before lined the path the boy chose. 'Come on,' he said, so Zara followed. Until he stopped at a metal bench set in the shade of a bush topiaried into the shape of a perfectly crenellated wall, and indicated that Zara should sit.

'No,' she shook her head. 'Not here.' A quick, almost embarrassed flick of one hand indicated him, then herself, the bench and its obvious seclusion. 'How can I?'

The boy looked surprised, but not irritated. 'We can walk,' he said simply and so they did: down another path until they reached a small lake with a fountain. Three stone women wearing very little stood, facing out, with their backs to each other. One of them held an apple and the other two, who were without the first's discreet stone drapery, used their hands to hide stone pudenda.

'Nakedness is not always a sin,' said the boy lightly. Then he smiled and shrugged, before adding, 'But, of course, that sentiment is probably heretical . . .'

He led her round the fountain and then down another path that doubled back inside the vee of greenery that the General had carved for himself out of a section of public gardens.

'So tell me,' said the boy. 'What is so important that you need to see the General?'

'I'd prefer to tell him . . .'

'No,' he said seriously. 'You misunderstand. The General is

unable to see you, so I am seeing you instead. Now, what did you want to say?'

Haltingly, occasionally exasperated with herself, Zara began to tell him about Ashraf. Not everything, because she didn't mention his time in prison or Raf's belief that he wasn't really a bey. But she told the boy about Felix, about how Ashraf swore that his aunt's death was neither suicide nor his doing. Zara talked about how he'd cleaned up the house and asked her father to get rid of the office where his aunt had been killed so as not to upset Hani. And she spoke of Hani and how the child was afraid to leave Ashraf's side . . .

Halfway through, the boy insisted they find a bench and walked away without waiting to see if Zara followed, though the bench he found her was out in the open, unscreened by hedges and in full view of the house. 'This man,' said the boy, when Zara finally finished. 'You know where he is hiding?'

The boy sighed at her silence, then shrugged.

'You don't know, and if you did, you wouldn't tell me?'

'Right.'

'Wrong. You do know and you still won't tell me . . .' He looked at Zara, his gaze steady. 'I guess that makes it love.'

After he'd listened to all the reasons why he was wrong, they changed the subject and Zara sat down again. 'America,' said the boy. 'You've been there. What's it like?'

'New York,' she corrected, and then she explained in detail why the two were completely different. How New York was really a part of Europe that Europe had mislaid. Explaining this took more time than she intended.

At the front door, as he was showing her out, Zara paused. 'You *will* tell the General what I said about Ashraf being innocent . . . ?'

'Of course.'

'And there's no chance of my seeing the General himself?'

The boy sighed. 'What do you want with Koenig Pasha,' he asked, sounding slightly wistful, 'when you've already seen the khedive?' And he shut the door, politely but firmly in Zara's face.

Chapter Forty-three

1st August

'Ashraf Bey,' said Raf into a brass grille set in a white pillar on one side of a large metal gate. Above the grille a discreet *se vende* sign from an exclusive realty agent in Rue de L'Église Copte had a simple strip neatly glue-gunned across the top. When Raf put his hand up to check the *sold* sign, he discovered the glue was still sticky.

There would be a small CCTV watching his every move. Up in a tree, probably, though he hadn't been able to spot it. Unless, of course, the Minister linked direct to a spysat, which was possible. At least ten private houses in Iskandryia were meant to be protected that way.

That it was only ten said something . . . On the Upper East Side whole blocks relied on nothing but spysats and a direct line to one of the top-end private police units. His mother had given him the details in one of her last e-mails, he forgot how many years before. She might have written a few more times, of course. Raf didn't know, he hadn't bothered to check that account much.

Static cracked from the speaker grille. 'Ashraf Bey,' said Raf for the third time. So far no one had showed much interest in letting him in. He could scale the gate, no problem. Even the spikes along the top wouldn't give him trouble unless he actually managed to fall on one. Weather, old age and too many coats of paint had made them blunt, almost rounded.

'The Minister isn't here.'

'I know that,' Raf said. 'I want to talk to Lady Jalila.'

There was another burst of static and then silence.

'The question,' said a different voice when it came, 'is

whether Lady Jalila wants to see *you* . . .' The words were cool, ironic.

'I don't know,' said Raf. 'Do you?'

The click of a bolt recessing was his answer, though no one appeared to show him the way and the mastiff that lolloped across a gravel path towards him seemed not to have been told he was allowed to enter.

'Heel.' Letting his hand brush the mastiff's head, Raf kept walking and heard rather than saw the animal fall into step beside him. No fear, at least not of animals. Let Lady Jalila make of that what she liked.

The house was old made modern. Once-stuccoed walls stripped back to stone and a roof retiled in pale grey slate. Old-fashioned windows had been sandblasted back to bare metal frames, glazed with smoked glass and covered with wrought-iron bars that were ornate and obviously handmade to order, but were bars all the same.

The front door was heavy and studded, pale oak polished to a shine. This could be her taste, or maybe not. It seemed a little too self-consciously modern and American for the Minister but perhaps Raf had misunderstood him.

'Your Excellency is most welcome.' It was obvious from the quiver in the maid's voice that he was anything but . . .

'I don't bite,' Raf told her, 'whatever you've read in the papers.' He waited for the French girl to stand aside and when she didn't he pushed gently past, eyes instantly adjusting to the darkness. The decor within was as ruthlessly modern as without. Black floors, glass walls, the only nod to classical taste being two large abstracts, one each side of the hall, on walls that were otherwise bare.

'Rothko,' said Lady Jalila. 'Mid-period. Not his best work but that's all locked up in museums.' She had a glass of clear liquid in one unsteady hand and a tiny pearl-handled revolver in the other.

'Medicinal,' Lady Jalila said, holding the glass up to the light. 'You can ask my doctor.'

'And the gun?'

'Safety, darling. You're a dangerous killer – or don't you catch the news . . . ?'

'I've been busy . . .'

'Tell me about it. Apparently that little girl you almost married now thinks you're innocent . . .' Lady Jalila lowered the revolver and took a gulp from her glass. When she surfaced the glass was empty and even at a distance Raf could smell the gin on her breath. 'But we both know different, don't we?'

The only thing Raf knew was that she was drunk and armed. And if anyone had come up with a more lethal combination than alcohol and a gun then Raf had gone through remand with his eyes closed. 'Look,' said Raf, 'I need to ask you some questions about my aunt.'

'About Nafisa?'

'That and a few other things . . .'

Lady Jalila laughed. 'Oh,' she said as she gently touched the barrel of her gun to Raf's cheek, 'I can talk about *things* for ages. You'd better come up.' She turned towards a rise of open steps, only to turn back. 'Take the afternoon off,' she told her maid . . .

'In here.' Lady Jalila threw open an upstairs door and Raf found himself in a drawing room with a white suede sofa, a long onyx table and floorboards of stripped cedar. Another, much smaller painting decorated one wall. A simple slash of red above a slash of dark blue, the paint thin, uneven and not quite covering the canvas.

'Unique,' she said heavily. 'Worth more than both of the ones in the hall. He didn't see it, of course. Thought it should be cheaper because it was smaller.'

He was the Minister, Raf decided, not Rothko.

Lady Jalila sighed. 'You have no idea how tiresome life can be . . .'

Raf looked round at the tiny but priceless Persian rug hung in one corner, the impossibly rich Moroccan burgundy of a leather beanbag big enough for a giant. At the single sprig of flowers in a Venetian vase filling the whole room with a perfume headier than incense.

'No,' he said. 'Probably not.'

Lady Jalila poured him a gin and tonic, dribbling Bombay Saphire over three lumps of ice and adding not enough tonic. A dash of bitters from an unmarked bottle finished the preparation. There was a fresh lime cut into slices on a saucer at the side but she didn't bother to add it to his drink or hers. 'I'd ask you to make them,' she told him, 'but you'd probably only get it wrong. Men do.'

Lowering herself carefully onto the suede sofa, Lady Jalila crossed one leg over the other. She wore a tight blue jacket and matching skirt, which rode up enough at the side to show a long expanse of nylon from knee to hip.

'Well, do you like it?'

Raf dragged his eyes away from her.

'What do you think?' Casually, Lady Jalila uncrossed her legs and leant back, head turned towards the tiny Rothko. Her knees parted. Only slightly, but enough for Raf to see clearly the white thong beneath her tights.

'Interesting,' said Raf.

'Mmmm,' Lady Jalila smiled slightly. 'Public exhibitions bore me, but there's always something about private views . . .' She shifted lower in her seat, arms coming round to hug herself until her full breasts were pushed together and outwards.

Raf wanted to keep talking, to keep up the pretence that this was just a conversation but proper words wouldn't come so he just nodded sagely. And all the while, Lady Jalila squeezed at her breasts and squirmed forward on the sofa until both gusset and thong edged up between swollen folds of flesh.

'The Rothko,' asked Raf shakily. 'When did you buy it?' But Lady Jalila wasn't listening. He could see her nipples hard beneath her jacket and each time she hugged herself they scraped against cloth, making her hiss between open lips.

Her foot rubbed his ankle and before Raf could protest her heel had climbed the side of his leg and rested on his groin, grinding down against him. He could have touched the dampness between her legs just by reaching forward. But all he did was watch as she shifted on her seat until the thong stretched so tight it vanished altogether. She was gasping, breathing through her mouth as she stared blindly at a ceiling fan. Lost to the gin and to what was going on between her legs and inside her mind.

She came silently, biting down on a cry as she jacked forwards and then sprawled back, knees wide and arms still clutched across her front.

A lavatory flushed and water ran. A hammering in the pipes went on for too long for it to be a basin being run. Which meant Lady Jalila was taking a bath or shower. For a moment, Raf wondered if he was meant to have joined her under the water, but decided that was unlikely. Most probably she'd forgotten he was even there. She'd certainly forgotten her revolver which rested on the white sofa next to a sweat patch in the shape of Lady Jalila's buttocks. Just as she'd forgotten the handbag beside her discarded shoes on the floor.

Driving licence, snakeskin wallet with mid-denomination notes and three credit cards. Gold but not platinum. So either they weren't as rich as she pretended or else the Minister was less lavish with his bounty than Raf had imagined from seeing them together. There was make-up – Chanel and Dior, predictably enough. A packet of sterile tissues, a packet of Durex Vapour with one condom missing and a half-empty plastic tube of breath mints.

Raf made a note of Jalila's credit-card numbers, wondering as he did so whether Hani would be able to do her magic with them. He looked inside the wallet for a photograph of the Minister, but she carried nothing sentimental except a small colour shot of herself standing on the Corniche. She was a teenager and the smiling woman behind her looked familiar. It was only after Raf had slipped the picture back into Lady Jalila's wallet that he realized the woman was Lady Nafisa, looking younger, happier and almost coy.

Putting aside the wallet, Raf sorted quickly through the remaining objects. A Lotus organizer, a penknife with a mother-of-pearl handle, a pepper spray and a little suede case for holding business cards. Inside were three cards of her own – *Lady Jalila, deputy head, Cross & Crescent* – an official laminate for entering the Precinct, one of the Minister's own cards, tattered at the corners, and an even more tattered card belonging to Felix.

And then Raf got the information he'd come for, without even having to ask. The last card in the holder advertised an alternative-heath clinic and five dates were scrawled on the back, four of them crossed through, with one due the following week.

Raf slid the card into his pocket, just managing to scoop the rest of the contents back into Lady Jalila's bag and get the bag back on the floor before the door opened.

'How thoughtless,' Lady Jalila said. 'Anna's forgotten to bring you coffee.'

'You told her to take the afternoon off,' said Raf.

'Did I?' Lady Jalila sounded puzzled. She wore black slacks and a white sweat shirt that might have suited a teenager if they were drunk, over-developed and vacant. 'How odd . . . So what was it you wanted to ask me about Nafisa?'

There were a dozen places he could start. Beginning with the fact that his aunt had apparently been refilling her personal account with money from a charity of which the woman opposite was now acting head.

The first sum taken had been repaid in full, with interest. The second sum had just been repaid. Half of the next sum was still outstanding and Raf doubted that even Nafisa had been able to convice herself that the following sums were loans only . . .

'Well?' Jalila asked. 'What was your question?'

No one Raf recognized stared out of her eyes. The wanton who'd sat opposite him with open knees had gone to be replaced by a prim but slightly swaying woman who smelled of soap, mouthwash and toothpaste.

'Probably not worth troubling you,' said Raf. 'But I'm just tying up odds and ends and I wondered if you knew of a Madame Sosostris?'

'No. I'm sorry.' Lady Jalila shook her head, her blonde curls still damp but already falling perfectly around a face innocent as an angel's. 'That rings no bells at all.'

Raf shrugged. 'Worth a try,' he said. Then he told her he knew exactly who had killed his aunt and asked her to fix him a meeting with her husband. Somewhere neutral. When he let himself out, she was still reciting digits to her wall phone.

Chapter Forty-four

1st August

'I'm armed,' said Hani. 'And I'll fire.'

In trembling hands, the child held a vast pistol with rubber handle and fat red barrel. The kind used to launch distress flares. Pulling the trigger would be enough to toss her backwards across the cabin, if not break both wrists. That it would leave a large hole in whoever was on the other side of the door was a given.

The door to the VSV stopped opening.

'Hani,' said Zara, her shock at meeting the khedive suddenly forgotten. 'It's me . . .'

The door started opening again and Zara put her head through the gap, her glance taking in the flare pistol and the tears streaming down Hani's face. 'Hani, put that down, okay?'

The child shook her head. 'Step inside, slowly.' It sounded like something Hani had heard while playing *Killer Kop IV*.

Zara stepped forward, her hands held up where Hani could see them.

'Right inside,' said Hani. 'Then shut the door.' She was watching not the woman who'd just entered but the space behind her.

'You're alone.' Hani's words were pitched somewhere between statement and question. Only Zara didn't need to reply because Hani was her own answer. Slumping to the floor, Hani pulled her knees up under her chin and wrapped her arms tight round them, the flare gun still held in one hand.

Whatever the fear was, it had the child rocking backwards and forwards, eyes screwed shut.

'Honey.' Zara kneeled in front of the girl. 'What's wrong?'

One eye opened. 'It's been h-h-hours,' Hani said furiously. 'I thought you were d-dead.' She stopped rocking and somehow her absolute stillness was almost worse. 'Lady Jalila called me . . .'

'Here?'

'Called Ali-Din.' She nodded to the rag dog thrown in one corner. 'The Germans are coming to kill me. You're to take me straight to her house . . .'

Which Germans . . . ?

'No one's trying to kill you,' Zara said firmly. 'She's got it wrong.'

The flare gun wasn't even loaded, Zara discovered when she finally worked out how to flip down its barrel. The sobbing child had discovered the device in a watertight cupboard set into a bulkhead. What she hadn't found were any flares. But then, maybe there weren't any, because Zara couldn't find them either.

'We'd better leave,' announced Zara, after she'd wiped the pistol with a rag and put it back in the cupboard, pushing the door so that it popped shut. Quite where they were going was another matter. She only knew it wasn't anywhere near Lady Jalila's house.

Chapter Forty-five

1st August

No signal. No up-link. Nothing.

Raf should have started getting worried when he noticed his Omega had stopped receiving, he realized afterwards. But at the time he figured it was just the usual crap connection.

So he kept heading north towards the address on the card he carried deep in his pocket, cutting through an area north-west of Place Orabi where child brothels used to be, back in the days Constantine Cavafy wrote his poems and Isk was where every would-be aesthete from New York, Berlin and London gathered to savour the exotic. Which usually translated into a taste for young Arab boys, rot-gut arak and opium.

Now the district was filled with hip boutiques, where the swipe of a credit card and the purchase tax-free of this season's Nikes gave jet-trash travellers a similar, more legal thrill.

Half hoping to get a working connection, Raf made his way up a side street towards the Corniche, passing an ancient mosque and a school, coming out at the fish market where picturesque boats were moored off shore to bobbing floats of blown glass. His phone functioned no better there than it had before.

The boats were mostly clinker-built and wooden, brightly coated in blood reds and deep blues, with painted eyes that stared forward. It didn't matter that some had satellite navigation and a few used echo-location to hunt bonito and shark: every family knew that the boats needed to be able to see their way home when the fishing was done.

It made sense to Raf who, by then, was standing with his back to the market, glancing between the card in his hand and a bank of buzzers on a wall. What was Tiriganaq if not his version of those eyes?

No one had answered when he pressed the right button, so he punched five or six wrong ones at random, ignoring the increasingly irritated voices demanding to know what he wanted until eventually someone hit enter, just as Raf knew they would, because someone always did.

He took the back stairs up to the fourth floor because, once again, most people always used the lift. Then he took the lift down a flight to the third floor and knocked on an unmarked cream door.

When no one answered that either, Raf whipped a new screwdriver out of its packaging and positioned it over the point where a strip of wooden frame obscured a Yale lock. One hit with the heel of his hand and the lock was sprung. Which told him two things. Not everything taught at Remand University was bullshit, and Madame Sosostris was nearby. Out for a coffee, maybe, or collecting laundry – whatever . . . People gone for longer usually remembered to double-lock their front doors.

A quick glance inside revealed a reception room that could have been for a brothel, a therapist or a chiropractor's. Copies of glossy magazines, a handful of leaflets, mainly about acupuncture. A blank screen on one wall, two crystals dangling on thongs from its bottom corners. Wicker armchairs that looked newish but were already well used.

Then a treatment room, which looked like a coprophiliac's paradise. Raf headed for a filing cabinet, ignoring the four polythene barrels atop metal scaffolding, with gravity tubes that fed down to end in surgical-steel twist joints, just as he ignored a kidney dish – next to a couch – that held various sizes of chrome speculums, each one double-tubed so water could feed one way and bodily waste the other. He needed more proof than a business card that Lady Jalila had been lying.

Raf found what he wanted in a bottom drawer, marked *dead accounts*; though he didn't think that was meant to be a joke, sardonic or otherwise. Lady Nafisa had been a client for ten years and there was a long and obsessively regular list of appointments to prove it, written by the same hand using a wide variety of different pens. There was a pattern, Raf realized, and an easy one to break. The pen used to record payment was inevitably the same pen used to make a note in the diary of the next appointment.

But the note declaring the file dead and the line scrawled through Nafisa's records were in the same ink as the last record of payment, dated the morning she died. Madame Sosostris had known Nafisa wouldn't be coming back.

And Raf didn't know if it really surprised him or not, but the person who'd originally introduced his aunt to the clinic was the person who said she'd never even heard of Madame Sosostris.

So all he needed to find was—

'Looking for something?'

The question came from behind him and the voice was confident. Which was probably reasonable, given the automatic in the blond man's hand. Though maybe the gun-toting woman at the man's shoulder was also a factor. Both were tall and fair and the last time Raf had noticed either of them they'd been standing by the harbour wall, studying a fold-out map headed *Ägypten – Kairo & Alexandria*. Something in their smiles told Raf they'd always known exactly where they were heading. And, more to the point, where he was headed as well.

Dancers, Hu San would have called them. Or rather, a dancer and a ballerina.

The woman kicked the door shut with her heel. She wore a straw Panama tipped over one eye and a pale scarf tucked into her silk blouse. They shared the same wiry build, the same almost white hair cropped short at the sides and left to flop forward over pale blue eyes . . .

In fact, they looked just like him. Give or take the slightly longer hair and his beard.

'Can I help you?' Raf asked politely.

Neither answered. Neither moved. But it didn't matter, because the fox was awake. *Disarm yourself, disarm your enemy,* said a tired voice in his head. It sounded cracker-barrel, but Raf recognized it as a koan from the old rasta he'd trained with while on remand.

Raf put up his hands and watched both dancer and ballerina suddenly relax.

'Yeah,' said the man, coming closer. 'We were told you'd be sensible.' He sounded disappointed.

'That's me,' said Raf, stepping forward to sweep aside the man's automatic with his left hand, while swinging in with his right elbow, catching him across the throat.

Sometimes you've just got to dance.

Raf uncoiled, right elbow returning to spread the man's nose sideways across his once-handsome face. Balance Raf took out with a simultaneous clap to both sides of the man's head, rupturing the eardrums. He was spared having to thumb the dancer's eyes because the man was already headed floorwards, Raf following hard behind.

As they landed, Raf put one elbow through the dancer's rib cage, driving a fat splinter of bone deep into a suddenly very shocked heart. The stink of open bowels filled the room but by then Raf had rolled sideways across the carpet, the dancer's automatic already in his hand, coming to rest beside a filing cabinet. Either it would give him cover or fill him with shrapnel, depending on what loads the ballerina carried in her gun. It gave him cover, though the only thing to be said for the sudden stench of cordite was that it swamped the smell that came from the body between them.

'Hey.' Raf's voice sounded better than he'd expected, given someone was using him for target practice. 'You want to tell me what this is about?'

He wasn't fussed about giving his position away. She already knew exactly where he was, she just couldn't reach him. 'Well?' Raf said.

Her answer was another slug, slammed into the filing cabinet. In at the front but not, thank God, out at the side. Her big problem was her slugs were small calibre, their load almost subsonic. She'd come carrying brass designed to fire at close range, then rattle round inside Raf's skull magimixing.

'You can put that gun down or I can kill you,' said Raf. It was, he realized, probably the wrong time to start enjoying himself; but knowing that didn't change a thing. His thoughts felt as clear as they'd ever been. And for the first time in years, he wasn't standing on the outside watching himself.

'Make your choice' said Raf, noisily jacking back the slide on his newly borrowed automatic. 'It means nothing to me.'

A slug fired into the filing cabinet gave Raf his answer.

Shaking dust from his short hair, Raf took a look around him. The ballerina had a door behind her to give an exit, if that was what she needed: this he already knew. He had a wall, a filing cabinet and a blind corner without door or window. Not good at all.

On the other hand . . . Raf smiled. 'I hope they're paying you well,' he said, doing his best to sound genuinely concerned. 'And I hope you've got insurance. Because the hospitals round here are likely to slice you up for body parts if you look like you can't meet their bill . . .'

He paused to let the silence build, thinking himself inside her head until he finally, briefly became her. 'You've still got a chance,' he said. 'Which was more than your friend ever had.'

The answering shot that Raf expected didn't come. And it didn't sound like the ballerina was changing position or anything, because he could hear silence, devoid of even the faintest tread of feet moving carefully over a carpet.

The woman was listening to him, which was her first mistake – probably the only mistake Raf needed. 'Look,' said Raf. 'You've been set up.' He paused again, as if hit by a sudden thought. 'You got a mobile there?'

The woman would have, undoubtedly. A Seiko wrist model or a Paul Smith wallet, the chrome flip-open kind. Something classy but anonymous to let her call in the cleaners when her job was done.

'Call home,' he told her. 'Have your handler access the precinct files, check out Ashraf al-Mansur.'

Nine, three . . . three, nine, two . . . two, two, five, four, zero, three. She was using something with a keypad and it was a local number, Raf decided, following the dial tones in his head. What was more, she got a connection first time which told him all he needed to know about his own situation.

The woman spoke rapidly, her intonation rising towards the end. Twice she stumbled over her words. Being scared made her unpredictable, which made her dangerous; and Raf seriously didn't want to be on the wrong end of a gun held by a frightened ballerina. Not when more triggers got yanked in panic than ever got squeezed with intent.

'*Schisen*.' The word was soft, spoken with feeling.

'Ashraf al-Mansur,' said Raf, 'special forces, explosives expert, advanced weapons training . . .' He paused, trying to remember what else the kid had put on her list, because it was Hani who'd faked his CV, Raf was certain of that. 'Crack shot, proficient in close combat.' And there was other stuff, real facts that Hani didn't know or couldn't imagine.

'Acute hearing,' said Raf, 'enhanced vision, eidetic memory . . . How am I doing?'

He wasn't expecting an answer yet and didn't get one. All the same, the woman's breathing grew shallower, more ragged. Right about now should be when she'd start thinking about how to bring this deal to an exit.

'There's a door behind you,' said Raf. 'Feel free to use it.'

'And get killed on the way out? Spend the rest of my life looking over my shoulder?' The blonde woman spat out her words, bitterness battling fear. 'You killed Marcus.'

'I'm sorry,' said Raf. What was more, he meant it. Killing the blond man hadn't been an accident but equally it hadn't been entirely from choice. 'You were set up, both of you. Because whoever sent you knew you wouldn't walk away from this alive . . .

'Think about it,' he said as he stood up, staying pressed back against the wall. 'You're disposable. Not to me but to whoever hired you.'

'That goes with the territory.'

'Yeah,' said Raf, 'but what was the franchise? To kill me or get killed yourself? Think about it,' he repeated. Surrendering the protection of his filing cabinet, Raf stepped carefully over the dancer who lay face up, blindly staring at a cracked ceiling. And the bullet he'd been waiting for all his adult life never came.

She was smaller than Raf had thought. Older, too. Her eyes only half watching Raf's gun.

'Your husband?'

'My brother.' She tossed her own weapon onto a nearby chair and peeled off latex gloves. Glancing at Raf for permission to approach the body.

The woman didn't touch the corpse, just kneeled beside it and looked. Her eyes were as dry as her face was impassive. But when she spoke her voice was cracked with tension and raw with anger. And the anger was not directed at him.

'Bastards.'

Raf gave a long low, silent sigh of relief and put the dead dancer's automatic in his jacket pocket. What he'd just achieved was the cerebral equivalent of reversing a throw hold. 'You want to tell me who hired you?'

She didn't, which was exactly what he expected. He wouldn't have believed her anyway. That would have been too easy and these things never were.

'Fair enough,' said Raf. 'But I'd like you to be very clear on one point. I'm already dead. And I'd like you to pass that on . . .'

The ballerina glanced up at that and saw Raf's smile. A smile so wintry she wanted to shiver. Very briefly, she wondered what his face would look like without those shades and decided she didn't want to know. Never would be too soon to see him again.

From the bullet-riddled filing cabinet Raf took the files for Nafisa and Jalila, ripped the page that contained Lady Nafisa's last appointment from the clinic diary and grabbed a manila envelope as an afterthought. When he shut the door behind him, the ballerina was carefully picking up her spent brass. One less collection of calling cards for forensics to consider.

Time to change camouflage, Raf decided. The building's

elevator only ran as far as the fifth floor, after that it was stairs all the way up to the eighth. On the sixth floor was a communal bathroom for men and a separate one for women, which probably meant no hot water at all on the floors above where the hall carpet grew stained, the paint peeled and the doors became narrow. More importantly still, the locks became old and cheap . . .

Raf posted the files and appointments page to Zara, c/o Villa Hamzah. Then, wearing his new washed and untorn jellaba, he ordered a coffee at a café next door to the apartment block and waited. When the dregs of the first coffee got cold, he ordered another and took the offer of an ornate sheesha and the evening paper. For once he wasn't on the front page or on pages two and three. Page four had a small paragraph, no picture. Someone somewhere had taken a decision to turn down the heat.

Raf smiled.

An hour after he'd left the clinic, a black van turned up outside. Largish, oldish, anonymous . . . The man in the driving seat clambered out, brushing cake crumbs from dirty blue overalls. Licking the suction strip on an on-call sign, he slicked it to the inside of his windscreen and wandered up to the main door, large toolbox in hand.

Cable repairs . . . air-conditioning experts . . . 24-hour electrics . . . From city to city, the cover rarely changed. The only thing unusual was that it had taken the van an hour to arrive. Since it was unlikely that the firm for which the dead dancer worked was that inefficient, it meant the woman had needed time to say goodbye to her brother. Which was a good sign. At least, Raf thought so.

The coffee was bitter and what little Raf had of the hashish was home-grown and too sweet. But when the man in overalls reappeared Raf knew it had been worth his wait. So he tossed a couple of notes onto his café table and pushed back his seat.

What was left of the dead dancer was being carried out, cut up and jointed in those black bags. And from the frozen stare on the blonde ballerina's face as she trailed after the clean-up man down to his van, it was equally clear she'd been present when the butchering had been done.

That was love of a kind.

Cleaner and woman held a fleeting discussion on the sidewalk. More a quick question and an emphatic answer, really. The man wearing overalls shrugging and pulling himself up into the driver's seat. The ballerina didn't acknowledge his nod or even glance at the vehicle as it slid into the traffic, positioning itself behind a rattling green-painted tram.

She was good at blending, Raf had to give her that. From the flash of a packet, it was obvious her cigarettes were local. Except that no local woman would have smoked untipped Cleopatras; but then, no local woman would have smoked in public. Only she was a tourist, wasn't she? And tourists did stuff like that out of ignorance. Showed their bare arms on the streets, didn't cover their hair, smoked in public. What she didn't do nearly so well was validate her surroundings.

Her gaze slid over Raf. A man, a striped jellaba, spent sheesha in front of him, settling up with the waiter of an Arab café. It wasn't what she was looking for and so she didn't see it. In non-eidetic people, the cortex was wired weird like that.

Cigarette in hand, she flipped open her wallet and made a call, lighting and discarding a second Cleopatra before her handler called her back with whatever information she'd asked for. An address, most probably, given the way she promptly yanked the map from her bag.

Raf and the ballerina moved off together, joined by their invisible thread of anger and need. Raf following twenty paces behind, his head half buried in an evening paper. Moscow Dynamos had destroyed Belgrade Eagles, Danzig had drawn with Naples. Montenegro had been thrashed by Tunis. That particular game was being replayed on café screens everywhere, the fact the score was known in no way diminishing the cascade of outrage when a player from Tunis got fouled inside the penalty area.

The Ottoman provinces kept their dislike of Berlin under control but their contempt for Austria-Hungary was legendary.

The significant difference being that the Kaiser had few, if any, Islamic subjects while whole areas of the Austrian Balkans were Muslim . . .

The woman went in through one revolving door and came straight out of another, barely bothering to pause in the foyer of the Suq el Meghreb. She was checking for a tail, but Raf was so far back that he'd barely turned towards the first door when she reappeared from the other muttering angrily.

She was coming unravelled in front of him, the slow burn of her shock overriding common sense to such an extent that she patted a bulging pocket and tossed her map into a bin, doubling back barely fifty paces before hanging a left into a blind alley so narrow it was more of a gap between the Suq el Meghreb and a neighbouring warehouse.

There was no way Raf could follow her into the gap without being seen, so he strolled past its narrow entrance, counted sixty and doubled back, glancing in as he walked by. The ballerina had vanished, the *cul de sac* was now empty.

Raf really didn't like what that said at all, because what it said was that she'd gone upwards and he was going to have to climb . . .

Chapter Forty-six

1st August

Only tourists ever bothered using the black carriages that plied their trade along the final sweep of the Corniche. Which meant that no one paid much attention to an ancient caleche being pulled past the fish market by an elderly mare: one of a dozen carriages working the Golden Crescent, that strip stretching up from the new Bibliotheka towards the headland and the heavy grandeur of Fort Quaitbey.

'What are we going to do?' Hani demanded, as the leaf springs of their carriage squeeked ratlike over the cobbles. 'Well?'

Zara said nothing. She just watched fishing boats depart, with their square nets raised and the lamps that would lure catch to their net unlit, but Hani wasn't fooled for a minute.

Behind them, Place Orabi burned its eternal flame in the tomb of the unknown warrior, up ahead was Shorbagi mosque, famous for lacking a minaret. Its muezzin called from arcades that looked out over a market square. Just another useless fact her aunt had insisted she know. Hani shrugged. None of it mattered now.

'Well?' she demanded.

'I don't know,' Zara said crossly, but she did. They would go to the address they'd been given. Maybe she should have taken Hani to Lady Jalila's house when the first message came. That way, maybe Raf would still be . . . Surreptitiously Zara checked the text she'd copied across from Ali-Din fifteen minutes before, even though she already knew it by heart. *Raf murdered. Hani in terrible danger. Meet me at* . . . No key accompanied the words and at the top the *from* field was blank. But the text itself was signed LJ, which Zara took to be Lady Jalila. The only relative Hani had, now that Raf was . . .

'You're crying again.' Hani said.

Zara shrugged. So what if she was? Stranger things had happened.

'Thought so . . .' Hani swapped seats so she could sit next to Zara and put one arm round the elder girl's sore shoulders. 'I'm sorry.'

I don't know how to handle this, thought Zara. She desperately wanted to tell Hani it was all right to cry. Only then there would be two of them turned inside out, exposing their bare flesh to the world. It was unbelievably selfish, but Zara didn't think she could cope with that.

Beyond the mosque was the fish market, shutting up for the night. The cobbled square already hosed down and the kiosks locked shut. What vans were there waited for morning and the new catch. The hum of their refrigeration units a reminder that come dawn the bustle would begin again. Then the catch would be gutted, packed in ice and trucked out along the desert road to Cairo, where it would go on sale in the kind of fishmongers that required those serving to wear striped aprons and use French names for everything. The kind of place her mother talked about without ever having been to one.

'Faster,' Zara told the coachman, who scowled but still cracked his whip at the grey. He'd spent a good hour taking his caleche slowly up and down the Golden Crescent at Zara's request and now she wanted speed. Reluctantly, the grey rose to a trot.

'Turn here,' Zara ordered but the coachman shook his head, reining in.

'Can't leave the Corniche,' he protested. 'Regulations. I can take you further up or I can take you back, but I can't leave the esplanade.'

'Great,' Zara muttered, but she was talking to herself.

'It's all right,' said Hani, stuffing Ali-Din into a new rucksack, bought that morning. 'We can easily walk from here.' The child wore new jeans that matched her rucksack, and a white Hello

Kitty tee-shirt still creased from its packet. Her usual buckle shoes had been replaced with stack-heel orange flip-flops and her long hair had been cut until it was as short as Zara's own.

Zara wasn't sure about that last touch. But Hani had demanded it, sitting on a stool in the VSV until Zara hurriedly used scissors to send long dark strands tumbling to the floor. And, in a way, Zara was flattered: they looked more like sisters now – and that had made shopping for clothes less risky.

Normality was difficult for both of them, Zara discovered. Almost everything Hani knew about life she'd learned through a screen. The crowds worried her, the noise worried her, the street smells she found so fierce that she took to holding her nose until Zara told her to stop. Too many people were watching. She didn't understand that money had to change hands before something could be taken from a shop. Somehow, it was as if many of the most basic rules weren't in her book. On the other hand, she could date buildings just by looking at the brickwork. She knew exactly who or what every street had been named after. And passing a Radio Shack with a flickering screen in the window, Hani dashed in to reset it almost without breaking stride.

As for her, Zara knew she belonged to Isk, but the Isk she belonged to didn't yet exist. Hers would be a city where men of her own race didn't expect her to step into the road so they could pass. Where robed clerics didn't glare to see a woman and child out on the streets alone. And where shopkeepers didn't look over her shoulder to see who was paying.

But they tried hard to be normal and blend in. Together they ate crêpes from a market stall like tourists, drank warm mineral water that fizzed from its bottle and glued their fingers together with sticky almonds. Standing with their backs to Place Zaghloul, they'd watched grown men crash stunt kites into the waves and then jerk the kites skywards, swirling tails scattering silver drops of water.

Happy almost.

Until news of Raf's death came and their fragile, almost-happiness fractured down the middle as Zara suddenly found herself more scared and more alone than she dared admit . . .

Seventy dollars for a caleche along the Corniche was outrageous. Snapping shut her wallet, Zara took Hani by one hand and walked away without a backward glance. Less than five minutes later they were both stood in front of an oak door so sun-blasted the last traces of paint had peeled away to leave only bleached wood cut by darker grain.

'Is this it?' Hani asked doubtfully.

Zara checked. 'Yes,' she said, trying to sound confident. 'We're here. Do you want to ring the bell?'

Hani shook her head. 'You do it.'

Zara didn't recognize the grim-faced blonde woman who answered the door. But it was hard not to notice that she was holding a flick knife and that there was blood on the blade.

Chapter Forty-seven

1st August

Hell didn't reside below any more than paradise resided above, whatever stories that child spun her rag dog. Hell was being suspended, like pain, between dirt and a darkening sky.

Someone up there was screaming, but Raf kept telling himself it wasn't a voice he knew. A bloody cut disfigured his mouth where he'd chewed his bottom lip ragged with frustration. He wanted to climb higher, needed to. Because he had to follow the ballerina, but his arms would no longer work and his legs were far too busy holding him fast to pay too much attention to any orders his mind might send.

Raf wasn't afraid of heights. He'd never been afraid of heights. What he was afraid of was falling. Falling and flames. But above and beyond need and fear, what he really wanted to know was just where the fuck the fox had gone now . . .

He was breaking into a spice house by levering himself up a narrow gap between the spice house and the facing wall of an adjoining suq: that was the theory, anyway. Proper climbers had a name for gaps like that. Only, proper climbers also carried equipment and, on the whole, didn't spend their entire lives terrified of falling from high places.

Sweat stained his shirt. He could feel the perspiration beneath his hair, under his arms and in his groin. A long slick of wet enamelling his spine.

Beyond scared, you reach a place that is almost beyond being ashamed. But only almost. Hani was up in that room, Zara too. From the moment Raf had recognized their voices he'd known that up there was where he had to be, desperately had to be, and only a memory of silver rain was stopping him.

And the really sick joke was, Raf wasn't even sure the silver rain was real. He, who never cared enough about anyone to be truly afraid for them, was terrified that Hani might be killed. And as for Zara . . . If he hadn't vomited already he'd be doing it again, beyond doubt.

Below him, between the suq and the spice house was the tiny blind alley down which the ballerina had vanished. At its end was a tiny courtyard belonging to the spice house. One back door, padlocked, one CCTV camera for security, nothing fancy; even adjusting his eyes across their whole spectrum hadn't revealed any trace of hidden beams.

As for dealing with the camera, Raf had justified being there by clumsily yanked up the front of his jellaba and unlaced his fly, at the same time as snatching a quick look around. To his right had been the red-brick wall, to his left the yard, little more than a token reminder of a larger one that had existed back before the suq was built. Above him a distant cast-iron loading boom jutting from the side of the spice house, its wheel rusted tight. The open window just below it had looked very far away.

Ambling back up the alley until he was out of camera range, Raf had jumped, feet jamming against the wall on both sides. He'd seen it on screen, mountaineers straddling a gap and climbing effortlessly, leaving the ground far below them. He managed four, maybe five awkward hops.

It wasn't pain in his ankles or lack of skill that stopped him. It was looking down. Down onto a drop of no more than three metres, but it was enough. Vomit rose barometer-like in his throat, spewed between rictus lips and trickled to the ground below, leaving memory etched on his palate as an aftertaste.

Open the door.

Can't.

Open the door.

No.

The voice of waves, other children shouting. Later on, in another place, he'd had to push one of them downstairs to cure that. Threw a knife across a crowded dining room so that it nailed a wooden beam beside another's head. Sheer luck but impressive.

Fear of heights or fear or falling? They were different. That difference had been explained to him at length by a psychiatrist at Huntsville, who masked her stink with cologne and scuttled sideways into rooms like a crab, because that was the only way she could fit through the door.

Apparently the height/falling difference mattered. Until he recognized which one it was, nothing could be done to cure what was a simple, almost boring phobia. All he had to do was watch some films and tell the fat woman what he felt.

Only Raf felt nothing as he looked at pictures of smiling children climbing frames or slides, shinning up ropes and leaping off walls. He didn't know any of them. And how he felt when he looked down couldn't be described. Not in words a child might use and certainly not by the adult that child became.

If he fell now and rolled on landing, he could walk away with nothing worse than a few bruises. Every shuffle upwards increased that danger. A few more shuffles and it would be a broken ankle rather than bruises, then a leg or hip. Much higher than that and his spine would concertina. At the top, where he needed to go, where muted screams broke through the open widow – fall from *there* and his vertebrae would be crushed on impact. He knew that for a fact.

Very carefully, Raf twisted round until his back pressed against the suq's brickwork and his feet jammed hard against the crumbling warehouse wall. It felt safer than straddling the emptiness. By shuffling his back and straightening his legs he might be able to inch his way higher. All it would take would be for him to conquer one simple, irrational fear.

All. Darkness swept in against the edge of his thoughts every time Raf glanced down. And the alley floor sucked in his concentration like a singularity swallowing light. Until looking away became nearly impossible, climbing ditto.

Crying with frustration, Raf made himself stare up at the window, its shutter swinging slowly in the evening breeze.

Everything he needed to become was on the other side of that. Zara, Hani, the ballerina . . . And whatever the ballerina was doing, that was something he needed to know about.

Hey, dead boy, the voice in his head was mocking. *Recognize where you are?*

Raf did. He'd been there before.

Chapter Forty-eight

Switzerland

Outside was silver rain.

Inside a fox cub coughed, thin shoulders heaving and skull flat to the floor. The door stood ready to be opened, buckled by the noise and anger of what waited on the other side.

He touched the handle.

Skin seared and the boy's fingertips vaporized, fragments of skin left sticking to the red-hot door knob as he yanked back his hand. He wanted to cry but he was doing that already.

It was nothing, he'd been telling himself . . . Nothing seeping under the door, nothing pushing past the sodden towels he'd used to close out the gap; but he could no longer pretend. Tears dripped unnoticed onto his red wool dressing gown.

He could smell burning and the smell came from him.

All the boy had to do if he wanted to live was turn the handle and yank back the door. It was that simple. The alternative was to die in peace, letting go any last shred of hope that stuck to his soul the way his burnt skin was glued to the door handle. Die, or walk out into the silver rain. Into the Hell pastors talked about in chapel.

Water still trickled from the cold faucet but it was boiling now, steam rising from the basin as he turned on the tap. A gravity-feed cistern in the roof behind him supplied water and the noise had not yet reached his stretch of attic.

Stripping off, the boy screwed up his dressing gown and held it under the water, burning his already burnt fingers. When the cloth was completely sodden, he wrapped it around his body. The dressing gown wasn't long enough to protect his ankles or calves but it would cover the rest of him, for what that was worth.

He opened the door by gripping its handle through cloth from his gown and twisting. And when steam hissed from beneath his fingers, the boy knew he should have dealt with the door first, when the dressing gown was still dry, rather than this way round. Logical rather than lateral, he wasn't as good at that as his mother's friends expected.

But this wasn't a test.

Taking a deep breath, he threw back the door and stepped out. There was no ground, no walls, no roof above him. Only a red glow. A darkness of night sky held back by flame. The silver rain had almost finished, thick drops of lead trickling down from gutters to evaporate into dark smudges on fire-scarred walls. Surrounding him was what was left of one attic and between him and the next surviving attic lay nothing but a smouldering pit of fire bisected by a black steel girder that stretched over empty space.

The noise of the flames had grown softer. Burnt out, along with the west wing of the school. There was fire behind him, scavenging its way like cancer along the building, shattering walls, melting lead and eating through wooden beams to drop the blazing remains noisily into orange cinders below.

Firemen had seen him now. That became obvious when a spotlight almost bowled him backwards with shock. Someone swore, their words made puny by distance and flame, and the light snapped out. So the boy shut his eyes and let them adjust, calling up darkness in his head. Waiting until the extraneous noise died and the orange glow behind his eyelids slid away.

When he looked again, the pit was back, framed round with darkness and night, while tiny grey bats of ash spiralled high into the air.

'Stay there.' Words loud enough to come from God bellowed from a hand-held loudspeaker somewhere below. 'You're safe there.'

The boy shook his head. The man lied, probably not intentionally. But only because the man wasn't where he was, so didn't know any better.

He was going to die or he was going to live: the choice was his. Not their choice, his choice. He and the fox were the ones who had to walk the abyss.

On the far side of the attic, a tall ladder was sliding upwards in a fluid sweep of hydraulics, a man balanced at its top. The man wore dark blue overalls and a yellow helmet with a bump across the top like a ridge of bone. A night visor covered his eyes and nose, and on his back was an oval oxygen tank. One of the new models, doughnut-shaped with a hole in the middle. He was mouthing words the boy didn't wait to hear.

'Time to go,' said the boy.

Claws needled into the flesh of his shoulder as he tightened his grip on the scrabbling animal. Of course the cub wanted out of there, so did he, and that meant crossing the iron beam. He didn't blame the fox for not being happy, but it wasn't helping.

The iron beam was recent: put there within the last seventy years to brace internal walls of a Swiss arms dealer's mansion originally built for show rather than quality. The beam and its bracing were the only thing stopping the wing of the Swiss boarding school falling in on itself.

Flames flickered below him, held in check by fire hoses but waiting, gathering themselves to explode upwards and sweep away the last fragments of his attic. This was life.

He shook his head crossly, flipping blond hair into already stinging eyes. He didn't like the school and didn't want to be there. He couldn't see the point of useless tests or running through brambles in the rain. It wasn't even the exercise he minded. It was the other pupils. The ones who never saw what he saw.

There were tears in his eyes again, but he couldn't work out why. Maybe he was just scared. That was allowed, wasn't it?

Except it wasn't.

Boys like him weren't scared. They did the stupid, the splendid and the impossible without making a fuss. They walked out along red-hot—

'Enough already,' said the fox. 'Move it.'

The beam was sticky underfoot. But that was the soles of his slippers melting, each step leaving a black footprint on the beam behind him.

Heat rose as if from a furnace, billowing his dressing gown until it blew out like a limp balloon. It was hotter than the wall of heat he'd hit that time stepping off a Boeing onto the tarmac in Singapore.

His mother had been photographing tigers then. Not the original singha *after which the island had been named, but the new ones, the re-introduced ones that kept dying because there was nothing in the wild for them to eat. The director had offered to pay for her to bring her kid along: it added human interest to the other sort.*

Bubbling step followed bubbling step. The next one would take him to the middle of the scorching beam, then he would have to do what the fox said. Not that he could turn round; any more than he could stop the soles of his slippers bubbling, molten rubber blistering the bottom of his feet.

Going on was his only option. The burning pit wasn't there. The beam was just a line he'd scrawled on a floor to amuse himself, a crack along the edge of some floorboard. Reality was what he wanted it to be, what he made it.

Staring straight ahead, the boy wrapped the struggling fox tight in his arms, buried his cheek into hot fur and walked across the remaining stretch of beam onto the front page of next morning's papers.

Fox Saves Boy – only the Enquirer *got it right.*

Fear, shadow and tears gave his childish face the tortured beauty of an El Greco saint. No one mentioned that he owed the anguish which twisted his mouth to a terrified fox cub chewing chunks out of his shoulder.

By the time a teeshirt was being faked in sweatshops in Karachi and sold on street stalls in London and Paris, he was gone. No longer aware of the fuss, no longer watching the screens. He had more important things to talk about – his mother was coming herself to collect him.

She flew into Zurich first-class on Lufthansa and the ticket was free, like the cars and hotels. Reporters met her at Kloten and photographs of him being hugged by a thin woman in a long black coat with shades, were syndicated worldwide. There were some long-lens pap shots from a brief stay-over at the George V in Paris – all flat surfaces and squashed depth of field – but no one got real access until London.

A man Raf didn't recognize – who called his mother Sally a lot and looked at her ankles – sat on a chair in a BBC studio on the outskirts. Hot lights blazed above the boy, raising beads of sweat under his newly cut hair. The fox cub sat on his lap, pinned by his hand to the grey flannel of his school trousers.

The trousers and tweed coat were a compromise. He wore school uniform for the interview and the school in Zurich didn't charge a term's notice for removing him as a pupil.

Everyone won except Raf.

On the studio wall was a bare blue screen. On it the people at home would see whatever the producer wanted them to see. Mostly this was a long shot of the boy balanced high on the iron beam, his face raised to heaven.

When the man had finished asking his mother how she felt about having a child who was a hero . . .

She was glad he'd rescued the fox.

What was she photographing now . . .

An endangered seal colony on the Falklands.

What would she and Raf be doing next . . .

Spending some quality time together at a friend's apartment in New York.

When all that was over, the man who called his mother Sally turned to the boy and, pasting on a sympathetic smile, asked how he'd felt up there on the beam.

The man wasn't happy with the boy because the producer had already halted the interview once, after a sound man complained he kept unclipping the button mike fixed to his school collar.

'Well?'

What had he felt? He wasn't too sure he'd felt anything at all. Mostly he'd been busy keeping his head empty.

'Were you scared?'

Only of having nearly killed the fox. Despite himself, despite not allowing himself feelings, the boy's eyes misted and for the first time since he'd reached the top of the fire truck's ladder, his mouth trembled.

It was like punching a button. Repressed irritation segued into instant sympathy as the interviewer's face softened. The man rephrased the question, glancing only once at the camera.

The boy thought about it. He still didn't know how he felt but now everyone was waiting, his mother's pale eyes fixed on him, her face tense.

'I can't sleep,' said the boy finally. That at least was true. Always had been. Darkness unravelled in front of his eyes in minutes that ticked by so slowly it was like living inside freeze-frame.

'Dreams,' said the interviewer. 'I can understand that.' He glanced at Raf's mother, his look conveying just the right amount of compassion mixed with an unspoken question.

'He'll be seeing the best child therapist in New York.'

The interviewer nodded. Debated the propriety of asking his next question and asked it anyway. 'When you do sleep,' he said, 'what exactly do you see?'

Nothing, that was the real answer. A brief darkness that swallowed emotion, fear and guilt. But, glancing round the studio, Raf knew that wasn't the right answer and he was learning fast that 'real' and 'right' were different things.

'Flames,' he said simply. 'I see flames.'

The producer brought the interview to a quick halt after that. Time was needed in the cutting suite and they had an actor from the National standing by to voice-over the links needed to tie the interview into existing footage of the fire.

In the hospitality room afterwards, hardbitten hacks wrapped heavy arms round the boy's tense shoulders and told him how brave he was. And all the while, the boy stood clutching a glass of orange juice and wondering why none of them had thought to ask him how the blaze got started in the first place.

Chapter Forty-nine

1st August

Some sense of meaning was there, just about. Hidden beneath animal howls that ended in choking silence. *Stb pzzz.* But the German ballerina had no interest in stopping, not yet. Not until Madame Sosostris told the ballerina why she'd been hired. Only Madame Sosostris wasn't saying, because refusal was the only thing keeping her alive – although that definition was becoming increasingly loose.

Sighing, the ballerina lit another Cleopatra and inhaled deeply, letting the smoke dribble from her mouth. Then she inhaled again, and stubbed the cigarette out in the screaming woman's navel.

Zara put her hands over her ears.

Ashraf was dead. Someone she knew and liked had been murdered. Maybe more than liked, if she was honest. Now she'd walked Hani straight into a trap. Zara had brains, she had courage, she should have been planning their escape but somehow . . .

All she wanted to do was cry. Zara was disgusted at her own cowardice. The kid, on the other hand seemed almost oblivious, only glancing up from where she squatted beside Ali-Din whenever another cigarette went out.

Outside, late evening leeched daylight from the sky. Lights would be coming on along the Corniche, the fish restaurants shuffling tables as tourists finished their supper and locals arrived to eat, children in tow. And, sitting alone in his study, nursing an illegal whisky, her father would be checking his messages and trying not to worry. She could look after herself, that was what he would tell himself because that was what she'd spent the last five years telling him, every opportunity she got.

She was sorry to have let him down.

'It's okay.' Hani squeezed Zara's hand. 'Raf will be here soon.'

'Raf's dead, honey.'

'No,' said Hani, as she tucked her wriggling rag dog tight in her arms and stroked its ears. 'He's just late, as usual . . .'

They both waited at one end of a spice-drying attic, or maybe it was a mezzanine. Whatever, it filled a third of the length of the building and was a simple platform, hung under the roof and anchored to an end wall. Slit windows in that wall let in air and would have looked down onto a street if only the street hadn't been so narrow or the windows set so high. That was the end where rickety stairs led up from ground level. At the other end of the platform, a simple rail separated the edge from a drop to the floor of the warehouse far below.

Light came from a single bulb that hung like a fat water drop at the end of an age-blackened twist of flex. The room it revealed was functional. A place of sour-smelling leaves drying on canvas tarpaulins, of peppery herbs hung from crude beams, each brittle bunch lashed together with rough string. The same type of string that bound the elbows of Madame Sosostris tight behind her as she lay quivering face up on a medical couch, knees wrenched back and ankles lashed to her elbows so that her arched body was taut beneath a short Muji vest which was all that she now wore. In Berlin that position was called 'Teasing the Rat'.

The more Zara tried not to think about what that couch was actually doing there, the nastier her suspicions became. Full pharaonic circumcision, which used to be called female infibulation was illegal in Iskandryia. But then, so was abortion and the little silver trolley with the surgical trays could have been for either – or even for both.

Beside her, Hani suddenly sneezed at the dust in the air.

The ballerina paused. *'Gesundheit'*, she said, sounding distracted. And then went back to heating the tip of her flick knife with a Zippo.

Black carob, henna and oregano, chilli and ginger. Their scents clashed with each other and with the smell of cumin, coriander and frying garlic that drifted up from a distant street stall. But rich as the mix was it wasn't enough to hide the stink of fear that rose from the tethered herbalist.

'Tell her,' Zara pleaded.

The ballerina smiled.

'Please.'

'*Ja,*' said the blonde German, as she pressed red-hot metal into the inside of the bound woman's thighs. 'Explain who really hired me and maybe I'll let you live . . . But then again, maybe not.' She jerked the blade sideways.

Blood ran between Madame Sosostris's legs in a trickle like scarlet tears.

'Tell me,' suggested the ballerina.

'What's to tell . . . ?' The question bubbled between bitten lips. 'I hired you. I didn't know he was dangerous . . . I made a bad mistake.'

'No,' said the ballerina. 'Not you. Someone else ordered you to hire me.' She pivoted on her heel and buried rigid fingers into the side of the arched woman, ignoring piss that spread across wipe-clean leatherette and dribbled floorwards, following blood down a crack in the boards. And in the silence between falling drips Zara heard a knock at the door below and then the sudden jagged trill of a bell, so loud that even the ballerina jumped.

'Expecting someone?' she demanded, holding her blade close to her victim's eye. Madame Sosostris shook her head.

'Well?' The question was shot behind her, at Zara.

'No,' said Zara.

The ballerina turned back to her victim. 'Well, now,' she said, listening to a second, more impatient ring from below. 'Maybe we can kill you, after all. Okay, *you* . . .'

Zara nodded.

'This is how it works . . . You answer the door and the child stays there. Any problems and . . .' She flicked her knife sideways, leaving Zara no doubt what would happen to Hani's throat.

Zara went. Walking slowly down the ancient stairs until she

reached the main door to the spice house. A big part of her wanted to keep walking, out of that door and into a world where upstairs wasn't happening. But she knew, stupid or otherwise, she'd probably die rather than leave Hani.

'Who is it?' she demanded.

'Me.' Lady Jalila's voice was scared or furious, but through an inch of sheet steel it was hard to tell which. '*Now open up, quickly . . .*' She pushed at the door, then visibly jumped when she saw it was Zara. 'Where is Madame Sosostris?'

Zara pointed to the ceiling.

'And you brought Hani?'

Of course she'd brought Hani. This was where the message had told them to come. Zara nodded.

'Good.' The woman pushed past Zara and headed towards the stairs without needing to be shown the way. 'I'll be taking her with me.'

'Lady Jalila . . .'

'What?'

What indeed. Zara thought of Hani upstairs and the blonde woman with her cold northern eyes and hot blade and said nothing. Besides, something was wrong. What did Lady Jalila mean, asking if Hani was there? Here, still? Here, now? Where else would the child . . .

'Lady Jalila.'

'Well?' The woman's eyes flicked from Zara to dark drips on the floor behind her. And when she stayed silent, Lady Jalila sighed. 'Leave it to me,' she said, reaching into her pocket. 'Just leave it to me.'

The rest Hani and Zara reconstructed from memory. Remembering most a *pas de deux* faster and more intricate than any they'd seen on a newsfeed.

Sound travels relatively slowly but, being cool-loaded and thus subsonic, Lady Jalila's first bullet travelled more slowly still, which meant it wasn't quite the surprise to the ballerina that it might have been. Though by the time Hani looked up, the German's blonde hair had finished streaming out behind in a sticky white, grey and red plume.

The .38 hollow-point entered the ballerina's head just below the jaw, passed through her soft palate and removed what had until then been the back of her skull, sucking out blood, bone fragments and grey jelly to splatter them over the brick wall behind.

A split second after her head flicked back, the woman's bowels and bladder loosened and her body stepped back, exploded blue eyes staring blindly at nothing. The crash the ballerina made as she hit the boards was loud enough to echo through the almost empty building.

'Mid-period,' muttered Lady Jalila, surveying the wall. 'Maybe mid-to-late . . .' Her eyes swept over the attic to take in Hani with her rag dog, the dead ballerina and finally, scornfully, Madame Sosostris hog-tied on the couch.

'Murderer.'

Before Zara could protest, Lady Jalila brought up her gun and yanked the trigger three times. Hollow-points took Madame Sosostris in the upper body, splintering ribs into bone fragments. Lungs collapsed as the first two bullets blossomed into sucking wounds in her side, the final shot taking Madame Sosostris sideways through the heart and blasting her off the couch onto the floor.

The gurgling stopped.

'She hired the German to kill Ashraf,' Lady Jalila said as if that explained everything, though whether it was said to Zara or herself wasn't clear. Walking over to the dead woman by the bed, Lady Jalila lifted a scalpel from a metal dish and slashed the twine binding her arms and feet. Then she rolled the sticky twine into a neat ball and dropped it into her pocket. She placed her own .38 in the dead herbalist's hand.

'We'll tell the police they shot each other.'

It wasn't a suggestion.

'Just leave the official stuff to me,' said Lady Jalila. 'Okay . . . ?' Without waiting for Zara's answer, Lady Jalila walked across to where Hani sat, hugging her knees and clutching her rag dog.

'Time to take Ali-Din home.'

Hani shook her head. 'You killed her,' she said, voice empty.

'Of course I killed her,' said Lady Jalila. 'There was no choice.'

Only the child wasn't talking about the blonde German, Zara realized. Or about Madame Sosostris. And everything fell into place as if the answer had always been right there, just waiting for Zara.

Cold.

Staggers.

Hallucinations.

'The pen was a side issue,' Zara said without thinking. 'Lady Nafisa died from poisoning.' And she suddenly knew exactly how the woman standing in front of her had done it. Except that by then Lady Jalila was crouching beside the dead herbalist, taking back her own gun.

The next bullet she fired took Ali-Din through the head.

Chapter Fifty

1st August

Always count the guns.

Crouching by the window, company to fat-toed geckos that had grown used to his stillness, Raf whispered it again – just in case he forgot. Counting the guns had been rule one, according to Hu San; and Raf had made a special point of remembering the things Hu San told him.

The automatic would belong to the ballerina, only she was dead. Raf had heard that happen. Lady Jalila had the revolver, subsonic slugs but unsilenced barrel, because silencing a revolver was a contradiction in terms. From an empty plastic coke bottle taped to the muzzle to the most expensive hand-turned tungsten mutetube, nothing actually worked. Some of the shock wave always forced its way between cylinder and chassis.

If you needed to mute a revolver then the answer was to self-load the brass and use less charge, which was what she'd done. Whether or not in imitation of *Thiergarten* dogma, Raf didn't know. But, either way, just knowing how to do it made her a professional in his eyes.

The ex-ballerina had a gun, so did Jalila and so did he . . . Three in total, if he didn't count the one he'd lifted from the dead dancer. Which made it four functioning weapons. Quite how knowing that helped him Raf had forgotten.

'Enough already . . .'

Old words but true ones. Bats echo-located around him through the warm night air, taking moths in mid-flight, each curving strike almost surgical in its precision. Their echo bounced off shutters, refracted from high walls or vanished through open windows to return milliseconds later. Cold and mysterious, like some distant music of the spheres.

There was a tom cat lurking in the dirt of the alley floor far below, its heavy shoulders hunched and thick muscles locked in anticipation as it walked, oblivious, round Raf's discarded jellaba and shades, tracking whatever vermin hid behind the rubble. If the cat was dimly aware of the spiralling almost-mice, it didn't allow them to put it off the prey within reach.

Yet another city within a city, world within world. A metropolis of wild dogs and feral cats, rats breeding beneath grain silos and mice infesting the cotton bales that waited to be loaded into containers along the dock. Spiders, scorpions, and millipedes fat as callused thumbs, safe from the frail, fly-hunting geckos that haunted the twilight edge of street lights.

Raf twisted his head to one side, easing an ache in his neck. Just holding himself secure in that gap between walls took effort. And if he waited much longer he'd have no strength for what must happen next.

Dead boy . . . It was an odd nickname for a man to give a child. He remembered the man well, with his faltering monitors and flat-lining neurofeedback machines. Remembering never had been Raf's problem. His first identity number, its position over a battered metal hook that took his school coat, the exact marble pattern of tiles along a hospital corridor – he knew them all. Far better than he knew himself, because Raf had been afraid there was no self.

We are the hollow men . . . Maybe now, but not back times . . . Back then he was just a hollow *child*, not English/not American, not rich/not poor, not wanted except for his logic skills. He could easily have passed that test. But he thought that if he failed they'd let him go home.

Live with it, as the fox would have said.

The silver rain was finished, almost twenty years before.

While Hani was in there. Zara, too.

And he was out here.

And they both undoubtedly believed he was dead and some days he still was. Some days it surprised him he even had a shadow or that when he stared in the mirror there was a reflection waiting to scowl back. But those days got fewer.

And the fear was gone, burned out. The fox dying too. He was going to have to make his own decisions. And this was the first of them . . .

Grabbing the rusty metal bar that had once supported a pulley, Raf kicked off from the spice house wall and let gravity swing him through the open window towards which he'd been climbing.

Things to do, people to become.

Hani was sure she saw a smoke-grey animal leap into the room, becoming Raf as it hit the ground and rolled. When he came upright, Raf's gun was already cocked, its muzzle pointed straight at Lady Jalila's stomach. What Raf didn't do was pull the trigger.

'You.'

He nodded.

'You're . . .'

'Dead,' added Hani and Raf nodded, watching the revolver pointed at his chest. Small, elegant, with pearl handles and an over-fussy blue finish that definitely didn't match the dark purple nails of the hand holding it.

Lady Jalila smiled. Her full lips twisting prettily.

'Darling,' she said. 'You kill me, I kill you . . . Such a waste, don't you think?' Lady Jalila meant it, too, Raf realized. Her greeting was real. In some warped way she really *was* pleased to see a man who only that morning she'd arranged to have killed.

'You murdered Felix,' said Raf.

Lady Jalila shook her head. 'Murder has to be intentional. That was an accident.'

'And you expected to get away with it?'

'Oh,' said Lady Jalila, 'I have got away with it . . . And I'll get away with this too. As will you. You and me, we're different.' Her pale blue eyes swept the room, taking in the dead ballerina and herbalist, then Zara. 'Whereas people like her . . .'

'What about people like me?' Zara demanded.

'Disposable.' Lady Jalila shrugged elegantly. 'What on earth made you think you deserved a pashazade?'

'Who said I wanted one?'

Lady Jalila ignored that. 'You know what you lack?' Lady Jalila said as the girl turned away. 'Breeding . . . That's why people like you never amount to anything. Ashraf, however . . . Who knows? With my help he could be the next Chief of Detectives.'

Looking deep into Jalila's pale eyes, Raf finally recognised the truth. She was barking, completely off the Richter scale. Dysfunctional, deluded, sociopathic . . . Exactly the kind of ally someone like him might need to reach the top of the pile.

'Jalila.' He nodded discreetly towards the far end of the mezzanine, where light from the single bulb barely reached.

'Tell me how I could get Felix's old job,' Raf said quietly when they got there. 'And then tell me what it's going to cost.' Both of them still held their guns, only now the muzzles pointed at the floor.

'The cost?' In her head, Lady Jalila divided the cost of a box of bullets, deducted the ten per cent discount she got at government shops and divided the remainder of it by fifty. 'In cash terms, about thirty-five cents . . .' Her tongue dipped out to lick her bottom lip, its tip moistening already glossy lipstick. 'The *how* should be obvious.' She glanced towards his gun.

'Kill Zara?'

'Too easy,' said Lady Jalila. 'I'll do that myself.'

The floor far below was in darkness. Hollow. Empty. She saw nothing and he saw the same. But with two more colours and in sharper focus. 'Why just Chief of Detectives?' Raf said. 'Why not Minister for Police?'

'What about my husband?'

'Accidents happen,' said Raf. 'Ask Felix.'

'You'd really kill Mushin if I asked?' For a moment Lady Jalila sounded almost interested.

'Why not?' Raf's voice was blunt. 'He's not that rich and I doubt he's much use in bed. What have you got to lose?'

Lady Jalila roared.

'Try me,' suggested Raf, seriously.

'Maybe I will,' said Lady Jalila laughing. 'Once you've met my reserve.'

'No problem.' Raf broke open his revolver as if checking the load. Blued, lightweight and virtually indestructible, the Taurus was a beautiful piece of work. It was also so much usless ceramic and tungsten with its cylinder flipped out to the side like that. Now was the time for her to shoot him if she wanted.

Lady Jalila just looked amused. 'When did you know?'

About the pen being Jalila's inability to resist an artistic flourish? 'Right from the start,' said Raf. He lied. It wasn't until the night on the VSV he'd realized his aunt had been poisoned first, then stabbed later. Two different methods, two different places, same person. And as for Jalila being responsible . . . Originally he'd been sure it was the General.

'And you know the really ironic touch?' Lady Jalila's eyes sparkled.

He didn't.

'Nas was mean as sin, but she still paid good money for that colonic . . . Of course,' said Lady Jalila, as she reached out with one finger to brush the back of Raf's hand. 'In the end she left me no choice. And she would keep sleeping with my husband.'

'*That* was your reason,' said Raf. '*Jealousy*?'

'No.' When Lady Jalila shook her head, burnished curls brushed her shoulders and framed an angel's face. 'But it didn't help.'

She stretched lazily, her silk shirt pulling tight. Hani and were Zara invisible to her, Raf realized. All her artfulness was reserved for him.

'Why, then?' Raf prompted.

'The Autumn Ball. No one's meant to hold the chair at the C&C for more than two terms. Nafisa had five and wanted six. It was my turn but she wouldn't resign . . .' Lady Jalila sighed, then brightened. 'You really must come. I promise you, this year will be the best ever. Everyone will be there.'

Of course Nafisa wouldn't resign. She couldn't, Raf realized. Not without admitting she'd plundered the accounts.

But what Jalila wanted, she was given. And if she wasn't given it, she took it. He'd known someone else like that: his mother. Raf flicked the cylinder shut on his gun, hearing it click into place.

'And the price I have to pay?'

'Don't be silly,' said Lady Jalila. 'You know it already.'

So he did. Hani.

'On the count of three,' said Lady Jalila. 'Okay?' Tightening her grip on the handle, she turned lazily to face Zara, trigger finger whitening at the knuckle. *One, two . . .*

She made it to the start of *three* before Raf thumbed back the hammer on his own revolver, swung round and watched Lady Jalila's baby-blues explode with shock. Very slowly, the woman tripped backwards over one kitten heel, and met the rail that might have saved her if Raf hadn't reached down to scoop both feet out from under her.

Time expanded, so that every action took longer than it should have done, including the fall. If she wasn't dead when she went over the rail, the wet thud as she hit concrete confirmed that she was once she reached the ground.

Raf stared briefly down at the smashed body, then back at the child who squatted by a broken rag dog and held the dead ballerina's smoking gun in her hands. She'd understood every nuance of the conversation. Which had been a risk Raf had to take.

'You missed,' Raf told her fiercely. 'Okay?'

Hani weighed next to nothing when he reached her. A bundle of sinew and bone. Terror holding her body so rigid that her arms and legs practically vibrated with fear.

'You missed,' Raf said more softly, stroking the back of her hair. 'I didn't. The police will tell you the same . . .' He kept his words simple, hoping that repetition would be enough.

'Do you understand? You missed . . .'

Disbelief slowly left the child's eyes and then vanished completely, replaced by tears as her sticklike arms snaked up to superglue themselves round his neck, almost choking him.

Later, when Hani's sobbing had stopped, Raf gently unpeeled her arms and sat himself back against the end wall, his spine pressed hard against rough brick.

Life felt real. This was who he was. He was Ashraf Bey, guardian to Hani al-Mansur and friend of . . . Raf looked across to the crude window where Zara stood staring at the wall opposite or half watching bats flitter over the rooftops without really seeing them. Well, maybe 'friend' was the wrong word.

'You should talk to her,' whispered Hani from where she sat next to him, knees drawn up, back also pressed to the wall. At her feet was what was left of Ali-Din. Scraps of rag, smashed memory, a cracked lens, fragments of ubiquitous phenolic circuit board . . . All that remained of the only real proof that Lady Jalila had stabbed Nafisa.

'Zara?'

When the girl stayed silent, Raf sighed and slowly pushed himself up off the boards. It was evident that she heard him coming from the way her shoulders stiffened at his approach. 'I thought you were dead,' Zara said. 'And then, when you finally turned up, I thought *I* was dead. I really believed you intended to let her kill me . . .'

Underneath the overwhelming smell of past fear was the residue of some cologne, oxidized and turned sour from sweat. But then, God alone knew how *he* stank – or looked, for that matter.

'So did I,' said Raf.

Zara glanced round at that and their eyes locked, her own dark with *felaheen* DNA, his chilly and pale as any dawn. He couldn't help it: that was the colour his pre-natal contract had specified.

'Only for a second, towards the end.' Raf shrugged and spread his hands in a gesture as old as humanity. 'Sometimes, believing is the only way to play a part.'

'And I'm meant to accept that?'

'Yeah,' said Raf. 'If I can I don't see why you can't.'

'So what happens now?' Zara's voice made it clear she reserved the right to disagree, whatever his answer.

'We tell the truth.'

'We *what* . . . ?'

'We tell the truth,' said Hani sadly. 'It's the one thing nobody can stand.'

Epilogue

Hani's spoon froze in mid-air. 'Zara would like this . . .'

'Probably,' said Raf, glancing at his Omega a second ahead of it beeping to remind him that he should be somewhere else.

Pashazade Ashraf Bey was in demand. Three weeks after the shocking murder of Lady Jalila by a renegade *Thiergarten* assassin, he was still a hero for the daring rescue of his niece, Hani al-Mansur, and of the daughter of Hamzah Effendi, a well-known industrialist. Charities begged Raf to be on their committee. There was the rumour of a Japanese miniseries. General Saeed Koenig Pasha called him almost daily. He had until two p.m. to decide if he wanted to be Iskandryia's new Chief of Detectives.

He didn't.

The only person not interested was Zara; not interested in Raf and not interested in the polite, handwritten little notes the Khedive had taken to having delivered to Villa Hamzah. As soon as she'd been polygraphed, her statement taken and affidavit signed, she'd stormed back to Glymonopolo Bay. Not to the Villa Hamzah but to a small summer house in the grounds. And since then she'd met Raf only once. At the office of her father, where she'd stood stiff-backed and formal while Raf politely refused Hamzah Effendi's offer of a reward for rescuing her and the big bear of a man had tried hard not to be offended.

'Look,' Hani said, spooning down another mouthful of ice cream hand-beaten from fresh milk, egg yoke and Caribbean vanilla pods. 'She's not going to call you. So you call her. It's not difficult.'

'Maybe . . . Later . . .'

Hani sighed and turned her attention back to her pudding. No matter how cold the vanilla ice was when Hani's bowl left the kitchen at Le Trianon, it still melted before she could take more than a dozen spoonfuls.

Still, they were small elegant spoons and she ate slowly. Her attention taken mainly by tourists who strolled the length of Rue Missala. Some smiled at the small girl sitting at her roped-off pavement table. Others glanced away, having decided the child in the Armani shades was famous and the man beside her was a bodyguard. In their next few steps they invariably decided who they'd just seen.

She'd been variously the child-model Isabella Cloud, a violin prodigy called x'Tra Sweet, known never to leave her compound in Wako and HRH Yasmine, only cousin of the young Khedive.

'Ready to move?' Raf folded his afternoon paper. He'd had the vending machine include downloads of anything personal and there were three snippets about him in the paper, none of them true and all of them highly complimentary.

'Sure.' Hani nodded at her bowl of melting ice cream. 'You want some?' She knew full well he'd say no.

Two small coffees had already gone cold in front of Raf, but he didn't mind and they weren't really cold. In Isk, in high summer, nothing was unless it came straight out of a freezer like Hani's endless supply of vanilla ice.

Raf thought Hani insisted on coming with him to Le Trianon every day because of the ice cream but he was wrong. What she liked was the bustle of the brightly dressed crowds, safely kept at bay by a rope that separated her table from the busy street beyond. And when she wasn't there, she was up in his office, being spoiled by Raf's assistant who'd suddenly revealed a side no one had ever before seen. It turned out the man grew up with three younger sisters and, bizarrely, had liked them all.

'Okay,' said Raf when his watch complained again. 'You need me to take you up to the office?'

She didn't. Not if her snotty look was anything to go by.

Finding her own way from the table up to his office was child's play to Hani. For a start, the Third Circle had its own private lift. And, as Hani had pointed out more than once, she didn't even have to climb the wire.

The girl was fine, Raf knew that. It was only anxiety that made him ask each day and that wasn't Hani's problem, it was his . . . Some day he'd have to stop trying to protect her. Not to mention stop letting her eat nothing but ice cream. But that time wasn't yet.

'You can get me—'

'. . . On your mobile. Yes, I know.' Hani sighed. 'Look, I'll call you if I need you. Okay?' She had to have borrowed that line from Zara.

'Make sure you do.' Raf watched as the kid threaded her way between two pavement tables and disappeared into Le Trianon's air-conditioned darkness. Maybe she knew he was watching her go, maybe not. Either way, she didn't look back.

'Car,' said Raf and seconds later the fat man's Cadillac rolled up to the kerb, white-walled tyres freshly washed. 'The precinct,' Raf told his new driver, 'and then home.'

'Whatever you say.' Skin like chocolate, eyes hidden behind mirror lenses, black cap balanced at an angle on his dreadlocked skull, Avatar nodded.

Zara's half-brother had recently got the Cadillac's shell sandblasted back to bare metal at a fly-by-night bodyshop out at Karmous. Then he'd had the twelve-cylinder super-tuned somewhere different. So now it roared like the devil and every surface burned with sunlight. The boy was arguing for a quad Blaupunkt sound system, flat speakers set into the leather door trim. To date Raf had been holding out, but it wasn't an argument he was about to win.

'You called my sister yet?' Avatar demanded.

Raf shook his head.

'You plan to call her?'

'We've got ten minutes to get to the Precinct,' Raf said firmly and pretended not to notice Avatar's grin.

It was only when the shining car overshot his turning and

kept gunning down Iskander el Akhbar towards Glymonopolo that he realized the boy intended that Raf should make a meeting all right, just not at the Precinct. And not with the Minister.

Raf could live with that.

Acknowledgments

Thanks to

Pathology guy Ed Friedlander MD for answering idiot questions on exactly what happens if someone sticks a spike in your heart. Everyone at rec.arts.sf.science for endless tolerance in the face of questions about genetic manipulation, wheelworlds, gravity and the nasty side-effects of vacuum (okay, we're going back some years here). The now-nameless Islamic academic who provided information on Sufism. I'm sorry my Packard Hell P3 trashed all your details. *New Scientist*, just for existing. Dick Jude, ex head-honcho of Forbidden Planet, New Oxford Street for taking a punt on *neoAddix* and declaring that 'Weird Shit' was a perfectly good publishing category. The Upper Street lunchtime crew, including but not limited to Pat Cadigan, Paul McAuley, Kim Newman and (Jay) Russell Schechter. John Jarrold, ace editor, drinker and quoter of Shakespeare. Maggie Noach (you said it would take four books and you were right . . .) A tip of the hat to Martin (Thraxas) Millar, whose novel *Milk, Sulphate and Alby Starvation* acted as a roadmap to the late 80s. Peter Sherwen, who froze on Bergen bandstand and crashed my bike in Morocco, then decided to ride it back to London because the forks 'weren't that bent.' And finally to my parents. Hindu shrines, Buddhist temples, deserted Far Eastern beaches and yet another bloody chateau . . . Much of these books I owe to you. (That's a compliment.)

And now . . .
Pocket Books is delighted to present
an exclusive extract from
Jon Courtenay Grimwood's second book in the
ASHRAF BEY series

EFFENDI

The Second Arabesk

Out now in paperback

Prologue

27th October

'Of course,' said Asharf Bey. 'We could just kill the defendant and be done with it . . .' He let his suggestion hang in the cold air. And when no one replied, Raf shrugged. 'Okay,' he said. 'Maybe not.'

It was getting late and autumn rain fell steadily on the darkened streets outside, while inside, sat around their table, Raf's visitors continued to chase the same argument in tight circles. A Grand Jury was in session. If three judges plus a senior detective in a damp, third-storey office could be called anything so imposing, which seemed doubtful.

'An accident,' suggested Raf. 'The steps in this precinct are notoriously slippery. Or perhaps suicide . . . Shoe laces, an unfortunately overlooked belt . . . ? One of my people would have to be reprimanded obviously.'

Raf looked from Graf Ernst von B, the German boy, to a sour-faced politician from New Jersey who insisted everyone call her Senator Liz, neither of whom met his eye. There was also an elderly French oil magnate, but he sat so quietly Raf mostly forgot he was there. Which was probably the man's intention.

'Alternatively,' said Raf, 'I could have him taken out to the courtyard and shot. Or, if you like, we could lose the body altogether and just pretend he never existed. One of the old Greek cisterns should take care of that.'

They didn't like this idea either; but then the young detective with the Armani wrap-rounds and drop-pearl earring hadn't expected them to . . . He was acting as *magister* to their judges. And no one as yet, least of all him, seemed very sure what that actually entailed.

'*Justice*,' Senator Liz said loudly, '*must be seen to be done.*' Her voice remained as irritating as when the session began several hours earlier.

'Lord Hewart,' Raf pulled the quote from memory. 'One of the worst judges in history. And even he never suggested putting a North African trial on American television.'

'That's not . . .' Ernst von B's protest died as Raf flipped up a hand.

'Let's hear what St Cloud thinks,' he said and turned to the Frenchman. 'Do *you* think justice needs to be televised?'

'Me?' Astolphe de St Cloud slid a cigar case from his inside pocket. And though the iridescence of its lizard skin was beautiful, even by the light of a single hurricane lamp, what they all noticed was the enamel clasp: an eagle spreading its wings, while jagged thunderbolts fell from between the bird's sharp claws.

As if anyone there needed reminding that St Cloud would have been Prince Imperial, if only his father had bothered to marry his mother.

'It depends,' said St Cloud, 'on what Your Excellency means by *justice* . . .' Shuffling a handful of prints, he stopped at one which showed a young girl with most of her stomach missing. 'If we decide the evidence is convincing enough, then obviously the prisoner must stand trial. Like Senator Liz, my only reservation is that, perhaps, El Iskandryia is not quite . . .'

Raf caught the wry amusement in the Marquis' voice and glanced round the room, trying to see it through the eyes of a man whose own business empire was run from a Moorish palace overlooking Tunisia's Cap Bon; and who now found himself in a third-floor office, without electricity, on the corner of Boulevard Champollion and Rue Riyad Pasha, in a tatty four-square government block built around a huge courtyard in best Nationalist Revival style.

At street level the exterior walls to Iskandryia's Police HQ were faced with cheap sheets of reconstituted marble, while glass hid the exterior of the two floors above. Black glass obviously. The architect had been on loan from Moscow.

It showed.

As for the level of comfort on offer . . . A fire burned in a bucket in the centre of the floor, filled with logs from a dying carob. Apparently, the tree had been not quite alive and not yet dead for as long as even Raf's oldest detectives could remember.

Two men from uniform had hacked it off just above the roots, using fire-axes. Now chunks of its carcass spat and spluttered as thin flames danced across the top of their makeshift brazier.

Directly above the brazier, suspended from the centre of the ceiling like an inverted red mushroom, hung a state-of-the-art smoke detector. Like almost everything else in Iskandryia since the EMP bomb, it no longer worked.

And behind Raf's head, a window unit that once adjusted electronically to lighting conditions had been rendered smoke friendly, also with a fire-axe. Through its shattered centre came flecks of rain and a salt wind that blew in from the Eastern Harbour.

'Justice,' said Raf, 'is whatever we decide . . .' His voice lost the irony, became serious. 'And since the killing occurred within the jurisdiction of the Khedive, I demand that the trial take place in El Iskandryia.'

Senator Liz shook her head. 'Absurd,' she said. 'We have to change the location. You cannot expect us to work in these conditions . . .'

'I don't remember anyone asking you to work on this at all.' Wrap-round dark glasses stared at the woman. The other two he'd chosen. The Senator was different, she'd practically demanded to sit on the Grand Jury.

Actually, there was no practically about it.

On her breath Raf could smell gin, while a non-too-subtle miasma of sweat rose from her compact body. If von Bismarck and St Cloud could manage to bathe in rain water, then so could the American.

'Your Excellency,' said Ernst von B. 'Senator Liz has a point. It will not be easy . . .' The young German spoke slowly, in schoolboy Arabic, supposedly out of respect for Ashraf Bey's position as *magister*, though Raf suspected his real reason was to annoy the American, who spoke no languages other than her own.

'Nothing is ever easy. But the decision is made.' Raf stood up from his chair. And it was his chair because they were in his office. His was the name engraved on an absurdly-long brass plate on the door. *His Excellency Pashazade Ashraf Bey, Colonel Ashraf al-Mansur, Chief of Detectives.*

He'd told his assistant a plastic nameplate was fine but that wasn't how things were done in El Iskandryia. The long plaque had turned up the day after Raf took the job, and once a week, on Thursdays, a Cypriot woman from maintenance came up from the ground floor to polish the sign.

'Excellency?'

Raf turned to find St Cloud stood next to him, leaning on a cane with a silver top.

'You *were* joking about those steps, the accidents . . . I have your word this trial will actually take place?'

The blond detective nodded. 'You do.'

The trial would happen and it would happen soon. In all probability the defendant, one Hamzah Effendi, would be convicted. Raf just wished Hamzah wasn't father to the girl he should have married.

Chapter One

18th October

Nine days before the Grand Jury met in an upstairs office at Champollion Precinct, Ashraf Bey sat through a warm Iskandryian evening, bombed out of his skull, at a pavement table outside Le Trianon, drinking cappuccino and listening to DJ Avatar wreck havoc on the words of a Greek philosopher.

The afternoon call to prayer had finished echoing from the mosque on Boulevard Sa'ad Zaghloul and the bells from l'Eglise Copte had yet to begin. If it hadn't been for a sense of dread hanging over El Iskandryia, this could have been a Monday in October like any other.

Horse-drawn calèches, their brasses shined and wheel bosses polished, rumbled up the Corniche, from the fat sea wall known as the Silsileh all the way north to Fort Qaitbey, where the ancient Pharos lighthouse once stood.

And at both ends of the sweeping Corniche, at Silsileh in the shadow of Iskandryia's famous library, and at Fort Qaitbey, groups of tourists watched as fishermen set hooks or mended and untangled nets, waiting for the evening tide.

It was a tourist who'd taken the taxi that stopped outside Le Trianon, with its window down and sound-system up too loud, giving Raf the chance to hear the city's favourite DJ one more time.

'And remember . . .' Avatar's voice was street raw. 'Rust never sleeps. Coming at you from the wrong side of those tracks, this for the Daddy, the Don . . .'

Most of Raf's officers thought DJ Avatar came up with *SpitNoWhere* on his own; if they thought at all, which Raf considered unlikely. So they happily stamped the corridors at Police HQ, humming along, not knowing that the unchopped original went, 'In a rich man's house, there's nowhere to spit but his face.'

Raf hadn't known that, at least not until recently, but the fox in his head did. And while the fox couldn't say why, the General's *aide de camp* had just delivered to Raf an engraving of hell, inscribed with the words, *'At its centre hell is not hot.'* It had at least been able to identify the picture as late Victorian, unquestionably by Gustave Doré . . .

'. . . *ou know*,' said the fox, before all this happened. '. . . *ese things, they occur.'*

The fox had a grin like the Cheshire Cat, except that no cat ever owned so many teeth or carried its tail wrapped up round its shoulders like a stole. Come to that, few cats took afternoon tea at Le Trianon.

These things could have been Raf becoming Chief of Detectives by default, or his recent refusal to marry the daughter of a billionaire.

'Why?' Raf asked. '*Why* do they occur?'

But the fox didn't answer.

Sighing, Raf took a gulp of cold cappuccino to wash away the taste of cheap speed and fixed his gaze on the pedestrians who streamed past his café table, separated from the terrace where he sat by a silk rope and the assiduous attention of two bodyguards.

The only pedestrians to meet Raf's stare were those, mainly tourists, who didn't realize who he was. They just saw a blond young man in dark glasses, wearing an oddly old-fashioned suit, the kind with a high collar.

'Come on,' said Raf, searching inside his head. 'You can tell me.'

He ignored his two guards, who looked at each other and then hurriedly looked away. Raf didn't doubt that they could see tears trickling from under his glasses, but he didn't much care either.

The fox was saying goodbye.

The beast had been dying for years. Its abilities limited by memory conflicts, failed backup and the fact that, these days, the animal could only feed on neon light.

Once Tiri had been state of the art. Feeding on daylight, infrared and ultraviolet, or so it told Raf. White light, black light – back then anything went. The fox sharpened Raf's reflexes, steadied his nerves and gave him good advice. It was what Raf had instead of parents . . .

A small ceramic box set into his skull behind one ear which kept him sane, sort of, and gave him a definable centre. And once, when Raf was very young and in another country, it had helped him walk out across a steel beam through flames and crumbling walls.

Only life wasn't simple; because the fox, of course, refused to admit that it existed. The fox's view was that Raf had a number of unresolved issues.

'Your Excellency . . . ?'

Someone hovered at his shoulder.

'Go', said Raf and the waiter went, grateful to have been waved away.

Raf went back to watching the tourists who fed off from Place Sa'ad Zaghloul, and headed south down

Rue Missala, searching for bars and theatres or just in a hurry to get back to their hotels.

After a hundred and eleven days in the city, Raf could now identify tourist groups as clearly as if they wore labels: waddling Austrians, dark-haired French men, the odd bunch of shore-leave Soviets in mufti and, rarer still, an occasional pink-skinned English woman with silk scarf and sensible shoes. But mostly Iskandryia got nice couples, as befitted a famously romantic city.

The fuck-me singles, with their piercings, tattoos and trailer chic, came out only after dark, and then only in closely-defined areas. Places like PeshVille, where Scandinavian kids hosed lines of coke off toilet rims, while girls shuffled in darkened corners on the unzipped laps of boys too blasted to know they weren't safely hiding out in student halls back home.

But that wasn't really Iskandryia, just how it went, with the limo-delivered international DJs as interchangeable as the clientele. It could have been Curitiba or Berlin, Punta del Este or Kota Baru. And anyway those clubs weren't Raf's business. The tourist police dealt with that stuff.

'You in there?'

Raf counted off the seconds, listening carefully for an echo inside his head. One winter night, when he was maybe ten and feeling sorry for himself, something that happened less often than Raf remembered, he'd asked the fox if he (Raf that was) had a soul . . . And the fox had gone all silent.

That was the weekend Raf refused to go to chapel. For five weeks he'd been made to run round a field in the sleet at the back of his school, while the others sang hymns in the dry. And the fox's only comment, months later, had been to point out that he should have waited until summer to lose his faith.

Maybe it was one of his schools that first put the fox in his head. Or perhaps it was his mother. Alternatively, just maybe the fox was right and it didn't exist, maybe it had never existed outside of Raf's imagination.

Raf sighed. 'Do I get an answer?' he demanded. 'Or do I sit talking to myself like an idiot?'

'*Your Excellency?*' It was the maître d' this time. Raf tried to wave away the thin man but the maître d' stayed rooted to the spot, urgency winning out over embarrassment. 'The General is on the line from New York . . .' In his hand the man held an old-fashioned telephone. 'He says it's very urgent.'

Raf shook his head and almost laughed as shock flooded the maître d's face. No one refused to talk to General Saeed Koenig Pasha, not even His Excellency Ashraf Bey.

'What do I tell him?' The maître d' begged frantically.

Raf thought about how to answer for so long that the thin man holding the telephone actually began to squirm with agitation.

'I know,' said Raf finally, 'tell him my fox is dying.'